Praise for
Stillwater: A Jack McBride Mystery

"An ingenious plot and a complicated protagonist with inner depths worth plumbing. Readers who miss Donald Harstad will appreciate this well-done police procedural."

—*Library Journal*, starred review and
November Debut Mystery of the Month

"The author strikes a delicate balance between the romantic aspects of McBride's life and the unsolved crimes swirling around him. Lenhardt weaves unpredictable twists and turns . . ."

—*Austin American-Statesman*

"Dallas native Melissa Lenhardt offers a punchy page-turner that's certain to draw a fan base. . . . I'm definitely awaiting the next installment of the McBride chronicles, promised November 2016."

—*The Austin Chronicle*

"Inspired plotting, fast pacing, sly foreshadowing . . . Lenhardt expertly sets the hook for the next installment."

—*Lone Star Literary Life*

"With a twisting plot, nonstop action, and a sexy, complex protagonist you'll root for from page one, Lenhardt brings the town of Stillwater, Texas (pop. 2,436), and all its long-buried secrets, to life. Fast-paced and tightly-written, *Stillwater* is a must-read for anyone who loves great crime fiction. Book two can't come soon enough!"

—Wendy Tyson, author of *Killer Image*
and *Deadly Assets*

"*Stillwater* runs deep with intrigue, passion, and long-buried secrets. Melissa Lenhardt weaves a rich tale of suspense as hot as the east Texas town in which it's set."

—Annette Dashofy, *USA Today* bestselling author
of the Zoe Chambers mysteries

"Small-town loyalties and long-simmering secrets combine for a compelling page-turner! Fast-paced dialogue, an authentic setting, and engaging characters—*Stillwater* is a one-sitting read."

—Hank Phillippi Ryan, award-winning author of *Truth Be Told*

"*Stillwater* is the perfect combination of a tightly plotted tale peopled by rich, complex characters (plus one or two deliciously hateful true baddies). Slashed budgets, racial tensions, messy pasts—this small town is anything but cozy. The mystery itself is a classic puzzle, though: clever and convincing. Roll on Jack #2!"

—Catriona McPherson, Agatha, Anthony and Macavity–winning
author of the Edgar-nominated *The Day She Died*

"Dangerous things lurk beneath the placid surface in Stillwater, Texas. Moody and atmospheric, utterly compelling, you don't want to miss Melissa Lenhardt's marvelous debut novel."

—Harry Hunsicker, former executive vice president
of the Mystery Writers of America, author of *The Grid*

"Secrets, lies, and betrayals run through *Stillwater* like irrigation through dry land. Melissa Lenhardt's writing drips with detail to create a story that rushes like a wave toward an ever-twisting ending. Don't let the name fool you; *Stillwater*'s threats lie right below the surface."

—Diane Vallere, bestselling author of the Material Witness,
Madison Night, and Style & Error Mysteries

THE FISHER KING

A JACK McBRIDE MYSTERY

MELISSA LENHARDT

Skyhorse Publishing

Visit our website at www.skyhorsepublishing.com.

10 9 8 7 6 5 4 3 2 1

Library of Congress Cataloging-in-Publication Data is available on file.

Cover photo credit iStock

Print ISBN: 978-1-5107-0729-0
Ebook ISBN: 978-1-5107-0731-3

Printed in the United States of America

For Mom

In olden times, the Fisher King was charged with keeping the grail. When the Fisher King was blighted by a wound that wouldn't heal, castles fell down and the land around was made infertile. There, he lived in a wasteland until the knight Percival came to the castle in search of the Holy Grail. Percival healed the king, and the land burst into blossom, and a time of plenty began.

PART ONE

Secrets and Lies

CHAPTER ONE

Fred Muldoon needed new shoes.

Leaves and twigs worked their way through the hole in the sole of his right shoe as he walked the woods behind Doyle Industries. He stopped at the chain link fence and stared at the gravel lot, dreading the journey across its uneven surface to his home for the night. He hadn't drunk enough to ignore the pain those damn rocks would put him through, lodging as they would beneath his big toe. Goddamn gout.

He patted his coat pocket for his bottle of Old Crow. He could sit here, against the fence, drink his whiskey. The night wasn't too cold, and this was as good a spot as any. He sat down against the sagging fence, unscrewed the cap, and lifted it to his lips. A low roll of thunder interrupted him. He took a quick gulp and replaced the bottle. He hated being wet. It used to be an occupational hazard for the town drunk until Fred stole a pair of wire cutters and used them to cut a hole in a remote corner of Doyle Industries' fence. Between sleeping in the cabs of Doyle's trucks and earning whiskey money from telling Jack McBride innocent lies and useless information about the seedier side of Stillwater, Fred Muldoon hadn't had it this good since 1969.

Tonight, Fred targeted his favorite Mack truck, which seemed to be doing longer and longer trips these past few weeks if its regular absence from the truck yard was any indication. He climbed into the cab and settled down for the night, the smell of wintergreen snuff reminding him of his father. He considered his fifth of Old Crow. It might not be enough tonight.

He took off his shoe and tried to flex his red, swollen toe. Goddamn gout. He lay down on the seat, propped his head on the armrest of the passenger door, and inspected his shoe. He'd had these shoes since the Reagan administration and, while the years told on the scuffed, faded leather, the uppers had twenty more on them, easy. These shoes were the last good thing Fred bought before his slide down the bottle, and he was attached to them. He didn't cling to them as a tether to a better, more successful past, but Fred figured these shoes would be there when he found the bottom of the bottle or the grave, and he wanted something familiar to keep him company when he got there.

Fred placed his shoe on his chest, drank his whiskey, and tried to imagine a way he could get to Yourkeville to have them resoled. He could probably hit the Methodist preacher up for a ride and maybe even the cost of the soles. He'd have to stay sober to do it—not an appealing thought at the moment. He'd worry about it later. The Old Crow wasn't going to drink itself.

Fred was well on his way to being drunk when he heard the low voices. Though the truck was high enough he couldn't be seen from the ground, Fred scrunched down into the seat anyway. He'd long since hocked his watch, and the security lights in the truck yard cut off any chance Fred had of telling time by the moon—not a skill he was good at anyway. He figured it was past midnight. In his seventy years, he'd discovered most bad shit happened after midnight.

Though muffled from the closed door and window, the voices were clear enough Fred could hear every word. He grinned and cuddled his bottle closer. He'd have enough money to buy its replacement, or two, very soon.

"I'm telling you, I don't trust him."

"And I'm telling you, I don't give a shit."

Fred's ears perked up at the sound of a woman's voice. He didn't need to see her to know who she was.

"You're only saying that because you're fucking him."

Fred shifted in the seat, not particularly wanting to hear more. His shoe dropped to the floorboard with a thud.

"Did you hear something?" the woman said.

Fred froze and pressed himself further down into the seat. If the woman stepped on the running board and peeked into the cab, he wouldn't live long enough to finish his Old Crow.

"Don't change the subject."

Fred's body sagged with relief. He sucked down the rest of his bottle, in case it was his last.

"Why would I change the subject? You're the one who sounds like an ass, not me."

"You're unbelievable."

"Jealousy doesn't become you."

The man snorted.

"I'll explain it again," the woman said as though talking to a child. "Having the chief's brother in our organization works to our advantage. If McBride takes us down, which won't happen, then he'll take his brother down with us. Pollard said McBride and his mother have bailed Eddie out of scrapes for twenty years."

"They won't bail him out forever. Everyone has a breaking point."

"You speaking from experience? Maybe you should take some time off."

"So McBride can waltz into my place? I don't think so."

The woman sighed. "God, why are men so fucking needy?"

"I'm not needy. I just don't trust Eddie McBride."

"Well, I do."

"Why?"

"I asked him to do something and he did it."

"What?"

"It doesn't concern you. Don't forget who's in charge. Are you done pouting?" After a pause, she said, "Good. I need you to set up a meeting with the Pedrozas."

"Why?"

"Because kids are overdosing on their dirty heroin, and I'm going to put a stop to it."

"You think they're going to stop selling because you say please?"

"No. I'm going to offer a truce."

"They're going to smell blood if you do."

"I hope so. That's when you let Jack McBride pick you up. He's been looking for you for weeks."

"What? I'm not going back to jail."

"You won't. You'll make a deal. The Pedrozas in return for an easy sentence. You'll get out, come back, and I'll give you the Cypress County operation."

"The whole thing?"

"Everything. Numbers, girls, drugs. Imagine taking it to your grand wizard. Y'all can fund your cause for years."

"Chris won't like giving up the numbers."

She laughed. "He'll do what he's told."

"What about Eddie?"

Fred heard a rustling, and the timbre of the woman's voice dropped. He almost didn't hear her next comment. "He's our protection from McBride."

"I've seen the way you look at him." The clink of a belt being released, then the man said, "Fucking's your answer to everything, isn't it?"

"You've never complained before."

The man moaned and, besides the sound of feet scraping for purchase on the gravel, Fred heard nothing for a full minute. He lifted his head from his prone position and saw the top of a man's head pressed against the door of the truck, his hand grasping the side view mirror as though hanging on for dear life. Fred lay his head back down and grinned. Someone was getting their pole shined. He might as well join in, if his old pecker would cooperate, never a sure thing these days. He tucked his empty bottle between him and the seat back and went to work.

Fred was at last getting somewhere in his efforts when he heard the man let out a long, low groan followed by the distinctive sound of spitting.

"Eddie will bring our next shipment in on Friday."

"That's my run."

"You're too important to be an errand boy. You have to get in touch with the Pedrozas and set up a meeting."

"I don't know. A lot can go wrong in this plan."

"If it goes right, we can get rid of two birds with one stone."

"The Pedrozas and who?"

"Jack McBride."

CHAPTER TWO

The house needed little coaxing to go up in flames.

One hundred years' worth of weather and Texas heat had baked the clapboard house to a brittle shell. It stood more from habit and memory than the skill of the one-armed doughboy who built the house on his return to Stillwater from the Great War. Fifty years of heartbreak, shell shock, the Great Depression, another war, and old age, and the soldier had died alone, willing the house and land to a woman no one had ever heard of or bothered to try to find. The house and land lay fallow and forgotten, blocked from sight by bushes and brush until only Stillwater lifers knew a neat little Craftsman was once out Old Stillwater Highway, just past the city limits, near the river.

Volunteer firemen soaked the surrounding field with water, more concerned with wildfire prevention and saving the pastures next door than an old ramshackle house long rumored to be a haven for hobos, hippies, satanists, wetbacks, or meth heads, depending on the decade.

Stillwater Chief of Police Jack McBride, eight weeks on the job, knew none of the history as he stood back, watching the heat pulse like a heartbeat on the fringe of the fire's aura. The mud-colored smoke hovered, as if reluctant to leave, before giving up and fading in the gray November dusk.

"Jack?"

Jack turned from the smoldering house to see Sheriff Ann Newberry approaching. As if on cue, the house's stone chimney collapsed into the scorched front yard.

"Ann, what brings you to Stillwater during rush hour?" He glanced at the steady stream of rubberneckers being directed past the scene by his two new deputies. "I hope you stopped by to take the case off my hands. It's outside city limits, after all."

"Doesn't look like there'll be much to investigate."

"Nope."

"Think it was deliberate? A belated Halloween prank?"

Jack took a deep breath. He coughed. "Smell that?"

Ann lifted her nose. She was experienced enough to know the smell of burning flesh buried beneath wood and brush. "Christ. Let's hope it's dead animals we're smelling." Ann turned her head away and coughed. "Why I'm really here is to tell you we've finished with Pollard's journals. I've brought you copies so you don't have to drive to Yourkeville every night."

Six weeks earlier, on suspicion of long-running corruption, Jack and Ann had searched former Stillwater Chief of Police Buck Pollard's house. Their disappointment at not finding trunks of cash and a ledger detailing who paid what and when dissipated when they found county police files, long thought lost, boxes of journals written in Pollard's hand going back forty years, and child porn on his computer. The next day, word had come from the Coast Guard: Pollard's boat had been found in the Gulf of Mexico, capsized in a September storm. Pollard's body had never been found.

"You didn't need to do that," Jack said.

"You like spending every night in the Yourkeville crime lab reading a dead man's journals?"

"I mean I could've sent Starling down to get them."

"Well, I wanted some fish at Mabel's," Ann said.

"I'm partial to her fried chicken."

"You can't go wrong with either." A lull followed and Ann said, "So, tomorrow we tell the others."

Because they weren't sure how far and wide across Yourke County Buck Pollard's corruption reached, only a handful of people knew about the search and seizure. Surprisingly, not a word had leaked. A silence that started out as a test of Jack's senior deputy Sergeant Miner Jesson's loyalty ended up being the confirmation that not everyone in Yourke County was beholden to Pollard. Though sometimes it felt like it. Tomorrow they would tell the other Yourke county police chiefs about what they'd found and hope they didn't resent being kept in the dark for almost two months.

A tall, thin policeman with lank hair sticking out from under his Stetson walked over to Jack and Ann. "Sheriff. Chief." Even though Jack saw him every day, Miner stuck out his hand. Jack wasn't sure if it was a sign of respect for his position as chief of police or merely a habit of Miner's, the bone-deep instillation of country manners into this thoroughly country man.

Miner looked at the house, which had burned itself out in record time. "Suppose it's a blessing in disguise. The tweakers'll have to find another hangout. Drove by Willow Street on my way over. There's a '84 GMC parked back there that's registered to Paco Morales."

"Name doesn't ring a bell," Jack said.

"He stays out of trouble. Been around for thirty years or more. Was legalized back in '86. Was a regular at the Chevron but's been working out at the country club for years now."

"The same country club Joe Doyle owns?" Jack said.

"The same."

"Willow Street?" Ann asked.

"Some'll park back there and walk across the pasture so as to not park on the road, draw attention," Miner said.

"This Morales ever been picked up for drugs?" Jack said.

"Not to my knowledge. I'll run him to make sure," Miner replied.

Ann shrugged. "I've never heard of him."

The firemen roamed over the wreckage, checking for and dousing hot spots. Jack looked down at his square-toed dress shoes, his recent polishing shot to hell, and, not for the first time, realized he wasn't dressed for real police work, or at least the kind he'd been doing in Stillwater, Texas, for the last two months.

As if reading Jack's mind, Ann said, "There's a uniform shop on the square in Yourkeville if you're in the market. It's gonna be hell getting the smoke out of that wool suit and silk tie. If you want, I can walk around the house so you don't get your shoes dirty."

"Ha ha."

"I'll go," Miner said.

When he was out of earshot, Ann asked Jack, "Debate starts soon. You gonna go?"

"I suppose I should, as chief, but I can't vote," he said. "Haven't lived here long enough."

"Do I need to ask who you'd vote for?"

The general consensus seemed to be Joe Doyle was about to be elected to the open city council seat. How it was even a contest, Jack didn't understand. Joe's opponent, Ellie Yourke Martin, was a pillar of the community. Joe Doyle was outwardly a successful businessman; behind the scenes, he was the biggest drug lord in Yourke County. It had only been a theory of Jack's until a week ago when he came across an entry in one of Pollard's journals that seemed to confirm it, justifying Jack spending the last six weeks holed up in the Yourkeville crime lab, pouring over the journals and tossing information to the DEA and FBI, who had been investigating Pollard for six months.

"Well, I sure as hell wouldn't vote for Joe Doyle." It was unconscionable to Jack for a crook like Doyle to hold a position of power, even in an insignificant small East Texas town like Stillwater.

"Ellie doesn't stand much of a chance, I hear," Ann said.

"I hear the same."

Ann paused and said, "Anything ever happen there, with Ellie?"

Jack jingled the keys and change in his pocket. Anything ever happen there? An easy question with a complicated answer.

The firemen at the back of the smoldering ruin raised their arms and waved them over as Jack's phone rang. His wife's picture flashed on the screen. He almost ignored it, but figured it was better to get it over with and answered as water sloshed over his shoes and seeped inside. "Shit."

"Nice," Julie said.

"I'm not cussing at you. What is it, Julie? I'm at a scene."

"I thought we were going to the debate together."

"I'm working."

"Really, Jack?"

"Yes, really. Would you like to talk to the fireman standing beside me, putting out a fire?"

"I thought the whole point of hiring new people was so you didn't work as much."

Jack sighed. "I'm still the chief, Julie. I have to go. We'll talk later."

"Jack, don't han—" Jack clicked off and put the phone in his pocket.

"Problems at home?" Ann asked.

Jack shook his head. "Second verse, same as the first."

Ann and Jack walked behind the wreckage and stopped next to Miner and the fire chief.

"Shit," Ann said.

The fireman looked at Jack. "You seem to attract 'em, don't you?"

The fireman walked off, leaving Jack, Ann, and Miner staring down at the charred, smoking remains of two bodies.

CHAPTER THREE

Jack left once the halogen lights were brought to the scene so Simon Jones, the lead crime tech, could sweep for trace evidence as late into the night as need be. The scene would be active for hours yet, though the officers would spend most of the time standing around, waiting for other people to do their jobs. Jack thought to use the scene as a way to get out of attending the debate, but with three Stillwater cops and half a dozen county deputies standing around waiting for something to do, he couldn't justify it. He'd make a quick appearance at the debate and still be back in plenty of time to see the bodies tagged and bagged.

Jack turned off Old Yourkeville Highway and onto Boondoggle Road. In a nod to its founding by a lumber baron, Stillwater's streets were all unimaginatively named after trees. Except Boondoggle Road. Only old-timers who remembered the fight against building the road during the postwar boom of the fifties said the name with any derision these days. Jack guessed the same residents who were against moving the main road a mile west of downtown back then would be voting on Tuesday for Doyle, the man who made his fortune from the move, and against Ellie, who wanted to pull businesses back downtown. Apparently Doyle's supporters' nostalgia for the good old days rested more on the status quo than in revitalizing downtown if it meant pulling in new residents and tourists. *Outsiders.*

When he couldn't put it off any longer, Jack pulled into Stillwater High School's parking lot and went inside. He opened the front doors to the school and wrinkled his nose against the faint, tangy aroma of teenage body odor hovering in the air. Chris Ryan, Joe Doyle's son-in-law, watched the debate through the rectangular window in the auditorium door. Chris was stocky, with a big head and a bull neck, an athlete gone to seed. "Hi, Chris," Jack said.

Chris jumped away from the door as though he'd been electrocuted. Confusion and fear flashed across his face before his expression fell into an easy grin. "Hey, Chief. You scared me."

"Obviously." Chris was dressed in khakis and a Nike half-zip pullover and smelled of grass and sweat. "Glad I ran into you," Jack said. "You know Paco Morales?"

"Sure. He's one of my groundskeepers. Head one, in fact." Chris wrinkled his nose and sniffed. "Why do you smell like smoke?"

"Came from the fire out on 107. We found Morales's truck parked back on Willow Street, behind DI. You send Morales to corporate for anything?"

Chris turned his hat forward and shook his head. "No."

"Seen Morales lately?"

"Today at work."

"Ever had any problem with him?"

The front door of the school opened and Miner Jesson entered.

"No, none. Very reliable. Why? Do you think he's involved in the fire?"

Jack shrugged. "His truck is abandoned where floppers tend to park." Jack jerked his head toward the debate raging inside. "Going in?"

"I guess I have to. Michelle's already ballistic I'm late. You?"

Miner walked up. "Hey, Chris. How's your game?"

"I'm winning more than I'm losing."

"Can't complain about that, huh?"

Chris shrugged and entered. When the door closed, Jack turned to Miner. "Let's go in the audio booth." Jack knocked on a windowless door next to the auditorium door and opened it.

A teenager swiveled in his chair as the two men entered. The kid's eyes widened, and he pulled his headphones off. "Sir?"

Jack pulled a couple of ones from his wallet. "Take a five-minute break. Get something from the vending machine."

Eyes bulging like golf balls, the kid took the money and bolted.

"What did you find?" Jack said.

"Esperanza Perez is Paco Morales's daughter."

Esperanza Perez had been an important part of solving Jack's first case in Stillwater, the murders of Gilberto and Rosa Ramos. She'd also been the alibi of their initial suspect, Diego Vazquez, who turned out to be the front man for the Pedroza drug cartel as well as the man who escaped Jack's custody his first day on the job. Every police department in Yourke County had been searching for Diego for the last eight weeks, and no one had been able to find him.

"What?"

"Yep. Said he hasn't come home. Usually gets home by six when it turns dark early. Sometimes he goes out again, but he never came home tonight."

"She seem worried?"

"She tried to hide it, but yeah. How soon will Jones get to the bodies?"

"He's sending them to Tyler," Jack said. "It's beyond his scope. Said he'd try to rush the bullets and the trace evidence, but considering his backlog, he didn't promise anything. Apparently, the Sheriff's department found a meth lab in some Dallas oil company executive's lake house. They cooked in it but didn't do a good job of cleaning up."

Miner watched the debate through the opaque glass.

"Set up in a house that's rarely used, leave before they realize. No one's the wiser. Surprised it took them so long to think of it."

"Maybe they're getting sloppy." Jack followed Miner's gaze but pointedly avoided looking in Ellie's direction. Joe Doyle watched Ellie with a condescending smirk on his tanned face. With a full head of silver hair styled in an elaborate pompadour and his dark suit and power tie, Doyle looked like a televangelist and was about as trustworthy.

Jack could look at Doyle's oily countenance for only so long. He stared down at the sound board.

"Wanna hear what they're saying?" Miner pulled the headphone plug from the jack before Jack could reply.

Ellie's whiskey-soaked voice filled the room. Jack focused on counting the number of bald spots in the audience until Joe Doyle started talking.

If you're such a pussy you can't even look at her, just leave, you idiot.

Jack jingled the keys in his pockets. He should leave. If he waited until the debate ended, he would get caught up with talking to residents and coming face to face with Ellie was almost guaranteed. Considering the size of Stillwater, they had done an amazing job of avoiding each other since September, the day his wife came home. He was strong as long as he wasn't anywhere near Ellie, but he wasn't a fucking robot.

He would leave.

His mistake was glancing at Ellie as she pushed a strand of hair behind her right ear. He was swamped with the memory of the first time he saw the mannerism two months earlier, when he sat across the desk from her and talked about Stillwater history and signed mortgage papers. The ache in the center of his chest, the one he had done a pretty good job of ignoring for the past six weeks, intensified. Ellie's eyes left Joe Doyle and moved to the back of the auditorium before fixing on the smoky glass separating them.

What was I thinking?

Ellie stood on stage in her high school auditorium for the first time in twenty-five years and listened to Joe Doyle slyly dredge up every scandal of her life.

It was, unfortunately, a long and varied list.

Her mother's suicide.

Her father's gambling, drinking, carousing, and his legendary hatred for his only child.

Witnessing the suicide of her best friend on a Lake Yourke dock in 1985.

The point-shaving allegations from the 1988 Girls State Basketball Championship.

Fertility problems. A lying, cheating husband who swindled Stillwater residents and was serving time in Huntsville.

Divorce.

Ellie doodled "Fuck you, Joe Doyle" on her legal pad. She clicked her pen, put it down, and tried to hide her smile. She always wondered what politicians wrote during debates. Now she knew.

Ellie's eyes roamed over the crowd. She knew everyone there, figured 30 percent would vote for her out of pure spite for Doyle. If dredging up tired old scandals was the best Joe Doyle could do to discredit her, maybe this election wasn't . . .

Oh, hell no. Did he call me a liberal?

Ellie removed her glasses and pushed her hair behind her ear. If that wasn't the nail in the coffin of her ill-advised campaign, she didn't know what was.

She should probably listen to what Doyle was saying, but what was the use? She wasn't going to win. She knew it. Everyone in this auditorium knew it. They all came tonight to witness her inevitable humiliation at Doyle's hands. There was too much in her history to overcome the modicum of respect she had been able to build over the last ten years. She knew plenty of people admired her, but those same people, as well as the ones who still held reservations about her, wouldn't be able to resist the sight of her disgrace. Stillwater residents had been the rubberneckers to her car wreck of a life for too long to change now.

The audience looked bored, and Ellie couldn't blame them. She glanced at the clock above the sound room window. Fifteen more minutes. She steeled herself to pay attention to Doyle so she could rebut when she saw Jack through the sound booth window. She didn't need to see clearly to know it was him; she knew his stance, the slope of his shoulders. His hands were in his pockets, absently jingling his keys, she had no doubt, but his eyes were on her.

The memory of those eyes raking over her, possessively, appreciatively, made her skin tingle, a welcome change from the intermittent nausea that plagued her all day. His hair was longer, a little disheveled, as though he'd been running his fingers through it—the long, square tipped fingers that had skimmed along her skin like . . .

"Ms. Yourke Martin?"

The debate monitor's nasally voice clawed through her consciousness like fingernails on a chalkboard. "Yes?"

"Your rebuttal?"

Of course. The debate.

In the audience, Julie McBride rose, walked up the aisle and out the door.

Ellie smiled at the moderator. "I'm sorry, Leo. What was the question again? I was too busy reliving my sordid past to take much notice of the points Joe tried to make. Or, maybe I'm correct in assuming his point was to merely distract this audience, and me, from the real issues?"

Jack couldn't breathe. Could she see him?

Ellie returned her focus to the moderator and broke the connection. Had there been a connection or did he just want there to be one? She couldn't possibly know he was here, at this spot, amid the hundreds of people in the audience.

Now that he'd looked at her, he couldn't stop. Though more than a hundred feet separated them, Jack knew the brown flecks in Ellie's green eyes were accentuated by the conservative camel-colored dress she wore, whose square neckline revealed enough to entice the men without offending the women. It dipped a shade lower than the First Baptist congregants would think appropriate, but the gemstone flag pin on her left breast and the single strand of pearls made up for it. The classically tailored dress stopped a few inches above the knee, but Jack's gaze continued down past her toned calves to the nude patent leather four-inch heels. Jack knew every red-blooded man in the audience had entertained the fantasy of seeing Ellie in nothing but those pearls, shoes, and the reading glasses she held in her left hand.

It kinda pissed him off.

"What did Doyle say about basketball?" Jack said, not taking his eyes off Ellie.

Miner nodded to the audience. "Here comes your wife."

Julie McBride smiled at him as she walked up the aisle. Talk about a study in contrasts. Where Ellie was tall and elegant, Julie was petite and a bundle of barely constrained energy. Jack wasn't surprised in the least she had been able to zone in on where he was, despite his best efforts at being incognito. He should have left earlier. Or not come at all.

Ellie's easy smile was now strained.

Julie entered the video booth without knocking and coughed. "It smells like smoke in here."

"I told you we were at a fire."

"Right. Hey, Miner. Good to see you." She smiled broadly at Jack's deputy, but the smile didn't reach her eyes.

"You, too," Miner said with a goofy, embarrassed grin. Julie had that effect on people, even men like Miner who were usually deceptively astute in reading people. Jack wanted to slap Miner and tell him Julie thought he was a rube without the sense God gave a slug.

"Hi, honey." She hugged Jack. The top of her head barely brushed the knot of his tie. He squeezed her briefly in return, grasped her elbow gently, and pulled her away from him as discretely as possible. She coughed and waved her hand in front of her face. "God, that's awful."

"Miner was about to tell me about Doyle's basketball comment."

"He doesn't like Ellie much, does he," Julie said with a wry smile.

"If Big Jake, Ellie's dad, would have gotten Ellie's property away from her," Miner said, "Doyle was set to buy it. Still hasn't forgiven her for having a backbone."

"The championship?" Jack said.

"Ellie was accused of throwing the championship game. Point shaving." Jack's head jerked back. "Impossible."

"She was the star, had the sweetest shot you've ever seen," Miner said. "She was money at the free throw line, something like 92 percent and still holds the UIL record for three pointers, I think."

"Impressive," Julie said.

"So, when she had a horrible game, people wondered, but no one believed it. Didn't help Big Jake was the biggest bookie in Yourke County. Everyone assumed he put money on the game. The coach kept her in until the end. With time winding down and losing by ten, Big Jake was poised to win thousands."

"He bet against his daughter?" Julie asked.

"He was a son of a bitch," Miner said, matter-of-factly. "Game's all but over. Ellie takes the ball down the court, everyone had given up, her team, the other team. She walked down the court, unopposed. She stepped inside the three-point line and dribbled once, twice, as the clock ticked down. Five seconds, four seconds. At three seconds, she stepped behind the three-point line and let it fly."

Jack leaned forward. There was a small smile on Miner's face. "Most beautiful shot I've ever seen, and I've seen a lot of basketball," he said. "Everyone in that field house held their breath as that ball arced through the air."

"Did she make it?" Jack said.

"What kind of story would it be if she missed?"

"She covered the spread, didn't she?"

"Yep."

"She went against her father?" Julie said, flabbergasted. Julie was too much of a daddy's girl to understand, or condone, a child betraying a parent's wishes.

"Of course she did," Miner said. "She's as honest as the day is long."

"I guess," Julie said, still unconvinced. "Jack, can I see you outside for a minute?"

Jack opened the door for Julie. "Bye, Miner," Julie said with a broad smile.

When the door closed behind them, Julie's smile fell from her face like rock slide.

"When did you get here?"

"Five or ten minutes ago."

"I saved you a seat."

"I didn't want to disturb the debate."

Julie scoffed. "It's a fucking city council debate."

"It's important to the people here and I wanted to respect that."

"Oh, and I didn't? Is that what you're saying?"

"That wasn't what I was saying, or even implying, Julie."

"That's what it sounded like to me."

Jack put his clenched hands in his pockets. Change the subject. Move on. "I didn't see Ethan. Is he here?"

"No. He was at Troy's doing homework."

For someone who wanted his parents to mend fences to restore the three of them to a happy family, Ethan was conspicuously absent from home a lot of the time. Jack was torn between wanting Ethan to spend time with his new friends, Troy, Olivia, and Mitra, and wanting Ethan to spend time with his mother to see that the last year without her hadn't been so bad after all. If Jack was honest, he missed having Ethan to himself, spending time with his moody 14-year-old son. He wondered if Ethan missed him or if he'd even noticed they'd barely seen each other these last few weeks.

"I thought he said he would get extra credit for attending," Jack said.

Julie shrugged. "Guess it wasn't worth it. Anyway, I want him to like me, not hate me for dragging him to this snoozefest. Your brother's here, though. Right down front, supporting his girlfriend."

"Is he?" Screw putting in an appearance with the community. The last thing Jack wanted was to run into Ellie with Julie connected to his hip. "Listen, I have to get back to the fire scene."

"Can't Miner take charge?"

"No."

Her face softened and she moved close to him. She ran her hand up and down the smooth, silk fabric of his tie. She bit her bottom lip and dropped her voice into the sexy baby-doll timbre he knew so well. "We've only made love twice since I came back. You know we work best when we have that."

When Julie turned on this persona, Jack could easily forget that hatred made his heart race when he was near Julie instead of desire.

"Maybe I want more than sex, Julie."

Her laugh was harsh. "You didn't before."

Before I didn't know there could be more. He looked away. "Why did you come back?"

"I told you. I missed my family."

"Bullshit."

"Jack, you and Ethan are the world to me. Tell me what you want and I'll do it."

Though they were alone in the foyer, Jack lowered his voice to a harsh whisper. "I want for the last year to have never happened. To not have had to lie to Ethan for a year about where you were, why you left. To never have been suspected of murdering you. To not have lost my career because you decided you wanted to 'find yourself.' Can you do any of those things?"

She sighed dramatically and rolled her eyes.

"You ruined my life, Julie. You're delusional if you think I'll take you back with open arms."

"Well, let me know when you're done punishing me," she said.

"I'm not punishing you."

"Then what do you call this? Because it's not a marriage."

The auditorium doors opened. Julie moved to Jack's side and intertwined her arm with his to meet the Stillwater residents, her demeanor now one of an enthusiastic resident.

Jack's soft response was lost amid the rumble of the crowd. "I call this temporary."

CHAPTER FOUR

Ellie walked to the center of the stage, hand outstretched. She met Joe Doyle's wolfish grin with a firm grip and a broad, fake smile.

"You bastard," Ellie said through gritted teeth.

"Welcome to the big leagues, Elliot." They held each other's hands and smiled while the newspaper photographer took their picture. As soon as she gave them the all-done thumbs up, Ellie dropped Doyle's hand, but the smile remained for the benefit of the lingering audience.

"Was that necessary?"

"No. But, it was fun," Doyle said.

"You lost as many votes as you gained by dredging up my past. It made you look small, Joe. Worse, you looked desperate."

"Oh, I don't think so."

"Of course you don't. You were too busy being pleased with yourself to watch the audience." Doyle's smile flickered. Ellie tilted her head and studied her late father's best friend. "Admit it, Joe. You're worried."

Doyle laughed and waved to someone over Ellie's shoulder. "How do you figure?" he said, scanning the audience as though her reply was so insignificant it didn't require his full attention.

"If you weren't worried, you would have never called me a Democrat." Ellie clapped him on the shoulder. "Don't worry, Joe. I'll be gracious in victory."

Ellie turned and walked off the stage, past Michelle Ryan, whose condescending grin was a mirror image of her father's, and Chris Ryan, who followed behind Michelle slowly, his head bent in concentration over his iPhone.

Ellie found the gap in the musty stage curtain and edged through it to hide in the darkest part of backstage. Eyes closed, she leaned her forehead against the cold, cinder-block wall and tried to breathe through her racing heart. Hoping for proof of a fever and justification for the sick feeling she'd had all day, she pressed her hands against her cheeks. She was disappointed. She wasn't sick. She was stupid. Maybe a little bit pathetic. Okay. Both.

The bravado she showed with Doyle was bullshit, and he knew it as well as she did. But, if nothing else came of this quixotic campaign, at least Ellie finally got to call Joe Doyle a bastard to his face, something she'd wanted to do for years. It was cold comfort when what she really wanted to do was to crush him at the polls, but she would take the small victory. She knew better than anyone a series of small, seemingly insignificant victories could lead to a coup. One had to be patient.

"Hey. What are you doing back here?"

Kelly Kendrick stepped out of the darkness, holding Ellie's notepad, a worried expression on her face.

Ellie smiled. "Reliving old memories."

"Do you feel okay?" Kelly asked. She put her hand on Ellie's forehead. "There were times you looked like you were going to puke out there."

"Was it that obvious?"

Kelly shrugged. "Probably just to me."

Ellie appreciated her friend lying to make her feel better. If Ellie were a better friend, she would tell Kelly what made her want to vomit wasn't the debate or even Joe Doyle's character assassination, but the sight of Jack McBride's silhouette in the sound room window and his wife walking out of the auditorium to meet him.

"I think I might be coming down with something," Ellie said. "I've felt bad all day."

Kelly nodded to the Exit sign glowing from the shadows. "Want to sneak out back?"

"More than anything. But, I can't."

Kelly nodded and handed Ellie the legal pad. "You did good. Doyle looked like an asshole for bringing all that stuff up."

"He *is* an asshole."

"You don't need to be a city councilwoman to make a difference in this town. You know it and I know it." Kelly held out her arms and waved her hands. "Come here."

Ellie let her oldest friend hug her. Kelly squeezed and patted her on the back, like a mother would. "Everyone in this town loves and respects you. They tolerate Doyle."

Ellie squeezed Kelly and released her before the urge to cry overcame her. "Thanks. Let's go glad-hand the masses."

Arm in arm, they walked onto the stage and were met by Eddie McBride. His eyes lit up when he saw the two friends. "What were you two ladies doing back there? Or should I ask?"

"God, men are so predictable." Kelly released Ellie's arm and walked on.

Eddie and Ellie watched her go. "Why does she hate me?"

They walked across the stage, down the stairs, and up the aisle. "She doesn't hate you. She hates your twin brother."

"Why?"

"Mike Freeman."

"And, I'm guilty by association."

Ellie shrugged.

"Does she know about you and Jack?" Eddie asked in a low whisper. Eddie opened the auditorium doors to a low roar of conversation amplified by the cinder block walls and tile floor. Ellie's eyes were drawn to Jack like a magnet. He stood with Julie and the Doyle entourage. Julie and Michelle looked over in her direction. Somehow she knew they were talking about her.

Ellie turned so she was facing away from Jack. "No."

Eddie raised his eyebrows. "I thought you two were best friends."

"We are."

She didn't feel like explaining why she didn't tell Kelly about her brief affair with Jack McBride, mostly because she couldn't explain it. At first, it was a matter of discretion. Jack was married, and Ellie didn't want another scandal. When Julie returned before Jack could file for divorce, Ellie and Jack decided the best thing to do was to break it off, at least until after the holidays, for Ethan's sake. It seemed pointless to tell Kelly after the fact. As time went on, the opportunity to tell Kelly faded until it was too late. Now the first reaction from her lifelong friend wouldn't be worry over how Ellie was handling the separation, but anger at not being told earlier.

Thank God, people came up to Ellie and congratulated her on a job well done, saving her from a more detailed answer. Eddie stood back, hands in his pockets (like his brother), smiled, and greeted people when necessary, acting more like a bodyguard than anything. When Matt Doyle walked up and shook Eddie's hand while his wife, Amy, hugged Ellie, a shiver ran down her spine at the coupleness of the scene. It wasn't helped by the fact Matt and Amy held hands throughout the greetings. Ellie shifted away from Eddie in case he got any ideas.

"Great job, Ellie," Matt said. He released his wife's hand and casually draped his arm across her shoulders. "I think you changed a few people's minds."

"We'll see."

When Ellie decided to run for city council, Matt and Amy had contacted her immediately and thrown their support behind her. On the one hand, it wasn't a surprise. Since Matt and Amy moved to town the year before, they'd been heavily involved in the Stillwater Historical Society with Ellie, and any campaign that focused on preservation and attracting young families to Stillwater would get their support. On the other hand, Matt was Joe Doyle's youngest child, the favorite according to many, and his defection had caused some strife in his family. His support of Ellie hadn't wavered, but when it came time to pull the lever, Ellie wouldn't be surprised if Matt voted for his father.

"Why didn't you mention the hotel?" Amy asked. She leaned forward and whispered, "I think the news would easily shave a few old-timers from Joe's supporters."

Of all Ellie's downtown property, the Henry Hotel was the biggest thorn in her side. It had been abandoned for twenty years since the management company contracted to run it went out of business. No other company had been willing to step in and manage an out-of-date hotel with low occupancy rates. Most people in town thought Ellie should have reopened the Henry instead of opening a bookstore. Ellie knew she needed to draw businesses into town before she could justify investing the time and money into a fifteen-room historic hotel with lead paint and mold. As luck would have it, a friend of Ellie's in Dallas was in historic renovations and had jumped at the chance to see the Henry when she mentioned it.

"I don't want to mention it until it's a done deal," Ellie said. "Plus, I don't want the opposition to find out and try to sabotage us."

"Good point," Matt said.

"Curtis has a chef interested in opening a small restaurant. An organic restaurant," Ellie said. "Your name might have come up."

Matt's eyes lit up. "No kidding?"

"He and the chef are coming on Tuesday to see the property. I know it's election day, but it's the only day that worked."

"What time?"

"They'll be at my bookstore at ten."

"I'll be there," Matt said. He and Amy shared an excited smile.

"We still on for tomorrow morning?" Ellie asked Amy.

Amy inhaled in fake apprehension. "I guess. Yes. Yes, we are. Four miles?"

"Yep," Ellie said. "You can do it."

"Of course she can," Eddie said, winking at Amy. She blushed and glanced at her husband.

Matt playfully punched Eddie in the arm. "Stop flirting with my wife."

Six weeks earlier, when Ellie's life imploded like a dying star, she had jumped at Amy's shy request to run together. Amy wanted to lose weight, and Ellie needed to get out of her head for an hour and focus on someone else. Amy was a bit of a chatterbox and a well-placed question would send her off to the races. Ellie thought for sure Amy would run out of conversation eventually, but so far she hadn't. Ellie, a solidarity runner for years, was surprised at how much she enjoyed running with Amy.

Julie McBride pushed into the small group, a bright smile on her perfectly symmetrical face. "Great job, Ellie."

Julie looked like the quintessential John Hughes movie villainess. The girl everyone hated but was too afraid of to confront. Ellie stared down at the petite woman and guessed she could pick up Julie with one arm and hurl her across the foyer with ease. Ellie inched away from Jack's wife before she acted on the urge and forced herself to be polite.

"Thanks, Julie. Do you know Matt and Amy Doyle?"

"No."

Ellie made the introductions. She stepped back while they made small talk and was plotting her escape when Julie said, "Miner told me and Jack about your basketball scandal."

Matt and Amy stilled. Ellie's smile stiffened. Everyone in town knew the story, but no one talked about it. At least, not to her face. "Did he?"

"It took courage to go against your family like that."

"You'd know all about that, I suppose." The jibe was out of her mouth before Ellie could stop herself.

When Julie arrived in town a week after Jack and his son, Ethan, the town swallowed Julie's story of being on a family-approved yearlong sabbatical like sweet tea on a hot summer day. Ellie was the only person in town who knew the truth.

Ellie hurried to cover her snide comment. "The difference being you have a supportive, forgiving family. My father never liked me much, so it didn't take as much courage as you think."

Julie's eyes narrowed, her face a mask of forced good humor. "Did your father ever forgive you?"

"No. He hated me until the day he died. Better him hating me than losing my self-respect. I've never regretted it."

"How admirable." The word twisted from her mouth, more insult than compliment. "Jack and I barely know you, but we know you'd never do something like throw a game."

You'd be shocked at how well your husband knows me.

"Thank you."

"Yeah, first impressions are usually *bang* on, aren't they, Jules?" Eddie said.

Julie turned to Eddie and narrowed her eyes. "Oh, I didn't notice you there, Eddie."

"Sure you didn't."

"If you'll excuse me," Ellie said. She felt sorry abandoning Amy and Matt, but they were by far the best people to handle Julie McBride. They would chit-chat about inconsequential stuff and let Julie lead the conversation around to her favorite subject—herself.

Not paying attention to where she was going, only the urge to get away, she pretended to wave at someone across the room and ran straight into Jack. Her legal pad fell out of her hand and slid across the floor.

"Oh."

Their eyes met and the leap of her heart triggered the memory of the first time she had been this close to him. How the bright lights from the football field threw his bruised face into shadow, how vulnerable he'd seemed, how she had been desperate to escape him and whatever it was she felt. Now, she wanted to bury her face in his neck, to nuzzle the soft spot behind his ear and breathe in his pine-tinged, woodsy cologne, which sent tingles up and down the inside of her left leg.

Christ Almighty. You're in the middle of the high school. Get a grip.

Jack stepped back, picked up her legal pad, and read the message on the top page. His eyebrow quirked into an incredulous arch. He pulled the page off, folded it, and put it in his coat pocket. "I'll trash this for you."

Ellie stepped toward him and away from the group. She took the legal pad and was impressed by how strong and clear her voice sounded when she thanked him. Ellie stared at the cleft in his chin and felt herself leaning toward him, as if an inexorable force pulled them together. She crossed her arms and pretended Jack was any other citizen, talking to her about the election.

"Why do you smell like smoke?"

"Do you know the One-Armed Soldier's home?"

"Out on 107? Yeah."

"It burned to the ground."

"I suppose it's a blessing in disguise."

Jack leaned forward and whispered. "Except for the two bodies inside."

Ellie's eyes widened. "Any ideas?"

"Not very good ones. You know Paco Morales?"

"Name doesn't ring a bell. Was he . . . ?"

Jack shrugged. "Maybe. I thought you knew everyone in town," he said with a wry smile.

"Almost."

"I don't need to tell you to keep this between us, do I?"

"No."

"Didn't think so." His gaze subtly traveled down and up her figure. "I like your dress."

Ellie looked down at the tan dress and touched her mother's pearls. "I look like Barbara Bush."

Jack chuckled. "I guarantee you, no man in that audience thought of Barbara Bush when they looked at you."

She laughed and leaned forward conspiratorially. "I guarantee you, you were the only one thinking naughty thoughts."

"Good."

She shook her head and glanced at the group behind them. Kelly had joined the group and eyed Ellie suspiciously, but thankfully Julie's back was turned. Somehow she and Jack had managed to avoid the attention of any of the other citizens. Ellie didn't know if she should be happy for the time with Jack or upset none of the residents cared enough about her campaign to talk to her. She decided to enjoy what conversation she could steal with Jack and try to prolong it as long as possible.

"How's your secret project going?" Their last night together, Jack had told her about Pollard's journals and sworn her to secrecy.

"I'm learning more about the residents of Stillwater than I ever wanted to know."

"As long as you don't use it against anyone."

"You know me better than that."

Her eyes slid down to his lips. "I do." It came out as a hoarse whisper. She dropped her gaze to the yellow legal pad, cleared her throat, and forced herself to meet his eyes. "I need to tell you—"

The rapid clicks of a camera interrupted her. The newspaper photographer was taking a picture of the group behind Ellie. Relief washed through her. Wouldn't that be the cherry on top of a disastrous night? A photo catching Ellie mooning at Jack McBride while his wife stood two feet away.

"What?" Jack said in a low, urgent voice. He touched her arm. "What do you need to tell me?"

She pulled her arm away but not before the familiar jolt of desire shot through her. She needed to get away from him. "Later. Thanks for coming," Ellie said and moved away.

CHAPTER FIVE

Jack was so bleary-eyed from his all-nighter, he almost ran over the drunk stumbling down the shoulder of Boondoggle Road.

The first time Jack stopped Fred Muldoon, he suspected he was being punked, that Fred was like all the other friends of Buck Pollard's who had made it their mission in life to waste as much of Jack's time as possible on groundless complaints. A few incoherent sentences into the conversation and Jack knew Fred didn't have the faculties to carry off any sort of grand plan, unless the grand plan was begging for money at the corner of Main and Old Yourkeville and buying a fifth of Old Crow with the proceeds.

Jack rolled down the window of his cruiser. "Fred, what are you doing out at this time of night?"

"That you, Chief?"

"Yeah, Fred. What are you doing out here on the highway?"

"Walking."

"Walking where?"

"Wherever."

Jack pulled off on the shoulder in front of Fred and got out. "Come on. I'll take you home." Jack grasped Fred's arm as he stumbled forward. "Have you eaten anything today?"

"It's tomorrow." Fred nodded to something over Jack's shoulder. The chief turned and saw a tinge of light breaking over the horizon.

"So it is," Jack said. He opened the back door to the squad car. "Come on. I'll buy you a honey bun."

"I ain't hungry, but I'm thirsty."

"Then I'll buy you a coffee. Abe'll have it on fresh, I bet."

"Abe ain't brewed a good pot of coffee since 1976."

"I didn't say it would be good. I said it would be fresh."

When Jack was settled in the front and driving off, Fred said, "Why you out patrolling at the crack of dawn. Ain't that some probies' job?"

"I like to pull my weight." *And avoid my wife.*

Jack turned into the Chevron and parked beneath the blazing lights. "Be right back."

The convenience store was empty save the large man behind the counter. Abe wore the same thing he'd worn every day Jack had walked through the doors—dingy overalls, an International Harvester hat, and a scraggly beard.

"Abe."

"Chief."

Jack made a beeline for the coffee counter, poured two large cups, and picked up a couple of honey buns on the way to the register.

Abe rang Jack up. "You really like them honey buns. I've had to buy a new case just last week. First time in years."

Jack paused. "How old were the ones I've been eating?"

"Oh, they weren't outta date. Don't you worry." When Jack didn't move, Abe continued. "You never got sick, didja?"

"No."

"Then, there you go. That Fred Muldoon you got in the car there?"

"Yeah."

"Huh. I figgered for sure he's one of the bodies you found out at the old soldier's home."

"Fred lives over on Birch."

Abe screwed up his face. "Fred ain't lived on Birch Street in thirty years. Don't live nowhere as far as I know. ID'd those bodies yet?"

"It's only been fifteen hours, Abe." Jack held up the buns. "Thanks."

"See you tomorrow."

Jack put the buns in his pocket, picked up the coffees, and left. He got in the car and tossed the two honey buns into Fred's lap. Fred held one of his shoes and was staring at the sole. The car smelled like stale Fritos.

"Jesus, put your shoe on, Fred."

"I need new soles."

Jack rolled down the windows to get some air flowing. "You need to wash your feet."

"Probably." He put his shoe back on and held up a honey bun. "Don't you want one?"

"I'm good."

Jack drove out of the parking lot. "Abe seemed to think you were one of those bodies out at the One-Armed Soldier's home."

"I've flopped out there before."

"Flopped out there lately?"

"Nah. Too many meth heads. Those people are crazy. I miss the hippies. Stoned and happy and fucking anyone willing."

"Hear any chatter about who the two unlucky ones might be?"

"Nope."

Fred finished the honey buns and was blowing on the surface of his coffee. He looked at Jack in the rearview mirror. "Surely that ain't it."

"Now Fred," Jack said, feigning offense. "Do you think I feed you so I could pump you for information?"

"It ain't the only reason you're nice to me, but it's a big part of it. Don't matter. As long as you give me my fee."

"You aren't spending your CI money on booze, are you?"

"Course not. Groceries and bills. Like I promised."

They went along with the lie because their relationship was mutually beneficial. Fred told Jack rumors he wouldn't normally hear, and Fred got to retain some dignity by not having to beg for drinking money.

"What's the word on the street, Fred?"

"Doyle's first order of business when he wins is to get you fired and put Miner in as chief. Probably fire your two new minorities, too. Why'd you hire the Mexican anyway? Ain't you fluent? Your mom's Mexican, ain't she?"

"Officer Malik is highly qualified. Speaking Spanish is a bonus." Jack parked in front of the house on Birch he'd been dropping Fred off at for weeks.

"Seen Kyle Grant around?"

Fred stopped blowing on his coffee and looked at Jack over the rim, his eyes calculating. *Interesting*, Jack thought.

Kyle Grant was a two-bit local hoodlum who'd followed in his father's footsteps down to Huntsville for assault and battery. He graduated from the pen harder and meaner, with rumored ties to the TexaSS, a white-supremacist prison gang with tentacles into the civilian world for drugs, girls, numbers, and murder for hire. For the last few weeks, Kyle Grant's name had come up occasionally, reluctantly, in minor drug busts around Stillwater. Fidgety meth heads were too scared to say Kyle supplied the meth or showed them how to cook it in batches or even asked them to go around town buying up the ingredients.

"Why don't you ask your secretary, Susan? She's married to Kyle's brother," Fred said.

"They don't have a close relationship, I gather."

"Rightly so. Brian Grant might be an unlucky son of a bitch, but he ain't stupid. It's an example you oughta take to heart. Kyle Grant is a mean motherfucker, like his dad."

"I appreciate the concern, Fred, but my job is to catch the mean motherfuckers, not avoid them."

Fred sipped his coffee then said, "I hear Kyle's branched out into heroin."

"Where's he getting it?"

"I ain't that tuned in. I stick to whiskey. It's legal and cheap. And I don't want to know. Quickest way to the grave, getting involved with drugs. Case in point, those two crispy critters at the One-Armed Soldier's house. Your brother better hope one was Kyle."

"Why?"

"Kyle has it out for Eddie. Thinks he's pushing in on his scene."

"I hope you're talking about his job at Doyle's produce company."

Fred laughed. "Shit, Kyle don't work for Matt. He splits his time working between the heavy equipment business and the country club."

"Where'd you hear this about Kyle and Eddie?"

Fred lifted his eyes from his coffee, looking more sober than Jack had ever seen him. "Here and there. Scraps on the street." Fred leaned forward and held out his hand.

"Tell me who said it."

Fred shook his head. "You may not think so, but my life is worth more than a honey bun and a cup of coffee."

Jack pulled out his money clip and removed three twenties. He held one of them out of Fred's reach. "Who?"

Fred licked his lips at the sight of the money, no doubt dreaming of all the whiskey it would buy. His eyes flicked between the money to Jack. He sighed. "I don't know who. I didn't see their faces."

"Where were you?"

"Like I said, here and there. I don't remember specifically."

"When?"

"Earlier this week. Tuesday. Wednesday, maybe."

"What'd you hear, exactly?"

"Christ Almighty, Chief. Ain't that enough?"

"You either give me the names of who was talking or you tell me exactly what they said."

Fred picked at the mole on the side of his nose, staring at the money. "They think having Eddie in their organization will keep you from coming down on them."

"They who? You need to give me a name."

"Can't do that, Chief."

Jack handed one twenty to Fred.

Fred scowled. "A single Jackson is hardly incentive to keep telling you stuff."

"Well, maybe this will incentivize you to pay better attention and tell me more." Jack held two more twenties between his thumb and forefinger.

Fred stared out the window of the car and nodded. "You know, it's coming back to me now."

"What is?"

"Where I mighta been."

Jack waited.

"Now, I ain't sure of it, might have got my days mixed up, but sometimes I sleep in the cabs of DI trucks."

"Doyle Industries?"

"I ain't saying that name. Plausible deniability in case someone tries to torture a confession out of me."

Jack drummed his fingers on the steering wheel. "So, if I'm hearing you right, Kyle Grant talked to someone in DI's truck yard earlier this week about not trusting my brother."

"That's about the sum of it."

Fred reached for the money but Jack pulled it back. "They talk about anything else? Mention anyone else by name?"

Fred dropped his head back on the headrest and stared at the ceiling. He closed his eyes and said, "They mentioned setting up a meeting with the Pedrozas to talk truce."

Jack peeled one twenty and handed it to him. "Was Kyle talking to a man or a woman?"

Fred took the money and sighed dramatically. "You gonna pay for my funeral when I turn up dead?"

"No one's going to kill you, Fred. Tell me what I want to know and I'll give you all of this money, *and* I'll pay to have your shoes resoled."

Fred held out his hand and wiggled his fingers for the remaining twenty. "A woman."

Jack held out the last bill. "Michelle Ryan?"

Fred nodded once and took the Jackson. He removed his fedora and put the money in the inner band and settled it back on his head. He started to get out of the car, but Jack put the car in gear and drove. "What're you doing?" Fred said.

"Taking you to jail."

"What? After all I gave you?"

"I throw you in the drunk tank, no one will think you're an informant, will they? Come sleep in the jail cell for a few hours. I'll bring you a burger and a new pair of shoes."

"Don't want a new pair. Want these resoled."

"If I bring you a pair of shoes, will you wear them while I get yours fixed?"

"You'd do that for me?"

"Of course."

Fred settled back in the seat. "I suppose."

Jack turned onto Main Street and drove through the square to the City Hall. When he stopped the car, he turned around and said, "One more question."

"You don't give up, do you?"

"Did Joe Doyle's name ever come up in the conversation between Kyle and Michelle?"

"No. Not once."

Jack should have been excited about finally getting a connection between Doyle's legitimate businesses and his drug business, but all he could think about was his brother's involvement in it all. As Jack ushered Fred to the holding cell and promised to bring him food later in the day, one thought was running through the back of his mind: it's time to see how serious Eddie is about going straight.

CHAPTER SIX

Eddie McBride was sitting at the kitchen table, drinking Dr. Pepper from a giant Whataburger cup and checking email on his phone when his brother came home.

Jack looked like shit; pale, dark circles under his eyes, his tie loosened, his collar unbuttoned. It was weird, disturbing, to see his brother look like a drunk coming home from a bender, like he was living in some alternate universe where Eddie was the responsible one, where Eddie cleaned up messes Jack made. Sure, Stillwater was different than most towns, but it wasn't *that* out of whack with reality.

Eddie watched as Jack made coffee as quietly as possible. "Hey, man. Brought you some taquitos," Eddie said.

Jack's brow furrowed. "You in Yourkeville this morning?"

"Had a hankering for taquitos. Sleep at the station again?"

Jack filled the coffee urn with water in silence. He placed the empty glass urn on the burner and clicked the pot on. "You off to work?"

"In a minute," Eddie said.

Jack sat at the table and fished a taquito out of the bag. He unwrapped one and took a bite. After he swallowed, he said, "We need to talk."

"About?"

"Your boss. Your job. Why'd you go to work for Joe Doyle of all the businesses in the county?"

"I saw their Now Hiring sign. I stopped in, and Matt hired me on the spot. The day Julie returned to the loving bosom of her family, as a matter of fact. I didn't even know who Joe Doyle was. Barely know him now. Why?"

Jack ate the taquito in three bites. He wiped his mouth with a napkin and reached for another. "I find it interesting my brother, who's been in and out of trouble with drugs for his entire life, so happens to go to work for the biggest drug lord in Yourke County."

Eddie laughed. "Joe Doyle's a drug lord? I don't buy it."

"Why'd you go to work there?"

"I told you why."

"I don't believe you."

Eddie lifted his hands in surrender. "I don't know what to tell you. Besides, I've never seen anything illegal going on."

"They're good. You being on their payroll gives them another layer of protection."

"How do you figure?"

"They think I'll go easy on them to save you."

Eddie laughed. "They don't know you very well."

"I bailed you out when you rode into town. Driving eighty with a gram in your pocket. If I didn't know better, I'd think you did it on purpose."

Eddie glared at his brother when what he wanted to do was smile. Jack was a damn fine cop. "I'll quit then. If Doyle is involved in drugs, I don't want to be involved. I get another strike and I'm going down for twenty years. Maybe Ellie will hire me as a barista."

"You're not quitting DI."

"Make up your mind, dude."

"You're going to let Joe Doyle reel you into his operation like a marlin. Make him work for it, but give in in the end."

Shock threw Eddie back into his chair. "You're asking me to work for you, against the Doyles?"

"Yes."

"Wow." Eddie's phone buzzed with a message. He swept it off the table and turned it off before Jack could see who it was from. Jack didn't seem to notice. "You trust me to do it?"

"I don't have any choice."

"That's a vote of confidence."

Jack leaned across the table, his bloodshot eyes blazing with determination. "This is where you make good on all the shit you've done the last twenty years. Pay me and mom back for bailing your sorry ass out of jail over and over. You help me bring Joe Doyle and his organization down or you ride out of town right now."

"Why do you want to take this guy down so bad?"

Jack sat back. "It's my job," he said, voice filled with incredulity at the question.

Eddie knew there was more to it but didn't press. He didn't want to push his luck and change Jack's mind. "I'll do it on one condition."

"You are hardly in a position to negotiate."

"I am anyway. Pull yourself together, man. You look awful."

"I'm fine." His voice was clipped, dismissive.

"Have you looked in the mirror lately?"

"You were always the mirror hog, not me."

Eddie ignored the jab. "I know you like it here and want to stick around, but these people are watching you. After all the shit with Freeman, they don't trust you. You looking like you're a walking ghost doesn't help."

Jack stood and took his time making himself a cup of coffee. He turned around and leaned against the counter. Jack sipped his drink but kept his eyes on his brother. "Who's trying to call you?"

"You noticed, huh?"

Jack raised his eyebrows and waited.

"It was a text and don't worry. It's nothing illegal." Eddie stood. "I have to go."

At the door, Jack caught Eddie's arm. "This is just between us. No one else knows."

Julie walked in the kitchen wearing running clothes and made a bee-line for the coffee. "Morning."

"Morning," the brothers said in unison.

Julie poured her coffee. "Eddie, isn't it about time you got your own place?"

"He can stay here as long as he wants," Jack said.

Julie replaced the pot on the warmer, picked up her cup, and turned to the brothers with a forced smile. "Of course he can. I figured he would want to have a place of his own to entertain his girlfriend."

"Thanks for being so concerned about my social life, Jules." Pebbles of ice ricocheted around his empty cup as he shook it. Eddie walked over to Julie, who leaned against the sink. He stared down at her with a knowing, private smile. "Excuse me."

She stepped aside, and Eddie tossed the cup in the trash beneath the sink. "Have a nice run. I hope you trip and break your ankle."

"I hope you get crushed under a crate of apples."

Eddie walked out the back door and to his bike, letting the screen door bang behind him. He turned his baseball cap backward, straddled his Harley, and revved the engine, just to piss off Jules. He drove slowly down the driveway and tried to get his head around the idea that his straight-laced, rule-following brother had asked him, the family fuck-up, to spy on Joe Doyle.

Instead of turning to the left and work, Eddie turned right, drove a few hundred yards, and turned left again up a steep, overgrown dirt track. Halfway up the road, he saw who he was looking for.

He shut off the bike, the silence always a little shocking. He smiled at Ellie Martin.

"Hey, Fabio," she said.

"You know you love it."

"I don't trust any man whose hair is longer than mine."

"So, if I cut my hair, you'll trust me?"

"Probably not."

"Where's Amy?"

Ellie jerked her thumb in the direction of the German church on the top of the hill. "She walks home down the other side. It's quicker."

"How was the run?"

Despite the chill November morning, Ellie wore thin running shorts and a half-marathon T-shirt from 2010. With her hair pulled back, her long neck and strong jaw were accentuated. Eddie had always been a sucker for swan-like necks, and the urge to pepper kisses up and down Ellie's had been a difficult thing to resist for the past six weeks.

"Good," she said.

"You ran before you met Amy didn't you?"

Ellie looked abashed. "Yeah. She's getting there, but she's still slow."

"It was a four-mile cool down for you."

"Pretty much." Ellie shrugged. "I enjoy her company."

"Want a ride?"

She raised an eyebrow. "The last time you took me for a ride on that thing, you almost killed me."

"In my defense, I didn't know where I was going and you were a shitty navigator."

"Your hair was blocking my view of the road."

Eddie nodded to the back of the bike. "I'll take you straight home, I promise. You're finished with your run, aren't you?"

"Yes."

"Come on. This bike isn't dangerous."

She stepped forward and Eddie knew he had her. "It's not the bike I'm worried about."

He grinned. "Smart girl."

She swung her leg over the bike and settled in as he started it. When he didn't feel her arms go around his waist, he looked behind him and saw her grasping the back of the seat.

"Don't trust yourself, huh?" He revved the engine.

"Shut up and drive," she yelled. But she was grinning.

He drove down the road, turned right, and passed Julie, in running clothes, leaving her driveway. Eddie gave her the middle finger with a smile.

"See what I saved you from?" he called over his shoulder.

"Thank you."

They were at the front of her store within a minute. Ellie got off the bike and thanked him for the ride.

"Want to catch a bite to eat tonight?" Eddie said.

"I don't think so."

"Come on, Ellie. Everyone thinks we're dating anyway. Do you want to make liars out of half the town?"

"Half the town were liars before you rode in, trust me."

"I'm going to keep asking."

"And, I'm going to keep saying no."

"Oh, you have no idea how good I am at wearing women down."

She laughed. "I bet I do."

"I'm going to keep teasing you until that laugh reaches your eyes."

She tucked her chin and narrowed her eyes. Her smile faded. "I don't need you to cheer me up, Eddie. I'm fine."

"Are you? Because my brother is miserable."

Ellie looked down the street at the stoplight. "I'm sorry to hear it." When she looked back at Eddie, her face was tight, her expression hardened. "But, there's nothing I can do about it."

"Maybe I can." Ellie crossed her arms over her chest and waited. "I've spent a lifetime getting away with shit, doing things behind people's backs," Eddie said.

"You've also gotten caught a lot."

Eddie waved his hand. "Doesn't even scratch the surface of what I *haven't* been caught for."

He stood and pulled her close. She stared him in the eyes, unblinking. Anger tinged her voice when she said, "What do you think you're doing?"

"Julie is about to run right around the corner. If you want to keep her beady little focus off of you, she needs to believe we have something going on."

"Why would she focus on me? I haven't been around Jack in weeks."

"Julie is suspicious of everyone." He saw Julie over Ellie's shoulder. He put his hand at the base of Ellie's neck, pulled her forward, and slid his hand down to rest below the waistband of her shorts. He whispered in her ear, "If you and Jack want to see each other, I can arrange it where no one will know."

"Oh, really? How?"

He massaged her neck and rubbed his cheek against hers. "Well, I haven't figured it out yet." He waved at Julie behind Ellie's back. Julie returned his middle finger from earlier and turned the other way.

Ellie chuckled. "It's tougher than you think to be devious in a small town."

"Maybe, but not impossible." Eddie pulled her tighter, felt her tense and try to lean away. "There is another option."

"For you to take your hand off my ass?"

"Take me upstairs. I'll help you forget all about Jack."

"Hmm," she purred and ran her hand up the back of his neck and into his hair. She gripped his hair and pulled his head back. Her eyes were dark with anger. "I would rather gouge my eyes out with a dull, rusty spoon."

He released her and laughed. "You're a goddamn amazing woman. The more I know you, the more I hate that bastard of a brother of mine. But," Eddie shrugged and leaned back against his bike. "Jack's the settling type. I'm not, and you need the settling type, don't you?"

"I don't need anyone."

"Aw now, don't get all independent on me. I'd like nothing more than to steal you from Jack, and, fair warning, I'm going to keep trying."

"Why?"

"Cause deep down, you like it."

"I do not."

Eddie swung his leg over his bike. "Yeah, you do. But, don't worry. I won't tell Jack. It might send the poor guy over the edge. Keep my other offer in mind. Between you and me, I don't think Jack will make it to January."

"What do you mean?" She stepped forward and placed a hand on Eddie's arm to keep him from starting his Harley. "What's wrong?"

"Nothing some time alone with you won't fix."

She sighed. "Eddie, the only way I can survive this is not to be around him." Her expression was so naked with fear and loneliness it took Eddie's breath away. For the first time, he saw in her what he saw daily in Jack. A steely resolve came over him.

He covered her hand with his and smiled. "Do you have a sister?"

She shook her head and forced a laugh. "Sorry."

He lifted her chin with his finger. "Hey. I think making the town believe we are circling each other is a good idea."

"No, it's not. If Jack and I do have a future, the last thing we need is for the town to think I've fucked both brothers. Play it up to Julie, fine. But don't you dare spread it around town that we're sleeping together."

Eddie held up three fingers. "Scout's honor."

She stepped back. "Thanks for the ride."

"Anytime."

Eddie watched her climb the stairs to her apartment until she was lost from view. He pulled out his cell phone and hit redial.

"Hey," Eddie said. "You won't believe the conversation I just had."

"With who? Doyle?"

"No. My brother. He wants me to spy on Doyle for him."

There was a beat of silence on the other end of the line.

"Fine. Everything still runs through me."

"I wasn't asking permission." Eddie hung up and pocketed the phone. "Bastard."

He watched Ellie's light turn on in her apartment, revved his Harley, and drove down Main to work.

CHAPTER SEVEN

Ellie Yourke Martin might have been the richest woman in town in terms of historic downtown property, but Joe Doyle owned west Stillwater. Metal buildings built by Doyle Construction lined Boondoggle Road on land bought by Joe Doyle during the savings and loan bust of the eighties. With one-hundred-year leases on the land and inexpensive metal buildings on top, Doyle lured downtown businesses—the pharmacy, the auto parts store, two florists, a mechanic, a café—to the Stillwater Business Park while his four businesses and his central office anchored the park at the corner of Boondoggle and Main. Eddie drove past the two-story main office, the heavy equipment yard, the feed store, and into the parking lot of Doyle Organics. He waved at a delivery truck as it left on its run to Tyler and pulled to the rear of the small building that held Matt Doyle's tiny office.

The rear yard was full of eighteen wheelers delivering produce from the Valley and the Houston docks, Doyle trucks loading up for daily deliveries, and a few local Fords and Chevys delivering the small amount of produce available in late fall in East Texas. In the middle of it all, Matt Doyle stood with a clipboard, checking off produce as it arrived in his warehouse and shooting the breeze with his workers. Eddie towered over

Matt, as did most of his workers, but Eddie was pretty sure Matt could kick his ass if his wide shoulders, bulging biceps, and muscular legs were any indication. If Matt wasn't such a health freak, Eddie would suspect he juiced to get his sideshow-worthy physique.

Everyone liked Matt. He was affable and honest, strict but fair. He was a shrewd businessman but a horrible judge of character who believed the best in everyone and was crushed when they turned out to have feet of clay. Eddie had been around enough shady businesses to know Jack was right—there was some serious shit running through Doyle's businesses. Matt, poor thing, was clueless. Eddie could easily take advantage of him, but he liked him well enough he didn't want to.

"Hey, man," Eddie said. "I can take over for you."

Matt didn't look up but smiled. "Almost done. Where've you been? Or should I ask?"

"You can ask, but I might not tell."

Matt shook his head. "You might as well give up there, buddy. You are way too much like Ellie's ex-husband to get anywhere."

"No kidding?" Eddie said, surprised. Sure, he'd heard snippets about Jinx Martin but never that he resembled Ellie's ex-husband. It explained why Eddie couldn't pry such a kick-ass woman away from his white bread, borderline boring brother. It also was a salve to his bruised ego.

"Yeah." Matt signed the invoice and gave it to the driver. "Thanks, buddy. See you tomorrow."

They started for the office. "What do you mean? I look like him or act like him?"

Matt opened the door and let Eddie pass through. "A little bit of both, to be honest. I didn't know him well, but talk about a rounder. I'm surprised she didn't give up men altogether."

Eddie flopped down into a chair. Matt moved around the desk, tossed the clipboard down with a clatter, woke his computer, and started checking email. He didn't have a desk chair because he didn't sit down. Ever. Eddie wondered if he ate dinner standing up.

Eddie crossed his ankle over his knee and picked at a loose thread on his frayed jeans. "You seriously going into business with her at the Henry?"

"Maybe."

"What does your dad think about it?"

"He doesn't know yet. All my dad cares about are results. Bottom line. If catering to the old-timers in town will get him elected, he'll say what they want to hear. But, if Ellie and Jane can make their plan for downtown work, he'll come around."

"Hmm," Eddie said.

Matt stared at the screen and clicked through email as he talked, his gold Texas A&M class ring glinting on his right ring finger. "So, hey, two things. Michelle needs you over at heavy equipment today."

"Okay."

"And Amy and I are having a bonfire out at the lake on Saturday night. On the lot we're going to build our new house on. Thought you might want to come."

"Sure."

"Bring Ellie. Amy invited her this morning. I think she's trying to play matchmaker with you two."

"Is she?"

"Yeah. I told her to back off, but she's a big fan of yours for some reason."

"It's the long hair and motorcycle. Chicks dig it."

"Like my sister?"

Eddie paused. "You know about that?"

"I knew my sister would set her sights on you as soon as you walked into my office." Matt shook his head, disappointment clear in his expression. "Be careful there, Eddie."

"What do you mean?"

"I don't trust my sister as far as I can throw her, and neither should you."

Eddie walked up the stairs of the business office and down the hall toward the only light in the building. He knocked on the open door. Red yard signs with JOE DOYLE, CITY COUNCIL in blue letters were leaned against every available inch of wall space. A big box of VOTE FOR JOE buttons were on the edge of Michelle's desk. Michelle, reading glasses perched on the end of her nose, looked up from her computer screen. She closed the laptop, took off her glasses, and put them on the desk.

"You're late."

Eddie sauntered over. "Don't take the glasses off on my account. I like them." He sat on the corner of the desk, picked up the glasses, and put them back on Michelle.

Eddie studied Michelle. He knew within a week of working at Doyle Industries she was in charge. Joe Doyle might bluster around and take credit for everything, but Michelle Ryan was the brains behind the legitimate business. Two weeks in, Eddie was fucking her. Three weeks in, he knew she was also the brains behind the illegitimate business. Now, they were poking and prodding each other, testing the limits of their trust in each other. Eddie felt sure he'd won her over. At the very least, she'd hesitate before ordering someone to kill him.

"Where've you been?"

He knew lying to Michelle wouldn't get him what he wanted. "I was with Ellie."

"Are you fucking her yet?" Michelle's voice was bland. Her gaze was too deliberate and even, as if beating her insecurities down with a hammer.

"Why do you care?"

Michelle stood and walked to the coffee maker on the sideboard. She poured two cups of coffee, picked one cup up, and leaned against the credenza. "I'm curious what you think. She couldn't hold her first husband's interest. Jinx said it was like fucking an ice cube." Eddie chuckled, walked over, and picked up his cup.

"Maybe the problem was him."

"Nope. Jinx knew what he was doing."

"What kind of name is Jinx?"

"A perfect one for him."

"Ellie told me your part in her divorce."

Michelle scoffed. "No doubt saying I ruined her life." She shook her head. "She hates me so much she can't see I did her a favor."

"You were fucking her husband."

"I was, and I enjoyed every minute of it. Everyone knew they were trying to get pregnant. One night, Jinx had too much to drink—he did that a lot—and he let slip he'd had a vasectomy. Laughed his ass off at Ellie." Michelle sipped her coffee and stared into space. "I've hated Ellie Yourke since I was twelve years old and will probably always hate her." Michelle met Eddie's eyes. "But to fuck with a woman like that? Bastard. So, I told her."

Michelle's eyes were a beautiful blue, almost violet, and completely clear. No doubt, no remorse, no guilt, no indecision. Eddie pushed the glasses up and said, "Matt says I remind him of Jinx."

"At first, yeah. But, if you were anything like Jinx Martin, I wouldn't have brought you in."

Eddie leaned forward. "You think I'm trustworthy."

Michelle's eyes settled on Eddie's lips. "You haven't betrayed me yet."

"And if I did?" He inched forward to kiss her.

"I'd cut your dick off and feed it to a wild hog while you watched."

Eddie stopped and leaned back until Michelle's face came into focus. Her eyes didn't waver. Her mouth didn't crack into a smile. "Jesus."

She pulled a set of keys from her pocket and slapped them into Eddie's hand. "There's a Mack truck out back with a backhoe on it. I need you to deliver it to Houston."

"Houston?"

"The address is in the cab. You'll pick up a different one and bring it back here. By tonight." She walked to her desk and pulled a burner phone from the top drawer.

"That's a ten-hour round trip. At least."

"Then you better get going." She tossed the phone to him. With one hand holding a coffee and the other with keys, he barely caught it. "Use this to do your civic duty and call in your hot tip. Toss it out the window on 45 when you're done."

Eddie stared at the phone. "Are you sure about this?"

"Yes."

Dread settled onto his shoulders. "You don't need to do it, you know. Joe's going to win."

"I do, if for no other reason than to prove you're trustworthy to your doubters."

"Who are my doubters?"

"All you need to worry about is what I think of you."

"Do you trust me?"

"Finish the job and I will. One hundred percent."

CHAPTER EIGHT

The tan uniforms and neutral walls gave the conference room at the Yourke County Sheriff's office an old-fashioned, sepia tone. The lone nod to modernity were the cell phones held in a few hands and Jack McBride, who preferred navy Hugo Boss to tan Dickies.

"Still aren't wearing the uniform, I see."

Yourkeville Chief of Police Harvey Dodd said it with a smile, but Jack saw the animosity beneath the good-ole-boy exterior.

"Tan isn't my color," Jack said.

"You should at least wear a vest," Lone Oak officer Tammy Cole said.

"You're right. But it'll mess up the line of my suit."

Cole saw it for the joke it was. Dodd turned away in disgust.

Jack held out his hand to the man standing next to Cole. "Hayes, good to see you."

"McBride."

Eric Hayes was a cop from central casting: stocky, with a crew cut and mustache. On the other hand, Tammy Cole, a lifelong Yourke County resident, looked like she was more at home on a horse than in a car. She was wide-hipped and bow-legged, with long brown hair pulled into a pony tail and a row of tightly curled bangs covering her tall forehead.

Sheriff Ann Newberry walked into the room, followed by District Attorney Oliver Pigeon. "Okay, let's get this started. Crime Stoppers'll be here in thirty minutes to talk about their public outreach program. Then the vultures descend." Ann moved to the head of the table and sat down.

"You invited the press?" Dodd said.

"Yep. The public needs to see what we're doing to address the drug problem in our county. McBride, why don't you fill everyone in on what you found out from the DEA?"

"Where *is* the DEA agent?" Dodd said.

"Couldn't make it." Jack moved on, not wanting to get into the age-old animosity between local and federal law enforcement. "Since the murder of Rosa and Gilberto Ramos, the incidence of drug crimes has risen 50 percent in Yourke County. Three hundred percent in Stillwater alone. The biggest problem has been the influx of heroin, especially in the high schools, as evidenced by the two ODs over in Yourkeville. Lucky they didn't die."

"They might as well have," Dodd said. Everyone around the table nodded, thinking of the two Yourkeville High School high-achieving seniors who were unlucky enough to have dirty heroin as their first hit and had become vegetables as a result.

"With the exception of a few fights and the explosion of the meth lab out your way, Hayes, the crimes have been nonviolent. Thefts, possession with intent to deliver, bike batchers. We've heard through the grapevine meth labs throughout the county are being destroyed, but of course, no one's going to report the destruction of an illegal drug lab. Still, it would fit in with the theory there's a turf war going on right now between the local organization and the Pedroza cartel, with the locals trying to protect their meth trade and the Pedrozas importing heroin. The Pedrozas are good, though. We haven't been able to catch a dealer yet."

"If the Pedrozas are involved, we're lucky no one has ended up in the county square holding their severed heads in their laps," Hayes said.

"True," Jack said. "We might yet." Jack passed out photos of the torched house and two charred bodies. "Two men were found in a fire out on 107 yesterday. We believe one of them is Paco Morales. Morales has lived, legally, in Stillwater for nearly thirty years. He did odd jobs for years before going to work full time as a groundskeeper at Stillwater Country Club. No arrests, though considering Pollard didn't arrest anyone for anything, it's not surprising."

Dodd scoffed, but Jack continued.

"So, clean on the surface. His daughter is Esperanza Perez, who was Diego Vazquez's alibi for the night Gilberto and Rosa Ramos were killed. He was low level with the Pedroza cartel, or at least the DEA thought when he came to them. Turns out, Vazquez was playing the DEA. They aren't sure how high up Vazquez is, but it looks like he's Pedroza's front man in Yourke County."

"And no one can find him," Hayes said.

"Not yet," Ann replied.

"Probably being hidden by the Hispanic community," Cole said.

"Maybe being hidden by Paco Morales?" Hayes said.

"Maybe."

Ann stared at the photo of the charred bodies as she asked, "You think the other body is Diego Vazquez?"

"If it is, we have to worry about retaliation."

"Bodies in the square," Cole said.

"Against who?" Dodd asked.

Jack glanced at Ann, who nodded. "Doyle Industries."

Jack and Ann waited for the indignant reaction they anticipated. Instead Dodd, Hayes, and Cole remained silent, contemplating the information. Dodd was the first to speak. "There were rumors of Doyle being in the trade back in the eighties, but it died out when the business park took off. I figured he made a wad selling weed then went legit."

"They would have the infrastructure to do it," Eric Hayes said. "Between their businesses, they're all over the county."

"The DEA has had them in their sights for a while now. In the course of his work with the DEA," Jack said, "Vazquez gave up Pollard. Told them Pollard had been running drugs for Doyle."

"Now, there I draw the line. I've known Pollard for fifty years," Dodd said. "No way he would run drugs."

"Yeah, I have a hard time believing that, too," Tammy Cole said.

"Pollard might protect the organization, but to actually run the drugs?" Hayes clicked his tongue. "It's a stretch."

"We have proof." Jack pulled out stapled photocopies and handed them out to his counterparts.

District Attorney Pigeon spoke for the first time. The melodious voice that had lulled many juries into trusting him, had sung newlyweds into their future and corpses into their graves, filled every corner of the room. "Six weeks ago, we received compelling evidence against Pollard for corruption. Judge Brockman signed the warrant to search Pollard's house. Under the house, we found boxes of journals, written in Pollard's hand, dating back to the sixties. In the storm cellar, we found filing cabinets full of documents we thought were lost in the fire back in the sixties."

"We've been copying the journals for the last six weeks," Ann said. "We finished yesterday. The originals went to the Feds, and the copies are in the evidence locker."

Dodd, Hayes, and Cole flipped through their amended copies. Sweat beaded at Dodd's temples. He leaned forward. "What else is in those journals?"

"Somewhere along the line, Pollard got smart and started using code for names. The latter journals are cryptic," Jack said. Dodd sat back, trying not to look too relieved. "But not before he mentioned catching Michelle Doyle selling weed in 1985. So, you were right, Dodd."

"To a point," Ann said. "Doyle's legitimate businesses were a cover for the drugs. With Pollard's protection, Doyle was able to build up an almost bulletproof organization."

"Which brings us back to Vazquez," Jack said. "The DEA turned him, he gave up Pollard, and the DEA and FBI started investigating. The start of their investigation coincides with Pollard's resignation."

"If Pollard was protecting drug dealers, you would think the cartel would want him in power," Cole said.

"Yes, but he was protecting the cartel's competition. The DEA theorizes the Pedrozas planted Vazquez with the DEA to get them investigating the local drug organization and dismantle it so they could move in, unopposed."

"Jesus," Hayes said.

"They sent Vazquez here to shake up the status quo. So far, the Pedrozas have shown surprising restraint, though. Focusing on hamstringing the drug organization and keeping the body count at zero. If it's Paco Morales and Diego Vazquez's bodies in that house, who knows what they'll do."

"Which is why we have to keep this theory about their identity right here, in this room," Ann said. "We don't want innocent people to get murdered based on a theory."

"If they're involved in the drug trade, are they really innocent?" Hayes asked.

"Why have you kept all of this from us?" Dodd said.

"We don't think Pollard's dead," Ann said. "With his contacts, it would have been easy enough for him to fake his accident. We figured if he thought we didn't have anything on him, he'd return."

"And what does any of this have to do with the drug task force?" Hayes asked.

"We bring down the drug organization in Yourke County—Doyle— they give us Pollard," DA Pigeon said.

"So, we take down the local organization—the largest employer in the county, by the way—basically doing the job for the Pedrozas so they can move in?" Hayes asked, voice full of incredulity.

"And we turn our focus to them," Pigeon said.

"Where the hell is the DEA?" Cole said.

"Trust me, they're as dedicated to this as we are," Jack said. "They have—" Jack stopped as DEA Agent Tom Hunter's words came back to him. *We've got someone inside. Close.* Jack's blood rushed to his head. He put his hands on the table to steady himself.

"Jack?" Ann asked.

"They have been working on this for months with the FBI, like I said. They're about to drop a warrant on them for financials."

"When?"

Jack shrugged. "They didn't say." When Jack balked at Hunter keeping mum on the when, Hunter said, flat out, that he was the only law enforcement officer in Yourke County the Feds trusted.

"In the meantime," Ann said, "we keep doing what we've been doing. But keep an eye out for Doyle rigs. If they drive even one mile per hour over the limit, stop them and pray there's a legitimate reason to search the vehicle."

"Whatever you do, have cause. We don't want anything we find to be tossed," Jack said.

"And we don't want Doyle to cotton on that we're investigating," Pigeon said. "We've kept it quiet for six weeks. If the Doyles somehow catch wind, we'll know where it comes from."

"Any questions?" Everyone shook their heads and Ann continued, "Good. Now, Cole, update us on your neck of the woods."

Tammy Cole flipped the stapled copies closed and pushed it aside. "Two drug arrests, both for small amounts of weed. Teenagers. Neither good candidates for CIs."

"We're pleading those kids out," Pigeon said. "Not worth the cost of going to trial. Probation, drug education classes."

"I'm sure you all heard about the meth lab set up in the empty lake house. The lab hasn't gotten around to the prints yet, so no news. I'm trying to stop by the weekend houses to check them for labs, but it's slow going. I could use some help."

"We'll help out," Jack said. "I'll put Bishop on it. Have him patrol out there."

"We should all be out there, except you, Hayes. That's out of your way," Ann said.

"We'll patrol out there, too," Dodd said. "Let's get together after and divvy it up so we don't miss anything."

"Sounds good," Jack said.

"Thanks," Cole said. "Also, seems like the high schoolers have remembered Cheyney's Field."

"Ah, yes. Cheyney's Field," Hayes said, a gleam in his eyes.

"What's Cheyney's Field?" Jack said.

"Pasture out near the lake that's been used for parties since I was a teenager," Dodd said. "'Bout halfway between Yourkeville and Stillwater, so it pulls kids from both towns."

"It'll be real popular for a time, then they'll get busted and move on. They always come back eventually," Hayes said.

"Haven't caught any out there yet. But they're leaving plenty of trash. I'm going to catch them tomorrow night," Cole said.

There was a knock on the door. Ann rose and went to open it. Ellie stood in the hall holding a briefcase. "Am I early?"

"No, you're fine," Ann said. "Have a seat."

Jack gathered the pictures of the charred bodies from the table together and shoved them in his folder. Ellie took the first available chair at the far end of the table. She smiled a greeting to the table in general and avoided Jack's eyes, focusing completely on Ann.

"Ellie, you have a house out at the lake," Ann said. "Have you noticed anything out of the ordinary?"

She leaned forward and folded her hands together. Like the night before, images of his time with Ellie in her lake house flooded Jack's mind. The last time he touched her. Kissed her. Felt her beneath him. He focused on the pen in his hands, hoping his face didn't betray the riot of emotions blazing through him, and wondered if Ellie was thinking the same thing and, if so, how she was so composed.

"I don't go out there much so, no," Ellie said. "I haven't seen anything."

"No increased activity? Vandalism?"

"Well, some kids are using my mailbox for batting practice, but other than that. No. Why?"

"We think cookers are setting up meth labs in abandoned houses, doing their thing, and moving on."

"I'll swing by and check my house on the way home."

"No," Jack said. Everyone stared at him. Ellie's face turned beet red. "Let one of us check it, in case someone's there cooking."

"He's right," Dodd said. "Let us check it out."

Ellie shrugged.

"So, Ellie." Ann smiled at her. "Thanks for joining us. Can you update us on your end?"

"Sure. Crime Stoppers has arranged for a former drug addict to speak to the high schools and middle schools. Give his testimony. First assembly is next week in Yourkeville. We're also working with the churches to start Narcotics Anonymous meetings. The DA," she nodded at Pigeon, "is making drug counseling part of the plea bargains. We're also meeting with the hospitals and local doctors to get their assistance. Sue Poole planned to come with me today, but had an emergency C-section."

Ann nodded, made a note. "What do you need from us?"

"We wanted to get an officer from each community to speak to the elementary schools."

"Excellent idea," Ann said. "I'll have my secretary get in touch with you. She'll organize it with the local police."

"Great," Ellie said. She reached down into her briefcase and removed a manila folder. She passed out a packet of information and said, "I put together a detailed outline of what we're doing on our end, as well as suggestions for the future. For your reference. If there's something I've missed, let me know and I'll take it to the Crime Stoppers board. We are all enthusiastic about helping out."

"Thanks, Ellie," Hayes said. "This looks great. Let me know whenever you need me to speak to a school. Or, anything." Hayes's ingratiating grin raised Jack's hackles. He was flirting with her.

Ellie returned Hayes's smile, too enthusiastically for Jack's taste. "Thanks, Eric."

"For ease of organization, we'll have it all go through the sheriff's department. Myrna will coordinate with you," Ann said.

"Whatever's easiest. I've also put together a press release. Sorry, but I can't stay to talk to the press. I have an appointment." She stood.

"Of course. Thanks for taking the time to come," Ann said.

Jack watched the door close behind Ellie. Ann started speaking and Jack's phone buzzed. He pulled it out of his pocket and saw Julie's number pop up. He stood and interrupted Ann. "I'm sorry, I have to take this."

He left the room. Outside the door, he punched the decline button on his phone and stopped cold. Reporters for every local newspaper in the county and one from Tyler waited in the hall. They looked up from their phones and tablets, as surprised by Jack's arrival as he was by their presence.

"Is it time for us?" the Tyler reporter said, standing.

"Not yet. Excuse me." Jack walked quickly out the front door. From the top of the courthouse steps, Jack saw Ellie getting in her car. "Ellie!" he called, running down the stairs and across the street.

She paused, halfway in the car. "Jack?"

He stopped at her door, slightly out of breath, but not from the short jog. God, she looked great. A little thin, but those eyes and that voice. Jack felt better than he had in weeks, just standing near her. Her confusion turned to realization. "You didn't just leave . . . ?" She pressed her lips together.

"No. I got a call. Ignored it. I wanted to talk to you."

"About what?" A slight breeze ruffled her hair. A few strands fell softly across her face.

"You were about to tell me something last night."

She brushed her hair out of her face, tucked it behind her ear, and turned her head away. "It must not have been important. I don't remember."

She fell silent, but didn't seem eager to leave. Jack stepped forward. "I miss you."

"Please don't do this. We agreed."

"You're right. We did. Worst decision of my life."

"No. We did the right thing."

"Right for who? Not me. Not you."

"For Ethan."

Jack looked away and thought of his son. Was it right for Ethan? Jack wasn't so sure. At first Ethan had been ecstatic. His parents were back together, he had friends, and he was settling into Stillwater. But recently Ethan had become more subdued, watching Jack with mixture of amazement and disbelief each morning at breakfast and evening at dinner. Jack tried with every fiber of his being to act normal, hoping Ethan believed he was truly trying to make his marriage work while guilt-ridden at living the lie of a happy family. How would Ethan react if he ever found out about the ruse, that he had no intention of staying with Julie? He feared it would irrevocably tarnish their relationship, more than going through with the divorce when Julie returned would have.

Julie, though, wasn't convinced. When Jack slept at home, he bunked on the downstairs couch, sure to wake up early enough to banish any sign before Ethan woke up. Mostly, though, he left the house after Ethan went to sleep and returned before he woke. Jack knew his avoidance of sleeping with Julie again was raising her suspicions about another woman, but he couldn't bring himself to do the one thing that would banish them. Whenever he thought of making love to a woman, he envisioned Ellie.

"Do you miss me as much as I miss you?"

She didn't answer for what seemed like an eternity. Finally, in a quiet voice Jack almost couldn't hear, she answered:

"No."

CHAPTER NINE

Ellie spent the ten-mile drive back to Stillwater alternately banging on the steering wheel and wiping tears from her cheeks, while a string of increasingly creative expletives streamed from her mouth. God, men were worthless. Why was it always the women who have to be so strong?

"FUCK." She banged her hand on the steering wheel again. This time, it tingled painfully up her wrist to her arm.

"Great. Just great. So, Ellie? How did you hurt your wrist? Oh, you know, banging my fucking steering wheel over a goddamn man."

She inhaled through her nose and exhaled through her mouth a few times. "Get a grip, Elliot."

She turned into a driveway almost obscured by trees, wild roses, and blackberry bushes. A crooked post stood at the end, a dented mailbox on the ground a few feet away. She stopped the car and got out. Fucking kids. She didn't know why she kept fixing it. No one lived here anymore, and the post office knew to forward the mail to her. Still, she picked up the mailbox and put it in her back seat before driving on.

The road wound through a tunnel of trees, the sight of their golden and red leaves soothing her fevered brain, before ending in front of an A-frame house. Trees dwarfed the house so sunlight rarely broke through, making it a perfect retreat during the long, hot Texas summers. Lake Yourke spread out behind the house, down fifteen feet from the long drought, but calm on this cool November morning.

She turned off the car and let her hands drop from the steering wheel. She closed her eyes. Jack's face floated before her, sad, strained, and pathetic. She jerked the car door open, got out, and walked around the house and down to the end of the pier. The lake was empty other than a small boat far across in a small cove known for catfish. The boat moved a bit and stopped. Moved and stopped. Checking a trot line, no doubt.

The house loomed behind her, full of memories she would rather not confront. That was a lie. If she didn't want to wallow in the memory, she wouldn't have turned off the highway.

When she and Jack said goodbye on that sultry, September night, she was full of hope. He loved her, and four months wasn't long to wait, but as the weeks dragged on, doubts crept in. They had known each other for seven days, for Christ's sake. They'd never been on a date. Eaten dinner together. Watched a movie. Debated politics. Argued. There was the real chance when they did fall into a normal relationship, they would realize they weren't compatible. Or Jack would discover the flaw in Ellie that seemed to repel men, to make it easy to betray and hurt her. Either way, there was an even chance all of this drama would be for nothing, the relationship wouldn't last, and she would be alone again. Best to move on. She had thrown herself into her business, the redevelopment of downtown Stillwater, and her campaign. Work and focus had gotten her through every other challenge in her life. Jack McBride would be no different.

But who was she kidding? She couldn't move on or forget. The memory of their last night together hadn't consoled her; it had tormented her. The knowledge that happiness had been right there, in her grasp—the kind of happiness fairy tales sell you, the kind that normal people don't really believe in but damn would they like to—had been one word away from being a reality. Instead, it was torpedoed by her fucking sense of right and wrong, by her concern for a fourteen-year-old boy who would hate her no matter what she did, by her knowledge that if she and Jack did the selfish thing, the thing that would make them happy, the fallout would only make them miserable in the end.

So, she did what she always did. Controlled what she ate, when she ate at all. Pushed herself every morning to run faster and farther. Drank more than normal. Let Jane Maxwell talk her into running for a city council seat she didn't want. At least she hadn't slept with Eddie, though she'd been sorely tempted to, especially on the nights the vision of Jack making love to Julie kept her from sleep. Instead, she went to Dallas one Saturday night and looked up an occasional lover she knew would be willing and whose only question would be, "How can I make you feel good?"

Control was the key. Anytime she'd allowed her control to slip, this happened. And, fucking shocker; it always involved a man. Daddy issues. Ha. How fucking stereotypical could you get?

Ellie turned to face the house. She wasn't there to confront her memories. She was there because she didn't want to be told what to do by anyone. Especially a man.

Especially Jack McBride.

She walked up the stairs to the deck and stopped. The glass sliding door was open a few inches. She knew she hadn't left it open last time she was here.

"'So, how was Ellie murdered, Chief McBride?'" Ellie said quietly in her best reporter voice.

Ellie lowered her voice in an impersonation of Jack. "'She specifically disobeyed my completely reasonable, professional suggestion to let the authorities handle it.'"

Ellie crept toward the door. "'So, she was hard-headed?'"

"'You have no idea.'"

The sheer curtains covering the sliding glass door blew gently in the breeze. When she touched the handle, she remembered a conversation she'd had with Susan and Kelly over wine once about how stupid horror movie characters were. Why do they always walk through the door? Just fucking run away, they all said, falling over in laughter. Here she was, walking straight into a stereotypical horror movie scenario.

"At least I haven't just had sex. I'd be a goner for sure."

She opened the door.

Enough light filtered through the sheer curtains to show Ellie she was alone. Instinctively, she pulled out her phone and called Jack. He answered in the middle of the first ring.

"Ellie?" Hope laced his voice.

"Jack, there's a meth lab in my kitchen."

Ellie leaned against her car outside the crime scene tape strung from tree to tree, twenty feet from the house. Jack, Ann and Tammy Cole ducked under the tape and walked to her. Ellie straightened to meet them.

"Well," Ann said, "the good news is they hadn't started cooking yet. Just set it up."

"We told you not to come out here." Anger laced Jack's voice.

Ellie crossed her arms and glared at him. Could he be any more obvious that his feelings about her actions weren't professional, but personal? She wanted to punch him in the chest, or maybe slap him, but knew it would be left up to her to deflect suspicion. "I'm sorry," she said, in as contrite a voice as possible. "It was on my way. I wasn't thinking, I guess."

"Did you see anyone around the house or on the road in?" Tammy Cole said.

"None after I got off the highway."

Ann pulled her phone out and held it up to Ellie. A phone number was highlighted in a text message. "Recognize this number?"

"No. Why?"

"About the time you called Jack, 911 got a call about suspicious behavior out here at your house. From this number."

"I'm pretty sure no one saw me. I know I didn't see anyone."

"Maybe you were distracted," Tammy said.

"Maybe," Ellie said.

"When was the last time you were out here?" Ann asked.

"A couple weeks ago?"

"I thought you said you didn't come out here much,"Tammy said.

"I don't. Maybe it was more like four or five."

"Were you out here alone?"

"No." Ellie paused. She felt Jack's gaze. Lied. "Sometimes I come out here with my friends, drink wine, visit."

"We're going to need the names of who's been out here. To account for their fingerprints."

"Okay."

Ann took out a small notebook and pen.

"Now?" Ellie asked.

"If there aren't many."

"Kelly Kendrick. Susan Grant. Barbara Dodsworth cleans it every month. I can call her and get the names of which maids cleaned it last."

"We can do that." She looked up. "Anyone else?"

Ellie looked at Jack and was about to speak when he said, "Me."

Tammy Cole rested her hands on her gun belt, shifted a bit on her feet, and looked away. Ann Newberry didn't say anything for a moment. Ellie closed her eyes, looked away and shook her head.

The sheriff flipped her notebook closed and pocketed it. "Okay, then. You can go. I'll be in touch with you later. Cole, want to take a look at this?" Ann nodded toward the house.

"Sure,"Tammy replied and followed.

Ellie turned away and cursed under her breath.

"It's fine. Ann and Cole won't say anything," Jack said.

She turned back to Jack, her face burning with anger. "Why did *you* say anything?"

"They were going to figure it out as soon . . ."

"No, they wouldn't have. The house has been cleaned since you've been here."

"There would have been a print."

"I doubt they're going to dust the bedroom."

"I wasn't only in the bedroom, now was I? Why are you so angry? When you looked at me, I assumed . . ."

"Well, you were wrong." She jerked open the car door and got in. Before she could close it, Jack grabbed the door.

"Whose prints are they going to find?"

"Eddie's."

Jack's face hardened. "What are Eddie's prints doing out here?"

All the anger at Jack from earlier came rushing back. "What do you think?"

Jack's face turned red. "Eddie wouldn't betray me."

"But I would?"

Jack opened his mouth, but closed it. *He wasn't sure.* Fucking perfect. Ellie laughed. "Trust me, your brother's been trying like hell to betray you since the moment he rode into town."

"I don't believe you."

"Why would I lie?"

Jack remained silent. Ellie started her car and tried to shut the door. Jack held on.

"Are you fucking my brother?" he said, as though he couldn't believe he was asking the question.

"No. But I'm pretty sure your wife has."

She yanked the door from Jack's grip, slammed it in his face, and drove off.

CHAPTER TEN

The last one hundred miles, Eddie struggled to keep his eyes open. All day he'd been fighting a crosswind, battling to keep his rig on the interstate. Because of the weight of the load, he couldn't drive over fifty-five miles per hour, and that fast only rarely. His arms were like jelly, and he was exhausted. He stopped for some stale coffee in Athens at 10 p.m., turned up the radio, and forced himself to keep going. The thought of his bed sustained him.

He turned into Doyle Industries' truck yard at nearly 1 a.m. Kyle Grant and a large bald man that might has well have had a swastika tattooed on his forehead walked out of the truck barn to meet him. Before Eddie could turn the rig off, Grant opened the driver's side door.

"Leave it running," he said.

"You need me to park it somewhere?"

"No. We got it."

Eddie feigned disinterest and gathered his trash from the cab.

"Don't worry about it," Kyle said.

Eddie shrugged and tossed the trash in the passenger seat. "Suit yourself." He climbed out of the cab. "Where you been, Kyle? Haven't seen you around much lately."

Kyle wore short-sleeved, blue Dickies coveralls. The long sleeves of his undershirt were pushed halfway up his forearms, revealing an elaborate tattoo that Eddie knew ran up his left arm, across his shoulder, and ended on his neck, peeking out of the collar of his overalls. "We'll take it from here," Kyle replied, ignoring Eddie's question.

"Don't take this the wrong way, but no one told me you'd be here to meet me. I don't feel comfortable handing my load to you without confirmation."

Kyle's face clouded. Eddie held his gaze but saw Kyle clench his fists while he considered how to respond. Kyle sneered and huffed but pulled out his phone and dialed a number. "Yeah. Just drove in. He wants to talk to you," he said, as if talking about a five-year-old.

"Hello?" Eddie said.

"Is there a problem?" Michelle said.

"I wasn't told they'd be here to meet me."

"Kyle's worked for me a hell of a lot longer than you have."

"You sure he's only working for you?" Eddie pointedly stared at Kyle's tattoo before moving his gaze to Kyle's face. He combated his adversary's anger with a wink and a grin.

"Eddie, don't be an idiot. You've done your part. Go home. Get some rest. Tomorrow is a long day."

"How so?"

"It's the Snipe Festival. Sidewalk sale. Ellie and my dad will be kissing babies and telling lies. Don't tell me your girlfriend hasn't enlisted your help in campaigning."

"She's not my girlfriend."

"Uh-huh. Matt said he invited you two to the bonfire. You coming?"

"Are you?"

"Yes."

"Then so am I."

Michelle chuckled. "Put Kyle back on."

Eddie handed the phone off and walked away, as if uninterested, but he managed to hear Kyle Grant say, "I'm still working on it. I don't have them on speed dial, you know."

He drove to the Chevron, gassed up his bike, and ambled past Abe's vintage green and white 1969 Ford on his way inside. Eddie'd been considering trading in the Harley. He still loved it, but it was inconveniently loud and conspicuous. Not necessarily good things in his line of work.

"Hey, Abe."

"Eddie."

Eddie walked to the cooler and pulled out a pint of chocolate milk. On the way to the register, he grabbed a honey bun. "Tell me, Abe, do you ever sleep?"

Abe rang Eddie up.

"Not much. What is it with you McBride men and honey buns?"

Eddie laughed, thought back to all the honey buns they'd eaten growing up. They should probably hate them, but both still loved them. Eddie was partial to the frosted tops, and Jack liked his plain. They each gave the other a case for Christmas ever year as a joke, but by February, they were gone.

"Breakfast of champions, Abe. Breakfast of champions. Tell me, is your truck for sale?"

Abe shook his head.

"Seems a shame for that beauty to sit in a parking lot all day."

"This way I can look at her."

"How about a trade. Straight up. My bike for your truck?"

Abe looked out the front window at Eddie's Harley. "I'd have to ride it."

Eddie peeled the wrapper from the sticky honey bun and took a bite. "How about we trade for a couple days. Drive and ride and see what we think."

Abe contemplated Eddie's bike for a few moments more and nodded his head. "Sure. Sounds good."

"Great. I'll pull the bike up."

He made the switch, climbed into the truck, and fell in love. It drove as good as it looked.

He drove out of the Chevron toward Jack's house. He turned on a side street and rolled as quietly as possible through the backstreets until he was on Willow Street, a secluded oil top road on the edge of town, bordered by vacant fields. He parked by a pasture gate, hopped the fence, and walked through the woods.

Eddie stopped at a barely camouflaged gap in the chain link fence and looked around. No one in sight. He crawled through and ran from truck to truck until he was at the truck barn. He flattened himself against the metal building, inched over to the back bay entrance, and looked around the corner. A radio was blaring the latest bro country song, barely drowning out the sound of Kyle and Baldy removing one of the skidder's front tires. A third man Eddie hadn't seen earlier was in the far corner pulling heavily taped bags of drugs from the wheel well. The man's back faced Eddie, and a Dallas Cowboys baseball hat turned backward on the man's head obscured any chance of identifying him.

Eddie felt something tap his shoulder. He jumped, lost his footing, and grabbed at the metal wall. Instead of stopping his slide, the slick metal rang like a bell. Eddie looked up from his crouch on the ground. Jack stood over him, his finger to his lips.

The sound of work stopped in the garage, leaving only the country bro singing about his truck and a bikini-clad girl.

"Did you hear something?"

Eddie mimed to Jack, *What are you doing here?*

The music turned down.

"What?" Kyle's voice sounded close.

"I thought I heard something."

Eddie motioned for Jack to go around the corner, stood, and walked into the barn.

"McBride?" Kyle said.

"I left my phone in the cab of the truck. Didn't think you'd mind if I came back to get it."

"Well, we do."

The mystery man in the Cowboys hat had vanished.

"It won't take but a minute for me to check." Eddie walked toward the cab. Kyle put his hand on Eddie's chest. Eddie looked down at his hand and back up at his rat-like face. "Get your fucking hand off me, dude."

"Or what?"

Eddie laughed, looked away and, with a practiced move, grabbed Kyle's wrist, twirled him around, and pushed him against the cab face first. "You don't want to fuck with me, Kyle."

"Or what? You'll shiv me like you shived my dad?"

"You heard about that, huh?"

The distinctive click of a gun being cocked and the cold steel of the barrel on his neck made Eddie freeze.

"Let him go, *dude*."

Eddie released Kyle and lifted his hands. "Look, I just want my phone. I think I dropped it when I dropped the trash. It's got some pictures on there I don't want getting in the wrong hands. You know, the incriminating kind."

Kyle rubbed his wrist and stared at Eddie. He made a motion with his hand and Baldy dropped the gun. Before Eddie could open his mouth, Kyle punched him in the stomach. Eddie doubled over, coughing, while Baldy opened the truck door and leaned inside the cab.

Baldy climbed out of the cab and held out Eddie's phone.

Eddie took the phone. "Want to apologize, Kyle?"

"Get out of here or I'll give you a beating you won't forget."

Eddie laughed. "You can't do shit to me that hasn't already been done. And there's a good chance I'll fuck you up instead." Eddie grinned and shook his phone. "Thanks. Michelle will be happy I didn't lose it. I kinda thought I left it in the gas station in Athens."

Eddie walked out the door, around the building, and out the front of the Doyle complex. He walked down the road, rubbing his stomach, when a car pulled up. He got in the passenger side and Jack drove off.

"Don't sneak up on people like that. What the hell were you doing there?"

"I saw you leave the Chevron and followed you."

Eddie paused. "Why didn't you talk to me? Do you not trust me?" He watched his brother drive for a moment. He wouldn't have trusted himself if he were in Jack's shoes, but still. It stung to have his brother's distrust confirmed. "Of course you don't."

"Where have you been?"

"On a run to Houston for Michelle. Delivering and picking up heavy equipment with wheel wells packed with drugs, looks like."

"What kind?"

"I didn't get a chance to notice, thanks to you."

Jack didn't apologize. "So, they're transporting it through the heavy equipment. Pretty fucking smart."

"Not the worst idea. Michelle's one of the best operators I've seen."

His brother's face was partially in shadow from the blue instrument lights on the dashboard. He worked his jaw, as if calculating. "Michelle? Not Doyle?" Jack said.

"No, man. I know you want JD to be in charge, but it's Michelle. Doyle's rarely around. She runs it all, legit and illegal."

"Matt's not involved?"

"Christ, no. He's way too straight-laced. Which makes him the perfect front. If she's not bringing drugs through the produce business yet, she will be. It's too perfect a set up."

Eddie pulled a scrap of paper from his pocket and handed it to Jack. "The place I went was down in Pasadena, not far from the ship channel. Guy I talked to said the backhoe would be fixed by Tuesday, ready for pick up. Wouldn't be surprised if Houston Heavy Equipment's owned by Doyle, too."

Jack raised an eyebrow, glanced at the address, and shoved it in his shirt breast pocket. "Why'd you go back?"

Eddie shrugged. "To snoop for you. I left my phone in the cab in case they caught me."

Jack looked at Eddie from the corner of his eyes. "You see Kyle Grant in there?"

"Yeah. Did you know he's a member of the TexaSS?" Eddie said.

"Yeah. Came up when I ran him. How do you know?"

"Tat. Not surprised. His dad was a big-wig inside."

"You knew his dad?"

"Briefly. TexaSS is a harsher crowd than I expected the Doyles to associate with."

"Me, too," Jack said. "But if Michelle's going to compete with the Pedrozas, she's going to have to have be ruthless. What better way than to bring in one of the most ruthless crime organizations in Texas?"

"Hey. Abe's truck's that way."

"We've got one more stop. Think Michelle will be suspicious? About the phone?"

"Yeah, but when I tell her I was making sure they didn't see the naked pictures she sent me, she'll forget her suspicions."

Jack jerked his head around. "You're sleeping with Michelle Ryan?"

Eddie leaned his head against the window and closed his eyes. "Almost from the moment I rode into town."

When Jack wanted to tell him where the hell they were going, he would. In the meantime, sleep.

There was a sharp pain in Eddie's shoulder.

"Wake up," Jack said.

"Did you just punch me?"

In the time Eddie had been asleep, ten minutes according to the dashboard clock, Jack's mood had changed from wary curiosity to anger.

"Get out." Jack got out of the car and slammed the door. He left the headlights on.

Eddie looked out the windshield and saw Ellie's lake house, circled with crime scene tape, and understood. He got out and walked to the front of the car.

"What happened? Is Ellie okay?"

He was staring at the front of the house and didn't see Jack's right hook coming. Eddie's head whipped to the left, but he held his feet. With his thumb, Eddie wiped away the blood trickling from his lip. Jack stood in front of him, hands balled into fists, his expression one of rage. Eddie laughed and looked over at the house. When he turned his head back to his brother, his own right hook came with it, quickly followed by a left uppercut to Jack's stomach.

Jack doubled over, coughing. Eddie leaned over him and whispered in his ear. "You've never been able to get the best of me, Juan Miguel, and you never will." He straightened. "You going to tell me what's going on?"

In a weak, breathy voice. "Ellie found a meth lab in her house."

Eddie laughed. "I guess that explains how she's so loaded."

"It isn't hers."

"Are you sure?"

Jack's withering glare was the only answer he would get.

"Yeah, you're right. She's way too straight and narrow to be a cooker. Whose is it?"

"Yours, probably."

Eddie laughed. "Mine? You aren't serious."

"That's what everyone is going to think since your prints are all over the house."

Eddie tried to suppress his smile. Finally, he was getting the reaction he'd wanted for weeks. "Is that why you sucker punched me? You jealous?"

"What's your game here, Eddie?"

"I have no game."

"Bullshit. You always have an angle, a game, an ulterior motive."

"Funny, you didn't mention it as a negative when you were asking me to spy on my boss this morning."

Jack spit blood from his mouth and wiped the remnants from his lips with the back of his hand. "Why would Ellie think you've fucked Julie?"

Eddie's smile slipped. He'd been to the lake house once with Ellie and, after killing a bottle of wine, Ellie asked about Jack and Julie's relationship. Somehow, his ramble about his brother's dysfunctional marriage led to him confessing about his night with Julie. It had been a miracle he and Julie had kept it secret all these years. Eddie had been sure Julie would throw it in Jack's face during one of their many arguments, but she never had. Eddie told himself he told Ellie the story so she would take comfort in knowing the kind of person Julie was and believe Jack wouldn't stay with her. Now, challenged by Jack, Eddie knew he'd been hoping for this confrontation.

"Because I told her."

"It's true?"

Eddie sighed. "Yeah. I met Julie at a bar on Sixth Street and one thing led to another. Of course I never called her after. That was a crazy time in my life. She came to Mom's fundraiser thinking I'd be there. I think I might have invited her. But, I was in jail, remember?"

"I left the fundraiser to bail you out."

"I never had a chance once Julie saw you, the clean cut, professional version of me, the version who had potential to be someone. Not that I wanted a chance."

Jack held up his hand. "Okay. I get it." He stepped forward. "Not since we've been married?"

Not for lack of Julie trying, Eddie thought. "No, Jack. I wouldn't do that to you."

"Then what the hell are you doing with Ellie?"

"Giving you cover, you idiot. Julie thinks I'm Ellie's boyfriend. She won't look twice at her. Julie's been fishing, trying to get me to tell her who you have on the side."

"What?"

"Come on, dude. She doesn't believe for a second you're working every night. She thinks you're off fucking your girlfriend."

"She told you that?"

"No, but every time she asks where I think you've been, she might as well be."

Jack ran his hands through his hair and looked away. "Thank you."

"For what?"

"Giving cover."

"You're welcome."

Jack stepped forward. "How many times have you been out here with Ellie?"

"Once."

"That's it?"

"Scout's honor."

"Leave her alone, Eddie."

"Why?"

"You know why."

"I want to hear you say it."

"Why?"

"Because maybe if you say it out loud, you'll finally fucking do something about it," Eddie hit Jack in the chest with his palms, "and stop walking around like a goddamn zombie." Jack stumbled but didn't strike back, pissing Eddie off even more. "I get what you're doing. Faking it with Julie long enough so you can tell Ethan you tried. That's it, isn't it?" Eddie shook his head. "Let me guess. Christmas, right? You're trying to get through Christmas."

"New Year's."

"God, you're a fucking idiot. Your plan only works if you try. Ethan has to see it and Julie has to believe it."

"I've been home every morning when he wakes up and I'm home every night for dinner. What more can I do?"

"Sleep with your wife, that's what." Eddie got close to his brother. "I get it, you feel guilty, probably because you like it so much." Jack tensed and Eddie thought Jack was going to take another swing at him. Eddie squeezed Jack's shoulder. "Ellie's awesome, dude. Perfect for you. You two will be ridiculously happy together. One day. Right now, though, Julie is determined to make it look like you're a happy family. She needs you to sell her story. Give Julie that for a few more weeks, then pull the rug out from under her."

CHAPTER ELEVEN

If Jack tried hard enough, he could trick himself into believing the last year and a half hadn't happened. That it was a typical Saturday morning in Emerson. He was making breakfast as Julie and Ethan slept in and planning how they would spend the day. Maybe go to the nature trail and let Ethan take pictures of the changing leaves. If the weather was bad, catch an early movie, sharing between the three of them the largest, butteriest bucket of popcorn available, Ethan going back for free seconds midway through the movie. Of course, it all depended on what time Ethan's soccer game was. Jack had spent hours and hours sitting next to Julie in canvas lawn chairs watching progressively better soccer, the smell of fresh-cut grass and the thump of the soccer ball being kicked as much a touchstone for Jack's thirties as it would be for Ethan's childhood. They had been happy. Not without troubles and disagreements, but nothing that couldn't be overcome.

Or so he thought.

It all started with an argument about money. Money and sex; those are the two big points of disagreements for married couples, so the studies say. Sex had never been much of a problem, thank God. But, money? Well, that was always an issue. Jack, coming from a single-parent home, decidedly middle class, always one catastrophe away from the lower end of the spectrum, was a saver. Julie, only child and daughter of an oil executive who was never told no in her life, was a spender. Julie had read an article about the value of being a stay-at-home mom and that their salary, taking all their tasks into consideration, should be somewhere around $100,000. Jack had laughed. That was his first mistake.

His second mistake was forgetting about it. In the middle of a big case, his hours increased, as did his distraction and his patience. His absence gave Julie free reign to stew in all the ways, real and imaginary, Jack took her for granted, which left the door wide open for another man to walk through and feed her narcissistic tendencies with attention and a way out.

After she left, it didn't take long for Jack to discover Julie's cheating. Her boyfriends left plenty of voice mails on the phone she left behind, which was probably her point. Julie would want to humiliate Jack as much as possible, to illustrate how totally he had been deceived.

But the explanation he preferred, the one that wouldn't wound his ego, was Julie's parents helping her financially while she took time to "find herself." They stonewalled him so completely he still didn't know what they knew, when they knew it, or what their involvement exactly was. They sure as hell weren't willing to deflect suspicion off of Jack when the police started asking questions about Julie's whereabouts and why he had lied and told everyone Julie was visiting her parents in Houston. Jack's reputation in the law enforcement community, and the investigators' own experience with their disgruntled significant others, meant the investigators accepted the fact he didn't search for Julie and lied because he thought she would be over her fit soon and return. When her parents didn't hear a peep from Julie during the holidays, the investigators couldn't look the other way. They contacted Jack's bosses, who were completely ignorant of Julie's disappearance. Jack's feeble excuses for why he lied and why he didn't let anyone at work know went from understandable to suspicious, with a healthy dose of guilty and pathetic. By this point, he was worried for Julie. He couldn't believe she would let Christmas pass without a word to Ethan. Something must have happened to her. He went to his partner, Alexandra Walker, and asked for help.

His partner's plan was ridiculously easy. So easy Jack felt stupid for not thinking of it himself. He had been emailing Julie regularly. The emails went from confused but understanding, to exasperated, to angry, to bitter, to furious, to the current state—worried. Jack, of course, hadn't thought of attaching read receipts so he had no idea if Julie had read them. If she had, the recent ones wouldn't encourage her to come home, Alex said. In fact, they would be excellent exhibits in a divorce. Cut that shit out. Now, Alex said. They attached an invisible file to Ethan and Jack's emails. When Julie opened the email, the bot would send her location and the time she opened the email back to Jack.

California.

That's when Jack knew Julie's parents were involved, at least funding her. They had probably encouraged her from the beginning. Jack, with his Hispanic heritage, his liberal politician mother, and low-class beginnings had never been good enough for their daughter. Jack went after Julie for Ethan's sake, at least that's what he told himself. Now he knew a big part of his motivation to get Julie back was to send a major *fuck you* to Tom and Cindy Lucas.

He had landed in L.A. with every intention to make it work despite his realization he didn't miss his wife at all, that life without her was easier in some ways. He was standing in the lobby of the hotel, ringing Julie's room on the house phone, his suit coat draped over the extended handle of his roller bag, thinking of what he would say, when he saw Julie walking around the pool. The bikini she wore was impossibly small and she looked amazing. Tan, fit, her blonde hair even lighter than usual from exposure to the sun. He'd forgotten how beautiful she was. He put down the phone slowly. A smile spread across his face, the anger, humiliation, and worry of the previous four months forgotten. She looked in his direction and smiled. He lifted his hand to wave when a man walked up to her, put his arms around her, and slid his hand beneath the back of her

bikini bottom. Jack had stared at his wife kissing another man and felt
. . . nothing.

Back in his Stillwater kitchen, Jack smiled, remembering it as one of
the happiest days of his life.

"What's this? Breakfast?"

Jack looked over his shoulder at his wife. She was in running clothes,
her hair pulled into a ponytail. Her tan had faded but she was still ridiculously beautiful. No matter what Jack felt about her, and his emotions
were complicated, he couldn't deny the sight of her stirred something
within him.

He flipped the bacon. "Bringing back a family tradition. Breakfast
tacos."

She was next to him, rubbing her hand in circles across his back.
"What brought this on?"

He smiled down on her and hoped it didn't look as forced as it felt.
"You were right." He almost gagged on the words. "It takes two to work
on a marriage."

She wrapped her arms around his waist. "I'm so glad to hear you say
that."

He put the spatula down and returned the hug. He rested his chin
on her head as he had done a thousand times before and thought of how
foreign it felt to be holding her. How did he never notice how awkwardly
they fit together? She looked up at him. "Does this mean what I think it
means?"

Jack nodded. "Tonight."

"I've missed you."

He kissed her so he wouldn't have to reply.

"Hey."

They broke apart with a smack. Ethan was in the kitchen doorway,
staring at them with an embarrassed expression. Jack turned back to the
bacon and wiped his mouth.

"Morning, baby." Julie went around the table and hugged Ethan.

Jack could hear the elation in her voice. He kept his back turned and said, "I'm making breakfast tacos."

"Cool."

"I thought we could all go to the Snipe Festival together," Jack said.

When Jack first arrived in Stillwater, he had decided there could be no more perfect choice for the town and high school mascot than the snipe, an imaginary creature used to take unsuspecting visitors on a wild goose chase. It always ended with the poor mark standing alone in the middle of a pasture, in the dead of night, holding a pillow case. Jack had been the victim of one snipe hunt, headed by Eddie, of course, and had taken numerous other suckers on them in college. The University of Texas had been full of city kids and Yankees who'd never heard of the prank and were easy pickins. Then Miner had set him straight. The snipe was real, a marsh bird expert at camouflaging itself against predators. There are a fair few on the river and at the lake, Miner said, you just have to look real hard for them.

Jack had heard it before, said nearly those exact words to his marks (though the bird part was new), with a straight and disinterested face as Miner presented. Miner laughed and got Susan in on it, then Starling. Everyone backed him up, which only increased Jack's suspicions, until finally Starling pulled up a photo on his cell phone.

"I'm going snipe hunting with Troy," Ethan said.

"Ethan, it's the oldest trick in the book," Julie said. "He'll take you out in the middle of nowhere and leave you. Because you can't hunt snipes. They don't exist." Julie poured a cup of coffee and brought the pot over to refill Jack's cup.

"Thanks." Jack poured the excess bacon grease into a metal bowl, replaced the skillet on the gas burner. The eggs went into the hot skillet with a sizzle.

"That's what I said, too. Nearly got my ass kicked for it," Ethan said. He lifted his phone to show a picture of a brown bird with a long beak who blended into the background almost completely. "See?"

"He's right, Julie," Jack said.

"Have you not been paying attention to the festival signs at all?" Ethan said, looking at his mom in astonishment.

"No. It's a pathetic little small-town festival that will amount to a couple of church bake sales and the few downtown stores that exist selling their sad little wares on the sidewalk."

Jack and Ethan stared at Julie. "It's a big deal to the town," Jack said.

"They're talking about expanding it next year to include music. At least Olivia says Mrs. Martin wants to."

Julie saw the expressions on their faces and smiled. "I suppose I should withhold my judgement until after I go. I still wouldn't go snipe hunting at night," Julie advised Ethan. "Unless you're trying to get a girl alone."

Ethan blushed and changed the subject. "Don't you have to work today, Dad?"

"I officially have the day off. As long as nothing major happens, I'm all yours."

"A family day. What's wrong, Ethan?" Julie said.

Jack turned so he could see Ethan, Julie, and the skillet. Ethan shrugged his shoulders. "I was going to hang out with my friends today."

"Go on," Jack said before Julie could respond. "I'm sure we'll see you downtown." Jack dumped the eggs on a plate and set all of the fixings on the table. "I'll give you some money."

"Where's Uncle Eddie?"

"Upstairs in his room, I imagine," Jack said.

"No, I checked," Ethan said.

"I don't know." Jack saw Eddie go into his room the night before. "I guess he got an early start."

"Maybe he's with *Mrs. Martin*," Julie said.

It was the same disdainful tone of voice Julie had used in regards to Eddie for fifteen years, but Jack heard something different in it this time. Jealousy? Regret? Anger? Jack wished Eddie and Julie *had* been screwing behind his back for years so he could end this farce now. No way would Ethan blame his father if something like that came to light.

Jack didn't look up from fixing his taco. "Probably." He felt Ethan's eyes on him.

Julie put her mug next to the sink. "I'm going for a quick run. I'll eat when I get back."

"I'll leave it out for you," Jack said.

Silence followed her exit. Jack made another breakfast taco and waited. Since Julie returned to the fold, strain had become such a part of Jack's relationship with Ethan, he could hardly remember what it was like before. He realized now it was the strain of lying. He'd lied to Ethan for a year to save his son's feelings about the abandonment of his mother. Now that she was back, Ethan and Jack were keeping things from Julie. He longed for honesty.

"Doesn't it bother you?" Ethan said.

"What?"

The taco in front of Ethan was untouched. He'd obviously been staring at Jack for a while.

"Uncle Eddie and Mrs. Martin."

"They're friends."

"Why? Because you're still seeing her?"

"I'm not seeing her."

"You broke it off?" Ethan snapped his fingers. "Like that?"

Lie, and tell him there was nothing to break off, or be honest?

"Yes. You wanted me to give your mom another chance, so that's what I'm doing."

"Don't *you* want to work it out?"

Jack sighed. "Ethan, it's complicated, but I'm trying, okay?"

Ethan shrugged one shoulder, clearly wanting to say something but not knowing how. Finally, he said, "It's just, if you really like someone, not being around them is, like, torture."

Jack paused with his breakfast taco halfway to his mouth. A flush started on Ethan's neck and spread up to his face. He flicked his eyes up to Jack's face then back down to his plate. Ethan's phone buzzed. When he looked at the screen, a small smile tugged at his lips. Jack thought he saw Olivia's name at the top of the message list. Interesting.

He waited for Ethan to finish typing. "You like living in Stillwater?"

"Yeah, it's okay."

"Would you rather live here or the city?"

"Why? Are we moving again?"

"Not that I know of. But your mom doesn't like it here."

Ethan drank half of his orange juice, wiped his mouth with the back of his hand, and put the glass down. "Obviously."

"She mention it to you?"

"Every day."

"Stillwater's growing on me," Jack said. "Who knows, though. They may run me out of town one of these days."

"You could be a lawyer, couldn't you?"

"I suppose so. If we wanted to stay."

Ethan's phone buzzed again. Olivia's name was at the top, for sure.

"Mind if I go, Dad?"

"It's kind of early, isn't it?"

"I'm meeting Ol—Troy downtown to do real snipe hunting. Can I borrow some binoculars?"

"Sure. Bottom left desk drawer. Need a ride?"

"I'll ride my longboard." Ethan put his plate by the sink and left the kitchen. Jack heard him bound up the stairs and back down. He came through the kitchen with a string bag on his back and his camera slung across his body.

"Keep your phone handy. Pick up when I call."

"Okay, Dad." And he was out the door.

Jack rubbed his face. Jesus. One more thing to worry about. Ethan had discovered girls.

CHAPTER TWELVE

The first of November festival started how most small-town festivals do, as a way to drive customers to downtown businesses. In 1975, downtown businesses decided the answer to a new, unknown monstrosity of a store called Walmart that had opened in Yourkeville was to have a sidewalk sale in the square on the first weekend in November. Not only would it remind the residents of the quality, local downtown shops that had everything you could possibly need without driving the ten miles to Yourkeville, but the sale would also give the residents a chance to get a jump on their holiday shopping. After a few successful years, sales flattened, and someone had the idea of turning the weekend into a festival to bring in tourists from as far away as Dallas. It wasn't easy to find a unique autumn festival honoree when you lived in a state as large as Texas whose towns had been celebrating pecans, peaches, watermelons, rattlesnakes, ice creams, trees, cotton, corn, bluebonnets, and anything else you could eat, stare at, pet, or harvest for the previous 150 years.

About this same time, Stillwater suffered its worst defeat in football at the hands of its main rival, the Yourkeville Lumberjacks, and had had just about enough of the unimaginative jokes about the Snipes disappearing after the opening kickoff. To boost the spirits of the dejected team, which would go on to have the worst record in Stillwater Snipes history, the town decided to honor the lowly, misunderstood snipe, and the Stillwater Snipe Festival was born.

The festival decided the best way to head off being the butt of a joke was to be *in* on the joke, so the festival embraced the ambiguity and celebrated the mythical snipe as an amorphous animal instead of the very real snipe, a shy wetland bird expert at camouflage. Things went on happily for a few years, until Stillwaterites couldn't resist the draw of low prices at the store formerly known as a monstrosity that had become a weekend destination. Downtown Stillwater businesses started shuttering, or were lured by lower rents in Joe Doyle's new development on the west side of town. It looked as if the Snipe Festival was going to be a shooting star—rare, bright, and short-lived.

Then, the birders showed up to save the day.

As it turned out, the Stillwaterites had inadvertently stumbled on the most unique festival honoree in the country, most likely since no one believed snipes existed. But birders knew and, with only a one-line mention in the back of a September 1987 issue of *Texas Monthly* to go on, a small group made the trip to Stillwater to hunt snipe. There was a good deal of suspicion and skepticism when the birders arrived in their khaki vests, cargo pants, and Tilley's field hats with binoculars and cameras draped around their necks. And for the birders, there was a good deal of disappointment to find not a birding festival but a sad little sidewalk sale with an indeterminate animal mascot walking around an almost-deserted square trying to entice people to take photos with him. But birders by nature are an unflappable, patient lot so they dispersed throughout the area to look for birds and were pleasantly surprised to find enough variety to make up for the fact that not one snipe was spotted. Stillwaterites were so thrilled with the influx of strangers—and their money—that they showered them with Southern hospitality and made the birders feel so at home, they would have returned the next year even if they weren't driven by the innate competitive urge in birders to be the first to spot the shy snipe.

Stillwater adjusted its festival to cater to the birders while still retaining the good-natured joke of the mythical snipe for the kids. Slowly the festival grew, and though the square continued to bleed downtown businesses through the nineties, Texas artists arrived at the festival to sell their bird-centric arts and crafts.

And, though she didn't know it at the time, the seed idea for Ellie's cause to save downtown Stillwater in thirty years was born. It would take outsiders—new blood, innovators—to save her town from a slow death. Unfortunately, *change* as a political slogan, or even a byproduct of her plan, was toxic in Stillwater's neck of the woods. But Ellie was unflappable, patient, and determined—like the birders.

Ellie stood outside the Book Bank, glad-handing and greeting every person who passed even if they wore a VOTE FOR JOE pin—and an alarming number of people did. It was exhausting, but a necessary part of running for office. Though she had taken the challenge as a way to get her mind off her personal problems, as she talked about her vision of Stillwater, Ellie became more and more confident she was the right choice. Slowly but surely, her message of downtown revitalization was getting through to the town. But Ellie's message resonated mostly with the younger residents, and that was the demographic Stillwater had been bleeding for twenty years. If the fact that demographics weren't on her side didn't deter her enthusiasm, the number of questions about her lake house meth lab outnumbering the questions on her platform five to one did.

She peeked her head in the store. Kelly stood at the coffee bar talking to Paige. "Kelly!" She motioned for her to come over.

"Yes, ma'am?"

"Go upstairs and get me some different shoes. These are killing me."

"They sure look cute."

"I'm looming over men whose votes I need to win."

"Fine, fine. Trust my judgement?"

"It's not like there're a lot of choices."

"Good point," Kelly said. She disappeared behind the door to the side of the store front that led upstairs to Ellie's flat.

"Ellie."

Stillwater Mayor Jane Maxwell appeared as if from nowhere, surprising Ellie not only because of the stealth of the nonagenarian but also because she seemed smaller than the last time Ellie met with her, as if she would fade into nothingness before succumbing to death. If anyone could beat death, Ellie believed Jane Maxwell was the woman to do it.

"What's this about a meth lab in your lake house?"

Ellie smiled. Jane Maxwell had also mastered the art of straight talk. Ellie bet she'd never been good at small talk at parties. She would have been more likely to get on a soapbox and dress down the rest of the partygoers for having too much fun.

"They think meth cookers are setting up labs in abandoned homes, using them, and leaving before the owners find out."

"Hrmph."

"It's kinda brilliant when you think about it."

"Does Jack think they intended to use it?"

"What do you mean?"

Jane sighed and shook her head. "You're trusting nature is going to get you in trouble one day. A perfect way to discredit you before the election." Jane looked across the street. Joe shook hands with citizens while Mary Doyle handed out VOTE FOR JOE buttons to everyone who passed.

"Wh—" Ellie stopped as the idea took hold. Would someone have done that? But how could they have been sure she would go out to the house and find it? She never went out there. Then she remembered the anonymous tip the sheriff's department received about the meth lab in her house. Was it all a setup by someone who knew how ruthless the Stillwater rumor mill could be, and how effective it was for destroying your enemies? Did Joe Doyle want to win so bad he would stoop to ruining her reputation?

"Yes," Jane said, reading Ellie's mind. "The good news is he's underestimating my power over the city council. Jack doesn't need to worry about his job yet."

Kelly returned, holding a pair of loafers Ellie'd owned for fifteen years. "I can't believe I'm giving you these. We have *got* to go shoe shopping."

Ellie heaved a sigh of relief. "Thank you."

"I don't know what you're thanking me for. These are hideous. Hi, Jane."

"They're classic." Ellie took the loafers and kicked the wedges off, losing four inches. She held onto Kelly's shoulder to steady herself while she put the loafers on.

"Kelly," Jane said. "Thank you for being such a good friend to Ellie during the election. I'm sorry I haven't been able to help like I wanted."

Kelly waved the compliment away. "Of course. Where's Marta?"

"I left her at the fabric shop. I don't know why she buys fabric. She hasn't been able to sew for ten years. I better go get her before she wastes too much of my money." Jane looked up at Ellie. "I will see you at the polls."

"Okay."

When Jane was out of earshot, Ellie and Kelly giggled and rolled their eyes. "Is she shrinking? I think she's shrinking," Kelly said.

"Me, too."

"She's still a dragon, isn't she?" Kelly said.

"You have no idea. Will you take these back upstairs?" Ellie held out the wedges to her friend.

Kelly took the shoes and said, "You're a born politician, getting others to do you dirty work while you smile at the camera." Kelly's eyes shifted to something behind Ellie and her expression turned thunderous. She turned and saw Jack just before he spoke.

"Hello."

Ellie's knees liquefied at the sound of Jack's voice.

"Well, well. Look who's here," Kelly said, crossing her arms, Ellie's shoes dangling from her fingers by the ankle straps.

"Hello, Kelly," Jack said.

"Chief McBride." She stood between Jack and Ellie, inching closer to Ellie and, as a result, pushing her friend away from Jack. "Are you on duty? It's so hard to tell since you don't wear a uniform."

Jack's smile was thin. "As chief, I'm always on duty. But, today, I'm officially off. Unless something major comes up."

"Something major always does seem to come up on your watch, doesn't it?"

Kelly glared at Jack. Ellie knew her friend's initial good impression of Jack had been irreparably damaged when Mike Freeman killed himself. And, even though Ellie had never confirmed she had a relationship with Jack, Kelly had obviously read his interest easy enough and resented Jack toying with Ellie while he was married.

"How's the fire investigation going? Two more bodies on your watch. Brings the number to five, I believe," Kelly said.

"We're waiting on the bodies to be ID'd," Jack said. "Thanks for asking."

"Kelly, the shoes, please," Ellie said.

With a final glare at Jack, Kelly jerked open the door to Ellie's flat and stomped up the stairs.

"Sorry." A beat of awkward silence followed, which Ellie filled with more awkwardness. Her anger at Jack had dissipated in the night and she had woken up mortified at her behavior. "I'm sorry for yesterday."

"For what? Telling me you don't miss me or that my wife slept with my brother?"

Ellie crossed her arms over her chest. "I'm trying to take the high road here, but don't forget you all but said you didn't trust me to not sleep with your brother."

Jack clenched his jaw. "You're right. I apologize." He ground the words out, and Ellie realized with disappointment that the more she got to know Jack, the more she recognized how typically male he was.

"Is everything else okay?" Jack said.

Ellie cringed. From almost their first interaction, Jack had had an uncanny ability to read Ellie's thoughts. Surely he hadn't perceived the small death of her dream of him as an ideal man?

"What do you mean?" she asked.

"Well, I—" He cleared his throat. "I saw you talking to Jane from across the street. You looked upset about something. And now, you have this little," he pointed to the place where her nose met her forehead, then to the same spot on his head, "crease right there. That's your tell."

She smiled in relief. "Oh, is it?"

"Yeah."

"Here I thought I had a good poker face."

"Maybe to everyone else. What is it? What's wrong?"

He lightly touched her elbow and the thrill of connection she always felt with Jack pushed her disappointment out of her mind, to be revived one day in the future during a volatile argument, of which Ellie thought they'd have many. He had a temper, and she wasn't a pushover. It would either be a disastrous combination or a passionate one. Strangely, she looked forward to the discovery.

"Jane suggested the meth lab might have been planted in my lake house to discredit me. Before the election. What do you think?"

Jack tried to push his hands deep into his pockets but only made it halfway. Unlike most days, he had worn jeans. Ellie pressed her lips together to suppress a smile. He didn't even realize his habit of jingling his keys in his suit pants pocket when he thought.

"It's possible."

"I can't believe Doyle would stoop that low. And why? Even I know he's going to win," Ellie said.

"Let's hope not. He's determined to fire me if he wins."

"Oh, Jane won't let that happen," Ellie said.

"As city councilwoman would you vote for or against me? Think carefully. Your response will determine how I vote."

"You haven't lived here long enough to vote," Ellie said.

"Avoiding the question. You're a natural born politician."

Ellie laughed. "What an insult. Don't worry, your job is safe with me."

He grinned and, before she could steel herself against it, her melting heart trickled down to her abdomen and hit her with a jolt of desire so strong she clutched her stomach to contain it.

"You okay?"

"Fine. Cramps."

Jack grimaced and glanced away. Ellie resisted laughing. Chalk another one up for Jack being a typical man.

Jack stared at Doyle across the street and stepped forward slightly. "What would you say if I told you I suspected Doyle was involved in illegal activities? Like drugs?"

Ellie pursed her lips. "Should we be talking about this?"

"No." His eyes slid from her eyes to her lips and back. "Under other circumstances, I would be talking to you about this every night."

She swallowed and hoped her face didn't look as red as it felt. "Well, it wouldn't surprise me a bit. Doyle's a crook, no doubt."

"How do you know?"

"Everyone knows. We just look the other way because it doesn't affect us and he's a philanthropist. And he employs dozens of people. And he's one of us. But how do I know specifically? He was like this with my father." She crossed her fingers. "JD—that's what my father called Doyle, good ole JD—he probably kept my father from being destitute in the last years of his life. I tried to help, but he wouldn't take anything from me. Ironic, considering he spent my entire life trying to take everything from me."

"I'm sorry," Jack said.

"We all have our sob stories. I just have a larger share than most." She shrugged one shoulder. "My dad alluded to Doyle's activities but never specifics. I think he ran numbers for Doyle."

"And Michelle?"

Kelly returned, squeezed between Ellie and Jack, crossed her arms, and said, "Where's your wife?"

Ellie could tell Jack was making an effort to keep his composure. "She's around here somewhere."

Kelly's eyes narrowed and never left Jack. "Ellie, you should probably walk around the square, mingle, instead of standing here like a bump on a log."

"I will in a minute. We're talking about Crime Stoppers. Grab a coffee for me, will you? Might as well get some Book Bank pub while we're glad-handing."

Arms crossed and a scowl on her face, Kelly went into the store.

"Christ. She holds a grudge," Jack said.

"I think it's more about what Freeman's death did to her son than Freeman dying. Kelly will come around."

"So, about Michelle."

Ellie followed Jack's gaze across the street where Michelle talked and laughed to a group of people, her VOTE FOR JOE pin flashing in the sunlight. Michelle caught them staring and, with a mocking smile, waved like a politician and gave them a thumbs up. Ellie turned away.

"She's devious, manipulative, cunning, and charismatic. She was born to be a drug lord."

"Tell me what you really think."

"I can't stand her and the feeling is mutual. Honestly? You'd have an easier time catching Joe than Michelle."

"Do I detect a hint of admiration?"

"I guess the way you admire a tiger, from afar." She cleared her throat. She was done talking about Michelle Ryan. "Jack, about yesterday. I lied."

At that moment, Julie came up and put her arms around Jack. "Oh my God, alert the press. A politician *lied*." Julie squeezed Jack's waist with her pencil-thin arms. Her head barely came up to his armpit. Jack looked pained, but quickly changed his expression to a smile when Julie beamed up at him. Ellie suspected Julie's teeth would glow under a black light.

"Kelly tells me you're a runner," Julie said.

"I am."

"We should go running together."

It took all of Ellie's strength to say, as genuinely as possible, "Sure."

"Awesome!" Though her eyes never left Ellie's, Ellie sensed Julie sizing her up and finding her wanting.

Ellie stood to her full height. "I run between a seven- and eight-minute mile most days. Can you keep up?"

Julie's eyes narrowed, but her smile remained.

Oh, yeah, bitch. It's on.

Julie looked pointedly at Ellie's legs. "Well, with legs that long, you'd have to, wouldn't you?"

These legs have also been wrapped around your husband, you manipulative little bitch.

"Long legs do have their benefits."

Julie laughed. "I'm sure I can keep up."

"I look forward to it."

Jack was silent, his face a mixture of horror and fascination.

"Don't you want to know what I lied about?"

Jack's eyes widened, and he shook his head conspicuously in warning.

"I do," Julie said.

Ellie looked down on Julie with a mischievous grin. "Oh, it was white lie. I told the other police chiefs that I agree with them about Jack wearing a uniform."

"Oh my God, you didn't."

"I *did*. I did it to see Jack squirm." Ellie turned to Jack. Poor thing, he was completely lost. He either didn't know the subtext running through this conversation or was too horrified by it to do more than gape at the two women in his life.

"You better not ever wear one of those hideous uniforms," Julie said.

Come on, Jack. I've given you a hanging curveball. Please don't be too stupid to hit it out of the park.

"I might have to. To keep the peace."

Ellie did an internal fist pump. *That's my boy.*

Ellie was past her limit on time with Julie McBride. She was relieved when Kelly returned with her latte and they went off down the street to shake hands and kiss babies for a campaign doomed to fail.

CHAPTER THIRTEEN

Indoors or outdoors, party groupings always tended to segregate themselves by gender. The men stood together, drinking beer, talking about football, no doubt, and staring at the insanely large smoker hooked onto the back of a Doyle Industries' fifth wheel. The women stood by the rectangular table laden with cookout sides—potato salads, chips, dips, paper plates, and fixings for s'mores. Three large coolers sat beneath the table, full of drinks, beer outnumbering water bottles and Cokes two to one.

Amy crunched into a salsa-laden Tostito, covered her mouth to catch the crumbling corn chip, and said, "I'm sorry about Michelle being here."

"No worries," Ellie said, knowing the comment was primarily directed at her.

"Matt said he couldn't very well use the smoker without asking them, and I said, you sure as hell can. Brian and Michelle don't own it. The company does."

"Really, it's no big deal." Ellie glanced at the group at the smoker. "She'll hang out with the men all night anyway."

As if Michelle heard Ellie's comment and wanted to prove her wrong, she peeled from the men and walked to the table.

"Hi, Ellie." Every time Michelle greeted her, she detected a small, superior smile beneath the outward friendliness, a secret knowledge of Ellie only Michelle knew.

Ellie wanted to rip her face off every time she saw her, but instead she smiled broadly and faked it. "How are you?"

"Outstanding. Did you bring the meth?"

Ellie shoved her hands into the pockets of her faded Stillwater Snipes hoodie. "No, I assumed you'd bring the pot."

"Yeah, how much does it go for these days, Michelle?" Kelly piped in. "You're still an expert, right?"

Forty years of lies, betrayals, secrets, and rumors shimmered between the three women like heat on a summer highway while Amy, a Stillwater newcomer, stood a little apart, a puzzled expression on her face. Ellie seriously doubted Matt had ever told his wife about Michelle's stint selling pot in high school. Hell, Matt may not have even known about it. It was one of those rumors, substantiated not by words, but by raised eyebrows, knowing looks, and silence.

Shadows from the bonfire's smoke and flames danced across one side of Michelle's face. "You never have been able to take a joke."

"Maybe you're not very good at telling them."

"Do they have any leads on the meth lab?" Amy asked.

Ellie stared at Michelle. The breeze shifted, sending the pine-scented smoke in her nemesis's direction. Since Jane planted the idea in her mind that afternoon, Ellie hadn't stopped thinking of it, and the more she thought of it, the more she believed Michelle was behind it. Jack's suspicions of DI's involvement in the local drug trade only cemented the idea further. Ellie tinged her scrutiny of Michelle with humor.

"There's a theory it was set up to discredit me. Before the election."

"Who would do a thing like that?" Amy said.

The fire popped and crackled in the ensuing silence. Michelle's perfectly plucked eyebrows arched above her blue eyes. "And you obviously think of me."

"Hey," Eddie said, pushing into the group. "Chris wants the ribs," he said to Amy. She picked up a large aluminum pan and nodded to a second one. "Kelly, would you mind?"

"Sure." Kelly followed Amy to the smoker, leaving Ellie and Michelle in a stare off with Eddie standing between, bottle of beer held loosely in his hand, an expression of amusement on his face.

"Am I interrupting?"

"Your girlfriend thinks I set up a meth lab in her lake house to discredit her before the election."

"Actually, your dad. But you make more sense. Your hatred of me is almost as legendary as my father's."

Michelle looked at Eddie and raised her eyebrows, seeming to say "see what I told you?"

Ellie gave an unconvincing shrug. "But it's probably some meth head who saw a vacant house and decided to use it."

"If McBride's investigating, they'll never figure out who did it," Michelle said.

"It's the sheriff's department's case."

"Well, Ann Newberry has more sense than McBride."

"You do know I'm standing right here," Eddie said.

Michelle smiled sweetly up at Eddie. "I'm not calling you an idiot, just your brother."

"We're twins, you know. Insult one of us, insult us both."

"Hmm." She raked her eyes over Eddie from head to toe. Ellie rolled her eyes and shook her head. Christ, Michelle was transparent. Even more irritating—Eddie seemed to enjoy it.

Eddie squatted next to a cooler. "Want a beer?"

"Not right now," Ellie said.

"I do. You have a big race tomorrow?" Michelle asked Ellie, a mocking smirk on her face.

"No."

"You in training?" She took the open beer from Eddie and sipped, her eyes never leaving Ellie.

"No. Just not thirsty."

Michelle narrowed her eyes and pursed her lips. "Hmm."

"Is every conversation between you two like this?" Eddie asked.

"Like what?" Michelle said.

"Loaded with subtext no one else understands."

"Yes," Ellie said.

"Then I'm going back to talk to the men. There's zero subtext in those conversations."

They watched him walk off. "Then where's the fun in that?" Michelle said.

"I don't know."

For the briefest of moments, their eyes, full of humor, met, and the two women were in sync. Ellie could almost convince herself they would've been friends if different decisions had been made in the past. The feeling was fleeting, and the comfortable pall of animosity descended once again.

Thankfully, Amy and Kelly returned. "I don't care what Matt says, we're getting a security system." Amy shoved the dirty aluminum pans in the large trash bag tied to a table leg. She pulled two new pans from the back of her suburban, unwrapped them, and placed them on the table.

"He'll come around," Kelly said.

"He better."

"There's only so much money, you know," Michelle said. "It's called a budget."

Amy crossed her arms. "Thank you, Michelle, but I know what a budget is."

"Then stay within it. If you want a security system, which is probably wise, get rid of something else. Like your heated bathroom floors."

Amy narrowed her eyes "How do you know about that?"

"We went over the plans the other day."

"Why would Matt go over our house plans with you?"

"Because I'm helping him finance your dream home, that's why."

"What?"

Matt, poor guy, chose that moment to walk up and get another beer. Ellie and Kelly moved away to the bonfire and sat down on a log, their backs to the three Doyles. They hunched their backs against the cold, looked at each other with wide eyes, and remained silent, the better to eavesdrop.

"Why is Michelle helping us finance the house, Matt? You said we had the money."

"We do, but not in ready cash."

"Ready cash?"

"It's—"

"Shut up, Michelle. This is between me and my husband."

"Amy, we'll talk about it later," her husband said.

Headlights swept over the lake lot.

"Good, the McBrides are here," Matt said.

"Since when does McBride drive a dually?" Michelle said.

"That's probably the Grants," Amy said.

"What? You invited them?" Matt's voice sounded panicked.

"Yeah, Brian's our contractor, and Susan is my friend. Why wouldn't we?" Amy said.

"You haven't told her?" Michelle's voice was filled with incredulity.

"No."

"Told me what?"

Matt's voice dropped to a stage whisper. "We're not using Brian."

"What?"

"Hey, sorry we're late!" Brian called.

"We'll talk about it later," Matt said.

"This is going to be fun," Michelle said.

Ellie and Kelly glanced at each other, both uneasy at the new knowledge and the laughter in Michelle Doyle's voice.

"Oh my God, those baked beans smell heavenly." Amy held the pan of beans to her nose and inhaled deeply again.

Susan smiled. "Bacon makes everything better."

"Truer words have never been spoken," Kelly said.

"Sorry we were late," Susan said. "The beans had to finish up, and Brian felt it his fatherly duty to put the fear of God in Ethan McBride."

"Why?" Ellie asked.

The women, save Michelle, stood around the fire. Michelle stood by the smoker with the men.

"Ethan's spending the night with Troy, and he wants to make sure Ethan doesn't get any ideas about sneaking off with Olivia."

"I can't believe you left them alone," Kelly said.

"Troy's there and so is Paige. Nothing will happen. I trust Olivia. Anyway, we'll be home by midnight."

"Did I hear you say you invited the McBrides?" Kelly asked Amy.

"Yes, at the debate. I'm not entirely sure how it happened," Amy's brow furrowed as though trying to remember exactly how Julie McBride finagled an invitation out of her.

"Maybe McBride was beaten up by another suspect today and left for dead."

"Kelly!" Ellie and Susan said in unison.

"Oh my gosh, why would you say that?" Amy said.

"Kelly doesn't like the chief because of what happened to Freeman," Susan said.

"I don't see how you work with him on a daily basis," Kelly said.

"He's a great boss," Susan said.

"Well he's a shitty cop."

"No he's not," Ellie said. "You can't blame Seth's emotional state on Jack."

Kelly's son, Seth, had taken Mike Freeman's death especially hard. Freeman had been like a big brother to Seth, helping him with weight training to improve his chances of landing a football scholarship. Since Freeman's death, Seth's performance on the field and in school had nose-dived. More troubling to Kelly was the fact Seth had lost all interest in friends and had pulled away from her, too. Instead of focusing her anger and frustration on the source of the problem—Mike Freeman killing two people in cold blood—Kelly blamed Jack.

Brian walked up and sat next to Susan. "If McBride's coming, we better hurry up and smoke these." Brian pulled a baggie with two fat joints in it out of his pocket.

"Jesus, Brian," Susan said.

"Lighten up, Sue, it's two joints to share among what, ten people? You won't even get a buzz."

Michelle and Eddie rejoined the group. "Then why do it?" Michelle said.

Brian lit one joint, then another. "To be social." He passed one to Michelle, who took a hit and passed it to Eddie.

Brian held the other joint out to his wife.

"No, Brian."

"Come on."

"No."

"Do it."

Susan took the joint between her thumb and forefinger, inhaled deeply, held it, and released the stream of smoke. She handed it back to her husband. "Happy?"

Brian took the joint, leaned over, and kissed Susan roughly before handing it to Kelly, who took a hit without hesitation.

Ellie watched Eddie through the entire scene, curious about his reaction. Where Eddie had been relaxed, his eyes were fixed on Brian and his body had tensed like a panther ready to strike. Eddie McBride was much more intuitive, and protective, than he wanted anyone to believe. Both joints made it to Ellie at the same time, and she passed them across her body to Eddie and Kelly without a hit of either. No one noticed.

"Maybe we can finish them before they get here," Kelly said on its third pass.

As if on cue, headlights lit up the vacant lot.

"Speed it up." Brian motioned for the others to take their hit and pass it on. Instead of pinching them out and pocketing them, Brian tossed the joints into the fire. "Now we'll all get high."

Susan sighed and inched away from her husband on the log they shared.

"That was stupid," Amy said.

"Great," Michelle said. "Now the fire will smell like weed."

"Eddie can say it's his," Brian said. "Chief won't arrest his brother, or so I hear."

"You heard wrong." Jack's voice carried loud and clear across the sounds of crackling fire, frogs, and cicadas.

Before she could catch herself, Ellie looked up. Her stomach twisted at the sight of them—and the realization they were a ridiculously good-looking couple. She hunched further inside her hoodie and looked up at Eddie, unsurprised to find him watching her reaction.

"I'll take that beer now," she said.

CHAPTER FOURTEEN

Eddie and Jack hovered where the firelight met the darkness. Eddie told Jack about Brian, Susan, and the joint.

"Remind you of anyone?" Jack sipped his beer.

"Dad. I was in Huntsville with Brian's old man. He was proud wife beater. Think Brian beats Susan?"

Jack studied Brian Grant. He had a history of disturbing the peace and a few assaults, all involving alcohol and all involving men, none leading to charges once everyone sobered up. Nothing involving women, especially Susan. "I hope not."

"Why do women stay with men like that?"

Jack could answer with all kinds of statistics about domestic abuse, about the mental manipulation that was sometimes as bad as the physical abuse, but he remained silent, watching his wife. Why had he stayed with her? Because it was easier than leaving. Sometimes, it was as simple as that.

"What do you think she's talking about?" Eddie said, nodding to Julie.

"God only knows. Michelle Ryan has been staring at us off and on for ten minutes."

"I noticed," Eddie said. "She's probably gauging if we'd be interested in a threesome."

"No."

Eddie drank his beer and watched Michelle, who stood next to her husband, Chris, but didn't bother to avert her gaze from the twins. Chris, long BBQ tongs in one hand and his phone in the other, was focused squarely on the glowing four-inch screen of his phone.

"Chris is a moron," Eddie said. "I could screw Michelle right next to him, and he'd never know."

"Well, don't."

Eddie shrugged one shoulder and grinned, as though he wasn't committing one way or the other. "You know, I think she's fucking me because she thinks I'm with Ellie."

"That's twisted."

"It is. But I'm not complaining. Need another?" Eddie held up his empty beer bottle.

"Sure." Jack wandered over to the smoker to talk to the men, passing Michelle as she walked toward the others. Jack glanced over his shoulder and saw Eddie and Michelle standing apart from everyone, heads close together, talking. Michelle laughed and touched Eddie on his arm. Check that. Flirting. He turned his attention back to the men and thought he caught Chris duck his head down quickly. A muscle in Chris's jaw tensed. He wasn't as big a moron as Eddie thought.

"Hey, Brian. Seen Kyle lately?" Jack said.

Brian wore an aged Carhartt jacket and a retro Cowboys toboggan on his head to ward off the cold. He dragged on his cigarette and blew smoke out the side of his mouth. "My half-brother and I don't run in the same circles. Why?"

"I have a few questions for him."

"What about?"

Jack didn't answer and addressed Matt instead. "He still work for you?"

"He doesn't work for me. He works for the company. Floats around, doing what needs to be done."

"Who does he report to?"

"Whoever needs him," Matt said, eyes flicking to Chris and back to the grill. Jack watched Michelle's husband, who appeared to be enthralled with his phone, but Jack suspected he'd heard every word. "Chris, how about you?" Jack said. "You seen Kyle Grant lately?"

Chris looked up from his phone. "What?" He tried to feign ignorance.

"Kyle Grant. He ever work for you?"

"Some."

"I heard he'd been working for you almost exclusively these past few months," Brian said. He blew the cigarette smoke right at Chris's face.

"I thought you two never talked," Chris said. Jack had never seen Chris bareheaded and wondered if he was bald beneath his black Titleist hat.

"He comes around when he wants something. Not lately, though. Guess someone's been taking care of him," Brian said.

"How about Paco? Seen him lately?" Jack said.

"Not since before we talked. Do you seriously think he was one of those arson victims?" Chris asked.

"It's looking more and more likely. Weird that two employees of yours have gone missing lately," Jack said.

"Kyle didn't work for me," Chris said.

"Come on, let's eat," Matt said. He closed the grill and carried the overflowing pan to the table. Brian flicked his cigarette away and followed. Chris pocketed his phone.

Everyone loaded their plates with food and sat around the fire to eat. Much to Jack's relief, the only spot left for him to sit was next to Ellie. Maybe he imagined it, but he thought he could smell her perfume beneath the smoky, sweet aroma of the ribs. He focused so hard on not looking at her or talking to her, he worried his avoidance was counterproductive and a neon sign was flashing over their heads.

"You aren't eating much." His eyes were on the thick, white paper plate balanced on her knees. A small rib, maybe two tablespoons of potato salad, and a couple of chips were almost lost amid the white of the plate.

"I'm not very hungry."

Everyone around the fire was eating or talking to others so he took a chance and looked at her. He kept his voice low. "You look thin."

"That doesn't sound like a compliment."

"What was that this morning?"

"Me being petty. I can be that way sometimes. You didn't know that about me, did you?"

They held each other's gaze. The last time Ellie said those words to him was the night they decided to stay apart until January. The last night they made love. She looked away.

"What did you lie about?"

She poked at her potato salad and sighed. "When I said I didn't miss you."

Words tumbled out of him, tripping over themselves in a race to finally find their voice. "I was fine, or told myself I was, until I saw you Thursday night, and yesterday, and today. But, Christ. I can't do it anymore. I need to be alone with you."

"I don't mean to eavesdrop," Amy said.

Jack and Ellie's heads jerked up. His stomach twisted and the ground spun. Amy had been too far away to hear, hadn't she? Had they been talking too loud?

"Did I hear you say you're writing a book?" Amy looked across the fire, away from them.

"I am," Julie said. She raised her eyebrows at Jack. He had no idea what she wanted from him, had he ever? "Do you mind, honey?" she asked Jack in a sweet voice.

Everyone stared at him, except Ellie. Tension emanated from her. He resisted the urge to leave and take her with him, to stick a flag in their relationship for all to see. *This is the woman I love and want to be with*. He knew everyone around the fire, save one, would understand his choice. Unfortunately, that one was the woman he'd made vows to fifteen years earlier, the mother of his son, the woman he was trying to convince that he was making an effort with their marriage.

The woman he'd promised to make love to that night.

He had no idea what Julie was going to say, what fiction she would feed these people. But he had no choice but to go along. "It's your story. Tell it if you like."

"Well, about a year ago, or a little more, right honey?" She didn't wait for Jack to respond. "I went on a sabbatical."

Matt licked the sauce from his fingers with a smack. "I thought only professors and priests went on sabbaticals."

"Anyone can. It's a time of rest, reflection, and study."

"What did you need to rest from?" Brian threw a bare rib bone into the fire.

"Mine was more of a time of reflection. A chance to be by myself to find who I am again, to discover my identity. For so many years, I was Jack's wife, Ethan's mother, someone's neighbor, a beloved daughter, school volunteer, church volunteer."

Jack twisted his mouth to keep from smirking. Until they moved to Stillwater, Julie hadn't been to church in ten years.

"But, who was I, really? I needed time to find out."

"Jack, you were on board with this?" Brian asked. At that moment, Jack kinda liked him. He was obviously the only one of the group who was going to be willing to call Julie on her bullshit. Poor Julie. She had no idea how ridiculous she sounded, but Jack gave her credit for throwing the church in. She knew her audience, at least.

"Jack was 100 percent behind me. In fact, it was his idea."

Everyone turned their attention to Jack, expressions of astonishment on the men's faces and admiration on the women's. Grudging, in Kelly's case. Jack bit into the meat on the rib he held and ripped it from the bone so he didn't have to speak.

"You're a better man than me," Brian Grant said. "Or maybe just stupider, I can't decide."

"Yeah, I wouldn't have been behind that," Matt said. "A girls' weekend here and there, sure, but there's no way I could handle my job and the kids and everything else by myself for a year."

"Me, either," Chris said, not looking up from his phone.

"It's not rocket science," Michelle said. "I do it all day every day, career, family, volunteering, social life. So do Kelly and Susan."

"Yes, we know, Michelle," Chris said, tonelessly.

"Don't patronize me, Christopher."

Chris turned his head toward Michelle and glared at his wife, who glared right back.

"So, what about this book?" Matt said.

"It's going to be a bit like *Eat, Pray, Love*. Without the divorce and the Italian lover. My agent thinks it's going to be a bestseller."

"Sounds like a real snoozer," Brian said.

Eddie spurted beer from his mouth when he laughed. "Sorry."

Julie glared at Eddie. "And I couldn't have done any of it without Jack's love and support."

Ellie stood. "Anyone need a beer?"

Everyone raised their hands and started calling out their orders.

"I'll help," Jack said. He put his plate on the log and followed.

Ellie squatted in front of the cooler, her back turned to the fire. Jack squatted next to her, but angled so he could see anyone walk up. They were far enough away for their conversation to be unheard by the others.

"How much of it is true?" Ellie asked.

"None of it. When I found her, she was at a luxury resort in California, fucking an artsy photographer half her age. She believes it, though."

Ellie handed the beers to Jack, who opened them and placed them on the table. "It's killing me to be so close to you and not touch you," Jack whispered.

Ellie stood, her knees creaking. She held out an unopened beer to Jack. He wrapped his hand around hers on the bottle and twisted the cap off. He kept his hand over hers and remembered the first time they met, how her hands flowed across the papers on her desk, and the last time they touched, how she intertwined her hands in his while they made love.

Ellie took a shaky breath. "I need to tell you something. I should have told you that last night at the lake. But, I was too angry. Drunk. And, honestly? I wanted to make you suffer. To wonder. Have you suffered?"

"Yes. Have you?"

"Yes." She paused and looked off toward the woods. "I thought you were crazy, to tell me you loved me after a week. I still do." Their eyes locked and one side of her mouth curled up into a wry smile. "But damnit if I don't feel the same way." She shook her head and rolled her eyes to the heavens. "Not how or where I wanted to tell you."

Joy and guilt warred within him. Of course he had thought Ellie loved him; why else put herself through this separation? But to hear her say it made Jack feel like he could bench press Chris's smoker. Then, guilt of his betrayal of Ellie every time he slept with Julie overcame him. "Ellie—"

"I'm not finished. I don't know how things are with Julie, and I don't want to know. But you have to promise me something."

"Anything."

She looked at him full on. "If you decide to stay with her, you have to resign. Leave town. I can't bear to be around the two of you."

"I'm not going to stay with her."

"If you do, promise me."

Jack clenched his jaw. He should have never let Ellie talk him into this farce they were living. He'd been weak, willing to say or do anything to make her happy. This, though? This was a bridge too far.

"I've done everything you've wanted, even though it's made me miserable. Why don't you believe me when I say I love you and I'm going to leave Julie?"

She let out her breath, her eyes lingering on his lips. "I want to."

"I want you, too."

Her brows furrowed, then the corner of her mouth quirked up into a wry smile. "I said, 'I want *to*.' To believe you. Not 'I want you.'"

"You're killing me over here."

She looked down, a blush working its way up her neck, and looked at him from beneath her eyelashes. "The wanting goes without saying."

"You can say it."

Ellie's laugh died when Julie's voice rang out across the fire. "What's so funny?"

CHAPTER FIFTEEN

"Were you talking to us?" Ellie handed Julie a Shiner, the beer from the cooler with the most calories.

"You two look so cozy. I thought you'd like to share the joke," Julie said.

Julie's eyes were clear, calculating as they moved from Jack to Ellie, from suspicion to disbelief. Ellie could almost hear Julie's thought: "You're fucking *her*?" Sitting next to Julie, Kelly looked mortified.

"I was thanking Jack for offering to talk to the developers coming in on Tuesday to meet with me and Matt."

"Developers? What are you talking about?" Michelle's voice was brittle, her eyes blazing as she stared at her brother across the fire.

"An old friend of mine from Dallas is in historical preservation. He wants to restore the hotel. Curtis knows a chef who wants to open a small, locavore restaurant," Ellie said.

"Dad won't like that," Michelle said.

"Will your developer bring his own contractors into town?" Brian asked.

"We haven't gotten that far, but I'm sure he'll bid out the business."

Ellie's gaze wandered to Kelly, who studied her as though trying to put together a complicated puzzle. Julie's eyes hadn't left Ellie, either. Ellie met the other woman's direct gaze across the fire and didn't blink. She was not going to be intimidated by her.

"You're lucky you have Yourkie on your side, Matt," Brian said. "If anyone can close the deal, it's Ellie."

"Yourkie?" Julie said.

"It was her nickname in high school," Michelle said. "Go on, tell our new friends how you got it."

Ellie narrowed her eyes at Michelle. "And ruin your moment of fun? I'd never."

"She got it from basketball," Susan said, speaking up for the first time. "She was a tenacious defender. She would lock on her opponent and never let go. She was the best player Stillwater's ever had."

Ellie looked at the ground, barely resisting the urge to leave. She didn't like to think about it, and she definitely didn't like to talk about it.

"Not that there's much competition in that department," Michelle said.

Ellie gritted her teeth. *Control, control, control.*

"Too bad about the point shaving. How exactly does it work?"

Ellie lifted her head slowly to meet Julie's smirk.

"That was a bunch of bullshit," Brian said. "Everyone who knows Ellie knows it."

Ellie looked from Julie to her oldest and best friend, waiting for her to say something, to defend Ellie as she had so many times before. Finally, Kelly said, "It isn't something she likes to talk about."

That was her best friend's idea of defending her? The roar in Ellie's ears started low and grew, so she almost didn't hear the next comment.

"Guilty conscience, maybe?"

"I suppose a guilty conscience is something you would know a lot about, Julie." Ellie tossed her plate of uneaten food in the fire, turned, and walked off.

As she hit the treeline, Ellie heard Amy say, in a falsely bright voice, it was time for s'mores. She made it fifty yards into the woods before she threw up the little bit of beer she drank. She wiped her mouth and leaned against a tree, her stomach still roiling. She felt her forehead with the back of her hand for the thousandth time since Thursday.

"Ellie?"

Ellie closed her eyes and sighed. "Over here."

Kelly walked around the tree. Ellie could just see her through the darkness.

"What the hell was that back there?"

"I was going to ask you the same thing," Kelly said.

"My best friend sitting by and letting some stranger insult me, is what I saw."

Kelly stepped forward. Her face was silvery in the darkness, but her eyes sparked with anger. "Are you sleeping with Jack?"

"No. Why would you ask me that?"

"Julie was right. You did look awfully cozy."

"We were talking."

"You sure as hell weren't talking about business."

"Why would you care if I was sleeping with Jack? Worried about your new best friend?"

"You sound jealous."

"Hardly. I wouldn't want to be friends with that manipulative, vindictive narcissist if she was the last person on earth."

Kelly's head jerked as if she'd been slapped. "What are you talking about? She's nothing like that." She narrowed her eyes. "How would you know anything about her at all? You haven't even tried to get to know her."

"I've been busy. Plus, I thought I had friends. I don't need to try to make more."

"You certainly tried to be friends with Jack when he first came."

"Which you encouraged, if you remember."

"That was before I knew him."

"Oh, and what do you know about him?"

"Well, he's a shitty police chief and he's a philanderer. He cheated on Julie all the time. That's the real reason she left. She's telling the other story so she doesn't hurt Ethan."

"Why would you believe her?"

"Because I remember how he went after you when he moved here, or have you forgotten? Jesus, he hadn't even unpacked before he was trying to get into your pants."

Ellie's stomach churned as realization dawned. "You just told her."

"What?"

"You told Julie." Ellie pushed Kelly away. "How could you?"

"She has a right to know what her husband has been doing while she's been gone. While you two were talking about 'the Henry' she was telling me how he was a carouser before she left and I said I could believe it. What does it matter to you? Nothing came of it. I told her that in no uncertain terms."

Ellie shook her head. "You need to stay out of other people's business."

"Did I lie?"

"What?"

"When I told Julie you didn't sleep with her husband."

"Are you asking me again, if I'm sleeping with Jack? The answer is no. Again. Now fucking drop it. And don't you ever talk to Julie McBride about me again. Understand?"

"Why do you hate her?"

"The better question is, why do you like her? How could you possibly find anything in common with a woman who abandoned her son for an entire year?"

"She didn't abandon him. He had his father, and she was constantly in touch with him through email."

Susan walked up so quietly she was upon Kelly and Ellie before they knew she was there. "Hey, girls. Am I interrupting?"

"Yes, thank God," Ellie said. "I need to go home. I think I'm going to puke again."

"What's wrong? Are you sick?" Susan asked.

Ellie bit back a smart-ass comment. Susan and Brian had defended her against Michelle and Julie, a pair of women Ellie hoped never ganged up against her. Ellie was pretty sure they would destroy her, and smile while doing it.

"I think I'm getting the flu," Ellie said.

"I think the party's breaking up anyway," Susan said.

"Great," Kelly said.

"Are you blaming me?" Ellie asked.

"You said it, not me." With a glare, Kelly pushed past her oldest friends.

Ellie watched Kelly dissolve into the dark. She sighed and turned to Susan. "Was I wrong back there? Did I overreact?"

"No."

"She was baiting me, wasn't she?"

"Julie or Michelle?"

"Take your pick."

"I get Michelle, but why would Julie?"

"Kelly told her Jack flirted with me before she got into town."

"Ah. That explains a lot." Susan put her arm around Ellie. Ellie leaned into her friend. "Did you sleep with him?"

Ellie took a deep breath. She wanted to tell someone, to share the burden of the secret, to have someone to commiserate with, someone who would listen, let her vent and always tell her she was making the right decision. Susan and Kelly had always been those people. Until now.

"No." Ellie tugged at Susan's hand. "Come on. Let's help clean up."

The rustle of leaves kept Ellie from moving. "Did you hear that?" she whispered.

"What?" Susan whispered back.

"I thought I heard something." Ellie peered into the trees to their right. She thought she saw movement, but it was too dark to be sure. When she heard the crunch of leaves again, she tugged on Susan's hand harder.

"I heard that," Susan said. "Let's get out of here."

Though the mood was decidedly more subdued, the party wasn't breaking up. Ellie focused on toasting her marshmallow to a perfect golden brown while the others chatted about the snipe festival. By unspoken agreement, Jack and Ellie toasted their marshmallows across the fire from each other and pretended the other didn't exist. Jack stared blankly into the fire while his marshmallows burned to a crisp. Ellie tapped her marshmallow against his and his eyes met hers. "You like them burnt?"

Jack noticed his marshmallows and pulled them from the fire. Julie walked up and, with the ease and familiarity of years of marriage, they wordlessly went about making s'mores for each other. Julie sandwiched the graham crackers and chocolate around one marshmallow and pulled the complete s'more from the straightened wire hanger. She stuck it in Jack's mouth and repeated the process with the second. She glanced up at Jack and wiped a bit of melted marshmallow from the corner of his lips. "You're a mess."

Jack shoved the rest of the s'more in his mouth and Julie held out the second one. "You take it. I'll make another."

Ellie turned away, overcome with the feeling she had witnessed an intimacy, a familiarity, which would take years to develop with Jack, if ever. How much of Ellie's future relationship with Jack would be retreads of his time with Julie?

"I told Ethan it was a prank," Julie said to Amy. "He immediately showed me a picture and said he almost got beat up when he said the same thing."

The locals laughed. Amy said, "The same thing happened to me. Well, not the beating up part. But you'd have thought I called them all atheists, or something. These Stillwaterites get protective about their snipe."

"Why don't we go on one tonight?" Julie said.

Ellie smashed her marshmallow between two graham crackers and a slab of Hershey's chocolate. "A wild goose chase only works if someone isn't in on the joke," Ellie snapped.

Julie's expression was slightly vacant. Kelly opened her mouth to clarify when they were jolted by Brian's yell and the sound of fighting. Jack handed his half-eaten s'more to Julie and ran toward the scuffle.

"I can't believe you," Brian yelled at Matt. Chris strained to keep Brian in check. "I thought we were friends."

"It's business, man. I'm sorry." There was a note of pleading beneath Matt's anger.

"It isn't business! It's my life. My livelihood. I was counting on this deal. You knew that!"

"It's out of my hands."

"Oh, no," Susan said, heading toward her husband.

Ellie crossed her arms over her chest against a sudden chill and looked around, her instinct to find her best friend and be beside her. Kelly and Julie stood together, watching. Ellie turned away, and suddenly, Eddie was beside her, out of breath. "I heard yelling."

Ellie studied him. His face was flushed. "Brian jumped Matt."

Without looking at her, he nodded and walked to the men. Michelle walked out of the woods in the general direction Eddie came from. She winked broadly at Ellie, wiped the edges of her mouth, and followed Eddie.

Figures.

Brian jerked himself free from Chris and stormed to his truck, Susan on his heels. Susan said something over her shoulder to Matt. Brian stopped and turned so abruptly, Susan ran into him. Brian grabbed his wife by the arms, said something in a low voice to her, and dragged her to the car. Eddie jogged toward Brian, catching him before he got in his truck. He grasped Brian's shoulder, pulled him close, and whispered in his ear. Brian's face glowed with anger before slacking into shock. Eddie pulled away, a smile on his face, and gave Brian a genial pat on the back.

Chris closed up the smoker and opened the driver's door to the fifth wheel.

"What are you doing?" Michelle asked.

"Leaving. Get in or get a ride with someone else." He got in and slammed the door. Michelle walked around and got in the passenger seat and they drove off.

Matt walked over to the table and started packing up. Amy worked so hard to ignore her husband, but Ellie was sure she'd seen the blood stain on his shirt and the beginning of what promised to be an impressive shiner.

"What a way to end the night, huh?" Julie said when she and Kelly walked up. Everyone ignored her. Kelly didn't say anything either, but started helping with a puzzled look on her face.

"I wouldn't worry about it, Matt," Julie continued. "He seems like a bully to me."

Everyone stopped and stared at her.

"What? I know he's your friend and all, but take it from the one person here not weighted down with history and baggage, Brian Grant is a bully."

Jack and Eddie walked up. "Can we help?" Jack said.

"It's okay," Amy said. "We've got it. But thanks."

Julie paused, looked around the group of people, none of whom would look at her. "Okay. If you're sure. Thanks for inviting us. We had a great time."

"Yes, thank you," Jack said. He gently grasped Julie's arm and led her away.

The rest of them finished cleaning up without a word.

CHAPTER SIXTEEN

"Did you see Eddie slither out of the woods with Michelle tonight?"

Jack stopped, his shirt halfway off. "What?"

"No, I suppose you were too busy holding Matt back from Brian. What was that all about?"

"You know as much as I do. What about Eddie and Michelle?"

"They came out of the woods together. Well, almost together. Eddie was buttoning his pants and Michelle was wiping her mouth. She made sure Ellie saw it, too. Did you know they were sleeping together?"

"Yeah. He told me the other day."

"He'll fuck anything, won't he?" Julie threaded her jeans through a hanger and wedged it into the too tiny closet. "This house is awful."

"I like it," Jack said.

"The bathroom is down the hall."

"You'll survive." Jack pulled his money clip, keys, and change from his front pocket and tossed them on the dresser.

In only her panties and bra, Julie walked down the hall to the bathroom. Jack opened his mouth to remind her about Ethan when he remembered Ethan was sleeping over at Troy's. And that he had all but promised Julie they would sleep together.

Shit. How could Jack do that on the same night Ellie said she loved him?

He couldn't wait until January. He would call Bob Underwood tomorrow to start divorce proceedings. Ethan wanted to be treated like an adult; it was time to see if he could handle bad news with some maturity.

Jack would continue this farce until after Thanksgiving, but no longer. Continuing meant making Julie believe he wasn't cheating on her though. Which meant sleeping with her. Jack laughed, incredulous he was sitting there dreading the prospect of fucking a beautiful woman. He closed his eyes and reminded himself none of this had been his idea. Ellie knew what this ruse would mean and still insisted on it. That absolved him, didn't it?

Julie returned, face clean, hair brushed to a flaxen shine. Jack knew she would smell faintly of oranges thanks to the face moisturizer she used at night. Her breath would smell like Crest, her body would be smooth and silky. Jack's dick hardened.

She stood in front of him, between his legs. She ran her hands through his hair. "And it's a real shame, too," Julie said.

"What?"

"That Eddie's cheating on Ellie. Kelly's told me about her luck with men. Leave it to Eddie to pick a woman with more baggage than him."

"He says they're friends."

"Well, he's lying." She ran her finger over the scar above his right eyebrow. Jack rested his hands on Julie's hips and tried not to remember a similar scene at Ellie's six weeks ago when she removed his stitches.

"What were you two really talking about?"

"The Henry."

"Bullshit."

Jack unhooked Julie's bra, removed it, and tossed it aside.

"Kelly told me you flirted with Ellie when you moved to town."

"Did she." Jack took her breast in his mouth, hoping to distract her.

"I told her it was ridiculous." Julie gasped and clutched at his head, pressing him closer. "Ellie's not your type at all. Now, Kelly on the other hand . . ."

"Would you stop talking about other women while we're fucking?"

"We aren't fucking yet."

"Shut up and we will."

"Tell me you love me."

"You haven't earned it yet."

"Say it."

"Fuck you."

He flipped her on to the bed, pinned her arms above her head. He stopped, wanting her to do something that would make him want to stop. Her shocked expression morphed to one of triumph, pleasure. She wrapped her legs around him and pressed him closer.

She still liked it rough. Jack thought of all the men who'd fucked Julie in the last two years and decided to give her exactly what she wanted.

CHAPTER SEVENTEEN

Since when did they start locking the damn doors?

Fred tried truck after truck with no luck. He tucked his hands beneath his armpits to warm them. He needed gloves. A coat. Shoes. Damn, tramping had turned into a chore. He sat on the ground against the front tire of his favorite truck to think, shivering.

He'd run through the sixty dollars McBride had given him quicker than usual. Shouldn't have used that ten on food. The whiskey went quicker and quicker these days, and donations had fallen off to practically nothing. In exchange for a hot meal, churches wanted a tearful confession and his immortal soul, two things Fred couldn't give for the one thing he didn't really want. Too bad Stillwater didn't have a Catholic church so he could steal the wine. Just a bunch of teetotaling Baptists and closet drinking Methodists, neither of which would give money to a remorseless drunk. McBride was the only revenue stream Fred had left. Fred needed whiskey, food, and a coat. To get those, he needed information which, looking around at the deserted yard, wasn't going to happen on this cold Saturday night.

He stood and walked through the maze of closely parked trucks to the back of the nearest building. He paused, hand on the door knob. He'd never tried the buildings before. He didn't hold out much hope this tiny office would be more comfortable than the cab of an empty truck. The only chair he saw was plastic. Still, it looked warm. He tried the knob. It didn't budge. He spent the next fifteen minutes trying every one of Doyle Industries' buildings with no luck. He collapsed at the back of the last building from exhaustion, the long, cold night stretched in front of him. Thirty wasted years stretched behind.

He supposed it was time to come to Jesus.

Luckily, it was about to be Sunday, if it wasn't already. Fred had to make it until 8 a.m., when he knew Brother Dobson would get to the church. A few hours. He could do it. He closed his eyes and, with teeth chattering from the cold, started practicing his confession.

"I've seen the error in my ways, Brother Dobson."

The rumble of a Mack truck and the squeal and whoosh of air brakes engaging broke his concentration. The rattle of chain link fence, the truck moving through the gate, the rattle of the gate closing told Fred he wasn't alone anymore. He tucked his knees close to his chest and wrapped his arms around them, for warmth and to make himself as small as possible. He felt reasonably good about his hiding place between an AC unit and an electrical box at the back of the furthest building in the lot, but he didn't want to take any chances. His stomach flipped over in fear when he felt the vibrations from the front bay opening. The rumble of the engine echoed throughout the large building, through the wall, and burrowed deep into Fred's chest. His heart hammered in his throat. He stared at Doyle Industries' back fence. Of course his hole was at the opposite end.

Sit here. Don't move. They won't open the back bay door. It's too cold. There's no reason for them to come back here at all. You're fine. Sit tight. Plan your confession. Think warm thoughts.

"I've seen the error in my ways, Brother Dobson . . ."

The crunch of gravel, the sound of a car door closing distracted him. Christ. Fred squeezed his eyes closed. Footsteps. Voices inside. The sound of another car. More footsteps.

"I've seen the error in my ways, Brother Dobson . . ."

Talking. Tools clanging. Laughter.

Fred's eyes opened. Then again, maybe he should sneak around the side and listen in. The rest of his body might be breaking down from abuse, but his hearing was better than ever. His invisibility to the upright citizens of Stillwater and his good hearing had been keeping him alive for thirty years. McBride wasn't the only chief who had paid him to be his spy, but he was the only one too stupid to make the connection between Muldoon and Pollard.

Fred let his head fall against the metal building and smiled. Bingo. He didn't have to risk his neck by eavesdropping. He'd tell McBride about his deal with Pollard. Fred had some major shit on that old asshole. No telling how much it'd be worth. Fred smiled and thought about the pool of whiskey he'd be swimming in soon, which was why he didn't hear the new truck drive into the yard. But he did hear the yelling.

"Drugs, Michelle? Are you kidding me?"

The clanging stopped.

"Matt. Let's go somewhere to talk."

"Eddie? You're in on this, too? Jesus."

"Matt, out here. Now."

Fred used the wall to help himself stand. He inched over to the corner of the building and peeked around. This little drama would set him up for a while. He could keep the Pollard dirt in his back pocket.

"Calm down, Matt," Michelle said.

"Calm down? You're running drugs through our father's company and you want me to calm down?"

"God, you're such an idiot."

"Oh, really? I'm not the one breaking the law."

"Yes, you are. You just don't know it."

"What?"

"Why do you think we brought you on, huh? When you came to us with the idea, I knew it would be the perfect cover with you being such a goody-two shoes. You think we give two shits about your organic produce?"

"You mean dad knows about this?"

Michelle laughed. "Who do you think started the business?"

Matt turned and walked away a few feet, running his hands through his hair. "For how long?"

"Thirty years."

Matt's mouth gaped, then he laughed in disbelief. "Thirty years."

"You might not remember when he lost everything back in the eighties, but I do. Dad has always shielded his precious golden boy from the big bad world. It was either drugs or destitution. Like it or not, drugs have bankrolled your entire life. Even now."

"I can't believe this."

"Look. You don't have to worry about it. No one would ever think you're involved."

"You just said—"

"We've set it up so nothing will blow back on you. That's the only way Dad would bring you on, as long as you could remain blissfully ignorant. You're safe. Just keep your mouth shut and look the other way. If you don't, I will take you down with us."

"Are you threatening me?"

"You're goddamn right I'm threatening you. Do you really think I would let my pussy brother ruin everything I've built?"

"You said Dad built it."

Michelle laughed bitterly. "His operation was chicken feed when he brought me on. I'm the one who built it up into what it is. We're so fucking big, the Pedrozas want in on it. Dad takes all the credit while I take all the risks. So, if you think there's any way in hell I'm going to let your guilty conscience ruin what I've created, you're out of your goddamn mind."

Matt stepped back slightly. "You wouldn't hurt me."

"Just fucking try me."

A hand clamped down on Fred's shoulder. He jumped, turned his head to the side, saw the outline of an elaborate tattoo on the forearm of his assailant, and pissed himself.

CHAPTER EIGHTEEN

Ellie decided she had missed her calling. Instead of banking and business ownership, she should have been an actress. If the smiles from all of the elderly people she'd greeted were any indication, she was killing the part of a happy, healthy, Christian woman. She shook her old piano teacher's hand and breathed through her mouth, hoping the four doses of mouthwash and five Altoids, along with brushing her teeth four times, freshened her breath. It sure hadn't killed the horrible taste in her mouth.

"Good luck on Tuesday," the sweet old woman said. She leaned forward and whispered, "I'm voting for you."

"Thank you, Mrs. Hennessey." Ellie made the mistake of breathing through her nose and was assaulted by the smell of mothballs. She hoped her grimace looked enough like a smile to fool Mrs. Hennessey. The old woman turned, and Ellie grasped her roiling stomach and sat down. She leaned over to Kelly, who sat beside her. "I think I'm going to be sick."

"Buck up, little camper. You can do it."

"I only had two beers, for Christ's sake. Technically only one. Part of one. I practically didn't drink at all."

"Shh. You're in church."

Ellie rolled her eyes.

Reverend Woodard, worn Bible in hand, approached the podium. "Welcome to all of our members and guests!"

Ellie checked out. She'd heard this same song and dance every Sunday for forty-two years. The church was a little more than half full, everyone sitting in their regular spaces. Like every week, Ellie and Kelly sat together, midway down the left hand side. The previous night's argument hung in the air between them, but it wasn't big enough to break their routine.

Announcements ended. There was a rustling while everyone opened their hymnals to 335, "Standing on the Promises." Ellie and Kelly opened their shared hymnal, but neither needed it. Kelly's voice was beautiful, but it wasn't loud enough to overcome the cacophony of reedy, elderly voices around them. Like the town, First Baptist Stillwater needed an injection of youth into its congregation, and fast, or it would die out.

When they stood for the next hymn, Ellie looked back at Susan and Brian's pew. They weren't there. Kelly caught her eye when she turned back to the front. Their absence was not a good sign.

Kelly and Ellie had spent many, many hours discussing Susan and Brian's relationship, what they knew and what they didn't. Everyone in town knew the Grant men had tempers and were quick to fight each other and other men. No one knew for sure if it was true that Grant wives were more accident prone than other women or if they were helped down the stairs and into doors. If the emergency room doctors and nurses knew, they weren't talking.

Susan had, of course, always vehemently denied Brian abused her. Many times, Susan's facade had fractured, and her two best friends had thought she might be ready to confide, to do something, to leave. But Susan always closed back up, leaving her friends with the feeling of helplessness they'd carried with them since standing up with Susan as she promised to love and obey Brian twenty-four years earlier.

The congregation stood to sing "It is Well with My Soul." Not one of Ellie's favorites, but as she sang, the words comforted her. *Yes, it is well with my soul.*

Across the aisle sat Julie McBride, confused by the tune and clearly not a Southern Baptist. Ellie didn't know why the McBrides chose this church—she was relatively sure Jack was Catholic, but religion hadn't ever come up in their short time together. Ellie assumed they were at First Baptist because Ethan had friends there. Whether her membership in the congregation had any bearing on Jack's choice, she didn't know. She realized for the first time that she didn't care.

Gone was the queasy stomach that had been constant since the horrible night six weeks earlier when Jack told her his wife had returned. Well, Ellie was queasy at the moment, but it was a different nausea, the kind that would go away when she ate and got as far away as possible from the smell of mothballs wafting from Mrs. Hennessey. The thick carpet covering her tongue made her regret the beer she drank the night before, but she didn't regret telling Jack how she felt. She now felt as light and happy as she felt their first night together. She loved him. It was as simple as that. He knew now, though surely he had known before. What he did with the information was up to him.

She'd probably gone too far with the demand he leave town if he didn't divorce his wife, but the little amount of time she'd been around Jack and Julie was proof enough. Jack needed to know she wasn't some fucking doormat who would stand idly by while he built a life with Julie in Ellie's hometown. If he chose Julie, fine. Ellie'd had her heart broken before and had lived through it. She would again. But she'd be goddamned if Jack McBride rubbed her nose in it every day for the rest of her life.

Ellie prayed, asking God to forgive her for mentally cursing in church, sat, and passed the offering plate. Brother Woodard had stepped away from the pulpit in the middle of the last hymn. He returned, head bowed, and waited for the ushers to bring the plates to the front and for the final, solemn organ note to end. He peered across his congregation, taking in every single face. Checking who was there, Ellie thought.

"Brothers and sisters, I have been given some grave, grave news."

Kelly and Ellie clutched each other's hand, their thoughts immediately going to Susan. Bile, tangy and acidic, rose in Ellie's throat, and her mind flashed through the events of the night before and all the times she had been on the verge of confronting Susan about leaving Brian. Regret, heavy and cold, settled on her shoulders. For the second time in her life, she'd failed a best friend.

"A prominent, loving couple has been brutally taken from us." Brother Woodard paused. Red blotches crept up his neck to his face. He wasn't grieving; he was furious. "We don't have all the details, we will probably never know the why of this horrible, horrible tragedy. All we can do is trust in God that this is somehow part of His plan, and that the deaths of these two fine Christians were not in vain."

Oh my God. It's real. Kelly was squeezing so hard Ellie couldn't feel her hand.

"Let us bow our heads and pray for the dearly departed souls of Matt and Amy Doyle."

PART TWO

Snipe Hunt

CHAPTER NINETEEN

In his previous twenty-five years of police work, Miner Jesson had investigated two murders. Since Jack McBride took over as chief of police eight weeks earlier, he'd seen six dead bodies and a human skeleton. Publicly, he didn't put much stock in the grumblings around town blaming Jack for the increase in crime, but privately he started to wonder if a little corruption wasn't a small price to pay if it meant he wouldn't have to ever see another woman with her brains blown out.

He and Jack, gloved and booted, stood outside the door of Matt and Amy Doyle's bedroom and watched Doctor Sue Poole, the local ob-gyn who shared coroner duties with her husband, take a temperature reading of Amy Doyle's body. Simon, the crime scene tech—booted, gloved, and gowned—took pictures of every step.

Doctor Poole straightened and stared impassively at the body on the far side of the bed as though she saw this scene every day. Amy Doyle lay on her stomach under the blankets, her face turned toward the wall, one pajama clad leg cocked outside the blankets. From Miner's angle, there was only a round bullet hole, darkened with blood, in the center of the back of her head. If Miner leaned to the left a little, he could see where

Amy's face used to be. If he looked at the wall, he could see where it was now.

"Time of death sometime between 1:00 a.m. and 4:00 a.m. Gunshot wound to the back of the head would appear to be the cause of death. Of course, we'll have to confirm it in the autopsy." Sue shook her head and, as if shaking off her professional distance, her impassivity was replaced with sadness. Sue packed up her gear and moved out of the tech's way and into the den.

Matt's body sat upright in a recliner, his hands covered in plastic bags. The mirror image of Amy's wound, Matt had a bullet hole in his forehead, above a blackened eye, and the back of his head was blown back into the recliner. His vacant eyes stared into the kitchen, his eyebrows in a permanent arch of surprise. He wore a plaid flannel shirt over a t-shirt, jeans, and work boots, and smelled faintly of wood smoke.

"He's still wearing what he had on at the bonfire," Jack said.

"Amy went to bed and Matt stayed up," Miner said.

Jack nodded and watched Simon take pictures of Doctor Poole's inspection of Matt's body.

"Same as Amy," Doctor Poole said, voice flat. She twisted her mouth.

"What is it?" Jack said. "Do you see something else?"

"No." She replaced her instruments in her bag and faced Jack and Miner. "I hope murders aren't going to be a commonplace occurrence. I much prefer welcoming people into the world than seeing them out." She nodded to the two men and walked out the back door.

Miner thought he saw Jack's face tighten at the mild rebuke, but Jack turned away too quick for him to tell for sure.

"Simon," he called to the tech. "We'll be in the kitchen."

"Sure thing." The camera clicked and flashed behind them.

Miner marveled at the neatness of Amy and Matt's house. It looked like something out of a design magazine. Light poured in through the breaks in the curtains. Pillows placed just so. Canisters on the kitchen countertop that might be functional or might be decoration. He picked up a huge, well-burned Pumpkin Spice Yankee Candle from the middle of the kitchen table and sniffed, hoping to combat the smell of death hovering in the air.

His house looked nothing like this. It was small, old, out of date. Junk littered the kitchen counter, dishes were always in the sink. The lights were always low, the television always on. The smell of sickness everywhere. Miner sniffed the candle again.

"Miner?"

Miner looked up. "Hmm?"

Jack's brow furrowed. "Are you okay?"

"Besides seeing the body of a kid I watched grow up, you mean?" Miner put the candle down with a snap. "Right as rain."

"Sir, I can't let you in there." Officer Nathan Starling's voice carried through the house.

"Move out of my way, son."

"Sir, I . . ."

Jack nodded to Miner, who moved to the front door. Joe Doyle, dressed in his Sunday suit, loomed over Starling. "Joe, you don't want to come in here."

"I saw the bodies, or have you forgotten?"

Jack appeared next to Miner. "This is a crime scene. You cannot be here. Let's step outside."

"It's a zoo out there," Doyle said.

"Then let's go to the station. Even being in the foyer here is contaminating the crime scene. You don't want a defense attorney to use it as a way to throw out what we find, do you?"

Doyle considered. "No."

"Come on, Joe," Miner said. "I'll drive you. We'll meet you there?"

Jack nodded.

Miner ushered Joe out the front door and to his personal truck. He'd come straight from home when Jack called.

They were out of Matt and Amy's neighborhood and on Old Yourkeville when Joe broke down in tears. Miner squirmed in his seat.

"My son," Doyle sobbed. "My son."

"Joe, I'm sorry for your loss."

"Miner." He sniffed lustily, wiping the snot from beneath his nose. "You have no idea."

"How's Mary?"

"Sedated. I wish I could take a pill and know everything would be taken care of." His voice, so full of grief for his son, held no compassion for his wife.

"I'm sure Michelle'll handle everything."

They turned into the square.

"Yes. Michelle will take care of everything. Though if it wasn't for her . . ." Joe gazed out the window at the Book Bank, which was filled with people. "Look at them, gossiping, telling a bunch of damn lies. Spreading rumors. Of course, Ellie's in the middle of it. I can't wait to crush her on Tuesday."

"You aren't dropping out?"

Joe looked at Miner as if he'd lost his mind. "Drop out? Hell no. I'm going to win, and when I do, I'm going to make you chief."

"Mr. Doyle," Jack said in a smooth, complacent voice.

Doyle's eye twitched, his anger in Miner's truck carrying over into the station. "I want to know what's being done."

Jack motioned toward the chair in front of his desk. "As would I. Have a seat. I'll fill you in."

Miner stood back and rested his hands on his gun belt. Jack sat after Doyle had taken his seat. "I'm so sorry for your loss. I didn't know Matt very well, but I liked him a lot. I was looking forward to getting to know him." Doyle's rigid posture softened slightly. Jack should have stopped there. "It's a damn shame, a young man with so much potential dying so suddenly."

Doyle's eyes narrowed and his voice rose. "He didn't just die. He was murdered."

Jack nodded. "Not the way I would have expected someone like Matt to die."

"If you'd done a better job catching the drug dealers who've been terrorizing our town the last few weeks, this would have never happened."

Jack's eyes brightened. "What makes you think it was drug dealers? Was Matt mixed up in drugs? Maybe PEDs?"

Doyle lifted his chin, apparently aware his drug dealer comment had given Jack an idea Doyle would rather him not have. "I don't know what a PED is. Any two-bit criminal in the country knows they can commit all kinds of crime in this town and not be caught. Probably a robbery gone wrong."

Jack nodded. Miner knew as well as Jack that two-bit criminals don't rob occupied houses in the middle of the night. Nor do they kill the homeowners in their sleep.

"Robbery is a possibility," Jack said. "Obviously, the big stuff is still at the house. Computer, television, phones."

"Once we've finished processing the scene, we'll need you to look around, tell us if anything of value is missing," Miner said.

Jack twisted his head to glare at Miner. Miner shrugged and nodded in Doyle's direction.

"Yes. Of course, Miner. Whatever you need," Doyle said.

Jack turned back to Doyle. "Can you tell us what happened this morning? How you found the bodies?"

Doyle rubbed his face. "I didn't find them. My granddaughter, Madison, did. Christ. You aren't going to have to talk to her, are you?"

"We might, but right now, your version will do."

Doyle cleared his throat. "Right. I was at home, getting ready for church. Mary, my wife, was making pancakes for Charlie, that's Matt and Amy's son. He spent the night with us last night."

"And Madison? Was she at home?"

"No. She spent the night with friends. Madison forgot her Bible. She saw their cars and told her friends she'd ride with her parents." Doyle cleared his throat again. "She called Mary, hysterical. I told Mary I'd go right over."

"When I got there, I called out for Madison but she didn't answer. The house was eerie quiet. I called out for Matt and Amy, even though I knew they wouldn't answer."

"How did you know?"

"I suppose I suspected it when Madison called. She's not a hysterical girl. Level headed. Top of her class. For her to be like that . . ." Doyle coughed and covered his mouth with his fist. "The master is closest to the garage. That's the way I came in." He cleared his throat, struggling to hold back emotion. "After, I went looking for Madison. Found her in her bedroom closet, back behind her hanging clothes. Arms wrapped around her knees, talking to herself. I heard Starling downstairs."

"You called 911?"

"Yeah. On my way over." Doyle sat back in his chair. "Now you know what I know. What do *you* know?"

"Mr. Doyle, we've been at it six hours. I know it sounds like a long time, but we're still gathering physical evidence. Right now, we know cause and time of death definitively. Everything else is supposition. What we do know, we're going to keep under wraps for a while longer. Gossip spreads across Stillwater like wildfire. We'll keep you in the loop as much as possible, but this is a murder investigation. We won't share everything."

"I want Miner in charge."

Jack chuckled. "You don't have a say in who investigates what, Joe."

"When I become city councilman—"

"*If* you become city councilman, you still won't have a say. This is my department, and I make the decisions about who does what."

"We'll see."

The two men glared at each other. "When was the last time you talked to Matt?" Jack said.

Doyle looked down and away. After a pause he said, "I guess yesterday at the snipe festival."

"Talk about anything in particular?"

"The election. The bonfire they were having."

"Okay." Jack stood and held out his hand. "I'm sure I'll have more questions for you tomorrow, as well as the rest of your family. It goes without saying y'all need to stay close to town."

When Doyle stood, he seemed to take up the entire room. "You better solve this case, McBride, or there'll be hell to pay."

"Oh, I'll solve it. You better be ready for some uncomfortable truths to come out in the process."

Doyle scowled at Jack's offered hand without taking it, turned, and stalked out of his office.

"Shit," Jack said, his bravado slipping into weariness.

"You sure love to poke the bear, dontcha?" Miner said.

"Why did you interrupt?"

Miner closed the door to Jack's office. "Because you don't want him to suspect you're on to his drug operation. They're already gonna go turtle on us, leastwise that's what I'd do. You waving a red flag in front of Joe's face ain't gonna help none, either. Doyle doesn't trust you. He trusts me. We can foster it. Take advantage of it."

Jack turned his head and studied Miner so long, he wondered if he'd raised Jack's suspicions. "You're right. Good cop, bad cop. Oldest trick in the book."

"And, easiest to sell." *Especially when you've got an ego like yours.*

"Go on, good cop. Take your mark back home."

CHAPTER TWENTY

It was the busiest Sunday in the Book Bank's short life. Everyone who had tsk-tsked at Ellie being open on Sunday afternoons spent most of this overcast Sabbath loitering, drinking coffee, and gossiping, though since it was a Sunday, they called it fellowshipping. Some bought a cup of coffee and believed it bottomless. Others had the grace to pick up the nearest book and purchase it. They emptied the pastry case by three o'clock and Ellie was out of small to-go cups by five.

Paige Grant worked with Ellie in silence, save for whatever communication was necessary to get their jobs done. She was distracted, made the wrong order a couple of times, and had a furrow of concern on her brow that occasionally looked more like anger.

"Everything okay?" Ellie asked, early in the shift.

"Fine."

It was on the tip of Ellie's tongue to ask why her parents hadn't been at church, but as much as Ellie wanted to know, another part of her didn't.

They worked on.

The gossip—fellowshipping—was redundant. No one knew anything except Matt and Amy were dead and Madison had found them. Rumors swirled it was a copy-cat of the Ramos' murders from two months earlier, but those were quickly dismissed by others who didn't believe Matt was wrapped up in anything illegal, especially drugs. Others pursed their lips and stayed silent, pushing away the idea that their turning a blind eye to Doyle's shady dealings over the years might have somehow led to the death of a young, well-liked couple and orphaned two children. After all, if not the Doyles, someone else would fill the void. Evil abhors a vacuum, or some such. Besides, the Doyles were the biggest employer in town. Gave back to the community. Many had weighed the good against the bad and decided the bad could be overlooked for the common good.

Kelly walked in the Book Bank and wove her way through everyone, greeting people, smiling, lightly flirting on her way to the office. She jerked her head at Ellie to follow. "You got this?" Ellie asked Paige. "I'm going to check to see if we have more small to-go cups."

"We don't, but sure. I've got it." Paige kept her eye on the espresso machine, but her face hardened.

Kelly leaned against the desk, waiting. Ellie pulled the safe door almost shut. "Well?"

"Broken hand," Kelly said.

"Son of a bitch."

"She's in bed, drugged to high heaven."

"Did she say what happened?" Ellie asked.

"The usual. She slammed it in the car door. Accident. Yada, yada."

"They were in the truck last night."

"Exactly."

They stared at each other. "We have to do something."

Kelly threw up her hands. "She won't let us. Did Paige say anything?"

"Hasn't said two words other than work related all day, but she's not happy."

Kelly rubbed her forehead. "What do we do?"

Ellie sighed. "Be there for her. Try not to judge her. Hate Brian's guts."

Kelly dropped her hand. "I don't have any jobs coming up or I'd throw him one, to keep him happy. They're hurting for money."

"She won't take money from me. I've tried." The phone beeped. Ellie picked up. "Is it busy again?"

"Yeah."

"I'll be right there."

They walked out of the office. "Has it been like this all day?"

"Since I opened."

"You're the new gossip mill."

"I guess so. Shit."

Julie McBride grinned and waved at them from across the room. Ellie didn't look back at her best friend, but went straight behind the counter. Neither one had forgotten their disagreement about Julie from the night before.

Unfortunately, Julie and Kelly got in line for drinks. While serving the people in front of them in line, Ellie repeated, "Be polite. You can do it," in her mind like a mantra.

She plastered on a bright smile. "Hi, Julie. What can I get you?"

"Wow. You're busy."

"I guess murder is good for business." Ellie regretted it as soon as it was out of her mouth. God, this woman brought out the worst in her.

"Ellie!" Kelly said.

"I'm sorry. That was crass and unfeeling." She softened her voice, chastened. "Can I get you anything?"

"Um," Julie stared at the chalkboard, pursed her lips, and furrowed her brows.

"It's not rocket science," Paige said, low enough so only Ellie could hear.

"The Snickerdoodle is good," Kelly said, though she hated coffee and had never tried it.

"Sounds good. Low-fat!"

Paige jerked a lever, and an angry jet of steam cleared out the milk wand. She wiped the wand down with a towel and started the drink.

"Have you talked to Jack?" Kelly asked.

"No. I'm not surprised. He probably won't be home before midnight. Just when I thought our life would get back to normal, this happens."

"I would have thought you two slid right back into old rhythms when you came back, seeing as it was a mutual decision, you leaving," Ellie said.

"You'd think. A year is a long time. As you know, Jack was getting restless."

"How would I know that?"

"Well, he flirted with you when he moved here, didn't he?"

Ellie cut her eyes to Kelly, who had the grace to look abashed. "I'd call it being friendly."

"It doesn't matter what it was," Paige said. She placed the drink on the counter in front of Julie. "Auntie Elle would never, ever date a married man. That'll be $3.56."

Kelly and Ellie were dumbfounded into silence. Julie stared at Paige's outstretched hand, then dug into her purse and pulled a five out of her wallet. Paige made change and smiled. "Thanks. Ethan's such a sweet kid. So much like his father."

Julie jerked her head back. "You know Ethan?"

"I work at the middle school. And I'm Troy and Olivia's sister."

Julie lifted her eyebrows and nodded as she realized who Paige was. "How's your dad feeling this morning? He was pretty drunk last night."

Paige narrowed her eyes. "He's good. Thanks for asking."

"Paige, why don't you go on break. I can handle this."

"Sure."

Julie drank her coffee. "I guess the apple doesn't fall far from the tree. Though she does make a delicious latte."

"What does that mean?" Kelly snapped.

"She makes a good coffee?"

"Before that."

"She seems a little short-tempered. I don't know what I did to piss her off. I suppose it's not easy finding good help in this little town."

"She's protective of those she loves," Kelly said. She crossed her arms over her chest. "As we all are in this *little town*."

Julie held the cup up to her lips and studied Kelly over the rim. Ellie could tell Julie knew she was on thin ice. "I didn't mean anything by it. It was a stupid comment."

"Those seem to be thick on the ground," Ellie said, shocked she was playing peacemaker. "We're all on edge because of what's happened. Let's talk about something else. *Twilight* maybe."

"You hate that book," Kelly said.

"Have you seen Eddie?" Julie asked instead.

Ellie shook her head. "Not since he dropped me off last night. Why?"

"He didn't come home last night. It's probably just as well."

A group of Baptists came to the counter carrying Ellie's entire stock of devotionals and Christian fiction. She rang them up and Kelly pulled Julie away from the counter to make room. Ellie hoped against hope they would leave. She didn't want to know, or even think about why it was "just as well" Eddie hadn't been home the night before.

But Ellie wasn't that lucky. Kelly and Julie went to the home improvement section, pulled books on decorating, and went to the back of the store and the cushy couch in the children's section. Paige returned as the new cop, Lincoln Bishop, walked into the store. He held the door for a group of men and women who then introduced themselves to him. He smiled and laughed with a low rumble. He nodded the people out the door, laughing at a joke made by one of the men, and ambled over to the counter.

"Hey, Lincoln."

Since Jack hired him a few weeks ago Lincoln Bishop had become one of Ellie's best customers, buying a barbeque cookbook and coming in regular for coffee and Earline's apricot fried pies. He was tall, dark, and handsome with a deep voice that Ellie found incredibly appealing. Lincoln Bishop had charisma to spare.

"Ellie." He pulled a notebook from his pocket and opened it up. "I have a list for you."

"It might be easier if you tear it off for me," Ellie said.

"Right." He handed it over, and leaned against the counter as though settling in for a long chat. He looked around the store. Disorganized book tables, leftover sugar granules and stir straws on the café tables, and haphazardly placed chairs and tables spoke of a busy day. "Record day?"

"You could say that."

"And on a Sunday." He eyes twinkled. "I woulda never thought."

"How's it going out at the crime scene?"

"Wrapping up. Still hours of work, though."

"Hence, the coffee."

"Yes. Jack's treat." Lincoln waved a credit card.

Ellie nodded and focused on making the order.

"You're dying to ask me questions about it, aren't you?"

"Yes. But I won't."

"Thank you. Jack'd have my hide."

"We don't want that."

"You know them well? Matt and Amy?"

"Well, I know everyone fairly well."

"Jack said you were a lifer. Said you helped him quite a bit when he first got here." Lincoln smiled at Paige, who had returned from her break and was inserting Lincoln's completed order in a drink carrier.

Ellie smiled. "I heard you bought Brucilla's place."

He wiggled his hand. "She's my aunt. I'm living there with the option to buy. Thinking of doing some renovations. Recommend anyone?"

"My dad," Paige said. She placed the carrier in front of Lincoln and he handed her Jack's credit card.

"I'll give him a call."

The door opened, and in walked Eddie McBride, looking like he hadn't slept in a week. He saw Lincoln and grinned. "Are you flirting with my girl?"

Lincoln laughed. "Nah, nah."

"I'm not his girl," Ellie said.

"I meant Paige."

"You could be my *dad*."

"Ouch." He and Lincoln slapped hands and did some sort of hand shake that looked more like an arm wrestling position.

"You look awful," Lincoln said.

"Yeah, where have you been? Julie's looking for you." Ellie nodded toward the back of the store.

Eddie glanced toward the couches and focused back on Lincoln. "I know you're a big guy, but that's a lot of coffee to get you through the night shift."

"Not all for me." Lincoln picked up the carrier and studied Eddie. "Haven't you heard?"

"Heard what?" He looked from Lincoln to Ellie, a perfect picture of innocence.

Lincoln looked taken aback. "Amy and Matt Doyle were killed last night."

Eddie's eyes widened, and his face lost what little color it had. "What? How?"

Lincoln paused before he answered. "I suppose everyone knows this, at least. They were shot. I can't say any more." With his free hand, Lincoln signed the credit card receipt Paige offered, leaving a nice tip. "Thanks. I better get going."

Eddie watched him leave then, glanced at the back where Julie and Kelly were still engrossed in their books. He grabbed Ellie's hand and pulled her around the counter and into the store. "Let me help you clean up."

Ellie followed, curious. They moved some chairs and tables around and Eddie moved next to her. "When asked, I need you to say you were with me all night."

"What?"

"Say we went out to the lake house. Spent the night. I dropped you off this morning before dawn so you could run and go to church. You did go to church?"

"Yes, of course. But, Eddie, I can't lie."

"You can, and you will."

Ellie straightened and crossed her arms. "Why would I lie for you?"

"Do you think I killed Matt and Amy?"

"Of course not."

"Then it won't hurt."

"What were you doing?"

He pulled her forward and whispered in her ear. "Do this for me and I'll make sure Julie is out of Jack's life for good within a week."

Ellie jerked back. "What are you talking about?"

Eddie stared into her eyes. "I need you to trust me." His eyes were so much like Jack's there was no way she could say no.

"There you are!" Julie's voice rang out across the store. Eddie and Ellie were so close it looked for all the world like Julie had interrupted a loving embrace. Kelly's eyes widened with shock, then narrowed. *Christ*, Ellie thought. *When this is all said and done, she's never going to believe a word I say.*

"Hey, Jules." Eddie voice was teasing, sexy. "I hear you've been asking around about me."

"Jack was worried when you didn't come home."

"Funny he didn't text me. Hi, Kelly."

Kelly crossed her arms. "What will Michelle think?"

Eddie chuckled, but didn't deny his involvement with Michelle. "I suppose not much, considering she has bigger problems right now. I just came from home. What's wrong with Ethan?"

"Oh, he's mad at me," Julie said.

"What for?"

Julie's eyes darted in Paige's direction and back. "We'll talk about it at home." She started for the door. "You coming?"

"I'll be along in a bit, after I help Ellie clean up."

Julie looked as if she was going to offer to stay but seemed to think better of it when she noticed Ellie, Eddie, and Kelly in front of her with less-than-welcoming postures. "See you later."

When the door closed and the jingling bell faded away, Kelly said, "Okay, I see what you mean."

Ellie threw up her hands and gazed at the heavens. "Thank you, Jesus."

"What's going on?" Eddie asked.

"Kelly's finally seen through your sister-in-law."

Kelly moved forward, her arms still crossed, and whispered, "She actually told Ethan he couldn't go over to Susan's house. I mean, can you believe it? The nerve."

Ellie raised her eyebrows but didn't respond. Eddie said, "Why would she do that?"

"She doesn't want Ethan to be in that *environment*. Thinks Brian's a bully. I suppose last night didn't help."

"What happened after the bonfire?"

Ellie read the wariness on Eddie's face, the suspicion, before Kelly replied. She remembered seeing Eddie take Brian in a playful headlock and whisper something in his ear that turned Brian's face red the night before. She realized too late she needed to stop her friend from telling him.

"Susan slammed her hand in a car door last night, and Ethan was there when it happened."

Ellie watched Eddie leave with trepidation. The expression on his face was not one of a man who planned to go home, have a shower, eat a snack, and get some shut-eye. She saw murder in his eyes.

She stopped wiping the café table, shocked the thought had come to her mind. She didn't really think Eddie capable . . . but why not? For all their conversations and flirty banter, she knew little about him, except he was Jack's twin and went to extreme lengths to make people believe he was a self-serving rebel, out only for a good time. Ellie knew that man, had been married to that man. Had been destroyed by him. She knew Eddie was not that man. Call it a hunch. An intuition honed through hard experience of being bamboozled by people she loved. If Ellie got nothing else from her life, she'd learned how to read people. Eddie McBride was not a killer, but he might go to great lengths to send a message.

Patsy Cline crooned "Crazy" in the background. Ellie sang along under her breath as she straightened the café tables, dusted the bookshelves, and swept the store while Paige broke down the coffee bar. The lemon scent of Pledge and the tangy aroma of vinegar and water tried to overpower the smell of coffee that permeated the store, and almost succeeded.

Paige cleaned the front of the decimated pastry case. "I hope Earline's been baking."

"I called her a bit ago and told her we were bone dry. I'm afraid she's going to be up all night, cooking."

"She loves it." Paige lifted the arched glass and sprayed the inside.

"I know but she's got to be at least eighty."

"You could go over and help her."

"I like my customers too much to subject them to my cooking."

Paige laughed for the first time all day.

She finished cleaning the glass, closed the case, and straightened, Ellie put her arm around her shoulder. "That's good to hear." Paige put her head on Ellie's shoulder and sighed. "We need to talk," Ellie said.

Paige nodded her head and pulled away. "Olivia texted that Aunt Kelly went to see Mom."

"How's she doing?"

"Olivia said she's up and around. Still out of it, but switching to Advil so she can go to work tomorrow."

"What happened?"

"I don't know. She says she shut her hand in the door, like before."

"Do you believe her?"

"I saw her do it once. The door is loose, so yeah. Maybe. I didn't see it this time, and she swears he didn't do it."

"Did you take her to the hospital?"

Paige nodded. "She begged Dad to take her, but he refused. He never takes her when she has her accidents. He knows everyone thinks he beats her."

Ellie's stomach fluttered at the question she was about to ask, but Paige continued before she could. "The whole way there, Mom was crying. At first, I thought it was from pain, but she said something weird."

"What?"

"She cradled her hand and rocked back in forth saying it was all for nothing, she'd only made things worse. When I asked her what she meant, she clammed up. Stared out the window the rest of the way."

"Did you see your dad the rest of the night?"

"No. He wasn't there when we got home around 4 a.m. He got home around six, smelling like pot. I left without talking to him."

The flutter was back. "Paige, I have to ask you this. I probably should have asked you years ago." Ellie took a deep breath. "Has your father every hurt your mom? Or you kids?"

Ellie wasn't sure what reaction she expected from Paige. Anger? Fear? Indignation? What she didn't expect to see was misery. "He's never laid a hand on me or Olivia and Troy."

"And your mom?"

Paige shook her head. "I've never seen him lay a hand on her."

CHAPTER TWENTY-ONE

The shop door slid open smoothly. Eddie flipped on the flashlight and looked around. Neat and clean, like a workshop should be. He pulled one wrench after another off the peg board and dropped it onto the ground, then moved to the screwdrivers, and hammers. He hefted the rubber topped mallet in his hand and left it laying on the work table.

He turned his head at the sound of a door opening, a screen door squeaking and slapping shut. He clicked off the flashlight, walked calmly to the back door of the shop and through it. It snapped shut at the same time the main shop light went on.

"What the fuck?"

Eddie walked around the shop and back through the front bay door. "Grant."

Brian Grant wheeled around, holding a baseball bat. He lowered the bat, no doubt hoping Eddie didn't notice the nervous tremor in his hand. "McBride. What the fuck are you doing?"

Eddie closed the bay door and walked toward Brian. "Visiting you. Like I promised."

Brian scoffed and shook his head. "You're a real son of a bitch."

"So I've been told."

When Brian saw Eddie wasn't going to stop, he lifted the bat and readied a swing. Eddie neatly ducked beneath it and, when Brian was twisted around on his follow through, punched Brian in the kidneys three times quickly. Eddie jerked the bat out of Brian's hands and took a swing at the back of Brian's thighs. He dropped to his knees like a stone. Eddie walked behind him, grabbed his hair, and pulled his head back.

"Did I stutter last night?"

The whites of Brian's eyes were huge as he tried to look back at Eddie. "What the fuck do you care?"

"Wrong answer." Eddie released Brian's head, stepped back, and kicked him in the middle of the back. Brian fell forward, his face hitting the concrete floor. Eddie placed his boot on Brian's right hand with enough force to get Brian's attention.

"I could break your hand right now and sleep like a baby in thirty minutes. But I won't. You need to be able to support your family. The beating I'm going to give you will be between us. No external bruises, but inside you're going to be screaming in pain."

"I'll press charges."

"If you do, you'll have to explain why I beat the shit out of you."

"I didn't break her hand."

"Bullshit. I know guys like you. I've served time with guys like you." Eddie squatted on the ground. Brian inhaled sharply through his teeth as the pressure increased on his hand. "In fact, I served time with this one man. Reminds me a little of you. Jesse was his name. Boasted about how he used to keep his wife in line. He was so good at it, he rarely had to use fists, but when he did, he meant it. Went a little too far with the second wife." Eddie leaned forward. "Sound familiar?"

"You were in jail with my father?"

Eddie nodded. "I stood by and watched him bleed out. He begged for his life. In the end, he was a pussy. Like all wife beaters are."

"I don't beat my wife. Or my kids."

Eddie stood and released Brian's hand. He picked up the bat. "Stand up."

Brian got to his feet gingerly. The left side of his face was scraped from his fall. "Sorry, that might leave a mark. Tell Susan a squirrel got in your shop, messed up your tools, and you tripped over them in the dark. Stupid-ass excuse, but she's probably familiar with lame excuses as cover stories." He stepped forward so he was inches away from Brian. Eddie gave him credit—Brian didn't flinch. Eddie lifted Brian's chin with the end of the bat. "I hear Susan is accident prone. You better pray to God she keeps her feet while I'm around. If I even suspect you've raised your *voice* to her, I'll make you regret it."

"What's with the white knight bullshit? You don't even *know* Susan."

Eddie thought back to his childhood, the tension in the house when his father was home, how his mother did everything possible to make sure Sean McBride's life went smoothly. He'd wondered more than once if his father hadn't died when he was young if he would have turned into him. He feared he would have—that the fury he'd seen in his father sat coiled somewhere deep within him, ready to strike if set free.

"If you think you're somehow going to get in her pants with your chivalry, you're out of your fucking mind. Even if she was the type to cheat, she wouldn't get within a thousand feet of you after you've been sticking your dick in Michelle Doyle's pussy." Brian pushed Eddie away and laughed. "Everyone saw her follow you into the woods. I think Chris even looked up from his phone to see it. There's only a handful of men in this town she hasn't sucked off or fucked, so don't think you're anything special."

Eddie laughed. "You think I care?"

"No. You're as trashy as she is. You're perfect for each other. I told Chris he better watch out or she'd trade him in. Having the chief's brother in your bed and on your payroll is a trifecta any crook like her would want. And whaddya know? My suspicions were confirmed two hours later."

Eddie went still. "What are you talking about?"

Brian sneered. "I was there last night, at the truck yard. I saw Matt pull in and wanted to talk to him. To apologize for jumping him, the things I said. I parked by your truck, as a matter of fact, walked back and heard the yelling. Michelle and Matt. I heard her threaten her own brother. I mean, what kind of woman does that?"

Eddie stepped forward. "What else did you see?"

Brian's confidence returned. "Why, you worried your brother might find out the kind of people you're associating with?"

"Brian, listen to me carefully. You need to forget what you heard."

"Forget it? It's my ticket to solvency."

"Don't be an idiot. Michelle Doyle is a dangerous woman."

"More dangerous than you?"

"Yes."

Brian's smug smile faltered.

"Haven't you considered the possibility she had Matt and Amy killed? I mean, you heard her, too. If she did, do you think she would have one qualm about wasting you? Hell no. You're nothing to her. If you go to her with this threat, or the cops, you're signing your own death warrant, and probably your family's."

Brian paled. They turned their heads at the sound of the bay door sliding open. Susan stood in the door, in flannel men's pajamas, holding her broken hand across her stomach. She looked small and vulnerable. "Eddie? What are you doing here? What's going on?"

Eddie smiled and walked to Susan. "I came to check on you. Heard you had an accident. Brian was giving me the update since you were asleep."

"It's two in the morning."

"Yeah, I'm sorry. I was delivering an earth mover to Houston for Doyle. Just got home. Anyway." He lifted her hand gently. The ends of her fingers were bruised. "How are you feeling?"

Susan shifted away from him, glancing in Brian's direction. "Spacey. Why do you have Brian's bat?" Her voice was small, her face a mask of exhaustion.

"He's letting me borrow it so I can go to the cages with Ethan. You need to get some rest. Brian, thanks for the bat." He dropped his voice to a murmur only Susan could hear. "Call me if you need anything. Ever."

He walked out of the shop, placed the baseball bat behind his seat, and got into his truck. He drove off, hoping against hope Brian Grant listened to his warning. He didn't want to have to get rid of another body.

The warm water streamed down Eddie's neck, across his shoulders, down his chest and splattered onto the bathtub floor. He rolled his neck from side to side, trying to work out the tension that had settled there six weeks earlier and refused to leave.

He closed his eyes and turned around, letting the water patter on his face. This was it. He was done. Stillwater was his last job. He couldn't take the lying and manipulation any more. And, Jesus Christ, what he wouldn't give for a full night's sleep in a soft bed. Preferably with a warm body nestled against him.

A knock on the bathroom door startled him.

"Jack? Is that you?"

"It's me. Eddie."

There was a pause and Eddie thought Julie'd returned to her bedroom. "Can I come in?"

"Sure." He squirted soap onto the loofa, turned his back to the door and soaped up, hoping his erection would go down and not up at the thought of Julie being on the other side of a thin shower curtain. At least it was opaque.

He heard the medicine cabinet open, the faucet turn on, and the sound of Julie brushing her teeth.

"You're up early," Eddie said.

"Going running," came the muffled reply.

"With Ellie?"

Spit, rinse. "If I can catch her. I don't think she wants to run with me."

"I wouldn't take it personally. Some people like to run alone."

"Yeah. I guess." The medicine cabinet opened and closed. Eddie waited for the bathroom door to do the same. When it didn't, he stuck his head out of the shower and caught Julie pulling her shorts down to pee. He pulled his head back in before she saw him.

"You know, I didn't only suggest you get your own place because I don't like you. One bathroom with three adults and a teenage boy isn't the best set up." The toilet flushed.

"You're right." Eddie watched the water fall from his fully erect dick like a curtain. "I'll be out of here in a week."

"It's probably for the best."

Eddie knew Julie was batshit insane, narcissistic. He'd watched her torture his brother for years. Eddie had always wondered if she would have been different with him. If he hadn't gotten picked up on the bogus drug charge that set him on his path, if they would have made a go of it and been happier together than she had been with Jack. Now, they were different people than the two twenty-three-year-olds who had an instant connection and a perfect night together. He didn't want anything from her, hadn't wanted anything in years. She was nothing more than any of the other hundreds of women he'd fucked since. A means to an end, only this time, the end result wouldn't benefit Eddie, and it would most likely alienate him from the one person he loved unconditionally.

Eddie inhaled and pulled the shower curtain back. Julie washed her hands and watched him in the medicine cabinet mirror.

"Why don't you join me? We may never get another chance."

She wiped her hands on a towel, turned, and leaned against the sink. Julie appraised him, head to toe, eyes lingering on his erect dick, before moving back to his face. "What about Ellie? And Michelle?"

"Do you really care?"

He held out his hand and she took it, without hesitation. He pulled her shirt and sports bra off while she wiggled out of her shorts. His hands were between her legs before she kicked them out of shower.

He lifted her off the ground, pressed her against the shower wall, and entered her in one smooth, practiced movement. She clung to him as he fucked her, heedless of the water running down her face and across his back.

"You were always the one I wanted, Eddie."

Any qualms Eddie had about what he was doing evaporated. He pushed into her harder.

She never mentioned her husband.

CHAPTER TWENTY-TWO

The smell of burnt coffee permeated the second floor of Stillwater City Hall. The night before, after a brutal day, Jack fell asleep on his office couch and forgot to turn the pot off. Actually, it had never occurred to him. Every morning for weeks, it had been magically cleaned by coffee pot fairies who also prepped the machine so all the earliest shift had to do was flip a switch. In reality, the coffee pot, and the break room it lived in, had been taken care of by Violet, the night dispatcher, during her long, boring nights of intermittent calls. To find the money in the tight budget for his two new officers, Violet had been let go, and all calls were rerouted to the central dispatch station in Yourkeville. An unforeseen consequence of this fiscal belt tightening was a perpetually dirty break room and, on this Monday morning, a charred coffee urn. When Jack ran cold water in the hot pot to clean it, it exploded, leaving him holding the plastic handle and staring at a sink full of steaming, coffee-stained glass. He threw the handle away and had sent Bishop to the Book Bank with his credit card again.

Jack's four officers sat at the round conference table in the corner of Jack's office, the Doyle crime scene pictures spread before them. The newest Stillwater police officers, Lincoln Bishop and Andrea Malik, drank their coffee with the placidity of seasoned professionals who had no personal relationship with the victims, which is precisely why Jack had hired them. Bishop had been on the job for three weeks, Malik for one. Jack had heard some grumbling about him not hiring local men, as well as hiring two minorities. He'd argued that with the heightened racial tensions across the country, it only made sense to have a diverse force, to act as a bridge to the underserved, and underrepresented minority communities. Having a woman was especially important to reach out to the victims of domestic abuse, who were almost always women. Jane Maxwell had backed him up on his decision, as had most of the city council, though grudgingly. But, Jack knew he, Bishop, and Malik would be scrutinized by his enemies for months, waiting for one of them to make a mistake.

Officer Nathan Starling, the young, local good-ole-boy, couldn't keep his eyes from the bloody, full-body shot of Amy Doyle. Sergeant Miner Jesson, the senior officer, stared at his coffee without blinking, dark shadows under his bloodshot eyes.

"Miner, you start." Jack sipped black coffee and listened.

Miner didn't take his eyes from his coffee cup. He had no notes. "Matt Joseph Doyle, thirty-nine years old, born at Stillwater Hospital March 16, 1971, to Joe and Mary Doyle. Second of two children. Only son. Good kid. Rarely, if ever, got in trouble. Good grades in school. Involved in theater and FFA in high school. Strange combination, but apt for Matt. He was a sensitive kid, always saw the good in people, and he loved nature. Flowers, plants, all that. Very much like his mother in temperament, and Joe's favorite. Graduated Stillwater High School in 1991 with honors. Went to Texas A&M. Graduated in 1995 with a degree in horticulture and a minor in business. He stuck around College Station working for the Extension Agency until Amy graduated in June '96, and they got married. In 2000, they moved to Tyler for Matt's job with East Texas Produce. He moved up steadily, and by 2007 he was VP of Operations. Last year, Matt approached Joe about starting an organic produce company. Joe liked the idea and they moved to Stillwater. Though in business less than a year, it's been a bigger success than anyone thought.

"Amy Leigh Robbins Doyle got a degree in secondary education and taught freshman English until she had her first child in 1999. Since then, she's been a stay-at-home mom to two children, thirteen-year-old Madison and ten-year-old Charlie. She's been taking online classes to get her masters in counseling so she could go back to work full time. They were involved in Stillwater Methodist. Matt didn't have any outside interests to speak of. Sometimes he would play golf with his father and brother-in-law, but if he had time off, he usually spent it with his family. Amy was the social one. She went to bunko on the first Tuesday of every month and book club on the third. She volunteered with the PTA, and since they've moved here had been subbing pretty regularly at the high school."

"Starling?"

The young man sat forward and opened his notebook. "At 9:01 a.m. yesterday, Joe Doyle called in and said there'd been an accident at his son's house. When I arrived, I went into the house, calling out to Matt and Amy, then Joe. I found Matt's body in a chair in the den at about the same time Joe came downstairs with Madison, almost carrying her. I asked them to wait for me outside, found Amy in the bedroom, called you, Chief, then the crime scene and coroner."

"Okay," Jack said. "Sue puts time of death between one and four in the morning. The weapon used was a 9 mm, which probably 80 percent of the local gun owners have. Ballistics will be back on it in a few days. We're trying to get it rushed but the lab is swamped. It appears Amy was in bed, asleep when she was murdered. Matt was shot sitting in his recliner. We'll know more when we get the bullet analysis back, but I suspect Matt was killed first, with a silencer, then the killer shot Amy.

"As far as we can tell, no valuables were taken. We're doing an inventory of the house, but right now, robbery seems like the least plausible scenario. None of the neighbors heard anything or saw anyone suspicious, but the victims' house backs up to the woods behind the German church, which is how the murderer could have gotten access without being seen.

"Madison and Charlie weren't at home last night. Madison spent the night with a friend, who dropped her off for her Bible before church.

When Madison saw her parents' car, she said she'd ride with them. Charlie spent the night with Joe and Mary Doyle. Was it a lucky coincidence for the killers the kids weren't there? Or did the killer or killers know?"

"So, was it strangers, personal vendetta, or professional hit?" Lincoln Bishop said.

"Right," Jack replied. "We all know the chances of it being strangers out killing for the fun of it is unlikely. Which means personal vendetta or professional hit."

"Known Matt my whole life. Never been in trouble, or even the rumor of trouble. I have a hard time believing someone had a personal vendetta against him," Miner said. "Or he'd do anything to warrant a professional hit."

"Malik, go to the school and talk to the principal about Amy's work. See if there were any kids who had it out for her, any problems with other teachers."

"Sure thing, boss." Malik nodded and wrote something down in her notebook.

Jack drummed his fingers on the table. "I was with Matt and Amy Saturday night. They had a bonfire out at their lake lot. He and Brian Grant got into it over Matt not using him for a job."

"Got into it, how?" Bishop asked.

"Brian jumped Matt, gave him the shiner you see on the picture." Jack pointed at the table. "Miner, you interview everyone at the bonfire. I'll interview the family, including Michelle and Chris, who were at the bonfire."

Miner nodded. "All right."

"Starling, you go out to Doyle Organics and talk to everyone who works there, as well as the drivers of the trucks that bring produce in. Find out if Matt got along as well with everyone as he seemed to. He was a nice guy, but no boss is liked by everyone. It's impossible.

"Malik, after you go to the school, I want you to put some feelers out in the Mexican community. See what the word on the street is with them. Speaking of, has Paco Morales ever shown up?"

"No," Malik said. "They say sometimes he'll take off for a week or so . . ."

"And goes where?" Starling asked.

"They're cagey about that. No one'll say it aloud, but I can tell the community thinks one of the burned bodies is his. If they know who the other is, they're keeping mum."

Jack nodded. "Keep me posted. Bishop, put some feelers out in the black community, as well. You two switch off on taking calls. Keep your ears open for any bit of information. Small-town gossip usually has a kernel of truth buried in the hyperbole. Any questions?" When they shook their heads and remained silent, Jack continued, "The scrutiny on this case is going to be enormous. This isn't meth heads and drug dealers fighting over territory. It's a prominent white couple murdered while they slept. The town is going to explode, if it hasn't already."

Bishop and Malik exchanged a significant look.

"Oh, yeah, it has," Starling said. "I've received at least thirty messages from friends and family calling for your head. I don't agree with them," he finished, hurriedly.

"Thanks," Jack said. He'd suspected calls for his head would grow in volume but was jarred at hearing of it firsthand.

They all rose, took their coffee and notebooks, and left. "Miner. You stay. Close the door." Jack stacked the photos and put them in a manilla folder. Jack walked around his desk and draped his coat over his chair. He motioned for Miner to sit.

Jack waited. "Well?"

"Well, what?"

"What happened with Doyle yesterday?"

"Nothing. He was silent the whole way back to his car," Miner said.

"Really?"

Miner shrugged and nodded. "Well, he commented on the booming business the Book Bank was doing, but mostly he stared out the side window so I wouldn't see him crying."

Jack's shoulders slumped. He stared at the folder on his desk and chastised himself for forgetting Joe Doyle was a father who lost his son. His stomach twisted at the idea of losing Ethan. He cleared his throat.

"Do you want to interview me before or after you interview everyone else at the bonfire?"

Miner rested his ankle on his knee and drummed his fingers on his thigh. "All right. Tell me about the bonfire."

Miner jotted down notes as Jack gave him a play by play of Saturday night.

"Did Brian ever threaten to kill Matt?"

"Besides obviously wanting to beat Matt to a pulp, Brian never explicitly threatened him." Jack rolled a pen between his fingers. "How bad is the Grants' financial situation, do you know?"

Miner shrugged. "No. You know Susan doesn't make much here, and Brian's a good contractor, one of the best in the county, but when times get rough, people either stop making improvements or they expect cut-rate prices. How was Susan Saturday night?"

Jack waited until Miner's eyes met his. "You see her hand?" Miner nodded again. "Believe her story?"

Miner shrugged. "She's accident prone, for sure."

Jack thought back to Saturday night and Ethan staying at the Grants' house. Sunday morning, Julie had said in no uncertain terms she didn't want Ethan over there again. She saw enough of Brian and Susan's relationship at the bonfire for warning bells to go off and her protective mother instinct to kick in.

"Think Brian might be good for the Doyle's murder?" Jack asked.

"Not really. It sounds like any number of get-togethers I've gone to. Drinking, smoking too much, tempers flare. The next morning everyone feels awful about it and either apologizes or never mentions it again, hoping everyone will forget it."

"That's what I thought, until Matt and Amy turned up dead."

Miner clicked his tongue on his teeth. "I don't know. Brian'll get drunk occasionally, pick fights with other drunks out at the Gristmill. But, killing? That's a pretty big leap."

"Ethan spent the night with Troy Saturday. I'll see if he saw anything, what time they got home."

"Think he'll tell you?"

Jack thought of the tension hovering between him and his son. "I hope so." He leaned back in his chair. "You okay?"

"I'm fine," Miner said. Jack waited, wondering if silence would work on his characteristically taciturn Sergeant. Since hiring Malik and Bishop, Jack had switched Miner to mostly day shifts and given him a few days off to let him recuperate from the long hours Jack, Miner, and Starling had been working since Mike Freeman's death. Still, Miner looked exhausted.

Finally, Jack spoke. "No, you're not. What's going on?"

Miner shifted in his chair and finally said, "Teresa's medicine ran out two weeks ago. Doctors prescribed a cheaper drug, but it's taking a while for her body to adjust to it. Happens every time. It'll be fine."

"Are you sure?"

Miner stood and headed for the door. "Yep. Don't worry. I won't let my personal life get in the way of my job."

"Not what I was suggesting."

"Still." Miner stopped at the door. "I'm gonna interview Susan first. Can I use your office?"

"Sure thing. I'm heading over to the Doyles'."

"Want me to come with you?"

"No. With nine people to interview today, you've got enough on your plate."

CHAPTER TWENTY-THREE

Miner led Susan into Jack's office and closed the door. He sat in the chair next to Susan—he didn't want to get anywhere near the Chief's chair—and picked up his pen and rested his small notebook on the arm of the chair. He clicked the pen and said, "How're you holding up?"

Susan pressed her lips together and shrugged. "It's been hard." Her voice was thick with suppressed emotion. "We saw them hours before. I mean, how can you . . . I can't get my mind around the idea Amy was killed hours after I saw her."

"It's horrible when it's someone you know."

Susan sniffed. "What do you need to know?"

"Tell me about Saturday night."

"The bonfire? It was like any cookout. We drank some beer, ate ribs. Talked. Laughed."

Miner watched as Susan's shoulders dropped a bit. "How were Matt and Amy?"

"Same as always. Amy was one of the sweetest people I know. Knew. Matt never sat down once." Susan laughed again. "I think Eddie teased him about it."

"Did Matt seem distracted?"

"No."

"Amy?"

"No. They were perfect hosts. Talking a lot about the house they were going to build out there."

"How did everyone else get along?"

"What do you mean?"

"Well, when I saw the names, I thought it was a pretty interesting group. There's no love loss between Michelle and Ellie."

"Whatever they have between them wouldn't have anything to do with Matt and Amy."

"You're right. You're right," Miner nodded. "Eddie McBride? What was he doing there?"

"He works for Matt."

"That's right."

"I think he and Ellie came together."

"Eddie get along with Matt?"

"Yeah. They seemed to really like each other."

"What about Chris? He and Matt . . ."

Susan's laugh was more like a bark. "Chris barely got his head out of his phone long enough to flip the ribs, let alone get into an argument. Well, with anyone other than Michelle."

"What'd they fight about?"

Susan grimaced. "I guess it was your typical husband and wife thing. Honestly, Miner, I don't remember."

"Did Michelle argue with Matt?"

Susan shrugged. "There was something about the budget for their lake house, I think."

"Kelly?"

"Talked to Julie McBride most of the night about remodeling the Yourke House."

Miner tapped his pen on the table. "What about Brian?"

Susan's shoulders stiffened. "You know Brian."

Miner didn't respond.

"He had a little too much to drink." She fiddled with the sling her broken hand rested in.

"Is that all?"

"We smoked some weed. Except Ellie. Before Jack and Julie arrived."

"What time did y'all get home?"

"We left about midnight, so I guess we got home a little after 12:15."

"Were the kids there?"

"Yes. Asleep. Ethan McBride was there, too."

"Paige?"

"Yes."

"Awake or asleep?"

"Awake."

"When did you hurt your hand?"

"When we got out of the car. That damn door shuts on its own before I get my hand away. Brian's fixing it today. I've shut my hand in it twice now."

"Did you go to the hospital?"

"I did. Knew it was broken immediately." Susan stared at her ruined hand.

"Is it the same hand you've broke before?"

Susan nodded and looked Miner straight in the eye. "Same hand, same door."

"You gonna have to have surgery?"

Susan shrugged, but wouldn't look at Miner. He thought he saw tears pooling in her eyes. He pulled his handkerchief out and laid it on the arm of the chair. Susan took it without comment and dabbed her eyes. Miner gave her a minute to compose herself before asking his next question.

"Brian took you to the hospital?"

"No, Paige did."

"Oh. Where did Brian go?"

"He stayed home, with the kids."

"What time did you get home?"

Susan clicked her tongue. "I guess around four. Four thirty. They gave me pain pills at the hospital. Knocked me right out when I got home. Slept until after noon. That's when I heard about Amy and Matt."

"So, Brian was home when you got home?"

"Yes."

Miner wrote *lying* and underlined it in his notebook. He smiled at Susan and closed it. "That's all I've got for now."

Visibly relieved, Susan stood and started for the door. She turned back and held out Miner's handkerchief. "Keep it. I have two dozen, at least. Teresa's aunt gives me a package every year, whether I want them or not."

"Thank you."

Miner reached out and opened the door. Before she'd cleared the threshold Miner said, "Susan, I heard Brian and Matt got into an argument Saturday night."

"Jack tell you?"

"He did."

"It was nothing. Brian was justifiably upset about losing the job. It was a big one, and you know how times are. But on the way home, Brian told me about another job he has lined up, even bigger than Matt's lake house."

"Oh, well that's mighty fine. I might have some work for him to do on my barn. Need to replace some boards and such."

"I'm sure he'll be glad to."

"Well, you be sure to stay on top of that pain."

"I'm trying to stick with Advil, though I have the others in my purse, in case."

"Good idea. I'll walk out with you." Miner followed her down the hall.

"I'll just be a minute," she said, stepping into the bathroom.

Miner continued on to the front and relieved Malik, who had covered the front desk for Susan.

"How'd it go?" the young woman asked.

"Good," Miner said. "After you go to the school you should go on home. Get some rest. You've been on for a while."

"Thanks, Miner. Let me know if there's anything you need me to do."

"Will do."

Miner waved Malik out and was alone. He looked up the stairs that led to the City Hall offices. He heard distant conversation and laughter, but nothing nearby, nothing coming closer. With a brief look at the door to the police station, he opened the cabinet beneath Susan's desk and pulled out her purse. The prescription was easy to find. Ten pills. Miner silently cursed the paltry amount and shook two out onto his hand. He closed the bottle, tossed it in the purse, and was closing the door to the cabinet when Susan returned.

"Thanks, Miner."

"Don't mention it," he said.

He walked across the City Hall foyer and out the front door, shoving the two Oxycontin in his pocket as he went.

CHAPTER TWENTY-FOUR

Miner walked down the steps and across the square. He greeted the men planting pansies around the park gazebo. "Gonna freeze tonight," one man said.

"Hope so," Miner replied.

Miner looked forward to the year's first freeze. He loved the crunch of his boots as he walked across the frost-encrusted pasture to feed the horses. The soft nickers converted to steam as their warm breath hit the cold air. The pitter-patter of mice feet across the floor as he opened the tack room door. The smell of straw and manure as he cleaned the stalls. The crunch of sweet feed and oats as the horses ate. An occasional stamp of a back foot. The swish of a tail. Too bad he couldn't make a living with horses 'cause they sure as hell were easier than humans.

Miner entered the Book Bank to a chorus of greetings and good-natured ribbing from the group of old men who played dominoes at the café tables by the front window.

"Why ain't you out catching the bad guys?"

"A cop at a coffee shop, if that ain't stereotypical, I don't know what is."

"It's donut shops, not coffee shops, Walt," Miner called with a smile and a wave. He ambled over to the counter.

Kelly Kendrick leaned against the empty pastry case talking to Ellie Martin. "They clean you out yesterday?" Miner asked.

Ellie nodded. "Fellowshipping is hungry business. Earline should be here any minute."

He raised his eyebrows and patted his stomach. "She bringing fried pies?"

"She might be," Ellie said, coyly.

"Guess I'll have to stick around until she comes."

"In the meantime, you can grill us about Saturday night," Kelly said.

"Well, *grill* is a mighty strong word."

"I've seen enough cop shows to know what's coming. But shouldn't you have someone with you to play bad cop?"

"How do you know I'm not the bad cop?"

"Miner, you couldn't hurt a fly," Kelly said.

"I'm glad you think so. You two have a minute to talk?"

"Anything for you." Kelly's smile was winning and, if he hadn't known Kelly Kendrick his entire life, he would think she was flirting with him.

"I'll have to keep an eye out for customers and Earline," Ellie said. "Let's go to the back." Ellie led him to the children's section. Two chairs and a comfortable couch formed three sides of an area centered by a wooden train table. A bookshelf whose top row was low enough for toddlers to reach was on the back wall. Kelly took one of the chairs, Miner sat on the couch. Ellie went to the bookshelf and started organizing the books.

"I'm listening," Ellie said over her shoulder.

The radio on Miner's shoulder crackled. Bishop's voice replied, picking up the call. He turned down the volume. "Saturday night. Matt and Amy seemed normal?"

"Yeah," Kelly said.

"No arguments?"

"You know how people can get when they're, you know."

"Drunk? High?"

Kelly's face pinked from embarrassment. Her eyes darted to Ellie's back then to Miner. "People always do and say things they regret when they're drunk."

"People who?"

Kelly picked at the arm of the chair.

Ellie straightened from her task and turned. "Brian was a little confrontational."

Miner turned to her. "Confrontational with Matt?"

"Did Jack tell you what happened?"

"I'd like to hear it from you, too."

"Most of us were making s'mores when Brian jumped Matt over by the smoker," Ellie said. "Matt is using someone else for his lake house. Was."

"I understand why Brian was mad," Kelly said. "Matt'd told him he had the job. To go back on it . . . I think it was Michelle who made him do it."

"Why would she do that?"

"Who knows, with her?" Ellie said.

"How did Amy react?" Miner asked.

"She ignored it. Started packing everything up," Ellie said.

"Where were the others while the fight was going on?"

Ellie glanced at Kelly. "Julie, Kelly, Jack, Amy, and I were by the fire making s'mores. Eddie and Michelle were coming in from the woods." Miner filed the nugget away, as well as Ellie's apparent disinterest in the information, but didn't react. "Jack went to help break up the fight. Chris pulled Brian off of Matt. "

"Brian's been going through some tough times, hasn't he?"

"It's the economy," Kelly said.

Miner nodded, though he was tired of the economy being used as a convenient excuse for all manner of problems people had. People these days wanted to take all the credit when things went well but none of the blame when it didn't.

"How did everyone leave? Who left first and such?"

"Brian and Susan left first," Ellie said.

"In his truck?"

"Yeah," Kelly said. "Then Chris and Michelle left with the smoker. Matt and Amy gave me a ride home since we live in the same neighborhood. I helped Amy unpack her coolers then walked home."

There was a loud curse, and men at the front of the store whooped and laughed amid the click and clatter of shuffling dominoes. "Sorry, Ellie!" one of the men called.

Ellie waved acknowledgment and shook her head with a smile. "Poor Walt can't win to save his life."

Kelly continued. "I got home about 12:45. Talked to Seth, took the dog out, and was in bed by one. When I took Bruno out, I saw Matt drive out of the neighborhood."

Miner looked up. "Did he mention anything about leaving when you were in their house?"

"No. There was a lot of tension between Matt and Amy. They barely said a word to each other. I got out of there as quickly as I could." Kelly sighed. "Now I wish I hadn't."

"So you could be killed, too?" Ellie asked.

"No. Well, you never think it might be the last time you see anyone, or talk to them."

"Ellie, what about you and Eddie? When did you get home?"

"I got home about 12:30."

"Y'all went straight back to your place."

"Yeah."

"And, Eddie. Know where he went?"

Ellie paused. "He was with me."

"What?" Kelly said. "You didn't tell me that."

"All night?"

"Until about dawn, I guess."

"What?" Kelly crossed her arms.

"He slept on the couch."

Miner pursed his lips and wrote down *covering for Eddie* with a question mark. He closed his notebook, put it in his pocket.

"Okay, ladies." Miner rose. "Thank you for your time."

"Sure thing," Kelly said.

When they were near the bar, he said, "When does Paige get in?"

"Four-thirty or five," Ellie said.

"Susan says Paige took her to the hospital."

Ellie and Kelly exchanged a knowing look. Ellie said, "She did. She also said Brian wasn't home when they got back, about 4 a.m."

"Huh," Miner said. No surprise Susan would lie for her husband, but disappointing all the same. "Susan mentioned Brian got a big contract, bigger than the lake house."

Both women stopped and stared at him. "Did he?" Kelly asked.

"He told her on the way home Saturday night."

"Good for him," Ellie said.

Miner could tell they didn't believe it, and neither did he.

CHAPTER TWENTY-FIVE

Joe and Mary Doyle lived in a large, two-story house on a ten-acre lot where Boondoggle Road met Old Yourkeville Highway. A smooth, oil top driveway curved its way through the pasture to the four-car garage at the back of the house. Jack watched two mares and a colt bolt from their positions at the barbed wire fence when his patrol car passed. The older horses slowed down and stopped by the small pond in the middle of the field. Lagging behind, the colt finally made it, running around the two, mimicking their frolicking. The two older horses, done with their spurt of playfulness, put their muzzles down into the startling green grass and grazed.

Jack parked his patrol car at the end of the line of sedans, Suburbans, trucks, and minivans and got out. He let two middle-aged ladies carrying casserole dishes go ahead of him on the sidewalk and waited patiently behind them as they rang the doorbell. The aroma of roast beef surrounded their little threesome, making Jack's mouth water. Before the chime faded, a man opened the door. He wore khaki dress pants, an oxford shirt, and a sport coat, all well cared for but twenty years out of style. Jack immediately pegged him as a deacon.

"Ladies. Go on into the kitchen. Mrs. Pritchard is in there making sure everything is organized."

"Taking charge, more like," one of the women said.

"I told you we should have come earlier," the other countered.

"Well, you can't rush a roast, now can you?"

The women continued to bicker in the way old friends do all the way across the living room.

The man turned his benevolent attention to Jack. Jack knew his type. Ingratiating and selfless to an unnatural degree masking his true need to be in the middle of things. Useful. Indispensable. "Chief McBride. Don McNatt. Deacon at First Methodist. The Doyles' church. We met at the Rotary Club last month."

"Of course. Good to see you again," Jack said, though he didn't remember the man. Shocking considering McNatt wore an obvious, ill-fitting toupee.

McNatt grasped the collar of his suit jacket like a nineteenth-century robber baron standing for a dour picture and gazed down at the terrazzo tile. He made no move to escort Jack out of the entry hall. "Terrible, terrible thing." McNatt shook his head for emphasis. "I suppose you're here to talk to the family."

"Yes."

"Well, Mary's in bed. Old Doc Poole gave her a sedative yesterday. Joe's in his office with Brother Dobson. Our pastor. And Norman Davie."

"Where are the children?"

McNatt's head jerked up. "You can't possibly want to talk to the children."

"No, but you didn't mention them. Are they here?"

"Oh. I believe they're with Amy's mom. She came in from Houston."

"Where?"

"At a hotel in Yourkeville. The Best Western, I believe."

"Huh," Jack said. "I need to speak with Mr. Doyle."

"Can't it wait? It's all so fresh."

"I spoke with Joe yesterday and promised I'd keep him updated."

McNatt's eyes lit up. "Of course. Follow me."

They walked out of the entry way and into an open plan kitchen and living room. Floor to ceiling windows looked out over a swimming pool with a slide and diving board. Beyond lay a pasture the mirror image of the one Jack drove through earlier.

Though it was barely ten in the morning, the house smelled like a restaurant in the middle of a lunch rush. The reason was easily apparent; in the kitchen, elderly women with tightly permed gray hair were organizing enough food to feed the entire population of Stillwater: platters of sandwiches, barbeque, meats and cheeses, casseroles, cookies, cakes, brownies, bags of chips and dips, coffee cakes, Danish, donuts, urns of coffee, coolers of sodas and waters. Groups of men and women stood and sat all around, drinking coffee and talking in low murmurs. Their expressions on seeing Jack varied from curiosity, to relief, to suspicion, to outright hostility.

Jack knew better than to catch anyone's eye. He kept his gaze on Don McNatt's toupee. McNatt knocked twice on the door under the stairs, heard an abrupt "Come!" and opened the door.

Joe Doyle's office was what Jack expected. Wood-paneled walls, a large desk, leather chairs, bookshelves with more memorabilia and framed photographs—mostly of the hunting variety—than books. A small hammerhead shark hung on the wall behind Doyle's desk. The aroma of food couldn't banish the masculine scent of sandalwood and pine, as much a part of the room as Joe Doyle.

Doyle and a bald, hefty man sat in the two chairs in front of the desk. A slight man with thinning hair and small, square, gold-rimmed glasses hovered behind Doyle and to the side. The bald man stood when Jack entered. Doyle walked behind his desk and sat down. Don McNatt left and closed the door noiselessly behind him.

The bald man shifted his Bible to his left hand and extended his right. "Chief McBride. Frank Dobson."

"Nice to meet you."

"It's about damn time you showed up," Doyle said. "I want to know what's going on with the case."

Jack ignored Doyle's outburst and stared at the hammerhead shark on the wall. Doyle followed Jack's gaze. "Caught it in the gulf. Fishing for swordfish. Fought me like hell, but I got the best of it in the end."

"Fishing with Pollard?"

Doyle narrowed his eyes. "As a matter of fact."

"Talked to him lately?"

"Pollard's dead. We had the funeral to prove it."

Jack chuckled. The funeral of the century. Technically a "Celebration of Life," it'd been held at the football stadium to accommodate all the people. Town leader after town leader spoke about Pollard's contribution to Stillwater, his multiple Man of the Year awards, the low crime rate the town boasted while he was in charge (a not-so-subtle dig at Jack's short tenure), his philanthropic contributions. By the end, Buck Pollard's reputation had been burnished to a blinding shine. Jack had watched the mourners leave and couldn't detect a hint of sorrow or grief on even one face. Most looked relieved. Reading Pollard's journals every night for six weeks, Jack knew why.

"Never found a body." He turned to Dobson and Davie, "Would you excuse us?"

"They don't have to leave."

"Yes, they do."

"This is my house . . ."

Jack sighed, knowing every conversation with Doyle was going to be a battle. "And, my investigation."

Norman Davie spoke up, "I'm Joe's lawyer."

"It's fine, Joe. I'll be outside." Dobson put his hand on Jack's shoulder and bowed his head. "Lord, bless Chief McBride with the gift of discernment. Amen." He patted Jack on the shoulder and left.

When the door was closed behind Dobson, Doyle said, "Well?"

Jack sat down though Doyle hadn't invited him to. He crossed his legs and studied Doyle, trying to find the grieving father Miner alluded to the day before and couldn't. Doyle seemed to have jumped to the anger stage of grief in record time. Jack imagined Ethan sitting in a chair, his brains blown out, and understood.

"Matt and Amy were killed by one gunshot wound to the head, each, sometime between 1 a.m. and 4 a.m. Sunday morning. Matt was probably killed first, with a silencer, since the position of Amy's body suggests she was asleep. Nothing of value was taken and their home office wasn't disturbed in the least, which rules out robbery. Do you know, did Matt and Amy always lock their doors?"

"I assume so. Amy was from Houston. She was afraid of her shadow. Why?"

"There was no sign of forced entry. A keypad opens the garage door. Any idea who knows the code?"

"I do. Mary. The kids. Michelle and Chris."

"Anyone else?"

"Barbara Dodsworth cleans their house once a week. She might."

Jack jotted the information down on his notepad. "Was the garage door up or down when you showed up yesterday?"

"Up. But Madison was there before me."

"She would have gone in through the garage, not the front door?"

"The whole point of the keypad is so they don't have to keep up with a key."

Jack counted to five before he asked the next question. "Mr. Doyle, did you know of anyone who might want to harm Matt or Amy?"

Doyle glared at him for a full thirty seconds before answering. "Of course not."

"Matt had been working for you a little less than a year, correct?"

"Yes."

"How was the business?"

"More successful than I expected."

"Were you involved in the produce business?"

"Only generally, during the weekly management meetings. Managers for all four divisions met with me and Michelle to discuss business issues."

"And was Matt having any issues with his business? With employees, suppliers, customers?"

"No."

"What about with Eric Sterry, Matt's former employer? Any animosity when he left?"

"No. He understood Matt and Amy's desire to move back home."

"What about issues with employees, suppliers, and customers there?"

"You'd have to ask Sterry."

"Amy subbed at the high school, correct?"

"Yes."

"Did she have any run-ins with students or parents?"

"Not that I'm aware of, but I didn't talk to Amy about her job."

"Why not?"

Doyle looked at him like he was insane. "Mary might have."

"I'll need to talk to her."

"Not today, you won't."

Jack didn't push it. Mary Doyle wasn't going anywhere. "When you saw Matt and Amy's bodies, what was your first thought?"

Doyle twisted his head, looked at Jack from one eye. "What do you mean?"

"I mean, your instinctual reaction. A name, perhaps?"

Doyle sat back in his chair and clasped his hands together, resting them on his stomach. A tuft of gray chest hair peeked out from the top of his dress shirt. His hair was perfectly coiffed, but Jack noticed a patch of stubble on his chin he had missed when shaving.

"My instinct was to find my granddaughter and get her out of there."

"When Madison called you, what did she say?"

"Mary couldn't understand anything she said. I heard her screaming and sobbing through the phone. I told Mary to tell her I'd be right there. The call lasted seconds. Ten at the most." Doyle sighed. "I've told you all this."

"Mr. Doyle, in investigations like this you'll have to answer the same questions over and over." Jack wrote down the call details and asked, "What happened when you arrived at the house?"

"I went inside."

"Front door or back?"

"Back. Madison left the garage door up." Doyle swallowed and struggled to continue. In a weak voice he said, "I called out to Madison. Then I saw Matt"—he cleared his throat—"and Amy." Doyle put his face in his hands. "I can't believe that little girl saw that."

Jack remained silent to give Doyle time to compose himself. Doyle scrubbed his face with his hands and sniffed. His eyes were red and watery and his face was a mask of despair.

"I'm not sure what type of counseling services the county offers," Jack said, "or if they have a victim's advocate on retainer or not, but I have the name of one in Dallas that might be able to help Madison, or at the very least help you and Mary find someone to help Madison."

"Thank you," he said, his voice husky.

Jack cleared his throat. "After you found Matt and Amy, what did you do?"

"I went to find Madison. When we came downstairs Starling was in the living room, gun drawn."

"What did Madison say to you while you waited for Starling to check the house?"

"Nothing. She was practically comatose."

"When you were standing there, comforting your granddaughter, what was going through your mind?"

"Nothing."

"No name jumped out at you, no one who might be responsible for killing your only son and daughter-in-law?"

"Matt and Amy didn't have any enemies."

"What about your enemies, Mr. Doyle?"

In the following silence, the floor-to-ceiling grandfather clocked ticked away ten seconds, twenty seconds, thirty seconds. Doyle's eyes bored into him, the short truce they'd had over his grief gone. "I can't think of anyone who hates me enough to kill my children."

Jack raised his eyebrow in disbelief, made sure Doyle saw it, and moved on. "Are Amy's parents local?"

"No. She's from the Houston area. Her dad's dead. Her mom's here, though. She's staying at the Yourkeville Best Western. The kids are with her."

"Why?"

Doyle narrowed his eyes. Jack could tell he was about to lie to him. "Bea wanted them with her, and they wanted to be as far away from the crime scene as they could."

"Are Michelle and Chris here? I need to speak to them, as well."

"Michelle's at the office. I have no idea where Chris is. Probably playing golf."

"The day after his brother- and sister-in-law are murdered?"

"We all deal with grief in different ways."

"Michelle works, Chris plays golf, Mary takes to her bed, and your grandkids try to get as far away from you as possible. Why did Matt decide not to use Brian Grant as the contractor for his lake house?"

"It's news to me."

"Was the house being built with Matt's personal money or company money?"

Doyle smirked. Jack knew he wouldn't admit to laundering money through a construction project, but wanted to ask anyway. "His personal money."

"Then why would Michelle care who he used?"

"Michelle's controlling."

"Was that a source of contention in the family?"

"No."

"It seemed to be Saturday night."

"You said they were drinking."

"Not that much."

Doyle sat forward. His leather chair creaked. "What are you driving at?"

"How involved are you in the business these days, Mr. Doyle?"

"I'm the president and CEO."

"So, all decisions run through you. What's Michelle's role?"

"She's the CFO."

"So, she would be the final word on what happens with company money. What was Matt and Michelle's relationship like?"

"Typical brother and sister."

"Fights?"

"They were adults."

"That's not an answer."

"This is the direction of your investigation? Doyle Industries? Family issues?"

"Most murders are perpetrated by family members, Mr. Doyle. What was Matt and Michelle's relationship like?"

"It's because of your ineptitude we've had more crime in Stillwater in the last two months than in the last twenty years. It's because of you Matt and Amy are dead."

"As you know, the increase in crime is drug related. Once Pollard stopped protecting the local organization, the cartel moved in. You mentioned Mexicans yesterday. Are you saying Matt or Amy were involved in drugs?"

"No, that's not what I'm saying."

"It's what I'm hearing. I mean, my impression of Matt and Amy is they were about as straight-arrow as you could get. Now, I could see them being caught in the cross fire. Innocents are used to get to the core of the organization. Looks like they overestimated Matt's importance in the family. No one seems to be mourning them. At least, not the immediate family."

Doyle stood, placed his fists on his desk, and leaned forward. "You son of a bitch. After I win tomorrow—"

"Speaking of the election, I can't believe you're not dropping out."

"So that liberal can bring in a bunch of hipsters to take over my town? Over my dead body."

"I assumed after the death of your only son, your favorite child according to many, you would want to focus on your family."

"Get out."

"You never have answered the question about Matt and Michelle's relationship."

"We're done here," Norman Davie said. Jack had forgotten he was in the room. Davie walked to the office door and opened it.

Jack closed his notebook and stood. "Joe, you can rest assured, I'll do everything possible to find their killer."

"Why does that sound like a threat?"

"It's the same promise I make every family. I'll be in touch."

Davie held out a business card. "If you need to speak to Mr. Doyle again, you go through me."

Jack took the card and stepped out of the office. "Mr. McBride," Doyle called out.

Jack turned. The sun was shining through the partially opened wood blinds, throwing alternating stripes of dark and light across Doyle's face. His eyes were cold, hard and calculating. "You will answer to me. When I win tomorrow, my first order of business will be to destroy you."

Jack opened his car door and heard someone call his name. Norman Davie speedwalked toward him.

"Chief!"

Jack waited in the gap between his car and open door. Davie arrived out of breath. He put his hands on his hips and, with a sheepish chuckle, took a couple of deep breaths. "Don't get much exercise," he said.

Jack waited for Davie to say what he chased after him to say.

"Whew. Better now. About what Joe said when you left."

"Vowing to destroy me? I thought it was a bit melodramatic. What did you think?"

"Mr. Doyle is understandably upset at the death of his only son. You shouldn't put much weight in what he says."

"That's disappointing."

"Do you *want* him to threaten you?"

"I'm thinking of the answers he gave. Are you saying I shouldn't believe him?"

"No, no." Davie's expression hinted at panic. "Mr. Doyle was truthful in everything he said."

"I'm more interested in what he didn't say."

Davie shifted on his feet. "You mean about Matt and Michelle."

"Yes."

"You have a sibling. You know how volatile those relationships can be."

"Matt and Michelle had a volatile relationship?"

"No."

Jack didn't smile but he wanted to. Davie might be a good business lawyer, but Jack supposed he'd never been in court, much less questioned by the police.

"Did Matt ever come to you with a problem?"

Davie stiffened. "Why do you ask that?"

"You're the family lawyer. I assumed if Matt had a problem with someone or someone threatened him, maybe, he would come to you."

"Oh. Right. There was the issue with his former boss when he left East Texas Produce."

Jack sighed. Why couldn't people tell a story without dramatic pauses. Fucking *Law & Order*. "What was the issue?"

"Matt signed a noncompete when he went to work for Sterry—Eric Sterry, the owner—and Sterry sued him for violation when Matt left."

"What happened?"

"Since Sterry's business includes organic and nonorganic, we were able to get the noncompete voided because Matt's company was solely organic."

"How was Matt's relationship with his father?"

"You can't possibly think Joe . . ."

Jack knew better than to answer the question either way. Everyone was a suspect, especially this early in the investigation. But, if Davie and Doyle wouldn't tell Jack about Michelle and Matt's relationship, maybe insight into Matt and Joe's relationship would.

"They were close. Joe adored Matt. He'd been trying to get Matt to come to work for him for years, but Matt always resisted. Until a year or so ago when he came to him with the idea."

"Why did he resist, before?"

"Matt didn't want to have the business handed to him. He wanted to make his own way."

Jack struggled not to roll his eyes. Only silver-spooned spoiled brats ever thought that way. Jack would have been thrilled to have his way in the world paved with a few more golden bricks than potholes. "Would the business have been handed to him? I would imagine Michelle would have something to say about it."

Davie laughed. "Oh, yeah." Davie waved at a couple walking to the house holding a grocery bag and a tray of sandwiches. "Michelle promised to give him full autonomy and he agreed."

"So, Matt didn't want to work with Michelle."

Davie turned his attention back to Jack and narrowed his eyes. "I didn't say that."

"What about Chris?"

"Chris?"

"Michelle's husband? Doyle's son-in-law."

"I know who he is."

"How does he fit in? He doesn't seem very 'engaged' does he?"

Davie rolled his eyes. "Chris is a former athlete who can't get over the fact he wasn't good enough for the NFL."

"What's his side business at the country club?"

Davie furrowed his brow. "What do you mean?"

"Come on, Norman. You and I know a small-town country club is the closest these bumpkins get to a casino."

"Shreveport is an hour and a half away."

"You don't need to go to Shreveport to run numbers. Or place bets on games. He have a five-card stud game going on the secret room off the locker room?"

"I'm not sure where you're going with this."

"Trying to get a bead on the pecking order in this organization. How involved different family members and employees are in the—" Jack paused as if choosing his words, "operation."

"What does that have to do with Matt's murder?"

"Maybe nothing. Maybe everything. I'm going to take a close look at everything, personal and professional, to figure out who would want to murder in cold blood two of the nicest people I've met in Stillwater." Jack put one foot in his car. "You can tell Joe Doyle to take that as a threat."

CHAPTER TWENTY-SIX

Miner drove into Doyle Organics as Eddie left the warehouse after the morning rush. Eddie stuck his pencil between the band of his baseball cap and ear and walked to meet him.

"Hey, Miner. You looking for Starling? He's back in the warehouse trying to interview the Mexicans."

"Hey, Eddie." The police cruiser's door clunked shut. "Chief probably should've sent Malik out here."

"Probably."

"Got a minute?"

"Sure." Eddie jerked his head toward the office. "Come on. I'll buy you a cup of coffee."

"No, thanks. I'm gonna float away if I have any more coffee."

Eddie held the door open for Miner, walked around Matt's desk, and threw the clipboard on it. He paused. "Man. Déjà vu." He looked up at Miner and forced the memory of Matt out of his mind. "I gotta get a damn chair. Matt never sat down."

Eddie motioned for Miner to sit and leaned against the credenza wedged behind the desk.

"Understand you were with Matt and Amy Saturday night."

"With a lot of other people out at their lake lot."

"Anything interesting happen?"

"Lots of interesting things happened. Care to be more specific?"

"Anyone threaten to kill Matt and Amy? Maybe wave a 9 mm around for good measure?"

"No," Eddie said with a laugh.

"You took Ellie to the bonfire, right?"

Eddie lifted an eyebrow. "So I'm not the first person you've talked to."

"No."

He shrugged. "Yeah. Ellie went with me."

"Leave with you?"

"Of course."

"What time?"

"Midnight? Twelve thirty?" Eddie said.

"After?"

Eddie paused. Anyone at the bonfire could have told Miner he went with Ellie. If Miner questioned Ellie, did she cover for him like he asked?

"We went to her place."

"Which one?"

"Lake house."

"What time did you leave?"

"Early morning. I dropped her at home so she could get ready for church."

Miner nodded. "Where'd you sleep?"

Eddie laughed. "That's awfully personal."

Miner waited. Eddie narrowed his eyes. If Miner was testing his alibi against what Ellie said, she sure as hell wouldn't say Eddie slept in her bed. "I slept on the couch."

"You didn't go home?"

"No. I ran into Dallas for the day. To see a friend. I thought Jack and Julie might want the house to themselves for a little longer. Ethan spent the night at Troy's."

Miner nodded. "When did you hear about Matt and Amy?"

"Last night, at the book store."

"You didn't hear during the day? It's all the town could talk about."

"I was in Dallas."

Miner nodded again. "Nobody texted you? Called you?"

"My phone was dead, and I didn't bother to recharge it. Sometimes I like being out of touch, you know?"

"Not very convenient when there's a murder, though."

Eddie crossed his arms. "Surely you don't like me for their murders."

"More than some, less than others. Tell me about the fight Saturday night."

"I didn't see all of it. I'd gone into the woods to take care of some business."

"With Michelle?"

Eddie jerked his attention back to the officer. "Yeah."

Miner narrowed his eyes. Eddie could tell the more Miner talked to him, the less Miner liked him. Cops never liked him. If he only knew.

"Did Chris see you walk out of the woods?"

Eddie furrowed his brows. "I don't know. He had his hands full."

"So, he didn't see you and Michelle come out of the woods together?"

"Ah. You wonder if he's jealous."

"Or if he knows Michelle's cheating on him."

"Correct me if I'm wrong, but I'm not the first."

Miner bobbed his head from side to side, not committing to a yes or no.

"I don't know if he saw, or if he knows or if he cares. Michelle and I don't talk about Chris. What could this possibly have to do with the murders?"

"Probably nothing." Miner stood and went to the door. "Thanks for your time."

"I'll walk you out."

When they were outside, Miner said, "By the way, I'm going to need the name and number of who you were with Sunday."

"Why?"

"To check your alibi."

Eddie laughed. "For during the day?"

"Your brother expects me to be thorough." Miner coughed and spit on the ground. "Sorry. You driving Abe's truck these days?"

"Yeah, we traded."

"Straight up?"

Eddie nodded.

"You got fleeced, son."

"I don't think so."

Miner clicked his tongue on his teeth and pulled a notebook and pen from his front pocket. He clicked the pen and waited with it poised over a blank page.

Eddie debated what name and number to give him. There were so many choices. Fuck it. "Tony Hunt. 972-555-5208."

Miner clicked the pen, closed the notebook, put them back in his pocket, and patted it. "Thanks."

Eddie watched Miner turn his car around in the gravel yard and pull out onto the road. When he was out of sight, Eddie turned on his heel and walked to the main office, head down.

Eddie asked the receptionist, "She in?"

The woman, eyes watery and red nosed, nodded. "Upstairs."

He took the stairs two at a time and walked into Joe Doyle's office without knocking. Michelle sat behind her father's desk, her feet propped up on the corner, her face remarkably composed and free of signs of grief. "Father Dobson, I'll have to call you back," she said, hanging up the phone.

Her eyes traveled from Eddie's head to his toes and back. "What do you want?"

"I want to know what I'll get for lying to the police for you."

She dropped her feet to the floor, stood, and walked around the desk. "I'd say an obstruction of justice charge and jail time. But, since your brother is the chief, I'll say nothing."

She stopped inches from him. Her eyes moved to the baseball cap on his head. She pulled the pencil out and said, "Take that fucking cap off. It reminds me of my husband."

Eddie took the hat off and tossed it on the desk, his eyes never leaving hers.

"Where've you been?" she asked.

"Miss me?"

Michelle ran her hands through Eddie's hair to the nape of his neck. She rubbed his neck with her thumbs. "I needed you yesterday."

"To run an errand? Maybe knock someone else off?"

She seemed genuinely hurt by the comment. "No. I needed you. To help me forget."

Eddie knew manipulating people was second nature to Michelle. As was using sex to get what she wanted and to control others. Still, there was a vulnerability to her Eddie hadn't seen before. Against his better judgment, Eddie leaned forward, cupped Michelle's face, and kissed her.

They'd kissed before, passionately, hungrily, even angrily, but never like this. Her lips were soft and gentle beneath his, her tongue moved languidly around his mouth, her hands cradled the back of his head, and massaged it gently. When Eddie pulled away, his confusion at the kiss was mirrored in her expression. They stared at each other for a long moment, each trying to regain their breath and composure.

He pulled Michelle to him and kissed her hungrily, working on the buttons of her blouse as he did. When she reached for his belt, he pulled away. Her face was flushed, her lips swollen, her expression confused.

"Today, it's all about you," he said.

She arched her eyebrows and smiled slowly, almost sweetly.

Eddie pushed the papers, blotter, and pen holder off the desk and on to the floor and lay Michelle back on Joe's desk.

"You are, by far, the best hire Matt ever made." Michelle stood and smoothed her skirt down. "So, who interviewed you? Miner?"

"Yeah."

She cleared her throat and lifted her chin, regaining her professionalism. "Good."

"It's not good. He's damn astute, Michelle. Don't underestimate him."

She laughed. "I'm not. I'm going to buy him off. Pollard gave him hush money for years. I've let Miner swing in the breeze for a while, to squash any flash of conscience he might have had when your brother came into town. Teresa's probably screaming in pain by now. He'll be easy enough to get in line. Where did you tell him you were Sunday morning?"

"With Ellie."

Michelle's eyebrows shot up. "Is she backing you up?"

"For now."

"Well, I'll be Goddamned. Little Miss Honesty is lying for her lover."

"We aren't lovers."

"Then why would she lie for you?"

Eddie stared at Michelle and remained silent. He was tired of lying to everyone about everything.

"That's what I thought. Where were you yesterday? I tried to call you all day."

"Taking care of your problem, like you wanted."

"Where?"

"Somewhere there's not cell service."

"Where's Kyle? He's not returning my calls."

"Kyle went to visit a long-lost relative."

"Goddamn him! I didn't tell him he could do that. Who did he go visit?"

"His father."

"Jesse Grant's dead." Michelle stilled. "You killed Kyle?"

"I was taking care of Muldoon when Grant shot at me. Lucky for me he's a shit shot. I'm not. Did you tell him to kill me?"

Her head jerked back. "Of course not! Why would you ask that?" Her voice went up an octave at the end of the question.

"Why else send him with me?"

"So you could prove to Kyle once and for all you're on our side."

"I didn't realize Kyle Grant was in charge."

"Kyle Grant kept my hands clean. I guess you've promoted yourself to that job." She narrowed her eyes. "Has Jack connected DI to the drug organization?"

Eddie paused. "No."

She studied him before nodding. "But he will."

"Yeah. Jack's a good cop. He'll catch you eventually."

Michelle smirked. "We'll see about that." She patted him on the shoulder and tried to move past him. "I need to get back to work and so do you."

Eddie stopped her. "We've got another problem."

Michelle inhaled. "What?"

"*Brian* Grant."

She laughed. "How is he our problem? I'd imagine he's your brother's number one suspect after Saturday night."

"He may be, I don't know. But I do know he was here after and heard you threaten Matt."

"I didn't threaten Matt."

Eddie laughed. "Yeah, you did."

Michelle gripped the edge of the desk until her knuckles were white. "What does he think he heard? No, better question, why was he here?"

"He saw Matt pull in and wanted to apologize."

Michelle dropped her head to her hand, sighed and rubbed her temple. Eddie continued. "He didn't see anything, but he heard enough to know about the operation, or at least have an idea about it. He's easy to shut up. Give him a job." Michelle dropped her hand and stared up at Eddie. "Apparently they're hard up for money. Give him a job with your metal building business."

"How do you know this?"

"What?"

"How do you know Brian was here?"

"I saw him last night at the Book Bank."

"Brian at a bookstore? Try again."

"He was picking up Paige." Eddie mentally crossed his fingers he wouldn't be caught in these lies. The last thing he needed was for Michelle to read more into Eddie's protection of Susan than was there. "Want me to make the offer?"

Michelle pushed him away and sat down behind the desk. She picked up the phone. "No. I'll do it." Eddie pressed the disconnect button. "What?" She was pissed now.

"Chris saw us come out of the woods."

"So?"

"He doesn't care about us?"

"Seriously, Eddie? With all the other shit I have to do, like plan Matt and Amy's funeral, whether Chris cares I'm sucking your dick or not is down pretty far on the give a shit list. Okay? Besides, Chris knows he's got a good deal." She batted Eddie's hand off the phone. Michelle dialed and swiveled the chair around to stare at the back wall. "Brother Dobson, hi. It's Michelle. Sorry for the interruption. What time can I meet you at the funeral home?"

Eddie left and almost ran into the wide-eyed receptionist standing outside the door. "We made a little bit of a mess in there." He winked at her and the woman dropped the papers she was holding.

CHAPTER TWENTY-SEVEN

The Grants lived on ten acres of land east of town in a neat, square red brick house with three dormer windows above a white columned front porch. The flowerbeds were filled with colorful, winter hardy flowers, mostly pansies. To the right of the front door were two rocking chairs and a porch swing. Brightly colored pillows sat in the rocking chairs and were propped in the swing. A small round table sat between the rocking chairs with a potted ivy trailing down to the floor. A glass butterfly stuck out of the top of the ivy on a copper wire.

Parked at an angle in front of the large metal building behind the house was a white dual cab Ford pickup with a square magnet advertising GRANT AND SON CONSTRUCTION on the doors and tail gate. The large bay doors of the building were open. Miner's gaze traveled from the clean and organized garage area, to the tool-covered pegboard wall, to the jam box blaring hard rock and sitting on the worktable, to the rifles and guns next to it. Brian stood with his back to Miner cleaning what looked like a handgun.

Miner released the protective strap over his holster and kept his hand on his own gun. "Brian?"

Brian Grant jumped and turned, his fists moving up to protect his scratched face. He dropped his arms and with a slight limp, he walked over to the jam box, turned the music down, and said, "Damn, Miner. Don't sneak up on people like that."

"Sorry. You limping?"

"Getting old."

"What are you doing there?" Miner jerked his chin toward the guns.

"Cleaning the arsenal."

"You won't be offended if I ask you to step away from the table." Brian reached toward the table for his cigarettes and lighter. Miner tensed. "Keep still."

"Come on, Miner. I'm getting a smoke."

"Over there," Miner said, motioning to a stool across the room. Brian shook his head but complied. Miner put himself between Brian and the guns, picked up the cigarettes and lighter, and handed them to Brian.

He shook a cigarette out of a pack, placed it between his lips, and shoved the packet in his front pocket. He lit the Marlboro and took a drag. "Horrible habit. This is the only place I can smoke." He took another drag and flicked the ash on the ground. "Let's not waste any time. You heard I got in a fight with Matt and think I might have killed him."

Miner didn't say anything.

"I told Susan you'd suspect me. She refused to believe it."

"I want to hear what happened. From you."

"At the end of the party, Matt told me he was using another contractor." Brian took another drag. "I was mad, of course I was mad. I'd had too much to drink, smoked a little wacky tobacky, and took a swing at him. If I hadn't been drinking, I would have never done it. Next morning, I felt awful."

Brian rose and limped to a bucket of sand. He lit a new cigarette from the old one and snuffed the old one out. "I called Matt the next morning to apologize and ask for a job. If you can't beat 'em, join 'em, huh? A policeman answered. I hung up."

"Why?"

"Shock? I don't know. I just did."

"Sunday morning, you got home and went to bed?"

Brian dragged on his cigarette and studied Miner. "You've seen Susan today, Miner."

"Yep."

"Then you know the answer."

"I want to hear your version."

"She slammed it in the car door."

"Did you take her to the hospital?"

"No. Paige did."

"Why?"

"I'd been drinking. Susan was hurt. I knew which way the wind would blow."

"Where were you?"

"Here with the kids."

"Were you here when Susan got home?"

"I'd fallen asleep. When I woke up, she was next to me. Dead to the world. I took the kids to church and came back and fixed that fucking car door. I've been meaning to do it for months. Now, her pinky is probably going to be permanently deformed because of it." Brian held his cigarette deep between his first two fingers, so his entire hand covered his mouth when he took a drag.

Miner stepped toward Brian until he was only a foot away. Brian didn't flinch, but blew smoke out the side of his mouth and away from Miner.

"Did you shut Susan's hand in the door?"

"No."

"Did you take the car or truck to the bonfire?"

"Truck."

"How did she shut her hand in the car?"

"I guess she needed something out of it. I don't know, Miner. I was putting the cooler in the shop when it happened." Brian nodded his head to the corner of the room. Miner glanced over his shoulder and saw the cooler. "I heard her scream and came outside. She was holding her hand. Then Paige came outside."

"And took Susan to the hospital."

"Yeah."

"And you went inside to sleep."

"Yep."

"These all of your guns?"

"Yeah. Careful. They're all loaded," Brian said. "Safeties on, of course."

Miner went to the table and looked at the guns. "Why are you cleaning your Beretta?"

"Troy and I went shootin' yesterday afternoon."

"Before or after you heard about Matt and Amy?"

Brian sucked so hard on his cigarette it accentuated the hollows of his cheeks. He blew the smoke out in one long, lazy breath.

"After."

"Lift up your shirt for me, Brian."

Brian's face changed from defiance to incredulity. "What?"

"Lift up your shirt."

"Why?"

"I want to know why you're wincing every time you move."

"Ate some bad catfish at Mabel's last night."

"Mabel's catfish scrape your face, too?"

Brian placed his cigarette between his lips and lifted his shirt. His torso was slim and well defined and completely free of bruises. Miner's eyes found Brian's. The defiance was back.

He let his shirt fall. "Happy?"

"You seen Kyle lately?'

"Kyle? What's Kyle got to do with this?"

"Nothing, as far as we know. We've been looking for him, in connection with something else, for a few days now and can't seem to locate him."

"Who the hell knows, or cares?"

"Put your Beretta back together. I have to take it."

Brian lodged the cigarette between his lips, picked up the slide and barrel. "You know, you're wasting your time here, Miner." He inserted the barrel into the slide until it clicked, then attached the guide rod and spring. "You ought to be looking closer to home."

"What do you mean?"

Brian attached the assembled slide to the main part of the gun, pulled it back, and held the gun out to Miner by the trigger protector. "I didn't kill Matt and Amy. The sooner you figure out who did, the better my life will be."

CHAPTER TWENTY-EIGHT

Ellie balanced the cookie on top of the coffee cup in her left hand and opened the heavy front door to the City Hall with her right. Susan sat at the front counter, her phone headset nestled across the top of her blonde hair like the headbands she had worn in high school. She was talking low and Ellie hung back to give her privacy. Susan glanced up and Ellie lifted the cookie and coffee. A finger raise, a murmured goodbye, and Susan clicked off. Ellie hoped for a smile when her friend looked up again, but was disappointed.

"Thought you might want a snack," Ellie said. "Earline brought these cookies. Cherry chocolate chunk. They're divine."

"Thanks." She reached down. "How much do I owe you?"

"Susan."

Ellie heard her drop her purse onto the floor. Susan winced. "You don't have to check up on me."

"I'm not."

"Liar."

"Fine. How's your hand?"

"It hurts."

"Are you taking something?"

"Advil."

"Didn't Poole give you anything stronger?"

"Yes, but I can't sound like a drunkard when I answer the City Hall phone, now can I?"

"You shouldn't have come in."

"You know I have no choice."

"If you need money, you know . . ."

"No."

"Don't you have sick days? I'm sure Jack would . . ."

"Jack?"

"Chief McBride."

Susan stared at Ellie. She could read Ellie as well as Ellie could read her. They'd had lots of practice.

"Has he interviewed you?"

"Miner came by."

"Was Kelly there?" Susan, usually so guarded, wore her suspicion like a bridal veil.

"Yes. Getting coffee."

"Kelly doesn't drink coffee. I can see y'all now, sitting 'round talking about poor Susan. 'I wonder if Brian slammed her hand in the car door again?'"

Ellie chose to remain silent rather than lie.

"What'd you tell Miner?"

"Told him Brian and Matt got into it. There were too many people at the lake. I couldn't lie."

"Why would you?"

"Well." Ellie stopped herself. Ellie hated lying, was famous for her honesty. It's what came from being lied to and manipulated for years by people she loved.

With her good hand, Susan fiddled with the items on her desk; straightening the blotter, adjusting the location of her message pad, clicking closed her pen and placing it diagonally across the pad.

"They took Brian's gun."

"Susan . . ."

"Save it." She continued rearranging things on her desk, now with more force than necessary. She slammed her stapler down on the desk with her good hand. "You don't have any idea what it's like. People thinking bad of him because of his family. His dad. *Kyle*." She glared at her best friend. "Of friends thinking he abuses his family."

"Susan . . ."

"I mean, *you* of all people."

"What's *that* supposed to mean?"

"Why is it no one wonders if you're a gambler, a slut, or a drunk? God knows that's what the town thinks of your parents. You've got some crooked politicians in your family tree, too, but everyone thinks the world of you. Ellie Yourke Martin can do no wrong. You sure as hell aren't haunted by the sins of your parents."

"I don't know, Susan. Maybe it's because I don't sleep around, gamble, or drink too much."

"You sure part of that statement isn't a lie?"

Ellie straightened, the jab hitting the intended mark. Ellie had forgotten how cruel Susan could be when she wanted. She thought of watching Brian bully Susan into taking a hit of the joint on Saturday night, of seeing the same type of interaction between them for twenty-five years, of Susan's phantom car accident in high school, of Ellie's conversation with Paige, the misery on the girl's face, the confusion. She decided she was tired of looking the other way.

"How did you slam your hand in the car if you were in the truck?"

Susan narrowed her eyes.

"It's your car with the loose door, right? But you were in the truck."

"You need to mind your own business."

"I'm done with standing by while—"

"While, what? Brian beats me? He doesn't beat me. How many times do I have to tell you? You and Kelly are wrong about Brian. You've always been wrong. I mean, really. Do you think I would have married him? I would have stayed with him? I mean, what's worse? You thinking so little of Brian or so little of me?"

"Maybe because you're lying to me."

"You're the last person who needs to lecture me about lying."

Ellie held her hands up in surrender. "Fine. We won't worry about you anymore."

"Me?" Her laugh was bitter, condescending. "Have you looked at your life lately? You're sleeping with two brothers, one of them married."

"Enjoy your coffee."

"Take it. I don't want it."

Ellie reached for the coffee and cookie, trying to stay as far away from Susan as possible. She left, her stomach churning with nausea, and ran straight into the broad chest of Lincoln Bishop.

"Oh, sorry, Ellie. I didn't spill on you, did I?" He held Ellie's elbows gently.

"No. Thank you." She held out the coffee and cookie. "This is for you. Welcome to Stillwater."

Lincoln took the cup and paper bag with a perplexed expression on his face. "Thanks."

"Don't mention it."

Ellie made it out the door, down the steps, and halfway across the square before she threw up.

CHAPTER TWENTY-NINE

If Jack had been looking out the window of Bob Underwood's law office, he would have seen Ellie throwing up in the park. Instead, he was staring at the family pictures on the credenza, without seeing them, thinking of the similar display in Ann Newberry's office. Jack's office had one framed picture, of Ethan when he was in elementary school, in a frame Ethan made for Father's Day when he was five. Each year, Jules gave him a new picture to replace the old. Jack always kept the old ones in the frame behind, like his mother did, so frames ended up being a small time capsule, their own photo album. He couldn't remember when Jules stopped giving him a new picture. He didn't even know how old Ethan was in the picture he had.

Bob Underwood walked into his office, his thin hair flying away, his large square glasses slid halfway down his sweaty nose.

"Sorry I'm late, Jack." Bob flopped his briefcase down on the credenza and took a deep breath. "I was over in Yourkeville. Court. Motion to dismiss. Denied. Go to trial next week."

"What's the case?"

"Bounced checks." He removed his jacket and hung it on a coat rack in the corner. "I'm surprised you made this appointment, what with the murders and all."

Bob sat down, pulled a yellow legal pad toward him, took a pen from an old-fashioned pen stand on his desk and wrote *Jack McBride, Monday, 11/5* on the top of the page. He looked up and waited.

"I want a divorce."

Bob put his pen down and sat back. "I charge $3,000 for a standard divorce. Costs go up if it's contested and we go to court."

"Do you need a retainer?"

"Whatever's in your pocket is fine."

Jack fished a twenty out and put it on the desk.

Bob picked his pen back up and waited.

Even being succinct, Jack spent thirty minutes telling Bob the story of his marriage's dissolution. Bob took notes, asked a clarifying question or two, but mainly let Jack talk. It felt good to get it all out to someone who had no preconceived opinion of Jack and Julie's relationship, no personality conflicts, no special interest. Bob hadn't even met Julie.

"Do you have the note Julie left?"

"No. I tore it up."

"Did anyone else see it?"

"No."

"So, she can use any reason she wants why she left, and you can't contradict her."

"Yes." Jack could recite the note verbatim, but he doubted it would help so he didn't mention it.

Bob tapped his pen on the legal pad, leaving little black dots on the margin. "We had an appointment six weeks ago. Why did you cancel?"

Ellie convinced me it was the best thing to do. "Ethan was so happy to have his mother back, I thought I should at least give it a shot."

"Probably a mistake."

"What?"

"Well, though you couldn't have gotten an *uncontested* divorce because of her returning before the 365, you would have still had solid grounds for divorce. Would have been difficult for her to contest it. Now, she's back, trying, and you're initiating proceedings . . ."

"It doesn't change the fact she left and was gone for a year."

"I know, I know. But this six-week reprieve will have to be explained better." Bob made a note and asked, "That it?"

"Yes."

"Is there another woman?"

"Jules likes men."

"I wasn't talking about her and you know it."

"There were other women. In Dallas. I told you I went through a rough patch."

"How rough are we talking about here? A couple of one night stands? Bondage? S&M? You ever take your anger out on some hooker?"

"No."

"On anyone?"

"Not on a woman."

"How many other women are we talking about?"

"I didn't keep count."

"Anyone going to show up with a little Jack Junior in the oven?"

"No." Bob remained silent. Jack new the trick well, but it still worked on him. "There were probably ten or twelve women. I would pick them up at lunch."

"Same bar every time?"

"No. Different. They were waitresses. Bartenders."

"Julie friends with any of your former coworkers?"

"No."

"Any chance she'll find out about your peccadillos?"

"I wouldn't think so. Anyway, she was cheating on me, remember? I saw her. With my own eyes. Anything she might find would be hearsay."

Bob sat forward. "Well, let's hope she doesn't find out. Does she have any idea you're thinking of divorce?"

"I think she suspects. She's trying very hard."

"Are you?"

"Not as hard as she is."

Bob put his pen down. "Why do you want this divorce?"

"I don't love her."

"Try again."

"Isn't that enough?"

"If you go into this with the reason as 'I don't love her,' you won't get custody of Ethan. It will look like you're giving up on your marriage."

"She left. On his fucking birthday! Went off to God knows where, with a man, never contacted me or Ethan. No one. I bought Christmas presents for Ethan from her, lied to him for a fucking year so he wouldn't think his mother left him. Took care of him when he got the flu. I was questioned, suspected of murdering my wife, which pretty much ruined my career. Hell, she might not even be there when I get home. What judge in their right mind would give custody to her?"

"She left on Ethan's birthday?"

"Yeah. Classy, right?"

Bob cleared his throat. "It sure makes her look bad. I'd hate to get your hopes up, but I'd be shocked if you don't win this running away. You'll still probably have to share custody."

"No. I want full custody."

"Why? Joint custody would be best for Ethan."

Jack thought of Ellie's threat. *I can't live in a town with the two of you.* "Because I'm not leaving Stillwater and I don't want to give her a reason to stay. Living in a town this size divorced from her would be miserable. At least in the city there would be a million other people around as a buffer."

"Then move back to Dallas."

"I don't want to."

"You like us that much?"

"You're growing on me."

"What if you get fired?"

"I don't plan on letting that happen."

Bob smiled. "It might not happen today, this week, or even this month, but it'll happen."

"Thanks for your confidence, Bob."

"Don't be sensitive, Jack. You'll get fired with that attitude for sure. Hypothetically, let's say you get fired. You sticking around then?"

"I don't know what this has to do with my divorce or custody of Ethan. If I lose my job, Ethan will go wherever I go."

"But you'd prefer to stay here?"

Jack didn't respond. Bob continued, "Because of Ellie?"

"What?"

Bob laughed. "You youngsters. I might be an old man, but I got good eyes. Always have. Even if I was blind as a bat, I would have felt the electricity sparking off you two like a damn transfer station at her business launch back, what was it? Six weeks ago?"

Jack shifted in his chair. "It's that obvious?"

"Well, you don't have much of a poker face when you're around her, that's for damn sure."

"Jesus." Jack rubbed his forehead.

"How far has it gone with Ellie?" Jack nodded, and Bob continued. "Have you been around each other with Julie?"

"Once or twice."

"Think she cottoned on?"

Jack thought about Saturday night after the lake. Since he'd distracted Julie from questioning him too closely about Ellie, she hadn't mentioned her again. But that didn't mean anything. She'd kept her plans to leave Jack secret for weeks. Months. He wouldn't know what Julie suspected until she wanted him to know, which would be the worst possible time.

"I honestly don't know."

"Does anyone else know?"

"Eddie."

"Kelly? Susan?"

"I don't know. I don't think so. They wouldn't say anything."

"You wouldn't think, but I wouldn't count on it. Small-town gossips can make lies into the truth. They can take a suspicion with a kernel of truth and make it into scandal. They take a scandal and ruin lives."

"We stopped seeing each other when Julie got back in town."

"Good. Keep it up."

Jack nodded, though it was the last thing he wanted. Since Saturday night, he'd been trying to figure out how to meet Ellie alone. He needed to tell her he loved her, and hear her say she loved him, again.

"Sure," Jack said.

"I'm serious. You cannot see her at all."

"That's going to be hard in a small town like this."

"I know, but not impossible. You have to avoid her like the plague."

"Avoid her?"

"Don't go get coffee, don't make a point to talk to her when you do see her in groups. Whatever you do, don't be alone with her."

"I think that's a little drastic."

"Do you want custody of your son?"

"Yes."

"Do you think your wife is capable of doing anything possible, even something despicable, to keep you from divorcing you? From getting full custody of Ethan?"

"Yes."

"Then you have to cut Ellie out of your life completely."

"Until Julie's served the papers, right?"

"No. Until she signs them."

CHAPTER THIRTY

Jack sat in his car outside Michelle Ryan's house and absently watched the comings and goings of mourners.

You have to cut Ellie out of your life completely.

Ellie and Kelly walked out of the front door in deep conversation. Kelly gestured with her hands as she talked; Ellie listened, nodded, and interjected a few words here and there as they walked to Kelly's red Escalade. Jack waited to get out of his car until they were driving past his. He gave a brief wave in greeting as they drove by. Though he only glanced in her direction, Ellie's puzzled expression lodged in his heart and festered there.

Do you think your wife is capable of doing anything possible, even something despicable, to keep you from getting full custody of Ethan?

If Julie even suspected Jack wanted a divorce, or was in love with Ellie, she would do whatever she could to destroy him. His career. His relationship with Ethan. His relationship with Ellie. His reputation in town, though that was admittedly tenuous at the moment anyway.

Until she signs the papers.

Jack could easily imagine Julie dragging out the divorce, just to screw him. She had a bottomless pit of money, thanks to her parents. Jack didn't.

He had already depleted his savings with his three-month unemploy-
ment, road trip, and down payment on the house in Stillwater. He needed
to have enough proof of her cheating and abandonment when the papers
were served to entice her to sign. He had all of the unanswered emails
and their read receipts. He could talk to the cops in Emerson who investigated him regarding her disappearance last year. They would be more
than willing, considering they were dragged around by one of their own,
who was Julie's spurned lover. His former partner would vouch for his
version of events, as well, though Jack's professional relationship with
Alex might make her seem too sympathetic of a witness.

If only Julie would leave again.

Jack paused at the front door and rubbed his chest. He hated himself
for being thankful for a case to keep his mind off of his personal problems. It was a ready and believable excuse to give to Julie for not being
around, for avoiding an encore of Saturday night. Her flirty comments
and meaningful glances made it clear she expected more of the same. Was
she playing a part, faking her enthusiasm to keep him interested? Maybe
to a point, but he knew her physical cues and reactions well enough to
know much of what happened was real. Hell, physically he couldn't help
but respond—she was right; they always were great together in bed— but
mentally and emotionally he was wracked with guilt.

He shook his head to clear it and knocked on the door. Michelle
answered.

"Jack." She stepped aside to let him enter.

"Michelle. I'm so sorry for your loss."

"Thank you." Her voice was toneless.

The activity at her house was more subdued than at her parents'.
Based on the age of the mourners, this generation hadn't seen enough
death to be as good at grief as Joe's generation. Everyone looked uncomfortable, as if unsure what to do, or to say. A group of men stood huddled
around the big screen television, talking urgently and low. Jack imagined the conversation revolved around the appropriateness of turning on
Monday Night Football pregame in the middle of a death visitation. One

man checked his watch and looked at the TV. Another had his head in his phone. Texting Chris about his bet, possibly?

"Is there somewhere we can talk?"

Michelle opened a door to the right of the entrance. Jack stopped in the doorway of a guest bedroom, tastefully but generically decorated. Sports magazines were stacked on the bedside table next to a half-empty water glass, an empty beer bottle, and a large bottle of Advil. Michelle sat on the bed. Her eyes dared him to enter.

"I'm not interviewing you in a bedroom." *Especially your husband's*, he thought.

Her mouth curled into a smile equal parts calculating and manipulative, and more than a little erotic. "Don't you trust me?"

Jack leaned against the doorjamb. "You aren't acting like a grieving sister. Why is that?"

Michelle stood and stalked over to him. She wore a tight skirt and silk blouse. Her legs were bare and ended in four-inch heels. She was almost eye-to-eye with him. "Off the record?" She leaned forward and whispered, "I didn't like my brother or his wife much." She lingered close to him, her gaze roaming across his face, her lips turned into a playful smile. Michelle wore the same perfume as Julie—Eternity—and too much of it.

"So you're glad they're dead?"

"Of course not."

A couple paused at the front door. The man looked embarrassed, perhaps perplexed, to see Jack and Michelle standing so close together. The woman didn't seem surprised at all. Michelle arranged her face in a wan, grieving smile and moved away from Jack toward the couple. "Thanks so much for coming." She hugged the woman and kissed the man on the cheek, lingering a half-second too long.

"We're so sorry," the man said.

Michelle opened the door and herded them out. "We all are, Kirk."

The woman moved in front of the man. "Don't worry about the Meals Ministry. We've got tomorrow covered."

"Don't be ridiculous, Dawn," Michelle said. "Life goes on. Matt and Amy believed in the Meals Ministry as much as I do. I'll be there, as I am every Tuesday."

"If you're sure," Dawn said. The couple walked through the door.

"I'll see you then," Michelle said and closed the door with a snap. The knocker on the outside thumped against the door. When she turned back to Jack, her expression was once again blank. "Let's sit by the pool."

They sat at a round metal table with red Solo cups of iced tea in front of them. The automatic pool sweeper gurgled and sprayed water before submerging again. Jack sipped his tea and watched Michelle.

"Are you going to ask me questions or stare at me?" Michelle said.

"Does it make you uncomfortable?"

"No. I have things to do. A business to run. An election to win. A funeral to plan."

"I guess you're in charge while your dad deals with this and the election."

She chuckled. "Right."

"Does it drive you crazy people give him credit for the company's success?"

Michelle stared at Jack in silence.

"What's the Meals Ministry?"

"What it sounds like. Delivering meals to shut-ins, old people. Whoever needs them."

"Is that through your church?"

"All the Stillwater churches participate. Is this what you came to talk to me about? My Christian witness?" Michelle smirked around the last two words and drank her tea.

"It's something I didn't know about you. But it's not surprising. Crooks and liars have always been an altruistic lot."

"What makes you think I'm a crook?"

"You come from a long line of them, I hear."

Michelle laughed. "Are you seriously sitting there calling my father a crook? The man who will hold your career in his hand in less than twenty-four hours? I gotta say, McBride. You've got some balls."

"You don't deny the liar part."

She shrugged. "If it gets me what I want."

"Why would anyone want to kill Matt and Amy?"

"I have no idea. Isn't it your job to find out?"

"I find out by questioning people who knew them."

"Matt and I were not close. I have no idea who would want to kill him. I doubt Amy inspired enough passion in anyone to want to kill her."

"That's cruel."

"Amy is everything I hate in a woman. Deferential wife and helicopter mom whose greatest ambition is to be PTA president."

"I hear she was getting her masters."

"Because I encouraged her to do it. She was smarter than Matt, if you want to know the truth. But she wasn't interesting, or offensive in any way."

"So she was collateral damage? The killer was there for Matt?"

Michelle shrugged.

"You and Matt were brother and sister, work together, and live in the same small town, and yet you weren't close?"

"Not particularly."

"Because you didn't like him."

"The feeling was mutual, trust me."

"Why?"

"Matt and Amy were a couple of goody-two shoes. He'd always been judgmental, prissy. Like my mother."

"How is your mother doing, by the way?"

"I have no idea. I think she's drugged up."

"You haven't checked on her?"

"I've asked about her, but have I seen her? Checked her pulse? Made sure she's breathing? No."

"How was Matt's business doing?"

"Surprisingly well," Michelle said. She crossed her legs and sipped her tea, clearly more comfortable on the subject of business. "When Matt came to me with the idea last year, I knew it would work. I saw it as a good opportunity to diversify, expand our business. Matt was a good businessman; I'll give him that. Very forward thinking when he wanted to be. And also ruthless."

"Matt?"

Michelle smiled. "Shocking, isn't it? Have I mentioned he was also a hypocrite? Sitting in judgement of others when he wasn't shy about stealing his best friend's biggest customers."

"Eric Sterry?"

She nodded. "Almost put Sterry out of business."

"I had heard he stole a few customers."

"They were Sterry's biggest ones. I couldn't believe Matt went after them. Like I said, he could be ruthless. He was always a hypocrite."

"What do you mean?"

"Let's say Matt had a narrow view of right and wrong. There were no shades of gray with him. No extenuating circumstances."

"Did that cause problems with people?"

"It's a pretty common viewpoint in this town, truth be told."

"What about with you?"

She chuckled. "I couldn't care less what Matt thought of me."

Jack drummed his fingers on the table. "The first time I talked to him, your father connected the drug-related deaths to Matt and Amy. Why would he make that connection?"

"He'd just found his son dead. I'm sure he wasn't thinking straight. He's distraught."

"Is he? He seemed more angry than distraught."

"His son was murdered in cold blood."

"It would make me angry, too. But not at the man investigating the crime."

She leaned forward and whispered with a mischievous grin. "He doesn't like you. He's running for city council to get you fired."

Jack leaned forward and mimicked Michelle. "I'm not afraid of your father."

"He'll be disappointed to hear it."

Jack sat back and crossed his legs. "You on the other hand . . ."

"Me? But I'm just a woman. Why would you possibly be afraid of me?" Michelle said, mocking clear in her tone of voice.

"Powerful women are much more terrifying than men."

"Do we emasculate you?"

"Yes."

"Good." She leaned forward again. "That's our intention."

"Walk me through where you went after the bonfire."

Michelle inhaled and replied in a bored tone. "Chris drove me to my car at the truck yard. He took the smoker out to the country club."

"Why?"

"Because it's the country club's property."

"Where did you go?"

"Home."

"Anyone see you?"

"No. My kids were asleep."

"How old are they?"

"Sixteen and eighteen."

"And they were asleep at 1 a.m. on a Saturday night?"

"Their curfew is midnight."

"What time did Chris get home?"

"I don't know. I was asleep."

"Or do you not know because he sleeps in the front bedroom?"

One corner of her mouth quirked up. "I wondered if you noticed."

"I wouldn't be much of a detective if I didn't."

"True." With a mischievous grin she said, "Off the record: I'm not a good bed partner. I sleep like the dead but I steal all the covers, and I snore."

Jack mimed zipping his mouth. "Back on the record, did you see Chris yesterday morning?"

"No. He was gone by the time I woke up."

"You have no idea if he came home Saturday night?"

Michelle shook her head. "He might have spent the night at the club." Michelle sighed. "You're wasting my time, McBride."

"Kelly told Miner she saw Matt leave the neighborhood around 1 a.m. Did he come to the truck yard?"

The arm of the pool vacuum whipped up and sprayed water into the air. It resubmerged with a gurgle. Michelle crossed her arms and studied Jack. "If he did, I didn't see him. I was at home in bed at one. Remember?"

"Which no one can vouch for." Jack closed his notebook and stood. "Okay, Michelle. Thanks. As the case progresses, I may have some follow-up questions."

"I hope they're better than these were."

Jack smiled tightly at Michelle. "Oh by the way, we finally found Kyle Grant. Picked him up in Yourkeville selling smack. I didn't know y'all had branched out into heroin."

"Y'all? I don't know what you're talking about."

"Hmm," Jack said. "Well, regardless, you can take him off your legitimate business payroll."

"Thanks for the tip."

Jack stuck his hand out and smiled at Michelle. "I'll be in touch."

She stood and shook his hand with a vice-like grip. "For the next few days, I will be the point man for the family. Any questions you have should come through me."

"Funny, that's exactly what Norman Davie told me this morning."

Michelle laughed and released Jack's hand. "Sure. Call Davie first. Make him feel important."

"One more thing: do you own a gun?"

"A gun?" She laughed. "No. I hate guns. When we had kids, I made Chris get rid of his."

"What kind did he have?"

"I don't know. Hunting rifles, I think. I can't tell one from the other and sure as hell don't want to touch one."

"Well, thanks again. The funeral is Wednesday?"

"Yes. Four o'clock. First Methodist."

Jack nodded. "I'll see myself out."

Jack walked into the house. He shook a few hands and answered all questions about the case vaguely while keeping one eye on Michelle, who remained out by the pool. She was on her phone. Though her back was turned to the window, Jack could tell by the tension in her shoulders and the way she punched the air with her finger, his lie about Grant had shaken the tree. Now, to see what fell out.

CHAPTER THIRTY-ONE

Miner stood in front of the rolling white board set up in Jack's office and stared at the timeline he'd made. He tapped his lips with the Expo marker. Only three of the eleven people at the bonfire had airtight alibis—Jack, Julie, and Susan. Miner had talked to Kelly's son, Seth, and confirmed Kelly walked in the door about 12:45, took the dog out, and was in her room by 1 a.m. Seth didn't see her until morning, but considering Kelly had no motive to kill Matt or Amy, Miner considered her crossed off the list.

Ellie had no motive to kill Matt and Amy, but she was lying for Eddie McBride. The question was, why? They weren't lovers, or Ellie would have been upset at the mention of Eddie and Michelle in the woods at the bonfire. Plus, she made a point to say he slept on the couch. They were friends, but was a six-week friendship enough for Ellie Yourke Martin, a woman known for honesty, to lie for an ex-felon who Miner was sure was up to his eyeballs in no good? Miner didn't think so.

If Eddie wasn't with Ellie, who was he with? Michelle? Possibly. 'Course, they'd had sex not two hours prior to the beginning of Eddie's time gap. Surely they hadn't met for an encore. Miner shook his head. Men liked to talk and brag about going all night, multiple times, but the reality was those men were the exception, especially when you got into your forties like Eddie. But he sure seemed like the type whose bragging might actually be more fact than fiction.

Miner looked at his watch. Jack would be here any minute to fill in information on Michelle and Chris. Starling was down the hall, typing up his notes from interviewing Eric Sterry in Tyler and the workers at Doyle Organics. Miner's eyes kept sliding to Brian Grant and the huge gap in his timeline. He had motive, opportunity, a recently fired 9 mm, and a family history that made him the prime suspect. The problem was, Miner didn't believe Brian Grant was a killer. He'd been involved in fights in the past, but never with a weapon. Not even a baseball bat. It's a big leap from fistfights when drunk to killing two people in cold blood over a handshake contract. Brian might be a lot of things, but he wasn't stupid. With Matt alive, he still had the possibility of a job. With Matt dead, he was the prime suspect.

"Miner." Jack walked in, taking his coat off as he went. He draped it over the back of his chair and rolled up his sleeves. "Looks good," he said about the whiteboard. "Michelle says she got home at 1 a.m. And didn't leave. Kids were asleep and she didn't see Chris." Jack studied the whiteboard. "Nice timeline."

"Thanks. Tammy Cole called. Taylor and Andy Ryan were busted at Cheyney's Field at 1:30 a.m. Said she didn't let them go till two-thirty. Gave them a warning, so my guess is Michelle doesn't know."

"I'll talk to the kids tomorrow. See if they can pinpoint when their mother got home."

Miner noted it on the whiteboard. "And Chris?"

"I didn't have a chance to talk to him. He dropped Michelle off at the truck yard to get her car. She went home, he took the smoker to the country club. They sleep in separate bedrooms so she didn't see him come in."

"Or hear him."

"Says he might have slept at the country club."

"Hmm."

Jack waved his finger at Ellie and Eddie's timelines. "What's this?"

"Well, Ellie and Eddie say they were together Saturday night, Sunday morning."

"All night?"

"Yep. He didn't come home?"

"No."

"That normal?"

Jack jingled the keys and change in his pockets, brow furrowed. "Honestly, I'm not sure. I've spent most nights in Yourkeville, reading Pollard's journals."

"You weren't worried when he didn't come home?"

"No." Jack stepped forward and pointed at Eddie and Ellie's timelines. "Why the question marks? You don't believe them?"

"Nope. Ellie said they were at her apartment over the store. Eddie said they were at the lake house."

"Ellie's covering for him."

Miner nodded.

"Are you looking at my brother for this?" Jack said.

Starling barreled into the office. "Got my notes typed up." He dropped them on the conference table and caught sight of the timeline. He whistled. "Nice work, Miner."

"Tell us about Eric Sterry," Jack said.

"It was a waste of my afternoon, going down to Tyler. Eric Sterry is in the hospital. Fell off a ladder Saturday afternoon, compound fracture in his lower leg. He had steel rods put into his leg Sunday morning. He's still hopped up on drugs. I talked to his wife. She hadn't heard about Matt and Amy. Hadn't read the Tyler paper, I guess. She confirmed Matt stole some clients from Sterry. Big ones, like they said. But she said Eric never took it personally. Apparently, the organic produce trade is dog eat dog."

"Who knew?" Jack mumbled.

"I know, right? Anyway. I talked to some of the workers at Sterry's company. Matt was well-liked. Not so much as a complaint about him. Total dead end."

"Damn," Miner said.

Starling studied the timeline for a moment and tapped on Michelle's name. "That's a lie."

"What?" Miner said.

"Michelle's car was at Doyle Industries at 2 a.m."

"Are you sure?" Jack said.

Starling nodded. "I was coming home from," he paused and blushed, "visiting a friend."

"You sure of the time?" Miner asked.

"Yes." Starling was so red, Miner didn't have the heart to push him.

"Did you think it was odd her car was there in the middle of the night?"

"I've seen it there other times at night. Never thought much of it. Some people work late."

"At two o'clock in the morning?" Jack said.

Starling chewed his bottom lip. "You're right. I should have thought twice. It's just." His eyes darted to Miner and back to Jack. He inhaled and said, "I mentioned it once to Buck, the stuff that goes on out there at night. He told me not to worry. It was the nature of their business to get trucks in all times of the night."

Miner stared at the toes of his boots and waited for the question. When nothing happened he looked up. Jack stared at him. "It's one of the reasons I mentioned DI as the front," Miner said.

"The front for what?" Starling asked.

Malik breezed into the office. "Token Mexican woman reporting for duty."

Starling laughed and Miner grinned, despite himself.

Miner had been skeptical when Jack had hired a black man and a Hispanic woman for the force. He was worried he'd be walking around on eggshells, that Bishop and Malik would side-eye and judge his town on their old-fashioned ideals, but mainly he worried that he'd say something unintentionally offensive. So far he'd managed to keep his foot out of his mouth, but he knew he'd trip up eventually, as would the town. He'd spent more than a few hours alone with Jack Daniels in his barn, worrying over it. Stillwater wasn't good with meeting its flaws head on. Truth be told, neither was he.

"Not funny," Jack said, but Miner detected a repressed smile. "What'd you find out?"

"Nothing. Except all the Hispanics are taking note of how engaged you are with the rich white people murder versus the anonymous barbeque."

"We need an ID to investigate fully."

Malik raised her hand. "Preaching to the choir, Chief. I can tell you this much, none of the Mexicans think the Doyles' murder was connected to their community. Matt Doyle employed a lot of Mexicans around here and none of them had a bad word to say. Sounded like a fucking saint. Excuse my language."

"No one's a saint," Jack said. "Where's Bishop?"

"Called about twenty minutes ago on his way to a domestic," Miner said. "Said he's got no news. Sounds pretty similar to what Malik said. No one in the Bottom knows anything, and they're watching us closely."

"Great." Jack tapped Brian Grant's timeline. "No alibi after Susan slams her hand in the car?"

"No. Paige confirmed Brian wasn't home when they got back from the hospital at 4 a.m. She put Susan to bed and fell asleep. When she woke up at seven, Brian was in the kitchen, making pancakes."

"Okay," Jack said. "Good job, everyone. Go home and get some rest. Except you, Malik. Get to work."

Malik executed a mock salute. "The mean streets await."

"Night, Chief," Starling said with a yawn.

"Miner, before you go. Did you get a Sunday alibi for Eddie?"

"He gave me a name and number but I haven't called it yet."

Jack put his jacket on. "Leave it on the desk. I'll call it in the morning."

Miner narrowed his eyes and pursed his lips. Jack was skating close to unethical behavior.

"Feel free to call it, too. Night," Jack said and left the office.

Miner furrowed his brow. Didn't make much sense, but okay. He copied the name and number down and left it on Jack's desk.

CHAPTER THIRTY-TWO

"Something smells good."

Ethan stopped typing on his phone and looked up. "Hey, Dad. You're home."

Jack draped his suit coat over the back of a kitchen chair and tossed his keys on the table. "And just in time, it smells like."

Julie stood at the stove, a wooden spoon in her hand and a slow smile spreading across her face. She seemed genuinely happy to see him. Jack went to her and gave her a brief kiss. "What's for dinner?"

"Turkey meatloaf," Ethan said. Julie didn't see Ethan fake gag for Jack's benefit. Jack shook his head at Ethan. They hated turkey meatloaf and Julie knew it.

"And cauliflower mashed potatoes," Julie added.

"Need any help?"

Julie paused before answering. "Sure. Grab the plates? Ethan get drinks for us, would you?"

Jack pulled three plates from the cabinet. "Is Eddie here?"

"No," Julie said. "I thought you might know where he is."

"No. I haven't seen him since Saturday night."

"Oh, he was here this morning," Julie said, her voice falsely bright.

"You two still fighting?" Jack teased.

Julie laughed, but it sounded forced.

"How was your day, Ethan?"

Ethan stared at his mother's back, his mouth curled in disgust.

"Ethan?"

Ethan shifted his focus to his father. "Fine."

"Any tests?"

"No."

"Any papers?"

"No."

"What book are you reading in English?"

"*To Kill a Mockingbird.*"

Jack leaned against the counter and crossed his feet and arms. "In eighth grade?"

"Face it, Dad. Kids nowadays are smarter than you were."

"Maybe, but I'll always be smarter than you."

"We'll see," Ethan said. He placed three glasses of water on the table, sat down, and stared at his phone again.

Jack forced himself to meet Julie's gaze with a smile. "How was your day?"

"You know. Normal stuff. Made some progress on my book."

"Did you?" From the corner of his eye, Jack saw Ethan look up. "How far along are you?"

"What book?" Ethan asked.

"Not far," Julie answered Jack. "But it's pretty fast going. Since it's based on my blog posts . . ."

"You had a blog?" Ethan said.

Julie turned. "Yes, honey. I told you that."

"No, you didn't. You didn't tell me about a book, either."

It was the first Jack heard of the blog, too. He tried to mask the tension coiling inside him. No telling what she posted on her blog for the world to see. If there even was a blog. It was difficult to tell Julie's lies from the truth these days.

"What's the name of it?" Ethan asked, fingers poised on his phone.

"Oh, I've archived all of it on my agent's advice. We don't want the posts up there for people to read for free."

"Smart," Jack said. Ethan looked at Jack like he'd lost his mind.

"What's your book about?" Ethan said.

"Oh, you know. My sabbatical."

"Is that what we're calling it?" Ethan said.

"That's what it was."

Ethan gaped at Jack with an unmistakable "what the fuck" expression. Jack shook his head, slightly, in warning.

Ethan narrowed his eyes at his mother's back. "Don't forget to put in there how you left on my birthday."

Julie dished up meatloaf, fake mashed potatoes, and salad onto a plate and handed it to Ethan with a false smile. "I also came back on your birthday, or have you conveniently forgotten that little fact?"

"No. I haven't forgotten anything."

Julie stopped, stared at Ethan, who was looking at his phone, before dishing up her own dinner. She sat and they ate in silence for a minute. "This is good," Jack said.

Ethan put his phone down. "So, Troy and Olivia think Ellie—Ms. Martin—has a good chance to win tomorrow."

Julie raised an eyebrow. "I hear she's going to get crushed."

"What do you think, Dad?"

Jack shrugged. "I can't vote."

"But you want Ms. Martin to win, right?"

Jack furrowed his brows at his son. Where in the world was this coming from?

"I mean, she's young and pretty cool," Ethan said. "Olivia says she runs marathons and half-marathons every month. She's got a drawer full of medals. And she owns practically all of downtown."

Julie scoffed. "No wonder she wants to pull business back to the square. She's not as altruistic as she pretends."

"She's got better ideas for the town than that old goat Doyle," Ethan said.

"Since when do you care about what happens in Stillwater?" Julie said.

"Since I live here."

"If Joe Doyle wins, we won't live here for long."

Ethan picked up his phone and slumped down in his chair. "Speak for yourself," he mumbled.

"Get off your phone," Julie said.

Ethan put it down with a snap. "Troy's not replying anyway. I'm supposed to go over there after dinner to study."

"No, you're not," Julie said.

"Yes, I am."

"First off, it's too late. Second, I told you you aren't allowed to go to their house."

"Since when are you against studying? Was that one of your sabbatical revelations?" Ethan sneered the last two words. "Too bad you didn't have the realization your cooking sucks."

"Ethan!" Jack said.

"What? You hate this shit, too."

"Enough." Jack's tone of voice shut Ethan up. Ethan stared sullenly at his plate.

Julie put her fork down and wiped the corners of her mouth with her napkin. She folded it, placed it next to her plate, and stood. "And you wonder why I left?" She walked out of the kitchen.

"Did you leave or was it a sabbatical?" Ethan called. "Keep your story straight!"

Jack waited for the bedroom door to slam, but it didn't. Julie's calmness was more disconcerting than a fit would have been.

"Ethan, what the hell's gotten into you?"

"I wish I'd never emailed her," Ethan mumbled.

Every muscle in Jack's body froze, as if paralyzed. He tried to speak, but his mouth was dry. "What?" he managed to say.

Ethan pressed his fork into his fake mashed potatoes and wouldn't look at Jack.

"When did you email your mother?"

"After I caught you and Ms. Martin."

Jack swallowed with difficulty. "Did you tell her . . . what you saw?"

Ethan looked up. "No."

"When she came back?"

Ethan shook his head. Jack sighed with relief. "Good." His muscles relaxed. "Please don't, okay? It will complicate things."

"I'm sorry."

"For what?"

"Bringing her back. We were better off without her."

"What happened?"

"What do you mean?"

"Well, Saturday you act like you want our marriage to work and today you're being cruel and deliberately baiting her. Do you *want* her to leave again?"

Ethan sat back and crossed his arms.

"What is it? What's changed?"

"Do you agree about me not hanging out with Olivia and Troy? She wouldn't even talk about it."

"Is that it?"

"Isn't that enough? They're my best friends."

"Did she tell you why?"

"No. Parents never give reasons, just orders."

Jack pushed his plate away and stuffed his napkin under the plate. He leaned on his crossed arms. "I need to ask you some questions. Man to man."

"Okay."

"When you've been over at the Grants, have you ever seen anything that makes you uncomfortable?"

Ethan shifted in his chair. "Like what?"

"I'd rather you tell me."

Ethan shrugged. "Mr. Grant's pretty strict."

"With Troy and Olivia?"

"And Mrs. Grant. He's like the dad in one of those old movies. Comes home, sits down, and drinks a beer while everyone else tiptoes around him."

"Were you awake when they came home Saturday night?"

"Yeah."

"Tell me."

"Troy and I were playing video games in the family room. Olivia was in there, too, reading a book, or acting like she was. She kept making comments about our game. I don't know where Paige was."

"She was there?"

"Yeah. Babysitting." Ethan put a derisive emphasis on the last word. "I didn't hear the car pull up but I heard the yelling when they got out."

"Hear what they said?"

"No. It was Mr. Grant yelling. Mrs. Grant was quieter. Troy and Olivia sat there, hearing it too but trying to act like they didn't, or like it was totally normal. Then, we heard her scream."

"Mrs. Grant."

"Yeah. Paige comes running through the house and out the front door. Then she starts yelling. Troy gets up, turns off the PS3, and tells me to come on. I follow him back to his room. Olivia goes to her room, and we close the doors."

Ethan shifts in his chair again and clears his throat. "Troy doesn't say a word, just pulls his sleeping bag and an extra pillow out of his closet, puts it on the floor and gets in. He tells me to get the light. I do and lay down on his bed. I can't hear much—his room is at the back of the house—but I hear the car rev up and tear out of the driveway. Then another one. I assumed Paige left."

"Did Troy ever say anything?"

"Not a word. The next morning, Mr. Grant makes us breakfast and drops us off at church. He said Mrs. Grant was in bed and not to disturb her."

"Did he say what happened?"

"Said she accidentally shut her hand in the car door."

"What did Troy and Olivia say?"

"Nothing. We ate our breakfast." Ethan swallowed and looked at Jack with a stricken expression. "He hurt Mrs. Grant, didn't he?"

"What makes you say that?"

"When Troy and I got into that fight at school, Troy was weird about the whole thing. Begging his mom to believe he didn't intentionally hit anyone. You should have seen the expression on her face."

Jack nodded. He rubbed his neck and gathered his thoughts.

"Did you ever see Mr. Grant? After they came home?"

"No. Just Sunday morning."

"Did you hear Paige and Mrs. Grant come home?"

Ethan shifted in his seat. "Yeah."

"What time was it?"

Ethan shrugged. "I wasn't looking at the clock."

"What were you doing?"

Ethan shifted again and wouldn't meet Jack's eyes. Oh, Jesus.

"Were you with Olivia?'

Ethan nodded.

"Where?" *Please don't say in her bedroom, please don't say in her bedroom.*

"In the living room." Ethan glanced up at Jack and his eyes went wide. "Nothing like that, Dad! We were just kissing."

Jack thought back to what he would have tried to do alone in a house with a girl at fourteen years old and doubted it was only kissing.

"Okay, that's a conversation we'll have to have another time. For now, I think you should have them come here to hang out. Just for a while. And only when adults are here."

"So, you agree with *her*. You don't think I should be over there."

"Ethan, it's complicated. Right now, the best thing is they come over here, okay?"

"I texted Troy they should come over here tonight, and he hasn't responded. He always responds."

"Are you worried something's happened to him?"

"No."

Jack sighed. "His dad probably won't let them come over."

"Why?"

"We questioned him today about a case."

"What case? The double murder?"

"Ethan, I can't say."

"Like I won't find out."

"You won't find out from me."

"Great. My only friends are going to hate me because of my cop dad. Perfect." He pushed away from the table, stormed up the stairs, and slammed the door.

Jack sighed and rolled his eyes. He cleared the table and cleaned up the kitchen while his family pouted. He hated that Ethan was exposed to what seemed to be domestic abuse, but he hated even more that Troy and Olivia were growing up in the environment.

Up to his forearms in soapy water, Jack washed the dishes by rote, thinking of his father. A burly staff sergeant who wasn't afraid to use his booming voice to intimidate and abuse his wife and young sons. To Jack's knowledge, Sean McBride never used fists on his wife, but Jack didn't know what went on behind their bedroom door. He and Eddie cowered in bed, under the covers with a flashlight, reading Hardy Boys mysteries to each other to drown out the arguing. Jack knew with certainty, though, the relief that washed through their family when the news came Staff Sergeant McBride had lost his life in the Beirut embassy bombing. Life became harder in many ways but much happier in others.

Jack finished the dishes and put the leftovers in the fridge. He leaned against the counter and pulled his phone out of his pocket. His hand hovered over Ellie's number. The urge to call her and talk about what he'd learned, get her opinion of Brian and his potential for violence was almost impossible to resist. Any reason to hear her voice, though he suspected she would defend her friend's husband and be offended at the idea Brian Grant might have killed Matt and Amy. If Jack was honest, he thought it was improbable as well. Men like Brian Grant were more likely to kill a family member in a moment of rage than to methodically kill an enemy.

Still, Brian Grant was the only suspect with motive and opportunity, which made him the best suspect Jack had.

Eddie grabbed a beer from the refrigerator and walked into the living room. Jack sat on the couch in the dark, feet up on the coffee table, resting a beer on his thigh.

"Hey. Who's winning?" Eddie plopped down onto the other end of the couch, kicked off his boots, and put his feet up.

"Saints."

Eddie drank half of his beer in three gulps and sighed. "Damn, that tastes good."

"Where've you been?"

"Working. Thank God Matt was so organized or I'd be fucked tomorrow."

"You aren't making the run to Houston?"

"Michelle hasn't mentioned it. You didn't want to raid it tomorrow night, did you?"

Jack shook his head. "You need to work there a little longer or they'll figure you're working for us."

"Yeah. I figured. How's the investigation going?"

"Fine. Where were you on Sunday?"

"Went to Dallas to see a friend."

"Don't lie to me, Eddie."

"I'm not lying."

Jack turned to him. "You stayed at Ellie's Saturday night?"

"Miner told you?"

"He thinks you're lying. Are you?"

"Yes. I was with Michelle. She had a shipment come in."

"How long were you there?"

"I left about 2 a.m. I don't know when she left."

"Where'd you go?"

"Dallas, like I said."

"For Michelle?"

"No. Personal business. I gave Miner the number. He can call and check up on me. Better yet, you should call."

"I'm going to tomorrow."

"Good, maybe then you'll trust me."

"Why should I trust you when you're still lying to me? And you're getting Ellie to lie for you?"

Eddie sighed. "I didn't want to do it, but I need everything I can get to make sure Michelle trusts me."

"Having Ellie lie for you makes Michelle trust you?"

"Jesus, yes. You don't know how much Michelle hates Ellie."

"Why?"

"Hell if I know."

They watched the game in silence until Brees threw a fifty-yard touchdown pass. "Damn," Eddie said. "That dude is awesome."

"I had him on my fantasy team one year. Won five hundred bucks."

"My brother, gambling?"

"Shut up and get me another beer, will you?"

Eddie got two more Shiners and returned to the couch. "So, you're bluffing Michelle with Kyle Grant."

Jack's head jerked around. "How do you know that?"

"She called me."

"How do you know I'm bluffing?"

"'Cause I dropped Kyle Grant in Dallas Sunday morning."

"What? You know I've been looking for him."

"I know, and you'll get him. But you can't get him from me, now can you?"

"What did Michelle say?"

"Lots of profanity. I told her to play it cool. If you talk to her tomorrow, tell me how she does."

Jack's expression was curious. "You like her."

"I respect her. Grudgingly. She's got a chip on her shoulder the size of Gibraltar."

"What about?"

"Daddy issues, no doubt. Matt was the golden child."

"Think she hated Matt enough to kill him?"

Eddie sat up. "Seriously?"

Jack nodded.

"No way."

Jack's mouth quirked up. "That was a fast denial."

"Michelle'd much rather ruin your life and watch you suffer than kill you."

"And you like this woman?"

"I said it was against my better judgment."

"You aren't going soft on me, are you?"

"No. But I don't think Michelle killed Matt."

"Huh." Jack turned back to the game. "I think Norman Davie did it."

Eddie laughed. "What?"

Jack shrugged and drank his beer. "If this case were a novel, he'd be the killer for sure. It's always the most innocuous person. They come on stage for a few pages, do enough to be noticed but not so much to raise suspicion, then they're forgotten."

"Have you run him?"

"Yeah. He's clean. Dammit."

They drank in silence. "Where's the fam?" Eddie asked.

"Upstairs."

"Did you go through with it Saturday night?"

Jack nodded.

"And you're avoiding her now."

Jack picked at the label on his beer and didn't answer.

"Or, you did your husbandly duty and are now sitting down here, feeling guilty you're cheating on your girlfriend. Guess you're not as white bread as I've always thought."

"Fuck you."

Eddie stood and stretched. "Well, I'm beat. This working for a living shit takes it outta you."

Jack stared up at his brother. "I want to know why Ellie would lie for you."

"I promised to get her what she wants most in the world."

"What's that?"

"You."

CHAPTER THIRTY-THREE

Overnight the temperature had dropped twenty degrees, but if the forecast was correct, it would rise forty degrees over the course of the day. Ellie didn't mind running in the heat or the cold, but she wished the weather would make up its damn mind and stay one way for a while.

Ellie adjusted her gloves, pulled her toboggan down over her ears, and stepped out into the cold November morning. She jumped off the curb and ran down the middle of Main Street toward the light at Yourkeville Highway. She was running through her list of things to do for the day when she saw the small figure standing at the corner. Ellie's stomach turned when the woman looked up at her and smiled.

"Hi!" Julie waved and walked toward Ellie.

"Hey."

"I hope you don't mind. You said we could run together, but we never set a day or time so I thought I'd ambush you." Julie's disarming smile almost took Ellie in.

"I run six miles."

Julie's smile faltered, before returning. "That's fine."

Ellie opened her mouth to warn Julie about her pace, but changed her mind. She grinned and said, "Let's go."

They'd jogged about a hundred yards when Julie spoke. "Aren't you cold?"

"Nope." She always wore shorts, no matter the weather. The cold air on Ellie's legs was a welcome contrast to the warmth of her upper body. Plus, the colder her legs, the faster she ran.

"I hear you run every day."

"I do."

"Impressive. I suppose it's a challenge, keeping the weight off."

Ellie cut her eyes at Julie. Her face was calm, slightly red from the cold, but not in danger. She was keeping up rather well. "It's all about discipline."

"You're so right. I can't tell you how bad I'd like to eat a chicken fried steak and mashed potatoes. If I did, it would go right to my ass and thighs. It's not worth it. Try telling that to Jack and Ethan, though."

Ellie glanced at her watch. Two minutes and she'd already brought up Jack. This was going to suck.

"Did Kelly tell you about my weight loss?"

"No. Michelle."

"Ah."

"She also told me about your ex-husband. What a dick. Makes me realize how lucky I am."

"Did Michelle mention she was one of the ones fucking my husband?"

"Um . . ."

"And she was the one who told me about Jinx's infidelities? With great detail, I might add."

"No," Julie panted. "She seemed happy to hear about you and Eddie."

Ellie laughed. "I bet she was."

They ran to the stoplight at Boondoggle and Main and stopped. "You don't think she purposely . . ."

"Gave Eddie a blow job Saturday night? Yeah."

"That's awful."

"That's Michelle for you."

"You don't care?"

The light turned red and they crossed. "She can screw Eddie if she wants. We're just friends."

"I'm glad to hear it."

"Why?"

"He's not right for you. You're too buttoned-up for Eddie."

Ellie stopped abruptly and turned to Julie. She was gratified to see Julie's face turn red. "Why does that sound like an insult?"

"I don't mean it to. Eddie's always liked more gregarious women."

"Really? 'Cause it seems to me his primary consideration is how quickly and far apart a woman will spread her legs. How long did you know him before you spread yours?"

"Excuse me?"

"He told me. One night out at my lake house. We'd had too much to drink and he started talking. Told me all about the two of you. Don't worry." She patted Julie on the shoulder. "I'm good at keeping secrets."

Ellie took off running, this time at her normal pace, and tried to forget Julie was running with her. After a few dozen yards, it wasn't difficult. She'd left Julie in the dust. Ellie glanced over her shoulder to see how far back Julie was and was surprised to see her gaining. She was a determined little thing, Ellie gave her that. She slowed so Julie could catch up.

"Why don't you like me?" Julie asked, panting slightly.

"Why would you think that?"

Julie rolled her eyes. "I thought you, of all people, would understand. I expected us to be friends."

Ellie laughed. "Why?"

"You're single, independent, successful. You don't need a man to take care of you. You'd probably cut the balls off of a man who tried."

"It's always a compliment for a single woman to be called a man-hater."

"That's not what I mean." Julie put her hands on her hips. "I get it. I understand why people judge me for leaving last year. I mean, never mind that men do it all the time. Mothers aren't allowed to stand up for themselves when they're being mistreated."

"Mistreated? By Jack?"

"There are more ways to be mistreated than by being a bully like Brian Grant, and trust me, Jack is the master of many of them."

Ellie narrowed her eyes, questions dancing on the tip of her tongue. But it wouldn't do to be too interested in Jack and his supposed failings as a husband. "Are we going to run or not?"

Julie waved her hand like Vanna White. "Lead on."

They ran for a while in blessed silence, but Julie seemed to have an agenda with this run, and she spoke up. "Neglect is a form of abuse, you know."

Ellie sighed. God this woman was a narcissist. "He wasn't paying enough attention to you?"

"To either of us. He worked constantly, late at night, on the weekends."

"He was supporting his family."

"Wow. You, too. He was avoiding his family. But men are allowed to wrap their faults in a blanket of dedication to their career, which of course they're only dedicated to for the good of their family."

"Careful, Julie, your bitterness is showing. Why did you come back then?"

"I hoped Jack would have a new appreciation for the job I did for thirteen years."

"And does he?"

"It's hard to tell. He's never around. Regression to the mean in action."

Ellie stopped. "Excuse me?"

"Regression to the mean," Julie said, breathing heavy. "It means—"

"I know what it means," Ellie snapped.

Julie lifted her head and her mouth opened in a small "o." "Oh, so you're surprised *I* know what it means, is that it?" Julie smirked. "Well, at least you have the politeness to look ashamed. I graduated with honors from UT, for your information. Major in finance, minor in economics. You just assumed I was an airhead. Or did Jack tell you that?" She crossed her arms and appraised Ellie. "How close *are* you to my husband?"

Ellie skirted the question. "What do you mean, regression to the mean in action?"

"Jack didn't want his wife back; he wanted his nanny, housekeeper, and cook back."

"If it's so horrible being married to him, why not just divorce him?" Ellie said.

"For a few reasons, but honestly?" she leaned forward and kept her piercing eyes on Ellie's. "Every time I think, *it's over, I'm done,* Jack fucks me so well I forget all of his faults. I wouldn't have thought he'd be faithful to me for a full year; he wasn't before I left, why would he be when I was gone? But if his fucking is any indication, he hasn't been thoroughly laid in a year. Trust me, there's no other motivation not to take Ethan and leave this town."

Ellie didn't know if a sob or a laugh was working its way up her throat until she turned, bent over, and vomited. She kept her hands on her knees and her head down. She spit bile from her throat and took a deep breath. Julie placed a hand on her back. "Are you okay?"

Ellie stood and shifted away from Julie's touch. "I'm fine. Just a bug I can't shake."

Julie studied her with a good deal of suspicion. "You aren't pregnant, are you?"

Ellie stared at Julie. "I can't have children."

"I'm sorry. I didn't know."

"Don't take this the wrong way, but I'm used to running by myself. It gives me a chance to plan out my day. So, I'm going to go on. I have to be at the polls at seven."

"Yeah. Sure," Julie said. "Sorry if I slowed you down."

"It's fine. Can you find your way back home?"

Julie tilted her head to the side and, her voice dripping with sarcasm, said, "In a town with two red lights, I think I can manage."

For the first time in three years, Ellie cut her run short. She bounded up the stairs to her flat two at a time, rushed through the door, and was barely in the bathroom before she vomited again. When all that was left was dry heaving, she flushed the toilet, closed the lid, and collapsed back against the bathtub. She stared straight ahead, seeing the past instead of the present. She stood in front of Jack, removing the stitches over his eye while he admired her naked breasts. She closed her eyes and remembered how he took her into the bedroom and made love to her slowly, deliberately, tenderly. He had been insatiable that night, and the other two nights they had been together.

Three nights. That was all they had. Three nights.

The pregnancy test lay where she left it the night before, on the edge of the sink, next to the toilet, its double pink lines appearing ten years too late.

Six weeks of pent up emotion exploded from her, her sobs ricocheting off the walls like shrapnel. She clutched her stomach, lay down on the cold, tile floor, and gave in to a level of despair she hadn't allowed herself to feel for thirty years.

When Jack walked into the kitchen, Julie and Eddie were pointedly ignoring each other.

"Good morning," Jack said.

"Morning." Their replies were mumbled and out of synch.

Jack noted Julie's clothes and said, "You go running?"

"I did."

Jack poured his coffee. He held the mug out to Julie. "Want a cup?"

"Thanks."

"She went running with Ellie," Eddie said.

Jack was glad his back was to his wife. "How was it?" he asked, trying to lace his voice with boredom. "I hear she's fast." He turned and leaned against the counter.

"She's not that fast."

Jack hid his smile behind a sip of coffee. Julie's petulant voice told him she'd had a hard time keeping up with Ellie. No surprise since Ellie's legs were about five inches longer than Julie's. The memory of those long, toned legs wrapping around him flashed through his mind. Her mischievous eyes. Her crooked smile. Her throaty laugh.

Guilt stabbed at his chest. Fuck staying away until Julie signs the papers. He needed to see Ellie. Alone. Today.

"If nothing else, it confirms what I suspected. Ellie Martin does not like me."

"She hardly knows you," Jack said.

"Doesn't matter. She's jealous."

"Why would she be jealous of you?" Eddie asked.

"Women like her who don't have a husband or children are always jealous of those of us who do."

"That's a gross generalization," Jack said.

Julie shrugged.

"She isn't jealous of you—she doesn't understand how someone who has a loving husband and great kid would abandon them for a year," Eddie said.

Julie narrowed her eyes. "Did she tell you that during one of your wine-soaked nights together?"

"As a matter of fact, she did."

"I can only imagine all the deep, dark secrets you shared."

Jack's head was moving back and forth between his brother and his wife as though he were at a tennis match.

Eddie smirked. "A fair few."

"I can imagine what else came up during those nights."

"It was one night."

Jack tamped down his jealousy. Eddie'd assured him nothing was going on, that he and Ellie were friends. His phone buzzed. He fished it out of his pocket and saw Ann Newberry's number.

"That's all it takes."

Jack answered his phone and said, "Hang on, Ann." He placed the phone against his chest and said, "What are you talking about?"

"I didn't stop running with her because she was too fast. She got sick. Puked on the side of the road." Julie stood, coffee mug in hand, and glared at Eddie. "I'd bet my life she's pregnant. Congratulations, Eddie. You're going to be a father."

Eddie lay on the bed, his legs crossed at his ankles when Julie walked into the bedroom, hair wet and wearing only a towel. She paused, then went to the dresser.

"You're going to be late for work," she said. She opened a drawer, dropped her towel, and stepped into a thong.

"This is more important."

She made an indistinct noise in her throat. She put on her bra and walked to the closet.

"I never had sex with Ellie."

"Please, you have sex with anyone who'll let you."

"True. She wouldn't let me."

"What? Eddie McBride losing his touch?"

"Rumor is I'm too much like her ex-husband."

Julie looked over her shoulder. "Really?"

Eddie shrugged.

Julie turned back to the closet. "Well, she's fucking *somebody*."

"How are you so sure she's pregnant?"

"Women's intuition." Julie pulled a T-shirt over her head. "Plus, she's fine in the afternoon and evenings. It's not rocket science." She walked to the dresser, picked up a brush, and ran it through her hair.

"Come here."

Julie looked at him in the dresser mirror. "Are you still fucking Michelle Ryan?"

"Are you still fucking my brother?" She focused on her task and didn't answer. "No need to respond. These walls are paper thin, you know."

"Fuck you."

Eddie got up from the bed and moved next to Julie. "You getting a charge out of fucking both of us? Want to do us together? Jack might go for it. We did it once in college."

"Shut up."

"Before we met you, of course."

"I said shut up."

"I don't think Jack would go for it now, though. He's pretty big on monogamy."

Julie slammed the brush down and tried to turn away. Eddie grabbed her by the arms. "You have to choose. Me or him."

Julie laughed. "Then what? You abandon your tomcatting and settle down with me?"

"Tomcatting?"

"Can you think of a better word?"

"No."

Julie looked at Eddie's hands on her arms. "You're hurting me." He released her, but stayed close. Her voice softened and she lost a bit of her combativeness. "Eddie, I've watched you screw up your life for twenty years. Why would I choose you over the stability I have with Jack?"

"Have you forgotten what you said to me yesterday?"

She shook her head.

"Say it again," he said.

"No."

" 'You were always the one I wanted.' Have you changed your mind in the last twenty-four hours?"

"It's going to take more than a quickie in the shower to make me give up my life."

"Bullshit. You gave it up last year for less."

"Yes, well last year my father bankrolled me. He won't bankroll you."

"Did you come back because your daddy cut you off?"

"Please. My dad wouldn't cut me off if I were a serial killer."

"Then why?"

Julie cleared her throat. "I missed my family."

"Ha! Try again."

"Why is that so hard to believe?"

"Because I know you, Jules."

Julie pursed her lips and narrowed her eyes. "Ethan emailed me and told me about Jack's plan to divorce me. I divorce him. He doesn't divorce me."

Eddie stepped back. "You couldn't stand the idea Jack and Ethan were getting on with their lives, could you? As long as you thought they were waiting for you, pining for you, you had no qualms about staying away."

"Come on, Eddie. You aren't the committing type. Why can't we enjoy each other occasionally?"

"I won't do that to my brother."

"You've already done it once."

"And if I tell him about it, he'll use it as grounds for divorce."

Julie's face tightened. "You wouldn't."

"Yes, I would. And I'd testify against you for custody. Wouldn't be a very good ending for your book, would it? Or is the whole book thing bullshit, like everything you do?"

"It's my word against yours. No one's going to believe you."

"Yeah they will, and you know it. With my reputation and yours, they'll be more shocked we haven't carried on for your entire marriage."

She lunged forward, hand pulled back to slap him. Eddie caught her wrist. He pulled his phone out of his pocket and revealed the open voice memo app. "Say hi to the mic, Jules."

"You son of a bitch. Get out."

"Gladly." He turned off the voice memo. "You're going to give Jack the divorce he wants and you aren't going to contest full custody."

"Like hell I am."

"And you're going to leave Stillwater."

Eddie's phone buzzed with a text from Michelle:

Where are you? You're late for your run.

Eddie suddenly felt bone tired. He was ready for this to be done. All of it. He wanted to be alone and away from all the crazy fucking women in his life.

He pocketed his phone.

"Which girlfriend was that from?" Julie said.

Eddie put his finger in Julie's face. "Don't fuck with me, Julie. Give Jack his divorce and get the hell out of Stillwater."

"Or what?"

"Or I tell Ethan we've been sleeping together for your entire marriage."

"You wouldn't ruin your relationship with Ethan like that."

"Maybe, maybe not. Trust me. You don't want to take the chance."

CHAPTER THIRTY-FOUR

Jack stood on the sidewalk across from the street from the Yourke County Courthouse and absently stared into the shop window at a uniformed mannequin.

Congratulations, Eddie. You're going to be a father.

Jack almost dropped his phone when Julie said it. Pregnant? He'd looked at his brother, panic clutching his chest, and was slightly relieved to see as much shock on Eddie's face as Jack felt.

"Take your call." Eddie had motioned to the forgotten phone Jack clutched to his chest.

"Ann." Jack's voice was a croak.

"Simon wants to see us ten minutes ago. Can you get down here?"

"Yeah. I'm on my way."

Eddie clutched Jack's shoulder. "Consider the source here, bro. There's no way Julie knows for sure." He dropped his voice to a whisper. "Could she be?"

Jack thought back over the last few days, Ellie's behavior, the bug she couldn't shake, her weight loss, not drinking at the bonfire. Calculating days to weeks. But, they'd been careful, used condoms every time.

Jack's eyes widened. Except the first.

"Christ. Maybe."

"I'll take care of Julie. You go do what you need to do. Hey." Eddie snapped his fingers in front of Jack's face. "Are you okay to drive?"

"I have to see her."

"I know. I'll arrange it."

"Tonight."

"I know, bro. I'll text you the where and when later today. You go solve Matt and Amy's murder."

Ann Newberry patted Jack's shoulder, jolting him out of his trance.

"Taking the plunge?"

"What?"

Her brow furrowed in concern. "Do you feel bad? You're pale and sweaty. And you sounded strange on the phone."

Jack swallowed down the lump in his throat and forced a smile. "Bad eggs."

She didn't buy it. "Uh-huh. Come on, then. Simon's bursting with news."

"Know what about?"

"He wouldn't tell me. Wanted to tell us together." They walked across the street and down the sidewalk. "He's about the only person in the county who's happy with all the crime going on. My guess is he's ID'd our fire victims."

They stopped in front of a windowless metal building two streets behind the square. Ann pressed the buzzer and looked up at the security camera. The door buzzed, and she opened it for Jack. Simon stood in a doorway halfway down the hall, motioning for Jack and Ann to hurry up. "Lots of things to cover," he said, not even attempting to control his excitement. Once inside, Jack spotted a 9 mm in a bag lying next to the microscope. Jack thought he recognized the handwriting.

"Did Miner drop it off?"

Simon glanced at the gun and dismissed it. "Yeah. Yesterday afternoon."

"Is it for the Doyle case?"

Simon huffed in irritation. "If you'll be patient, I'll get to it. First, the fire victims. They've ID'd one of them. Paco Morales, like you suspected. Dental records confirmed it. There was nothing identifying on the other man. So, he's still a John Doe."

Simon swiveled his stool and rolled to a table holding a microscope. "But when we swept the area for trace evidence, I found this." He held up a baggie containing a charred metal circle. He turned the baggie around to show the clasp on the other side.

"It's a pin," Ann said.

"A campaign pin."

Excitement coursed through Jack's body. *This was it. The piece of evidence that would unlock it. Don't jump to conclusions. Listen. Think.*

"Like this one." Simon held up a red, white, and blue VOTE FOR JOE pin and held it next to the charred one. Their sizes matched perfectly.

"I'll be damned."

"Sorry to burst your bubble, boys, but there are hundreds of those pins in Stillwater," Ann said. "Was it found on either body?"

"No. In the area."

"The killer might have dropped it," Jack said.

"Or a random flopper dropped it emptying out their pockets while searching for a lighter to get high. They've been handing those things out like candy canes at Christmas. It's thin, and you know it."

"You're right." Simon adjusted his microscope and said, "Look."

Ann let Jack go first. He leaned in. The underside of the pin contained a clearly defined partial print. Jack stepped back.

"Whose print is it?"

"Michelle Doyle Ryan's."

"How are her prints in the system?" Jack said.

"She was busted in college for vandalism. The charges were dropped but not before she was processed," Simon said.

Ann raised an eyebrow, but her response, if she had one, was cut off by Simon. "That's not the most interesting thing I have for you."

He opened a manila file folder and pulled out three sheets of paper. "Now, don't go expecting this kind of turnaround in the future, but I had a hunch." His laugh sounded like a goose honking. On one sheet, two bullets with identical markings were pictured. "The fire victims." He put down another sheet with two bullet markings. "The Doyles." The final sheet was from the Bureau with a picture of a single bullet's rifling markings. Jack didn't need to see the name at the top of the page to guess whose it was.

"Son of a bitch," Ann said.

Jack grinned and nodded. Finally, a direct connection between the Pedrozas and fucking Joe Doyle. "They were all shot with my gun."

CHAPTER THIRTY-FIVE

Five miles south of Stillwater, a white plantation-style house sat on the western bank of the Cypress River. A crushed gravel drive lined with cypress trees veered off into a sparsely filled parking lot before circling under a porte-cochère and back toward the highway and past the sign marking this as CYPRESS COUNTRY CLUB, EST. 1954.

Jack walked up the AstroTurf-lined stairs and shook his head at the sight of the two black lawn jockeys guarding the front door of the clubhouse. A fat man with the ruddy complexion and wide nose of an alcoholic held the door for Jack, sloshing pale yellow orange juice out over his hand.

Inside, the clubhouse smelled of stale beer, cigar smoke, old grease, and sweat. Jack followed the sign to the golf shop down a hall to his left, past a bar with men playing cards while the Golf Channel played low on the television behind them. The smile the golf pro had on his face when he looked up from his paperwork dropped when he saw Jack's badge.

"Can I help you?" The man's country drawl was clipped and hostile.

"I'm looking for Chris Ryan. He here?"

The man paused as if debating how much he should stall, or if he should stall at all.

"He's out on the course."

"When will he be done?"

"His teed off at 7 a.m. He's probably about to make the turn."

"He come back here for the turn?"

"Yes."

"I'll wait."

Jack wandered around the pro shop, stopping to hold up a navy blue golf shirt with the Cypress Country Club logo on it. Khaki pants, Foot Joy golf shoes, straw hats, and conservative ball caps were the sum total of fashion offerings. The golf pro kept peeking at Jack, as though wanting to say something. More likely he wanted to be interviewed so he would have an interesting story to tell his buddies over beers.

"You know Matt and Amy?" Jack ventured.

"A little."

"They members out here?"

"Sure. All the Doyles are."

"Matt play golf?"

"Not much. He would occasionally come out with Chris."

"They get along?"

"As far as I could tell."

Jack leaned against the counter and picked up a VOTE FOR JOE button from the box on the counter. "Can I have this?"

"Take the box. I'll have to trash them tomorrow."

"Thanks." Jack made a show of pinning the button to his coat. "Is there a bathroom . . . ?"

"Yeah, locker room is down the hall on the right."

"Thanks."

Jack went down the hall, peeked into the locker room, and kept going. The next door was a cleaning closet, but the next one was what he was looking for. He opened the door to Chris's office and flipped on the light. A desk was wedged into a space only marginally bigger than the cleaning closet next door. A filing cabinet, a number of single golf clubs in various states of repair, and a couple of folded metal chairs took up the back wall.

A dusty Dell desktop sat on the corner of the desk, looking like it hadn't been used in five years. No sofa. Jack flipped off the light and went back into the hall.

He walked back to the nineteenth hole slowly, taking in the pictures and plaques on the walls. One name dominated the Club Championship plaques from the mid-1980s to the early 2000s. Jack stopped in front of a fairly recent picture of Joe Doyle, Chris, Matt, and an older man Jack didn't recognize.

"That's Big Jake." Chris stood in the doorway of the nineteenth hole, holding a cup filled with tomato juice. "Red beer," Chris explained. "Want one?"

"No. Should I know who Big Jake is?"

"Jacob Yourke? Ellie's dad."

Jack nodded and turned his attention back to the man in the picture. He was big all right. He towered over Joe, Chris, and Matt. A large nose anchored a face covered in broken blood vessels. A cigar was stuck in the corner of his mouth but couldn't hide his smirk of self-satisfaction. Jack saw where Ellie got her height but nothing else about this man reminded him of her.

"He spend a lot of time out here?"

"He called it his office."

"I suppose, for a gambler like him, a country club is a good place to spend your time."

Chris sipped his drink and stared at Jack over the rim. "What can I do for you, Jack?"

"I'm here to talk about Matt and Amy."

"You are?"

"Why are you surprised?"

"I assumed y'all weren't interested in what I had to say since you didn't come see me yesterday."

"Lots of interviews to get through."

"And I'm at the bottom of the list. Come on. Ride a few holes with me."

Chris didn't wait for Jack to answer. He was out of the bar, through the door, and outside in five long strides, in his golf cart in ten. Jack sat in the passenger side.

Chris punched the gas pedal and the golf cart jumped to life. Jack grabbed the roof of the cart with his free hand. "You play golf?" Chris asked.

"Some."

"You should come play with me. Five a hole, usually, but I can go richer or poorer, whatever you want."

"Probably shouldn't be gambling, as chief of police."

"I won't tell."

Chris was out of the cart before it completely stopped at the tenth tee. He pulled a driver out of his bag, teed his ball up, took two practice swings, and hit the ball straight down the middle of the fairway.

"Nice shot," Jack said.

Chris put a stuffed bear head cover over his driver and shoved the club into his bag. "Thanks." He punched the gas and the golf cart lurched again. "What do you want to know?"

"Why are you playing golf when your brother and sister-in-law have barely been dead forty-eight hours?"

Chris checked the GPS for distance and stopped the cart by his ball. "Two-oh-five. Slight headwind. Looks like a four to me."

Jack waited while he hit a solid shot. It landed on the left edge of the green with a right pin placement.

They drove to the green.

"I guess it does seem cold, me golfing after my family's been murdered. It isn't because I didn't like Matt and Amy or because I'm not sad. They were the only two people in this whole damn family with a bit of decency."

Chris got his putter, two putted for birdie, and returned. He drove the cart to the eleventh tee, stopped at the tenth tee box, and picked up his cup. He sat back and stared at the river to their left.

"Peaceful, isn't it?" Chris said.

"It is."

"Nothing like what's going on at Joe's house."

"No."

"Or mine, I imagine." Chris spread his hands as if it explained everything. "There's nothing I could do there. They've got all the bases covered."

"What do you mean?"

"My father-in-law is all blustery and indignant, threatening for heads to roll if the murder isn't solved yesterday. My mother-in-law's sedated. My wife is methodically taking care of everything but letting her father take the credit. There's nothing for me to do."

"Be a comfort to your family."

He scoffed. "Mary is the only one who needs comfort, and she's got Prozac for that. She'll probably be drugged up for a year. She is most of the time as it is."

"What about Matt and Amy's children?"

"Being taken care of by Amy's mom, no doubt. She'll probably push for custody, which will be granted because Mary can't take care of them and Michelle won't want them. Joe will probably put up a fight because it's expected, but he doesn't want the hassle, either."

"You aren't painting your family in a very rosy light."

"It's not a rosy family. I have no doubt Michelle and Joe are livid. But grieving? Not in the typical way."

For all of Chris's distance and apparent disinterest, he saw right through his family.

"You have any theories on who did it?"

"No."

"I don't believe you."

Chris Ryan put his arm across the back of the seat and turned toward Jack. "Who do you think did it?"

Jack smiled. "Norman Davie."

Chris's eyes bulged and he guffawed. "Davie? You're shitting me, right?"

"Yes. He has a rock-solid alibi. About the only one close to Matt who does."

Chris tossed his empty cup in the trash and pulled out his three iron. After he made the shot—straight down the fairway, again—Jack said, "Tell me about Saturday night, Sunday morning after the bonfire."

"Michelle and I left together. I dropped her at her car and brought the smoker out here."

"What time did you get home?"

"I don't remember. Late. After two, probably."

"Where were your kids?"

"Home. In bed. I checked on them before turning in."

"Asleep?"

"Yes. Or pretending to be. You know teenagers."

"And Michelle? Was she home when you got there?"

"I don't know. We don't share a bedroom. She snores like a locomotive."

"When did you see her next?"

"Sunday afternoon."

"You didn't talk to your wife until the afternoon? She didn't call or text you about Matt and Amy?"

"She texted me, but there was nothing I could do."

"No one can confirm where you were from 12:30 until Sunday afternoon?"

"I was here Sunday morning."

"Who did you see first and what time?"

"I honestly don't know. I took a shower in the locker room and got out on the course about seven."

"I'll need the names of your foursome."

"I played by myself."

"Not busy on Sunday morning?"

"Not particularly. It picks up after church."

"What was your relationship with Matt like?"

"We weren't close, but we didn't dislike each other."

"How about Matt and Michelle? They get along?"

"No. Michelle resented Matt because he was Joe's favorite, and Matt thought Michelle was a raging bitch and a bully."

Finally, a family member willing to tell it like it is.

"Then why did Matt come to work for DI?"

"Joe promised him autonomy from Michelle."

"Did he get it?"

"He thought he did. My wife can be subtle when she wants to. They needed him to stick around and be happy, so she made sure he was."

"Why did they need Matt happy?"

Chris's golf shoes clicked on the cart path. He leaned one arm on the roof of the cart. "You know I have a pretty good life. Hell, I basically play golf for a living. For the privilege, I look the other way when my wife fucks other men, and I do exactly what Joe and Michelle tell me to do."

"And they've told you to keep quiet."

Chris's laugh was bitter. "I'm so insignificant, they haven't told me shit."

"You know about Michelle's infidelities?"

"Everyone knows about my wife's infidelities."

"And you don't care?"

"Like I said, I have a good life. I have my share of secrets." He pulled his driver out of his bag, walked to the tee and teed up his ball. Chris addressed the ball and wiggled his club. With a fluid motion, he sent the ball flying, a perfect draw.

"Remind me never to play golf with you," Jack said. "Tell me about Paco Morales."

Chris covered his driver and pushed it in his bag roughly. "Paco? Old bastard hasn't shown up for work in five days. If he wasn't the best groundsman I've ever had, I'd fire his ass."

"When was the last day he was here?"

"Thursday, I think. Maybe Wednesday. I'll have to check the timecards."

"Ever have any trouble with him?"

"No. None. Reliable. Great worker."

"We've ID'd one of the bodies at the 107 fire as Paco's."

"Ah, shit." Chris rubbed his hand over his mouth. After a moment, he shrugged. "I guess I'm not shocked. He'd occasionally ask me to hire friends of his, pay them in cash. I know it's illegal, but I would. Only short term. I caught one of his friends living out in the groundkeeper's shed out by the twelfth green. I tore into Paco. He stopped asking after that."

"When did that happen?"

"A year ago?"

"No one recently?" Jack said.

Chris frowned, shook his head, and looked away. "Not here."

"Did Michelle know Paco?"

"Sure. He did our yard, too. Are we about done here? I need to get home and get ready for visitation tonight."

"Sure."

They drove the length of a hole before Jack said, "Do you own a gun?"

"No. Michelle made me get rid of them. She has one. She doesn't think I know about it."

"How do you know about it?"

"I saw her hiding it in her dresser, Sunday night."

CHAPTER THIRTY-SIX

Ellie wondered how much longer she needed to continue with this farce. She looked at her watch. Eleven in the morning, and if the lack of eye contact from the voters as they exited the Rock Gym was any indication, Doyle was going to win in a landslide. Ellie felt like a criminal standing before the bar, waiting for the jury to read out the sentence.

Jane Maxwell and her sister, Marta, exited the gym. They, at least, made a beeline to her, heads high.

"Don't look so downtrodden," Jane chastised. "Voters who are on the fence as they go in will surely not be encouraged by your defeated expression."

Ellie plastered on a smile. "Better?"

"No. We knew it would be a long shot. You made people think, which will help you when you run for mayor to replace me."

Ellie laughed. "I'm not running for mayor. This little endeavor has cured me of any desire to be in politics."

"Nonsense." Not for the first time, Ellie got the impression she was playing a part in a script written long ago by Jane Maxwell. "You look terrible," Jane said. "Are you sick?"

"Don't spare my feelings, Jane."

Jane gave Ellie a look that said she was too old and time was too short to spare feelings.

"It'll pass. How are you feeling?"

"I'm ninety-two years old." It was apparently all the explanation Ellie was going to get. Jane glared at someone over Ellie's shoulder. She followed Jane's gaze. "Look smug all you want, Joe Doyle," Jane said, voice low. "Your days are numbered."

Joe and Michelle walked on either side of Mary Doyle, holding up her and her grief. Joe and Michelle looked appropriately subdued as the relatives of recently murdered family members, but Mary was the only one who looked truly wrecked at the loss. Joe smiled tightly and waved at voters, and Michelle kept her arm around her mother but her eyes found Ellie. Grief couldn't mask the knowing smirk Michelle always threw Ellie's way. She knew Michelle's mind wasn't on her mother, her dead brother and sister-in-law, or the vote she was about to cast but was on all the ways she had bested Ellie over the years. Ellie turned her back on her lifelong nemesis only to see Jack McBride drive up and park across the street.

"Christ," she murmured. She closed her eyes, lifted her head, and inhaled deeply. When she exhaled and opened her eyes, Jane's ice blue eyes met hers. Too much knowledge resided there. Ellie looked away, the opposite direction from where Jack came from.

Jack stopped at their little group. "Ladies."

Ellie put a smile on her face and turned to face him. "Chief."

"How is the case going?" Jane asked.

"I expect to make an arrest today or tomorrow."

Ellie couldn't hide her surprise. "So soon?"

Jack's eyes held hers and he nodded.

"Good job," Jane said. "That'll be an important notch on your belt before Doyle gets on the council."

"We'll see. Is he here?"

"Inside voting." Ellie said.

"It will," Jane said, ignoring Jack's question and Ellie's response. "As long as I'm mayor, you'll have a job. Don't you worry about Doyle's threats. Bombastic rhetoric from a blowhard." Done with Jack, she turned to Ellie. "Are the developers from Dallas coming today?"

"No. I rescheduled."

"Why?"

"Because Matt was murdered. The Henry isn't going anywhere. They'll be here next week."

"If we keep pushing them off, they might lose interest."

"They won't lose interest." Ellie rubbed her forehead. A headache was coming on. "It's under control, Jane."

"You should go home," Marta interjected. "I will come over with some soup. You will feel better soon."

"Thank you, Marta, but I'll be fine. You two should get out of this cold. I'll call you later, Jane."

The two walked off slowly, leaving Ellie alone with Jack. Ellie kept her gaze fixed on the two elderly German women for as long as possible to avoid looking at him. She felt a slight pressure on her elbow and turned to face him. Concern and pity were clear on his face.

"Don't look at me like that."

"Are you okay?"

"No, I'm not okay. I'm losing, badly."

"I'm not talking about the election."

Ellie raised an eyebrow. "Julie told you about this morning."

Jack nodded. "Is there something you need to tell me?"

"Is there something *you* need to tell *me*?"

Jack's expression morphed to puzzlement.

"Julie could barely run today she was so sore. *Insatiable*, I believe is what she called you."

Jack shoved his hands in his pockets. He couldn't meet her gaze. "Christ."

Ellie swiped her fingers under her eyes to banish the unwanted tears. "I don't want to know. Here come the Doyles. I'm leaving. I have a business to run."

Jack stopped her with a hand on her arm. "Ellie, we need to talk."

She stared into his eyes, hating herself for crying, for showing any emotion at all, and wondered if this would be the last time she would be close enough to smell him, to see the golden flecks in his brown eyes. "I don't know that we do."

CHAPTER THIRTY-SEVEN

Jack didn't have time to fully comprehend what Ellie said before she was walking off and the Doyles were walking up. Mary Doyle wore a vacant, drug-induced expression. Michelle tried to hide her revulsion, which Jack suspected was directed at her mother.

Doyle's commanding voice shattered the crisp morning air into a thousand pieces. "Do you have news, McBride?"

"I do." Jack turned to Michelle. "Could you come to the station?"

For the first time since he'd known her, Michelle looked surprised. "Me? Why do you need to talk to me?"

"Just a few questions. Clarifications."

"Ask them here," Doyle said.

Jack glanced at the steady stream of voters coming and going. The VOTE FOR JOE signs that outnumbered Ellie's ten to one. The campaign buttons seemingly on every voter's lapel. Jack'd had the foresight to remove his before he got out of the car.

"How many buttons did you buy?"

"What kind of question is that?"

"Five thousand." Mary Doyle's quiet voice broke in.

Mary Doyle was one of those older women you see who are always perfectly put together, whose clothes somehow always looked like they just came from the cleaners. Her hair and makeup would always be perfectly in place despite humidity, heat, wind, or cold, and she probably hadn't ever left her house without her lipstick on. Her perfume was faint, but notice-able, and tasteful one-caret diamond earrings were clipped on each lobe. She was a woman whose quietness either confirmed a timidity or masked a deep-seated strength. She met Jack's eyes steadily. "I ordered them."

Jack smiled encouragingly at the grief-stricken woman. "Mrs. Doyle, I'm so sorry for your loss."

"Thank you, Chief McBride." She sniffed. "Despite what Joe and Michelle say, I know you'll catch whoever did this."

"I will."

Mary Doyle nodded and slumped back into her trance.

"Michelle, are you ready?" Jack said.

"Yes."

"I'm coming with you," Doyle said.

"No, Dad. Take Mary home."

"I'll bring Davie."

"No need."

Michelle and Jack walked to his car. "You don't want a lawyer?"

"I have nothing to hide."

Jack opened the passenger side door of his personal car. He closed the door behind her and said, "I doubt that."

"No, in here."

Michelle stopped outside of Jack's office and glanced at the break room, which doubled as the interview room. She shrugged, entered, and sat down. Jack closed the door and sat across from her. He placed a manila folder on the table between them. Michelle pointedly didn't look at it.

"First things first. You have the right to remain silent."

"What?"

"Anything you say can and will be used against you in a court of law."

"Are you arresting me?"

"You have the right to an attorney. If you cannot afford one, one will be appointed to you. If you give up this right—"

"You really don't want to keep your job, do you, McBride?"

"No need to worry. I Mirandize everyone. I had a problem with that in a case once. I told myself never again. Do you understand your rights as I've told them to you?"

"Yes."

"Good. Do you want a lawyer?"

"I don't need one."

"Do you know Paco Morales?"

"My lawn guy?" Michelle said, nonplussed. "What does this have to do with my brother?"

"Did he work for Matt?"

"Sure. Paco did Matt and Dad's yard, too." Michelle leaned forward. "I'm confused. Why are you asking me about Paco?"

Jack pulled a photo from his folder and slid it to Michelle. "One of these bodies was Paco."

Michelle wrinkled her nose at the charred bodies and their melted faces. She turned her head away. "I think I'm going to be sick."

Jack removed the metal trash can from beneath the sink and set it next to Michelle's chair. "In case you're being sincere."

"Of course I am." She was pale. Jack sat down.

"When was the last time you saw him?"

"I have no idea. Months probably."

"But he did your yard weekly?"

"It's November, in case you haven't noticed. They did the yard when we were at church."

Jack placed a picture of the scorched button in front of her. "You don't remember giving him a VOTE FOR JOE button?"

She laughed and regained a bit of her color. She flipped over the picture of Paco's charred body. "McBride, I haven't handed out any of those stupid buttons. They were Mom and Dad's idea." She focused on the second picture. "Why don't you cut to the chase and tell me what's going on?"

"We found this campaign button at the scene of the fire, with the bodies. It has your fingerprint on it."

"Bullshit."

"You haven't asked who the other victim was."

Michelle crossed her arms and remained silent.

"Diego Vazquez."

It was a small lie. Jack and Ann weren't sure who the second victim was, and might not ever know, but all signs pointed to Diego Vazquez: there was a direct connection between him and Paco Morales through Esperanza Perez; Morales was known to harbor illegals; and Jack's gun had been the murder weapon. Vazquez was either victim or perpetrator, and making him the victim suited Jack's game at the moment. He was pleased to see his bluff hit the mark.

"I don't know who that is," she said, shifting a little in her chair.

"Everyone in Stillwater knows who Diego Vazquez is."

"I know the name but I've never met him."

"How do you think it is that a known cartel assassin and your lawn guy end up murdered together?"

"I guess Paco sold drugs."

"Could be. But how does a campaign pin with your print get there, too?"

"Chris probably gave them out to all of his workers."

"But it wasn't your husband's print we found on it."

"I'm not saying another word until my lawyer arrives."

Jack put the paper back in the manila folder, closed it, and leaned back in his chair. "Suit yourself."

He wondered if she would remember she told her father not to bring Davie. After a few minutes he leaned forward. "You want to call him?"

"Who?"

"Your lawyer."

Her eyes widened slightly. She had forgotten. Jack slid his phone across to Michelle. "Use mine. If you like."

Michelle reached into her purse, pulled out her phone, and called Davie. "He's on his way," she said when she hung up. She looked out the window.

Jack flipped over the photo of the charred bodies and placed pictures of Matt and Amy's dead bodies on the table next to it. Unable to control her curiosity, Michelle glanced down. She gasped and her face paled. Michelle swallowed a couple of times but couldn't overcome her disgust. She bent over the side of her chair, and threw up in the trash can.

She sat up and wiped her mouth. "Fucking asshole." Michelle crossed her arms and clenched her jaw so hard a muscle pulsed near her ear.

"Logic would say Matt and Amy were payback, but I have evidence it's not."

The break room door clattered open, and Joe Doyle barreled through, a flustered Norman Davie on his heels. "We're done here," Joe said.

"We are," Jack agreed.

"She can leave?" Davie asked.

Jack nodded. "She could have left ten minutes ago."

Michelle huffed in irritation and pushed herself away from the table, scraping the metal chair across the industrial tile floor. She walked out the door, pushing it against the wall with a bang.

Doyle stepped right up next to Jack and said, "You're going to pay, McBride."

"Yes, yes. I know. When you win, you're going to fire me. I've heard it before."

"It's a promise."

Jack got in Doyle's face and said in a low, threatening voice. "Good luck doing that from jail, you son of a bitch."

Doyle's eyes widened slightly, before his face turned a mottled red.

"Come on, Joe," Davie said, pulling on Doyle's arm.

Doyle let his lawyer pull him out of the office. Once Doyle was on his way down the hall, Davie returned.

"I told you yesterday everything goes through me. Nothing said here is admissible." He caught sight of the photos and visibly recoiled. "Oh, Lord."

Jack held up the metal trash can. The tangy scent of Michelle's vomit almost sent Davie over the edge. Davie stepped back and waved the trash can away.

Jack carried the trash can out of the break room but stopped in the doorway. "You might want to get Michelle a lawyer with a stronger stomach."

Miner watched the interrogation through the double-sided glass window in Jack's office. There was an arrogance in Michelle that showed itself in an eerie calm and directness Miner'd always thought off-putting, but would she kill someone in cold blood? If her nausea at the sight of the burned bodies and Matt and Amy was any indication, she wouldn't have the stomach for it, which was shocking. Michelle fostered the image of being a bad ass, tougher than anyone else. Miner bought most of it, but everyone had their weaknesses, and it seemed as though gore might be Michelle's.

Which only meant she would order a hit, but she wouldn't do it herself.

Jack entered the office. "You get it on tape?"

Miner shut down the camera. "Yep."

"What do you think?" Jack went to his computer and opened his email program.

"You rattled her, for sure. I guess your gun rules out Brian Grant as a suspect for Matt and Amy?"

"It would seem to. I can't imagine a scenario where Brian would get my gun from Diego Vazquez. Unless Kyle killed Morales and Vazquez and gave my gun to Brian. But why would he do that? They weren't close and my gun wasn't with Brian's guns."

"Don't mean he didn't have it somewhere else. I didn't search."

"Maybe Brian was with Kyle when he killed Paco and Diego," Jack mused. He shook his head immediately. "No. I don't buy it. Last week, Brian still thought he had the Doyle job. He wouldn't've been desperate enough to get involved in his half-brother's illegal shit."

Miner chewed the inside of his mouth. "The button bothers me."

Jack looked up from his computer screen. "Why?"

"Doesn't make sense it only has her print on it."

"You're right. It doesn't."

"You think someone is trying to frame her?"

"Who would hate her that much?"

"Well, most every woman in town hates her, but few have the stomach for four murders and arson. My money is on the Pedrozas."

"But, why kill your own man if you're wanting to send a message to the local organization?"

"Maybe they found out Diego was a DEA informant." Miner's phone vibrated in his pocket. He ignored it.

"But we think the Pedrozas planted him with the DEA. And why would the Pedrozas kill the one Doyle who isn't involved in drugs?"

"To make their enemies have to live with it."

Jack nodded almost in agreement. "I'm not ruling out the Pedrozas, but Matt and Amy's murders feels more personal. There was no sign of forced entry, so the killer either knew the garage code, which would mean family, or Matt had to let his killer in the house. Why would he let a cartel man in? No. It doesn't make sense."

"Of the four people without alibis Saturday night, which one would have access to Diego's gun? Your gun?"

"Who wanted to set up a meeting with the Pedrozas?"

"Michelle."

"Whose fingerprints were found at the scene?"

"Michelle's." Miner clicked his tongue against his teeth. "It's too pat," he mumbled. "Why would she kill Matt? What's her motivation?"

"Jealousy. Resentment. Daddy issues."

"Does Michelle Doyle strike you as a woman with daddy issues?"

"Christ, yes. Classic daddy issues."

Miner shook his head. "Nope. Not buying it as motivation." Miner rested his hands on his holster. "Matt left the neighborhood about one. What if he drove by DI, saw some activity, and stopped to check on it?"

Jack's eyebrows raised. "And confronted Michelle."

"And threatened to expose them?" Miner felt a kernel of belief bloom in his chest. "That I'd buy."

"So would I." Jack sat back and rested his ankle on his knee. "Would a woman who vomited at the sight of gore have the stomach to blow two people's brains out?"

"No, but she'd sure as hell tell someone else to do it."

"Kyle Grant."

"Or your brother."

Jack remained silent.

"Have you called his alibi yet?"

"Going to do it after this. You?"

"Today."

"We'll compare notes. Go on. Your phone is about to buzz a hole in your pocket. Now, you go fill in the blanks for the Doyles. But not too many."

Jack fiddled with the piece of paper with his brother's alibi written on it and thought back to six weeks earlier. Eddie showing up right as the drug war started, getting a job with Doyle Industries, agreeing with little encouragement to spy on Doyle, sneaking back into the yard Friday night, the phone ruse. But, most importantly, the quality of information he'd given Jack. No superfluous details, succinct and to the point.

Jack laughed as his memories and reality of the last twenty years shifted, then fell into place. He shook his head and dialed the number.

"Hello?"

"Hey, asshole."

"Eddie?"

"No, Tom. It's Jack."

In the drawn-out pause, Jack imagined the internal calculations run-ning through the mind of Tom Hunter, his old DEA counterpart, the agent who was supposed to be working with the Yourke County Task Force. The son of a bitch who'd been running his brother as an undercover agent for years, probably, all the while working with Jack and making snide jabs about his loser, ex-con brother. Fucker.

"Jack, how'd you get this number?"

"Eddie gave it as his Sunday alibi. Tony Hunt. Not very imaginative. I suppose you have to keep it simple."

"Now, now. Don't be all bitter. You would have done exactly the same in my place."

Jack clenched his jaw to keep from saying something he would regret.

Tom chuckled. "It's just as well. Your brother's burned out. He's the best agent we have. The one with the best cover."

"You mean me and my mother."

"Yeah. Came in handy quite a few times."

Helping his brother get out of jail might have been good for Eddie's career but had been a weakness in Jack's for years. "Was he with you?"

"Yeah. I can vouch for him."

"Starting when?"

"He made contact with our dead drop about 2 a.m."

Relief coursed through Jack. He'd never truly thought Eddie had killed Matt and Amy, but to have it confirmed was heartening.

"Where are you holding Kyle Grant?"

"You figured it out?"

"Don't act so surprised, jackass. Eddie said he dropped Kyle in Dallas and gave your number is his alibi."

"You're right. It's not rocket science."

"Fuck you. I want to talk to Grant."

"He wants to talk to you. Says he knows who killed Diego Vazquez."

Jack shot up out of his chair. "I'm leaving now."

"Fine. I'll meet you in Segoville. You want to talk to Muldoon, too?"

"Fred Muldoon?"

"Yeah. Your brother didn't tell you he shot him?"

"What? No."

"Good boy. I told him not to."

"Why?"

"Old rivalries die hard."

Bastard. "I'll be there in two hours."

"I'll be waiting for you."

CHAPTER THIRTY-EIGHT

Miner felt like he was in a scene from *The Godfather*. Joe Doyle brooded behind his desk. Norman Davie leaned against the credenza, his eyes never leaving Michelle, who paced the office, phone against her ear. Chris sat on the couch, near the door.

"Eddie's not answering." She stared at her phone. "He's probably in the middle of Houston traffic. He'll call when he gets there." She glared at Miner. "McBride seriously thinks I killed my brother?"

"Of the suspects, you're at the top of his list."

"Who are the other suspects?" Chris asked.

"The other three people who don't have an alibi."

Michelle threw up her hands. "Who are . . . ?"

"There's a limit, Michelle."

She walked toward Miner. "Oh, really? How does your wife like her pain meds, huh? Because I can make sure she never gets another Oxycontin in her life."

"Do that and I'll make sure Jack and Sheriff Newberry know everything I know about your little organization."

"Little organization? You don't know shit."

"Pollard told me more than you think."

Michelle laughed. "Pollard thinks you're an idiot."

"Sure you want to take that chance?"

"Enough," Joe said. "Why does McBride like Michelle for this?"

"No one else has a motive. Except Brian Grant."

"What exactly is my motive?"

"Daddy issues."

Michelle's laughter was harsh. "Are you fucking kidding me?"

"Daddy issues?" Doyle said. "That's what McBride is basing his case on?"

Michelle turned to her father, a bit of the tension easing out of her. "He's got nothing. When Eddie gets back, he'll confirm my alibi, and McBride will have to move on to someone else or have to look into his brother for it, which he won't do."

"Did Eddie do it?" Miner asked.

"No. And neither did I," Michelle said.

"Who were you with?" Miner asked.

Michelle pursed her lips. "With Eddie, like I said."

"Why didn't you tell Jack the truth from the beginning?"

"Because I thought my husband would be my alibi."

"Maybe next time give me a heads up on what lies I'm supposed to tell," Chris said.

Michelle rolled her eyes. "Don't you have a golf game or something?"

"Already played." Chris stood. "I'll get the kids to Matt and Amy's visitation. You obviously don't need me to plot world domination."

"I don't need you for anything," Michelle mumbled. Chris walked out, seemingly oblivious.

"Michelle, you've really fucked this all up."

Michelle rounded on her father, her face a mask of indignation. "What? I haven't done anything!"

"Two dead Mexicans and Matt and Amy."

"How are either my fault? I never had a meeting with the Pedrozas. It takes time for Kyle to go through his channels. It's not like I have them on fucking speed dial."

"Watch your language, young woman."

Michelle clammed up, but her face turned beet red.

"Where is Kyle?" Doyle said.

"He's dead," Michelle said.

Doyle's expression was like granite. "How do you know?"

"When they were dealing with Muldoon, Kyle went after Eddie, and Eddie killed him."

"Did he?"

"I can't hear this," Davie said.

"Then leave," Michelle shot back. "You're fucking useless anyway."

"Michelle!" Doyle roared. He stood and walked around the desk. He loomed over his daughter. Miner admired Michelle for not looking cowed, but he suspected the strength it took for her to stand toe to toe with Joe. "Did you see the body?"

Her brows furrowed in confusion. "Whose body? Kyle's?"

"Yes." Doyle's derision-filled voice made Michelle flinch.

"No."

"Then how do you know he's dead?" Doyle's eyes never left his daughter's. "Miner, do the Feds have an undercover agent in our organization?"

"Yes."

Michelle's head twisted around to Miner. "Don't you think you should have told me that when I gave you the big fucking bag of pills?"

Miner shrugged. "I'm telling you now."

Michelle lunged for Miner, but Doyle caught her. "Don't blame him for your incompetence."

"Me?"

"You've been too busy spreading your legs for Eddie McBride to see who he really is."

"That's not true."

Doyle still gripped Michelle's arms. "You even fucked him in my office, haven't you?" Michelle recoiled, but Doyle held her fast. "Where'd you do it? My chair? My desk?"

"You're hurting me."

"You've always been a slut, just like your mother."

Michelle's head jerked back, as if slapped.

Miner stepped forward. "Joe, that's enough. Eddie's not the narc."

"Who is?"

"I honestly don't know. McBride doesn't even know."

Doyle pushed Michelle away from him. She stumbled back and turned her back to the men, wiping at her eyes.

"You better find out, tonight, Miner, or I'll go and take those pills from Teresa myself. And I'll make sure no doctor within a hundred miles writes her a prescription for a fucking aspirin."

Composure regained, Michelle turned on her father. "You son of a bitch. I was setting up the truce with the Pedrozas for you! Get rid of McBride, crime goes down, you're the fucking town hero, and we grow our business without competition. Then, your golden child caught us at the yard Saturday night and was oh so shocked his wonderful, upstanding father would be involved in something so amoral." The derision in Michelle's voice dripped from every word like syrup. "I didn't kill your pussy of a son, but I'm not sad he's dead."

Miner saw the blow and watched Michelle fall to the floor in slow motion. Davie knelt beside Michelle immediately. Miner was too stunned to speak, let alone move.

Davie helped Michelle stand on shaky feet. She brushed him off roughly. Davie's face hardened, reddened, and he stepped next to Doyle, whose granite expression was tinged in red, whether in anger or embarrassment, Miner wasn't sure. Michelle's chest heaved and she touched the angry red welt rising on her cheek.

"Y'all are ignoring the real problem," Miner said. "McBride has evidence putting Michelle at the murder-arson crime scene."

"That's as much bullshit as me killing my brother." She glared at her father.

"Maybe, but it's enough to get a warrant."

"There's nothing to find."

"You better hope not."

Doyle finally turned to Miner. "It doesn't matter," Doyle said, "because Miner will make whatever they find disappear. Won't you, Miner?"

Miner thought of Teresa at home, pain free for the first time in weeks. Of his promise to Jack that he would tell him everything the Doyles asked him to do, account for every cent they gave him. Lucky for Miner, Michelle paid him in pain pills.

The answer rolled off his tongue easily.

"Yes."

CHAPTER THIRTY-NINE

Jack was being waved through security at the Federal Correctional Institution in Segoville when his brother called.

"Where are you?" Jack said.

"Buc-ee's parking lot on 45 with a load of DI drugs."

"Get me some Buc-ee's Balls, would you?"

"Sure."

"Ask me where I am."

"Where are you, Jack?"

"I'm pulling in to Segoville to talk to your two witnesses." There was silence on the other end of the phone. "You still there, Eddie?"

"You aren't angry?"

"I'm furious. But Buc-ee's Balls might keep me from kicking your ass."

"You tried that a few days ago and lost."

"Well, this time I'm on the side of righteousness." Jack parked and cut the engine. "Honestly, I don't know whether to hate you or be proud of you."

"I've hated myself enough for both of us," Eddie said.

"Mom included?"

"Probably not."

"When did it start?"

"The night you met Julie. Someone connected me with the son of the future lieutenant governor and brother of a law student. Recruiting you for the FBI was part of it, too."

The shot to Jack's ego was deep. "Nice to know our government has been manipulating us for twenty years."

"Well, we've done a little good, so I can forgive them." Eddie sighed. "God, what a weight off. You don't know how long I've wanted to tell you."

"Does Mom know?"

"No."

"Make sure I'm in the next state when she finds out." Jack got out of his car and locked it. "So, you were bringing Fred and Kyle to Dallas Sunday morning? Why the fuck didn't you bring them to me?"

"Michelle would have known you had Kyle Grant in custody. As it is, she thinks he's dead."

"What?"

"Dude, it's a long story. Hey, I'm sending you an audio file. Use headphones. I've got to get on the road and you've got to do your shit and get back to meet Ellie at ten."

"Where?"

"Her lake house. She'll think I'm meeting her, so be ready to have to convince her to stay. She is *not* happy with you."

"She can get in line."

"I've seen the error in my ways, nurse."

"Have you, Fred?" The nurse squeezed the bulb of the blood pressure cuff.

"I have, and it's all because of the attentions of a fine woman like you."

"I'm married, Fred."

Fred's arm tingled from the tightening cuff. "I won't tell him if you won't."

The nurse released the valve. "Uh-huh." She ripped the cuff off and stuffed it in the metal basket on the wall. "How's your pain, one being no pain at all and ten being excruciating?"

"Six."

"I notice you've eaten some." She jerked her head toward the plate on the tray table.

"The food here's terrible."

"It's a prison, Fred."

"I didn't do nothing wrong. Wrong place at the wrong time is all. Story of my life, if you want to know the truth."

"Have you gone to the bathroom?"

"No, ma'am. But if you'd get me some whiskey I imagine it'd go right through me."

"I thought you'd seen the error in your ways," the nurse smiled.

"I have, and that's a fact. But whiskey is proven for medicinal purposes."

"Maybe in the nineteenth century."

Someone knocked on the door and it opened. Jack McBride stuck his head in. "Is he decent, nurse?"

"As decent as he's ever gonna be. I'll check on you later, Fred."

"I'll count down the minutes."

She rolled her eyes as she walked past Jack.

"Well, well. Look what the cat dragged in," Fred said. Jack placed a box on Fred's tray table. "Those my shoes?"

"They are. I also brought you a honey bun." Jack pulled it from his pocket.

"I told you my life was worth more than a honey bun."

"You're still alive, aren't you?"

"No thanks to your brother."

Jack pulled up a chair and sat down. "How are you feeling?"

"I've got a bullet hole in my shoulder."

"So I see. Tell me what happened. From the beginning."

Fred sighed. He'd already told the story to the fat Fed and didn't particularly want to tell it again. He was tired, and his throat felt like sandpaper. Fred flipped the lid from the box and lifted out a shoe. The leather gleamed in the fluorescent hospital lights. The soles were smooth and thick. They looked brand new.

Fred dropped the shoe back in the box and slapped the lid down. He cleared the lump from his throat and started. "T's just trying to get warm. It was cold Sunday morning, you know? They'd locked all the trucks in the yard, so I went around the buildings to try to find one open. I didn't, and I'd hunkered down by an AC unit when I heard all the commotion. Couldn't hear a whole lot through the walls, but I heard plenty when they were outside, yelling at each other."

"Who?"

"Michelle and Matt."

"Sunday morning, you sure?"

"Considering your twin brother shot me that day, yeah. I'm sure."

"What were they yelling at each other?"

"Something about Matt not believing what he was seeing. Michelle telling him to keep his mouth shut or else."

"Do you remember specifically what she said?"

"No. About that time, someone grabbed my shoulder, and I pissed myself. Not my finest moment."

"Who?"

"That little shit stain, Grant. He's always been a little weasel. He frog-marched me into the truck barn, and there was Michelle and your brother, conferring."

"Where was Matt?"

"Didn't see him. Grant wanted to kill me right there, but Eddie talked them out of it. Make a big mess, harder to get rid of a dead body than to drive a live one to his grave. Well, it was a mess of an argument, but Eddie won. Michelle, though, I could tell she didn't trust Eddie 100 percent, so she told Shit Stain to go with us. I knew I was a goner for sure.

"We drove through Yourkeville, and Eddie stopped at the Whataburger to get taquitos. Asked me if I wanted any. Last meal and all. I didn't, though now I wish I had. A taquito sure sounds good right now. Damn sight better than a honey bun."

"I'll bring you some taquitos next time I come."

"Eddie ordered the most fool thing you can imagine and we drove on. Drove west all night until we were in the middle of nowhere, somewhere south of San Angelo, I think. Finally stopped next to a oil well, then we started walking. By this time, Shit Stain was pretty pissed off. Let's just kill the fucker and get back. Eddie told him sure, okay, if we wanted the body to be found.

"Shit Stain stopped to take a leak, and Eddie pushed me forward, told me to run, and to fall when he shot me. 'Shot me?' I said. 'Yeah, if you want to live, you've gotta play dead. Go.' So I ran and the sumbitch shot me in the shoulder. Damn fine shot, come to that. I fell and played dead, like he said. I heard some commotion, don't know rightly what happened since I was playing possum. Might have drifted off, not sure. Next thing I know, I hear a bunch of cars pull up, then leave. Then here comes your brother with a first-aid kit and some water. Takes care of me right nice, apologizes for shooting me and sends me along with some mouth-breathing Fed. No offense, Chief."

"None taken."

"They bring me here and operate on me, and here I am."

"So you heard Michelle threaten Matt."

"I did."

"This is important. What exactly did she say?"

"Jesus, Chief, I'm a seventy-year-old alcoholic. I can't tell you anything exactly."

"Fine. What do you remember?"

"Matt said something like, 'You wouldn't hurt me,' and Michelle said, 'Don't fucking count on it.'"

The chief stared at the shoebox as if it held the secrets of the universe.

"What do you care about that? Aren't you investigating the One-Armed Soldier fire?"

"I guess you haven't heard. Matt and Amy Doyle were murdered early Sunday morning."

"You don't say? And you think Michelle did it?"

"You know I can't tell you that."

"Well, I bet you're barking up the wrong tree."

"Why?"

"Once they decided to get rid of me, they were pretty free and easy with their conversation. Took a while for Michelle to calm down, but Eddie eventually got her settled. Encouraged her to have Joe talk to Matt, bring him around."

Jack stilled, as if holding his breath, or his excitement. "Did she call Joe while you were there?"

"Yep. She hung up and said her dad was going straight over."

CHAPTER FORTY

"Kyle Grant. I gotta say. You rock the orange jumpsuit. Brings out the crazy in your eyes."

Kyle leaned forward across the table and tried to grab at Jack, but his handcuffs stopped him. They rattled against the metal table. "Fuck you and your brother, McBride. These charges are bullshit. I didn't try to kill your brother, though if I saw him right now, I might."

His public defender put her hand on Kyle's arm. "Mr. Grant." When Kyle sat back, the woman extended her hand to the federal prosecutor sitting next to Jack. "I'm Andrea Armstrong. Mr. Grant's attorney." She was in her mid-thirties, at least, and didn't look harassed or beaten down by the system. Jack guessed she was starting her second career.

"Tanya Porter," the prosecutor said, her west Texas drawl as thick as the day-old coffee in the Styrofoam cups front of them. Jack had worked with Tanya many times. She was a by-the-book pitbull. He had done a mental fist pump when he saw her purposely striding down the hall to the interrogation room.

"Threatening to kill his best agent like that isn't the best way to endear you to Special Agent Hunter back there." Jack jerked his thumb at the glass behind him.

Kyle sat back. "I *told* Michelle not to trust him. But she was too busy sucking his dick to listen to reason."

"Really, Kyle. There are ladies in the room."

"Don't mind me. I'm not easily offended," Andrea Armstrong said. Jack didn't need to see Tanya roll her eyes to know she did it.

Jack tilted his head. "Or are you jealous? Michelle throw you over when my brother came to town?"

Kyle looked away. *Bingo.*

"You've been here before. You know how this works."

"I know the Feds lie, promise you shit they never intend to give, then throw you to the wolves."

"And that's not the way to ingratiate yourself to me," Tanya said.

Jack continued. "As soon as Michelle and Joe Doyle hear you've been picked up, they're going to pretend they don't even know who you are. Norman Davie will twist things around so much Ms. Armstrong won't know which way is up."

"Don't count on it." Jack heard the smirk in Andrea Armstrong's voice.

"You'll take the dive for everything we have on them, and they'll pin things we don't even *know* about on you."

"I don't think you have anything on them."

Jack knew the only bluffs that ever worked were the big bluffs. "You do know this investigation isn't just me and county, right? The DEA and FBI were looking at Doyle way before I ever even heard of Stillwater. They've got wiretaps, informants up and down Texas and down to Mexico. Heard of Diego Vazquez? He sang a good song about Buck Pollard and Joe Doyle. They've got Doyle for a laundry list of stuff. I couldn't care less. Let the DEA and FBI follow the drugs and money. All I care about is solving four murders. And Agent Hunter said you can help me."

"Here's the question, Mr. McBride. Why would Mr. Grant want to help you?" Andrea Armstrong said.

"Because if you don't, the TexaSS might hear you've been working with the Pedrozas. You're heading back inside for breaking parole."

Kyle lost some of his bravado. "No one'll believe you."

"You were supposed to set up a meeting between the Pedrozas and Michelle, right? How exactly would you do that? Through Paco Morales? He hid Vazquez at the country club, didn't he? When did you put two and two together?"

"Who's Vazquez?" Andrea asked.

Jack addressed the lawyer. "Diego Vazquez is the Pedroza's front man for Yourke County. He beat me up and stole my gun my first day as chief. That was a bad day." He turned his attention back to Kyle. "Did you contact Morales to set up the meet with Vazquez? Who went with you? Or were you alone?"

Kyle smirked at Jack. Jack knew Kyle had been in enough interrogation rooms to know they had nothing on him. Apparently, his lawyer realized it, too. "I think we'll take our chances," she said.

Jack shrugged and rose. "With what charge? Attempted murder against a federal agent?"

"I didn't try to kill him."

"Kidnapping Fred Muldoon."

"I wasn't kidnapping him."

"Right. I meant conspiracy to murder. Then there are your parole violations, Eddie's testimony about your involvement in the Doyle drug organization. You're absolutely right. Taking your chances is the way to go."

Andrea Armstrong leaned over to whisper into Kyle's ear. They conferred for a moment, before Kyle nodded. "I didn't kill Diego Vazquez, but I know who did."

"How do you know?"

"I was there."

Andrea Armstrong put her hand on Kyle's arm. "Nothing else until we talk deal."

Tanya took over. "He pleads guilty to assaulting a federal officer and he gets five years, minimum security, somewhere on the East Coast. Away from the TexaSS and the Pedrozas."

Kyle shook his head no.

"Six months," Andrea Armstrong said.

"The minimum sentence for all of his charges is thirty years. Five years is a steal," Tanya said.

"You're assuming I'd lose."

Tanya grinned like the cat that ate the canary. Obviously Andrea Armstrong didn't know her opponent; Tanya hadn't lost a case since 1989. She turned to Kyle. "Do you want to gamble thirty years of your life on a new lawyer?"

Andrea Armstrong bristled, but Kyle shook his head.

"Two years," Andrea Armstrong said, "minimum security."

Tanya narrowed her eyes and pursed her lips. Jack could tell she was disappointed at the lost opportunity to put Kyle Grant away for a long time. But she also knew how important it was to get Grant to talk. "Deal." Tanya opened her briefcase.

"Write it up," Andrea said, trying to take command. "Then he'll talk."

Tanya paused and glared at Andrea Armstrong. She pulled out a legal pad and clicked the end of her pen, still glaring at the young lawyer. She shook her head, wrote down the outline of the deal, and signed it. "Sign this. We'll work up the official form while you talk to McBride."

Andrea Armstrong read the form, nodded to Kyle, who signed it.

Tanya took the legal pad, tossed it in her briefcase, and left.

"Who killed Diego Vazquez?" Jack said.

"Michelle killed Paco and Diego."

"Michelle Doyle."

"With your gun."

"The gun Diego had. How did you get it from him?"

"I overpowered him."

"It was only you and Michelle there, meeting with Diego and Paco. No one else?"

"Nope."

"Why did you meet in the One-Armed Soldier's House?"

"Huh?"

"Why there? Why not out in the country somewhere? There's plenty of run-down barns and old houses in Yourke County. Why pick one on the edge of town?"

"Michelle wanted you to investigate it. Another example of you being incompetent."

"Why burn the place down? We would have ID'd Diego much sooner if he hadn't been burned."

"That was an accident. I tossed a cigarette and the place went up like a tinderbox."

"What happened to the gun?"

"Diego's? When I told her it might be yours, she kept it. As a souvenir."

Miner, case meeting w/everyone tonight at 8 p.m. Order in from Mabel's. It's going to be a long night.

Jack closed out the text app as Tom Hunter walked down the hall toward him.

"You may keep your job after all," Hunter said. When Jack glared at him, Hunter said, "Eddie mentioned you were under some pressure out there."

"You could say that."

"You like it? Small-town living?"

Jack thought of Ellie, of Ethan settling in and making friends, and of all the nice people he'd met in the last two months. They far outweighed the Doyles of the world. "Yeah. I do."

"Good. Glad you're happy."

Jack wouldn't have exactly used that word but let it slide. "You haven't let Grant make a call, have you?"

"I'm not a fucking amateur, McBride."

"Uh-huh. You ready to search DI?"

Hunter nodded. "Yep. Your ex-partner is working on a warrant for their financials."

"Alex is working this case?"

"Yep. Asked to be put on it. Probably hoping to run into you. You two had a thing going, didn't you?"

"No."

"Uh-huh. I've got a warrant being delivered to a federal judge right now to search DI's businesses. First thing in the morning. When's the funeral?"

"Tomorrow at 3 p.m."

Hunter nodded appreciatively. "They won't know what hit 'em."

CHAPTER FORTY-ONE

"Deciding against decorations was the best decision I've made in two months."

The Book Bank was officially closed for Ellie's postelection victory party, but since there was nothing to celebrate and no decorations, it looked like any other Tuesday evening, and thank God. Paige worked behind the counter, serving those few people who wanted a Snickerdoodle latte instead of the free tea or Cokes on the display table that usually held Christian fiction, Amish mysteries, and devotionals, which had been wiped out Sunday afternoon.

"It's a testament to how much people like you that they're buying stuff instead of taking the free," Kelly said.

Ellie drank the dregs of a Diet Coke from a red solo cup. The ice crinkled when she set it down. "I should have opened a bar."

"You might've won if you had."

Ellie's lips fluttered when she sighed. "I didn't want it anyway."

"Liar."

"I am a liar." Ellie stood. "But not about that. Once we get rid of everyone, I need to talk to you."

"Sure. Are we going to need wine for this conversation?"

You might. "I have some upstairs."

"Oh, good Lord," Kelly said.

"What?"

"Here comes Julie McBride."

Ellie turned and saw Julie and Ethan walk through the door. Her stomach clenched. She hadn't seen Ethan since the September night he caught her and Jack kissing in the Book Bank office. The horrified expression on Ethan's face had been what Ellie thought of when Jack told her his wife returned. Ellie had hoped if Jack made an effort with his marriage, Ethan might eventually come around to the divorce and them being together. Stupid idea, she now knew. Ellie didn't count on ignorance being one of the biggest drawbacks of staying away from Jack. She knew nothing about how the farce was going over, if Ethan was buying it. All Ellie could tell from Ethan's expression was this was the last place he wanted to be.

"I thought you and Julie were big buddies."

"She wants to be. She's called and texted me a hundred times since Saturday. She's the neediest person I've ever met." Kelly fixed her beauty pageant smile on her face. "Hey. What're y'all doing here?"

"We're on our way home from Matt and Amy's visitation. Did you go?"

"We did," Kelly said.

"It's just so sad. Those kids being orphaned," Julie said.

"Are you friends with Madison?" Ellie asked Ethan.

He shrugged. "We have a couple of classes together."

"I'm sorry about the election, Ellie," Julie said. "Though I'm not sorry for me."

Kelly bristled. "What do you mean?"

"Michelle told me the first thing her father wants to do is fire Jack."

"God, Michelle Doyle is such a—"

Ellie placed her hand on Kelly's arm. "Do you *want* Jack to get fired?" Ellie asked. After their little conversation that morning, Ellie knew the answer, but it wouldn't hurt for her best friend to get further confirmation what a narcissist Julie was, and straight from the horse's mouth.

"You know I wouldn't mind a reason to leave Stillwater."

Kelly's arm tensed beneath Ellie's hand. She did not like people trashing their hometown, though Ellie knew her best friend would be happy to see the back end of Jack McBride.

"A lot of people think Jack's doing a good job. What about you, Ethan? Do you want to leave?" Ellie asked.

Ethan studied his mother before turning his attention to Ellie. Had she caught a hint of irritation in his expression or was that wishful thinking? "I don't want to move again."

"How's your photography going? Still finding a lot of subjects around town?" Ellie asked.

"Yeah. Looking forward to the changing leaves."

"You have to catch it quick. They're here one day and gone the next. You should go out to the lake when they turn. You can get some great pictures out there, I bet."

"He's turned into quite the photographer since we gave him the camera for his birthday last year," Julie said.

"Um, you left on my fucking birthday, or have you forgotten?" Ethan said.

Julie's smile wavered. "Your dad and I agreed on it all before I left, remember?"

"Whatever." Ethan moved away.

Kelly recoiled visibly from Julie. Ellie knew that was it. Kelly Kendrick would be polite to Julie—she was a Southern woman after all—but she would never be friends with a woman who left her son on his birthday.

"I wanted to stop by to see how you're feeling, Ellie," Julie said, her voice pitched high. "She threw up on our run this morning," she explained to Kelly.

Kelly rubbed Ellie's back. "Are you still fighting that stomach bug?"

"I saw Sue today. I'll be better soon."

"You need a vacation," Kelly said.

"I don't think a vacation will f—" Julie began.

"Do you two want anything? Coke? Coffee? Paige'll make you something. On the house."

Ethan touched Ellie's arm. "I wondered if you still had that photography book you mentioned." He moved away from the group, but kept his eyes on Ellie, as if willing her to follow.

"Sure. Let me show you."

Ellie wanted to thank Ethan for saving her from his mother, but thought better of it. "I ordered a few for you. I didn't know what I was doing, so I ordered the ones with the best ratings on Amazon. Here." With Vanna White hands, she showed Ethan the books, felt stupid, and shoved her hands under her armpits.

"Cool. Thanks." His hair obscured part of his face when he dropped his head down and flipped through a book. Ellie waited. Did he bring her over here to talk or was he just saving her from his mother? He remained silent.

"Well, I need to start cleaning up." She stepped away.

"My dad said you two stopped seeing each other when my mom came back to town. Is it true?"

"Yes."

"So, you switched to my uncle."

Ellie sighed. "Dammit, I told Eddie people would think that." She met Ethan's gaze. "Your uncle and I are friends." Ethan looked like he smelled something foul. "You don't believe me. Why?"

"Why should I believe you?"

"Why shouldn't you?"

"Adults lie all the time."

Ellie couldn't argue with that. She glanced over at Kelly, who looked like she was about to explode.

"You're right. But I wouldn't lie to you."

"Why?"

"I want you to trust me."

"Okay. Are you pregnant?"

Ellie's breath left her in a whoosh, as though someone had punched her in the chest. Ellie'd never had a panic attack, but she wondered if this might not be the start of one.

"I—" The sound came out as a gasp. She could tell by Ethan's expression the answer was all over her face, but luckily Julie interrupted them. "Ethan, let's go," she called across the room while Kelly stalked over to Ellie.

Ethan put the book down. "So?"

Ellie cleared her throat and tried to speak again. "Yes."

His eyes flicked to her stomach. "Thanks," he said and left as Kelly arrived.

"What happened?" Ellie asked, still struggling for air.

"Is it true?"

"Is what true?"

"Are you pregnant?"

First Ethan, now Kelly. This was not how or where Ellie wanted to have this conversation. She motioned to Paige to get her attention. "We'll be in the back for a minute." Paige waved her acknowledgment and Ellie grabbed Kelly's arm and dragged her to the office and shut the door.

Kelly's arms were crossed over her chest, her hip cocked in her no-bullshit pose.

"Yes."

Kelly opened her mouth, closed it, opened it again. "I don't know if I should congratulate you or slap you. How long have you known?"

"For sure, today. I've suspected for a week or more."

Kelly pushed Ellie away. "And you didn't *tell* me?"

"I knew you'd react like this."

"What did you think, I wouldn't notice eventually?"

"No."

Kelly gasped. "You aren't going to get an abortion."

"No."

"Then why wouldn't you tell me? Better yet? Who's the father? Eddie? You said you weren't sleeping with him!"

"I'm not."

"So, what? This is the virgin birth?"

"No."

"Is it that guy you go see in Dallas? What's his name? Kirk?"

"No, it's not Curtis."

"Are you going to make me ask you twenty questions or just fucking tell me? Who's the fath—" She stopped cold. Her eyes widened, then narrowed. "No way. You told me you never slept with him."

Ellie nodded imperceptibly.

"Jack McBride? You've been fucking Jack McBride while acting like you're dating his brother?"

"If you would stop for a minute and let me explain."

"Oh, *now* you want to explain. Since I've confronted you about it."

"Would you shut up for one second? Huh? Jesus. This isn't about you, remember? It's about me. *Me.* I'm the one who's pregnant." Kelly crossed her arms over her chest again and waited. "It happened before Julie came back. When she did, we stopped seeing each other."

"You fucked him after knowing him less than a week?"

"You told me to!"

"I didn't think you'd actually do it! He's married."

"He was filing for divorce . . ."

"That's what they all say . . ."

"He could file uncontested when she'd been gone 365 days. She came back on 364. We decided he needed to try to make it work, for Ethan."

"For Ethan."

"Why is it so hard to believe?"

"Does he know?"

"Ethan?"

"No, Jack."

"I think Julie told him I was pregnant with Eddie's child. She believes we're together. Jack knows we're not."

"*The whole town* thinks you're sleeping with Eddie. But you're pregnant with Jack's baby. Jesus, you know how to create a scandal. Sometimes, I think you live for this shit."

"That's totally not fair."

"It would be best for everyone if Jack got fired."

"Not for me!"

"What, do you actually think he's going to leave his wife for you? They *never* leave their wives."

"Like you have so much experience with married men."

"I watched *Sex and the City*."

"Jesus Christ."

Kelly shook her head. "I cannot *believe* you lied to me for two months. Right to my face. Over and over. Ellie the Honest. You're a fucking hypocrite."

"Typical. I'm pregnant at forty-two years old, and all you can think about is how I didn't tell you soon enough. Here's a newsflash, Kelly: the world doesn't revolve around you. I don't tell you everything. I've never told you everything!"

Kelly's head jerked back as if Ellie'd slapped her. Ellie's instinct was to apologize. She always apologized, then Kelly forgave her and they moved on. This time, she didn't. Ellie matched Kelly's stance and waited. Kelly's face crumpled. She turned and walked out the door.

CHAPTER FORTY-TWO

Eddie pulled into Doyle Industries truck yard at 7:30 p.m. His timing was perfect. He'd run home, take a shower, and get to Ellie's before nine. He would have an hour to talk her into meeting Jack out at her lake house. He had no idea how difficult a job it would be. With a pregnancy, the election, downtown development, her new business, trying to lure new businesses downtown, Eddie was afraid Ellie was at the end of her rope.

Doyle Industries was deserted. Eddie was relieved. Michelle had been calling and texting him all day. He'd have to come up with a pretty creative lie as to why he didn't reply. Say he lost his phone and didn't realize it was gone until he pulled in. He'd put the metal down to make it back before visitation ended so he wouldn't run into Michelle.

The company was closed the next day, out of respect for Matt and Amy. The drugs would be safe in the wheel wells until the following night, after Matt and Amy were buried, and condolences were received. Then business could return to normal.

Too bad for Michelle that Tom Hunter planned to raid Doyle Industries at dawn.

Eddie jumped from the cab and closed the door. A few weeks more and he would be done with this life forever. It was hard to believe he'd been doing it long enough to get a pension from the government. It would be enough money for him to live on and take some time to figure out what he wanted to do. First thing on his agenda was getting his Harley back from Abe. He'd missed it more than he thought he would. Then maybe he'd take it across the country. Hit some national parks. Do some camping. Be alone. God, he wanted to be alone. He was sick of people, but more importantly, he needed to figure out who exactly Sean Edward McBride Junior was. He laughed. Maybe he should ask Julie for advice on how to take a sabbatical.

She'd probably want to go with him.

Eddie almost threw up at the thought. Sure, she was a good lay, but she was totally, 100 percent fucked in the head as well. Which made her his type, he knew. But he didn't want that type. He didn't want anyone. At least not yet.

Eddie twirled his keys around his finger as he walked to his '69 Ford. It was a great truck. He had some money saved. He'd buy a new Harley and keep this. Decision made, he rolled the truck yard gate closed and locked it. He turned around and almost ran into Brian Grant.

"Shit, Grant. You scared me to death."

The security light back lit Grant's face, throwing it in shadow. "Did I? Sorry."

"What are you doing here?"

"I came to thank you."

"For what?"

"For going to bat for me with Michelle. She gave me a job."

"Well, good. How's Susan's hand?"

"Good. Things are looking up."

"Glad to hear it, Brian. Michelle's a good boss."

"Oh, I'm not working for Michelle."

"But you just said."

"She thinks I am, but I'm not. Or, I won't be tomorrow when she's arrested for Matt and Amy's murder."

"Who are you working for?"

"Me."

Eddie turned his head to follow the voice and, too late, saw out of the corner of his eye a brass knuckle–covered fist rushing toward his temple.

PART THREE

The Fisher King

CHAPTER FORTY-THREE

Jack rang the doorbell four times before Michelle, hair twisted up in a clip, black-rimmed glasses over sleepy, hooded eyes, opened the door. She looked Jack up and down. "McBride? What are you dressed like that for?"

Jack looked down and was as shocked as Michelle to see himself wearing a tan Stillwater PD uniform. The gun belt creaked when he walked, and the bullet-proof vest pinched his underarms.

Jack ignored her question and held the warrant out. "We have a warrant to search your house and place of business."

Realization dawned and she laughed. "You are out of your fucking mind." She snapped the warrant from Jack's hand and glanced at it.

Chris appeared behind her, looking more hungover than sleepy. "What's going on?"

Michelle handed him the warrant. "I'm calling Davie."

Chris looked from the warrant to Jack and Malik, and the sheriff's deputies arranged behind them.

"We're searching your house, Chris. We need you to step aside."

He did, and he held the door open.

"Yeah, Norman, they're here, in my fucking house at six o'clock in the morning," Michelle said into her phone. "Get your ass over here now. I'm calling Dad."

"Mom? Dad?"

Two teenagers stood at the top of the stairs.

"Jordan, Andy, get some clothes on," Michelle said, then put her phone to her ear.

"Start downstairs," Jack said to the officers streaming into the house. "Malik, stay near Michelle." The deputy nodded.

"Dad, McBride is searching my house. He said he's searching my place of business, too . . . I don't know, I haven't heard from him . . ." Michelle's face tightened and she hung up.

Michelle put the phone down on the counter and studied Jack. Without taking her eyes from him, she held out her hand to her husband. "Let me see the warrant." Chris dutifully handed it to her.

"Evidence pertaining to the death of Diego Vazquez, Paco Morales, Amy Doyle, and Matt Doyle." Astonishment clear on her face, Michelle said, "The worst part about this is you have no *idea* who killed these people."

"Why don't you and Chris have a seat," Jack said. "This'll take a while."

"How dare you," Michelle said. She walked forward and stood toe to toe with Jack. He looked down on her with a placid expression. "You come into my house on the day of my brother's funeral and accuse me of murdering him? This town will never, ever forgive you."

Jack smelled her morning breath and tried not to gag. "When I catch Matt and Amy's killer, no one will care."

Michelle's lip curled. "You're not going to catch him in this house."

"We'll see."

"I'm going to change."

"Brush your teeth while you're at it."

He thought Michelle was going to claw his eyes out and was disappointed when she didn't try. Instead, she walked away. Malik followed. Michelle stopped at her bedroom door and saw the deputy. "What are you doing?"

"You can't be alone."

Michelle sighed in exasperation but went inside the room and let Malik follow.

Chris watched his wife with amusement, which he wiped from his face when he saw Jack watching him. "Funny?" Jack said.

"I'm not used to seeing my wife so flustered."

Jack tried to put his hands in his pockets but was thwarted by his holster on one side. He settled for resting his hands on the holster, felt ridiculous, and crossed them over his chest. With fifteen extra pounds of Kevlar, his crossed arms stuck out at a weird angle, making him feel like a genie about to work a spell. He dropped his arms down next to his side.

"Nice uniform," Chris said.

Jack didn't answer.

"I hate to tell you, but that isn't going to help you when Doyle comes after you."

"It's not why I'm wearing it."

Jordan and Andy Ryan, one of them wide-eyed and disbelieving, the other disdainful, came into the living room. Jordan sat next to her dad, and Andy sat on the fireplace hearth.

"What's going on, Dad?" Jordan asked. She was the classic cheerleader type; fresh-faced and innocent looking, but her expression at the moment was one of fear.

"They're searching the house, honey," he said.

"Why?"

"Because our family is a bunch of crooks."

Andy, on the other hand, looked like he would have fit right in with the hipsters in Brooklyn. Looking at the two of them, Jack would have guessed Jordan was watching over Andy in Cheyney's Field, not the other way around.

"Jordan, can I speak to you for a minute?"

Her eyes widened. "Why do you want to talk to her?" Chris said.

Jack smiled tightly at Chris. "I need to ask her about Saturday night."

"Sure." She jumped up and walked to the kitchen. She pulled a bottle of water from the refrigerator, opened it and sipped. Her hand shook when she lifted the bottle to her mouth. Jack moved around so Jordan had to turn to face him, placing her back to her father.

"I'm not going to tell your parents about Cheyney's Field, okay? Don't look so terrified or your dad will ask questions."

She nodded briskly.

"What time did you get home Sunday morning?"

"Three."

"Did you see your parents?"

"Yeah."

"You did?"

Jordan's brows furrowed. "Yeah. I saw my dad coming out of my mom's room."

"What time?"

"Three," she said, as if she couldn't believe he didn't remember she just told him.

"Did he see you?"

"I wouldn't be very good at sneaking in if he did."

"Was your mom here?"

"Why else would he be coming out of her room in the middle of the night?" Based on Jordan's expression, she clearly thought Jack was an idiot.

"You didn't see her though?"

"No."

"Okay. Thanks."

Jordan rolled her eyes and left as Michelle walked into the kitchen. She made coffee like it was any other day and there weren't deputies wearing surgical gloves searching every drawer and cabinet around her. Jack went over to the door to Michelle's room and saw Malik searching the bottom dresser drawer.

Malik stood and motioned to the drawer. "Chief."

Jack walked over and peered down at a 9 mm at the bottom of what looked like her athletic clothes drawer.

"That was too easy," Malik said.

Jack walked out of the room, found the crime scene tech, and motioned for him to follow. Jack stopped at the door. Simon entered and took a picture of the room at large before slowly narrowing his focus to the gun in the drawer.

Jack called Michelle over. She took her time. By the time she got there, Malik was holding the gun by the handle with two gloved fingers. Simon wrote on a labeled plastic bag.

"I thought you said you didn't have a gun."

"I don't. That's not mine."

"It was in your bottom drawer."

Michelle's face drained of color, her expression of bravado. "Jack, I swear. That is not my gun." Malik removed the clip and emptied the chamber and dropped it all into the bag Simon held open. He sealed it and walked past Jack and Michelle. Jack stopped him, took the bagged gun from him, inspected it, and gave it back to Simon with a nod. Simon had the tools in the mobile CSI unit to check for prints, but he would have to take it to Yourkeville for ballistics, not that he needed to.

Jack would know that gun anywhere.

Jack lowered his voice. "Michelle, you need to come with me." Her eyes were panicked, shifting from Jack, to Malik, and finally to her family, sitting silently in the living room. "I won't arrest you or cuff you in front of your family, but you have to come quietly and willingly."

She nodded. "Let me put my shoes on."

They walked out of the house and saw Norman Davie patiently waiting out of the way. When they got abreast of him, Michelle said, "Norman, meet us at the station."

"Michelle, I can't. I'm your father's business lawyer, and the company is being searched. You'll have to find another lawyer."

Michelle stumbled, stopped, and turned to Davie. A riot of emotions played across Michelle's face and, for a split second, Jack thought she was going to sob. Instead she straightened to her full height, said, "Tell Dad what's happened, and call Bob Underwood," and walked away, head held high.

Jack stared out the window of Ann Newberry's office, his phone held to his ear. "Hey, Julie. Is Eddie at home?"

"Where are you?"

"I'm in Yourkeville."

Julie sighed. "Of course you are. No. Eddie isn't here and as far as I know, he never came home last night."

"Have you talked to him?"

"Why would I have talked to him? What's wrong?"

Jack picked up a picture from the credenza. Ann, her daughter, and her granddaughter dressed up for Halloween. He smiled despite his concern for Eddie. The daughter and granddaughter were zombies, and Ann was dressed up like the sheriff from *The Walking Dead.*

"I've been trying to call him since last night and can't get in touch with him."

"He's probably with his girlfriend. Celebrating their good news."

"I'll call her."

"Did you even come home last night?"

"No. Sorry. I was in Dallas until late, then I had to get a judge to sign off on a warrant to execute this morning. I've hardly had time to eat."

"Jack, this is worse than when you were with the Agency. I can't live like this."

"This is how it is, Julie. If you don't like it, leave."

"I'm taking Ethan with me."

"Over my dead body."

There was silence on the other end. Jack knew she might be gone when he got home, and he wasn't sure if she could manipulate Ethan into leaving with her or not.

"Don't do anything until we talk, okay?" Jack said. "This should all be settled down by tomorrow. I promise."

Her laugh was laced with bitterness. "That's what you always say," she said and clicked off.

Jack let his phone fall to his chest. Should he text Ethan, warn him his mother wanted to leave Stillwater and take him with her? Hope she waited one more day? Hope Ethan wouldn't leave with her if given the chance?

He lifted the phone and placed the call he dreaded making, though when Ellie answered, his shoulders relaxed and he smiled.

"Hey. It's Jack."

"Hi." She sounded wary. Jack couldn't blame her. He expected angry. Wary he could deal with.

"I'm sorry about yesterday."

"Oh. Thanks. I didn't expect to win."

"No, not the election. About last night."

"The victory party?" He heard the air quotes in her voice. "You didn't miss anything. Though your wife and son came by. That was fun."

"No. I'm sorry I didn't make it out to your lake house."

"My lake house?"

"Didn't Eddie talk to you?"

"I haven't talked to Eddie since Sunday night. He texted he was coming by last night, but he never showed. Why? What's going on?"

"I'm looking for Eddie. He didn't go home last night, and if he isn't with you . . ."

"Why would he stay the night with me?"

"I don't mean it like that. It's just, where else would he be? Has he ever stayed out at your lake house?"

"No. But he might have seen me punch in the code. Do you want me to go check?"

"Can you?"

"Of course. You don't think he's in trouble, do you?"

"I doubt it, but still."

"I'll go right now."

"Thanks."

Neither hung up. Finally, Jack said, "Is it true? Are you—"

It took Ellie so long to reply, Jack thought she had hung up. "Yes."

"Oh my God."

"Is that a good 'Oh my God' or a . . ."

"Of course it's good. It's wonderful." He realized Ellie sounded subdued. "Is everything okay? Julie said you threw up. Have you been to the doctor?"

"Yes, everything's fine," she snapped. "Jack, this isn't a conversation I want to have on the phone."

"No. Right. I should have these cases wrapped up today. Tomorrow at the latest."

"Cases? Matt and Amy's case?"

"Yeah. I'll tell you all about it when I see you. Let me know when you get out to your lake house."

"Okay. Jack?"

"Yeah?"

"Be careful."

CHAPTER FORTY-FOUR

At first glance, Doyle Industries parking lot looked like it did on any other business day. Upon closer inspection, the cars parked in front of the buildings weren't minivans, trucks, and sedans, but crime scene vans, generic black Suburbans that could only be government issue, sheriffs' cruisers, DPS cars, and a lone Stillwater PD Tahoe.

Miner got out of his truck and inspected the scene. Men and women in FBI and DEA windbreakers huddled together drinking steaming cups of Abe's coffee and grimacing. They either hadn't discovered Ellie's coffee shop or were out here before she opened. Miner chuckled to himself; Ellie was one of the few people making out like a bandit from all the crime.

Miner ambled up to the group of agents. A DEA agent with a barrel chest and close-set eyes took Miner in from his Stetson to his cowboy boots and, by the wry expression on his face, slotted Miner in the bumpkin category.

"Miner Jesson," he said, holding his hand out.

"Oh, right! Jack's mentioned you. Tom Hunter."

"Nice to meet you."

"This is Special Agent Alex Dunne with the FBI."

A female agent with startling green eyes and a knowing smile held out her hand. "Deputy."

"Hunter," the DEA agent said into his phone. "What?" He walked a few feet away.

"Sergeant, actually," Miner said.

"Sergeant Jesson." A strawberry blonde braid fell across Agent Dunne's left shoulder from beneath the loose-knit toboggan she wore. "Mr. Doyle's been asking for you."

"For me."

She nodded. "When he's not cursing McBride."

"Where is he?"

With the hand holding her coffee, Dunne pointed behind Miner. Joe Doyle sat in his Ford about thirty feet away.

"Excuse me."

Miner walked around to the driver's side. Doyle rolled down the window. Waves of anger emanated from him. "Why didn't I know about this?"

"This is a federal operation. How would I know about it?"

"Don't bullshit me, Miner. No way the Feds raid a local business without telling the local cops."

Miner shrugged. "They may have told Jack, but he didn't mention it to me. What did the warrant say?"

"Which one?"

Miner raised his eyebrows.

"There's one for physical evidence of the intent to sell drugs and another for our financial records."

"Hmm."

"Hmm? That's the best you can do? Where the fuck did they get their information, huh? And why are they raiding on the day of my son's funeral?"

"Well, to the former, I can tell you they have someone in custody who's feeding them information."

"Who?"

Miner scratched his chin and looked away. He and Jack had gone over exactly what to divulge to Doyle, but he still didn't feel right about it. Jack was taking a couple of pretty big gambles on interpersonal relationships and human nature. "Kyle Grant."

Doyle clenched his jaw and exhaled. He stared out at the front door of his business. An FBI agent propped open the doors and stood aside as other agents walked out the front door with computers.

"Fucking Eddie McBride."

"Joe, I need to ask you a question."

Doyle glared at Miner. "Do you."

"Witnesses say Michelle called you Sunday morning and told you about Matt discovering the operation. Is it true?"

Doyle nodded.

"And you said you'd go straight over to talk to him."

Doyle returned his gaze to his company being dismantled before his eyes. "Yes."

"What time did you go over to Matt's?"

"One-thirty."

"How long were you there?"

"Thirty minutes."

"What happened?"

"I lied to him. I lied to my boy. He was going to leave, to move away, back to Tyler to work with Sterry, or Houston to be near Amy's mother. I couldn't have that. I told him I didn't know anything about what Michelle was doing and that together we'd fix it."

"Did you mean any of it?"

"No." He drummed his fingers on the steering wheel and stared straight ahead, his brows furrowed as if calculating. Finally, he said, "I called Michelle and told her it was time to move the operation permanently. She would move down there and run it from Houston."

"How'd she take the news?"

"Dead silence. But I knew she would come around eventually. She's always done what I wanted her to do."

"Why didn't you mention your conversation with Matt to Jack when he interviewed you?"

"I didn't see anything, and they were alive when I left. I couldn't risk Jack finding out about the drug operation."

"Well, the jig is up now."

Doyle watched more agents with computers file out and nodded.

"You haven't asked about Michelle," Miner said.

"If it wasn't for Michelle and all of her fuck-ups I wouldn't be watching the Feds raid my business."

"You realize you're giving McBride Michelle's motive for killing Matt and Amy," Miner said.

Doyle continued drumming his fingers on his steering wheel and stayed silent.

"She'll be charged with four murders, Joe."

"I know."

CHAPTER FORTY-FIVE

Michelle Doyle Ryan sat at the interrogation table, hands clasped together, trying and failing to be the picture of calm confidence. Bob Underwood sat next to her, a blue Bic pen poised over a yellow legal pad.

Jack leaned against the wall in the interrogation room while Ann sat across from Michelle and asked her questions, which Michelle stared at the corner of the room and refused to answer.

"Simon rushed ballistics on the gun we found in your dresser," Ann said. "It was a match."

Michelle's eyes flicked to Ann and away. Jack knew the question *for what?* tickled the end of Michelle's tongue. Instead, she clenched her jaw, and Bob Underwood asked the question.

"It's Jack's gun. The gun used to kill your brother and sister-in-law. And Paco Morales and Diego Vazquez. Your fingerprints were found all over the gun, as well."

Michelle opened her mouth, closed it, then decided to break her silence. "That's impossible. I hate guns. I haven't touched a gun in years."

"I'm not making this up," Ann said. She placed a copy of the fingerprint results in front of Michelle. She leaned forward and studied the paper. When she sat back, Bob inspected it.

"I'm telling you, I've never seen that gun before you pulled it out of my drawer," Michelle said.

"Yet, it was in your dresser and your fingerprints are all over it." Ann slid the fingerprint results away from Michelle. "We have witnesses who said you wanted to organize a meet with the Pedroza cartel and who heard you threaten your brother."

"Did you ask Kyle Grant to set up a meeting with the Pedrozas?" Jack said.

"Who are the Pedrozas?"

"We know you wanted to meet with the Pedrozas to talk truce, split up the drug trade in the county, maybe."

"I don't know what you're talking about. I'm vice president of the largest employer in Yourke County. Legitimate businesses that pay all of our taxes and do good in the community."

"Grant set up a meeting, and things went south," Jack said. "You executed Morales and Vazquez with my gun, that Grant was somehow able to get away from Vazquez."

"That's the stupidest story I've ever heard."

"I have to agree with Michelle here," Bob said, almost apologetically.

"Why?" Ann asked.

"Are these Pedrozas cartel?" Michelle asked.

Ann and Jack remained silent, their withering expressions of disbelief all the answer she would receive.

"Wouldn't killing them only bring more cartel to the area? More trouble for the local organization? It's a stupid business move and I don't make stupid business moves. But maybe the rules are different for illegal businesses. I wouldn't know," Michelle said.

"Michelle," Ann sighed, "you can stop the act. We know DI is the front from the local drug business. We have solid witnesses turning on you as we speak, and as your business crashes, more and more will come forward to save their own asses. The gig is up. We don't care about that, anyway. That's the Feds case. We're here to talk about four murders."

"Here's the thing, Michelle," Jack said. "Everything points to you. Evidence: the gun that killed Morales and Vazquez was found in your dresser with your fingerprints on it. Motive for the Pedrozas is easy. Dueling drug operations. But Matt was a bit tougher. Until our witness told us about Matt stopping by DI and discovered you unpacking drugs from your heavy equipment."

Michelle clicked her long red nails on the table and studied Ann and Jack. "Kyle's alive, isn't he? That's who you have in custody." She laughed in disbelief. "He was right. Eddie's a fucking narc."

"We wanted to give you the chance to tell your side of the story," Ann said. "Maybe Pigeon won't go for the death penalty."

"We haven't heard any physical evidence that even put Michelle *at* the scenes," Bob said. "It's all very circumstantial, relying on unreliable witnesses and a lot of supposition."

Michelle stared off into space, her nails clicking in a faster and faster pattern. Ann and Jack watched as Michelle calculated what to do. Bob leaned over and whispered in Michelle's ear. She shook her head and finally said, "Shit."

"You're good and cornered, aren't you?" Jack said. "On the one hand, both sides of your business are going up in flames, on the other hand, you're the suspected murderer of four people."

"Suspected," Bob said. "This is a very weak case, and both of you know it."

She leaned forward and hit the table with her fist. "Maybe if I say it enough, you people will *listen*. I didn't kill any of these people! I never met with the Pedrozas. Last I heard, they turned down the meet. Kyle was going to keep trying. As far as Matt and Amy go, Dad went by Matt's Sunday morning to talk to him. He was going to get in line. Anyway, I wouldn't have killed my brother. I can't even believe you would *think* that of me."

"Did your father tell you Matt was falling in line?" Ann said.

"Yeah. Dad called and told me he'd talked to Matt and he'd worked everything out."

"What time?" Jack said.

"Two? Two fifteen?"

Ann closed her file and Jack stared at the floor.

"What? Ask him! He'll tell you."

"We did ask him. He said he told you that you would need to move to Houston. Run your businesses from there," Ann said.

"And you were unhappy with the decision," Jack added.

"He's lying." Disbelief laced her voice. Her eyes moved back and forth as she stared at the table. Her head jerked up. "Who talked to him?"

"Miner," Jack said.

"Miner's being paid to feed you lies."

"Michelle, be quiet," Bob said.

"By whom?" Jack said.

"The company. He'll say whatever Dad tells him to as long as we keep giving him drugs for Teresa."

Bob sighed and leaned back in his chair, shaking his head. He capped his Bic pen, opened his briefcase, and started packing up.

"He's lying to you," Michelle continued. "That's not what happened. Dad wouldn't send me away like that. Our whole operation will collapse if I'm not there."

Ann stood and walked around the table. "Stand up."

Michelle looked up at Ann and shook her head in disbelief. "I didn't kill anyone."

"Evidence says you did."

"What are you charging Michelle with?" Bob said.

"Four counts of first-degree murder, and now bribing a police officer."

"What? Bob, I didn't kill any of these people."

Bob held up his hand. "What do you have besides the gun?"

"Witness testimony that says she pulled the trigger on Vazquez and Morales," Jack said.

"That is a bald-faced lie."

"A campaign pin found at the scene with her fingerprints on it," Ann said.

"And, at Matt and Amy's house?"

Ann patted Michelle on the shoulder. "Stand up." Michelle, panicky, looked to Bob for help.

"The gun," Jack said.

Bob shook his head. "Those murder charges won't stick, and you know it."

"The bribing a police officer will," Jack said.

"Bob?" Michelle asked.

"Go on. We'll get bail posted and have you out by tomorrow."

"*Tomorrow?*"

"You just admitted to bribing Miner. There's only so much I can do."

Her shoulders slumped. She exhaled, straightened, and stood, her chair scraping loudly against the floor. "Michelle Ryan Doyle, you're under arrest for the murder of Paco Morales, Diego Vazquez, Matt Doyle, and Amy Doyle, and for bribing a police officer," Ann said.

"Someone is setting me up," Michelle said, panic creeping into her voice.

"Who?" Jack said.

"Kyle Grant."

"Why?"

"I don't know, because Eddie was replacing him?" Michelle said.

"Personally or professionally?" Jack said. When Michelle narrowed her eyes, Jack continued, "Yeah, Kyle told me you were fucking him, too."

"He hated Eddie. Something to do with Kyle's father in prison. I don't know. That's why he was so mad about me and Eddie."

"So, Kyle killed Matt and Amy because he was jealous?" Ann asked.

"Yes."

"Try again," Ann said. She grasped Michelle's elbow and propelled her toward the door. "He was driving west with Eddie McBride when Matt and Amy were killed."

"Then he's working with someone." Michelle pulled against Ann's grip, which only made Ann use more force. "You're hurting me."

"Stop fighting or I'll cuff you."

"Hang on," Jack said. He stepped forward. "Who would hate you so much they would set you up for four murders?"

Jack could smell Michelle's terror. Her eyes rolled around the room, as if searching for the culprit in the corners. "Brian Grant!" she said triumphantly. "Because I made Matt use another contractor."

"The Pedrozas were killed before Brian knew."

"His brother did. Kyle. They're in on this together. How can you not see it?"

"How would Brian, or Kyle, plant the gun in your house?" Ann said.

"And get your fingerprints all over it."

Michelle was searching for a plausible answer.

"Michelle, stop," Bob said. "You'll be out of jail in twenty-four hours, tops."

"But I'll miss my brother's funeral."

Ann led Michelle out of the room, still reciting the warning. Michelle called over her shoulder, "I didn't do this. McBride, I'm going to destroy you when this is all over!"

Jack turned to Bob. "You know, you could have waited until after the funeral," Bob said. "The town won't forgive you for that."

"I'm here to do a job, not to win a popularity contest. My job is to solve crimes and stop crime when I can. I call arresting someone for four murders and playing a role, though small, in the search of the front of a suspected crime organization a pretty fucking good day at the office."

"Well, when you get fired, you can come work with me. Shirley is on me about retiring, and she's about convinced me." He opened his briefcase and took out a folded legal document. "Your divorce papers."

Jack pulled out his phone. "I have an audio file to send you. For our case."

Bob raised his eyebrows. "Should I be alone when I listen to it?"

"Nothing like that. But it's not good for Julie."

With a weary sigh, Bob patted Jack on the shoulder and walked down the hall to take care of his client.

Jack's phone vibrated with a text from Ellie.

–Eddie isn't here, nor does it look like he's been here.

–Thanks for checking. I'll call you later.

–K

He was putting his phone back in his pocket and adjusting his bullet-proof vest beneath his shirt when his phone rang. "McBride."

"Who's Brian Grant?" Tom Hunter said.

"Kyle Grant's brother. He was a suspect in the Doyle murders but he's been ruled out. Why?"

"Got a call from Segoville. Some dumbass let Grant make a call."

"And he called Brian."

"Looks like it. Have you talked to Eddie?"

"No. I've been trying to get in touch with him since last night. You?"

"No. We've tried to track his phone but it must be turned off or dead."

"Is there a blue and white '69 Ford in the parking lot?"

"Yeah. Damn nice truck."

Jack tried to ignore the stab of fear in his chest. "It's Eddie's."

Tom Hunter didn't reply for a moment. "Shit."

"Is Miner there?"

"Yeah. Talking to Doyle. They look awfully cozy."

"That cozy relationship gave us Michelle Ryan's motive. Pull Miner away and tell him to find Brian Grant. I'm on my way back to Stillwater."

CHAPTER FORTY-SIX

Miner leaned against the counter as Susan straightened and re-straightened the items on her desk with her good hand. She wore a black skirt and white blouse for Matt and Amy's funeral. Her daughter, Paige, stood beside her behind the front desk at City Hall. Paige wore Susan's phone headset and had a pad of paper lined with notes in front of her.

"Paige gonna watch the front for you while you're gone?" Miner asked.

"Yes."

"Ellie's closing the Book Bank for a couple hours," Paige explained.

"Can't very well shut down City Hall." Susan forced a laugh.

"No. I imagine calls will be light."

The phone rang and Paige picked it up. "Stillwater City Hall, how may I direct your call?" She paused. "I'll put you through to his voice mail." She punched buttons on the phone and looked at Miner. "I wouldn't count on it. Everyone's calling about Doyle Industries and the rumor Michelle's been arrested."

"Susan, where's Brian?"

"Why?"

"I want to talk to him."

"What about?"

"Have you seen him?"

"She hasn't seen him since yesterday morning."

"Paige!"

"Why would you lie for him?" Paige spat. "He broke your hand!"

"No, he didn't. How many times do I have to tell you?"

"Paige, if you've got this, I need to talk to Susan alone." Miner lifted the breakaway counter, walked to the door beneath the stairs, and waited for Paige to buzz him through. When the door clicked, Miner opened it and held it for Susan. Reluctantly, she followed.

Miner motioned for Susan to sit in a metal chair next to his desk then settled into his own chair. He leaned back and crossed an ankle over his knee. "Now, Susan, no more bullshit."

Susan's head shot up at the profanity. "I'm not—"

"Yes, you are and I'm not judging you for it. Trust me, I'm the last person on earth who would judge someone for lying or stealing or going against their morals for their family. But we're talking about murder here, and you've got three kids to think about."

"Brian didn't kill anyone."

"How are you so sure? He doesn't have an alibi for Matt and Amy's murders."

Susan closed her eyes and inhaled deeply. She didn't see or hear Jack walk in and stop at the door.

"If he would have just taken me to the hospital, none of this would have happened."

"What do you mean?"

She opened her eyes and saw Jack. "On the way home from the lake, Brian was livid. I've never seen him as angry as he was that night. He was almost as pissed at Eddie as Matt."

"Why?"

"Before we left the bonfire, Eddie told Brian if he ever hurt me, he'd make sure Brian regretted it."

"Are you close with Eddie?" Miner asked. He looked to Jack, who stared at the floor with a contemplative expression.

"No. I hardly know him. Of course, Brian got all kinds of ideas, based on Eddie's reputation. Between Matt and Eddie, I knew I had to do something to divert Brian's attention."

"You baited him to get angry with you," Jack said.

Susan shook her head. "I slammed my hand in the car door when he went into the shop. I begged him to take me to the hospital. I knew by the time we were done, he would have lost a bit of his high, calmed down, seen reason."

"But Paige took you," Miner said.

"Brian's never taken me. I don't know why I thought this time would be different." Her face tensed. "Even so, I don't believe Brian killed Matt and Amy."

"But he's involved somehow. Kyle's implicated him," Miner said.

"Of course he has." Her shoulders slumped and she sighed. "I came home yesterday, and Brian wasn't there. No note, wouldn't answer my texts or pick up when I called. I checked the caller ID on our home phone and saw the number from a jail and knew."

She fiddled with her cast. "Over the years, Kyle's tried to get Brian involved in his stuff, but Brian's always refused." Susan looked up and saw Jack. She spoke to Jack as much as Miner. "Brian's a good man, but sometimes it's a struggle. He'd see Kyle with a wad of cash after working fifteen-hour days on a job and still barely being able to pay the bills."

"Did you talk to Brian, after Kyle called?"

"He called. He was high. Drunk. Not making much sense."

"What did he say?"

"Things were going to be okay from now on."

"He didn't get more specific?"

Susan looked down and to the left. "No."

"Susan."

"He's my husband, Miner."

Jack stepped into the room. "Did he say anything about my brother?"

She closed her eyes, as if blocking out the world would make the truth go away. Finally, she nodded.

"What did he say?"

Her eyes met Jack's. "That Eddie McBride was our ticket to the good life."

Jack stared out the window of his office and tried to forget it was his brother who was missing and work the case like the objective cop he needed to be. He had to remind himself that his brother had been under-cover for twenty years and had no doubt gotten out of worse scrapes than this. What a conversation that would be, listening to Eddie recount the double life he'd been living for so long. Jack rubbed his face. He hoped they had the opportunity to have it.

Brian Grant was in the wind, with his phone turned off. Based on Brian's comment to Susan, Kyle's message had been about Eddie being a narc. If Brian had intercepted Eddie somewhere on his way home, where did he take him? Or, the better question, to whom did he take him? Michelle? Joe? The Pedrozas?

"Okay. I'll question Michelle about Eddie. How did Doyle react to Eddie being a narc?" Jack said.

"Not surprised. He suspected it. He blames Michelle for everything." Miner paused. "I think he's lying."

"About Michelle?"

"Yep."

Jack nodded. As much as he didn't want to, he believed Michelle's protestations of innocence. The question now became, *who's setting her up?* "Me, too. Do you think Joe killed Matt and Amy?"

Miner shook his head. "No. I think he's making her the fall guy to save his own skin."

"Christ, this family is fucked up. Doyle gave up his daughter for the murder of his son to save his drug business."

Miner nodded. "Suspect Joe was so mad about Eddie he didn't really think his lie through."

"It's a stupid play if so. Phone records are the easiest thing to check," Jack said.

"Criminals are never as smart as they think they are," Miner said.

Nathan Starling knocked on the door and entered without waiting for a response. His eyes were bright with excitement. "Chief? Sorry to interrupt. But you're gonna wanna hear this."

Jack expected Eric Sterry to be in late middle age, on the cusp of retirement. Instead, the man who sat in a chair in City Hall foyer was younger than Jack and much fitter. A cast covered his right leg from foot to mid-thigh. A woman hovered over him, concern written all over her face. They wore funeral clothes.

Jack went forward and held out his hand. "Mr. Sterry?"

"Jack McBride?"

"Yes."

Eric stood with less trouble than Jack would have thought. His wife was ready and eager to help, but Sterry ignored her. He shook Jack's hand with a vice-like grip. "Sheila?" Sheila Sterry fished an iPhone out of her purse and handed it to Eric.

"I fell on Saturday, as I'm sure your deputy told you. Broke my phone as well as my leg. Sheila went out and got me a new one, and my teenaged son restored it for me. With all the "get well soon" voice mails and texts, it took me a while to find this. Found it this morning. Came here as soon as we could." He held up the phone showing a voice mail from Matt Doyle. He motioned for Jack to take it.

Miner and Starling stood at Jack's elbows, silent, while he snapped a glove on his hand and held the phone up an inch or so from his ear.

-Eric, it's Matt. Sorry to call so late. I should have listened to you. You were right, I was wrong. Dad was just here. I can't believe I never saw through him before. God, what a mess. I'm such an idiot. I don't know what to do, who to trust. Chris, maybe, but he won't go against Michelle. He's on his way here. Who knows, he may be as crooked as the rest. Call me tomorrow.

The time stamp on the message was 2:35 a.m.

"What did you warn Matt about?"

"My grandfather told me not to hire a Doyle, that he would cheat me. I didn't believe him. After Matt told me he was starting his own organic produce business, bankrolled by his father, my grandfather told me he'd heard rumors about Doyle being involved in some pretty shady dealings, shadier than the savings and loan or hot oil. He wouldn't give me details, so all I could do was tell Matt he was making a mistake, that his family wasn't always aboveboard. Matt got defensive, as I would have. I knew when I heard the message that he'd found out what everyone suspected."

"He mentioned his brother-in-law. Did he ever talk much about Chris?"

"He liked him okay, but thought he was a pussy. Chris was content to let Michelle wear the pants, make the living, and skate through life. I was pretty shocked when he said he called him. Only thing I can figure is Matt thought he was outside the family business and he'd be an ally."

"Can I keep this for a couple of days until we can establish chain of possession and download the message."

"Sure. Whatever you need."

Jack motioned to Starling, who pulled an evidence bag out of his back pocket. Jack dropped it into the bag.

"I take it you're going to the funeral?" Miner said to the Sterry's.

"Yes."

"Don't mention the message to anyone."

"We won't," Eric said. "Is it going to help?"

"Yes, it is," Jack said.

Starling handed the bag to Jack and held the heavy front door open for the Sterrys. Jack turned to Miner and shook his head.

"They're never as smart as they think."

CHAPTER FORTY-SEVEN

Brian Grant made a production of checking his watch. "We missed the funeral. I'm sure Chris will tell us all about it. I wonder if Michelle made it?"

Eddie watched Brian through the slits of his swollen eyes. His captor sat on a wooden stool next to a work bench that resembled Brian's own workshop. Eddie wasn't sure where he was, but based on the distant thwacks and hum of motors, he guessed he was somewhere on the grounds of Cypress Country Club.

Brian inspected the baseball bat in his lap, the one Eddie took from him Sunday night, the one Eddie suspected would soon be stained with his own blood.

Eddie grunted through the duct tape on his mouth.

"You wanna talk?" Eddie nodded his head. Brian studied him and slapped the bat in his hand, like a cheesy movie villain. "You know if you scream, I'll kill you, right?"

Eddie nodded.

Brian ripped the duct tape from his mouth. Eddie opened his jaw and moved it around. "Thanks." Eddie twisted his hands, which were taped behind the back of his chair. His feet were taped to the back legs, pitching him forward into a miserable sitting position.

"What are you doing, Brian? You aren't going to get away with this. Either of you."

"Yes, we will."

"No, you won't. Jack'll catch you, figure it all out."

"If he does, all I'll be guilty of is kidnapping you."

"A federal agent, Brian. That means hard time. Think of Susan. Your kids."

"I am thinking of them. Michelle goes to jail, and Chris takes over the operation. I'll be his right-hand man. We won't have to worry about money."

"No, just you getting caught and going to jail."

"Your brother isn't that good."

Eddie remained silent. As the hours had ticked away, Eddie's faith in his brother wavered. He hoped Jack would figure it all out before the Pedrozas showed up to collect him.

"It won't just be kidnapping, Brian. If the Pedrozas execute me, which they will, you'll be charged as an accomplice. You're lucky the Feds don't have the death penalty, but you might as well be dead. You'll never get out."

"Do you want me to tape your mouth back up?"

Eddie shook his head.

"Then shut up."

Brian sat on the stool, took a tin out of his back pocket, and removed a joint from it, watching Eddie the entire time with something like wonder. "How long you been a DEA agent?" Brian lit the joint and inhaled deeply. He put the lighter in his front shirt pocket.

"Twenty years."

Brian whistled. "Long time. I guess you've done some pretty morally ambiguous things in your life."

"Morally ambiguous. Those are a couple of ten-dollar words for a Grant."

"What do you know about Grants?"

"I told you; I knew your dad in Huntsville."

Brian took a hit and held it. "He was a bastard."

"Yes, he was. I thought you were different."

"I am."

Eddie gave Brian what he hoped was an incredulous look. Pain shot across the back of his skull. "Look at what you're doing, asshole."

Brian shrugged. "A man's gotta do what's necessary to provide for his family."

"If you say so."

"I do, and you wouldn't fucking know about family, would you?"

"I guess not. Don't you think it looks weird, you not being at the funeral?"

"No."

"I wonder what Susan is telling people who ask about you. You know how small towns are. If they know you were a suspect in Matt and Amy's death, they'll assume you're not there because you're guilty."

"They'll know Michelle's been arrested."

"No one will believe that."

"Sure they will. With the evidence they have . . ."

"No one knows about the evidence yet. They're going off reputation. Between you and Michelle as the killer, everyone's gonna assume it's you."

"Shut your mouth."

"And Susan and the kids having to deal with the stares and whispers."

"Shut up."

"Her hand."

Brian came at Eddie. The brass knuckles crunched against Eddie's jaw and he toppled over. Unfortunately, the chair didn't break apart. *Shit only happens in movies*, Eddie thought.

Brian knelt down and blew the sweet smoke of his joint in Eddie's face. "I hope the Pedrozas torture you before they kill you."

"You gonna stay and watch? You don't have the stomach for it. You're a fucking coward, just like your dad."

"You think so?"

"I know so. You bully your wife and kids, probably beat them, too, but not so anyone can see it. Use your fists on their chests and stomachs. Maybe a belt on their backs. All wife beaters are cowards."

Brian stood, pulled his leg back, and kicked Eddie in the stomach with each word he said. "How many times do I have to say it? I. Don't. Beat. My. Family."

Brian walked away and picked up the bat. Eddie coughed up blood and gasped for air.

Two, maybe three ribs broken.

Brian knelt down again, holding the bat in front of Eddie's face. "Call me a coward again."

Though it hurt like a motherfucker and Eddie could barely breathe to do it, he laughed. "Yeah, prove me wrong. Beat up a defenseless man."

Brian pulled a knife out of his pocket and opened it. He waved it in front of Eddie's face. "Know whose this was?"

"Your dad's."

"Granddad's. He was a mean motherfucker, too." He cut one of Eddie's legs free, then the other. He cut Eddie's hands free, grabbed the bat, and stepped back. Eddie tried to stand and fell to the ground. Brian's laughter ricocheted against the metal walls of the shed. Eddie lay on the ground, waiting for his legs to stop stinging and wished he could lay there forever. His head pounded with each beat of his heart, one of his lungs had collapsed and he could barely see through his swollen, tender eyes. He pushed himself to his hands and knees and spit blood onto the concrete floor. He glanced over his shoulder, half expecting Brian to take advantage of his weakened state and go in for the kill. But Brian didn't. He took a hit on his joint with one hand and held the bat in the other. The knife was nowhere to be seen. Thank God for small favors, Eddie thought.

Eddie stood on shaky legs, turned to his opponent, and was overcome with a bone-deep weariness. How many times had he been in a similar situation? More than he could count. This had to end.

"Come on, Brian, let's leave. Right now. You and me. I'll testify for you, you testify against Chris, and we'll get you in a country club prison. You can be back with your family before Troy and Olivia are out of high school."

"Afraid, are you?"

Eddie sighed. "You're not going to win."

Brian laughed again. "If you could see yourself, you'd know how stupid you sound."

Eddie stumbled forward, as if struggling to stand. "If you kill me, Chris or the Pedrozas will kill you."

"Oh, I'm not going to kill you. This little beating will be between us." Brian placed his joint on the work table to save for later and stepped forward with the bat raised.

Eddie swayed and Brian pulled the bat back in the classic batter's swing, leaving the front of his body exposed. Eddie straightened, stepped forward, and kicked Brian in the balls. Brian's swing lost its force and the bat clattered to the ground. Brian doubled over. Eddie shifted behind him, wrapped his arm around Brian's neck, pulled him into a standing position, and squeezed. Brian flailed at Eddie's arm with little strength, his body struggling to cope with the shooting pains in his groin. Eddie squeezed harder and said in a hoarse voice, "You forget, Brian, I kick people's ass for a living."

Brian gagged and Eddie released the pressure, but only slightly. "I told you I was there when your dad died, and I was." Brian hands patted against Eddie's arms. "He came after one of the leaders I was there to get close to, and I stepped between them. Have a nice, long scar on my side to remind me of the coward. Killed him with his own shiv. He cried like a baby." Brian found a bit of strength and tried to kick at Eddie. Eddie squeezed his neck again. "Don't make me regret letting you live." Brian stopped kicking and flailing and went limp.

Eddie held up Brian and tried to catch his breath. Just a little bit more. He dragged Brian to the chair and dropped him into it. Brian's chin sank to his chest. Eddie went to the work bench, found the duct tape, and taped up Brian as he'd taped up Eddie nearly twenty-four hours earlier, ending with a piece across Brian's mouth. Eddie grabbed Brian by the hair and lifted his head. "Fucker." He punched him in the eye. "That's for my left eye." He punched him in the other and almost fell to the ground with the effort. "That's for the right."

He stumbled over to the work bench again, dumped packages of black plastic ties out, and noticed the joint. He put it between his lips and took a long drag. He closed his eyes and let the smoke settle in his lungs before exhaling. He kept the joint between his lips, took the plastic Lowe's bag and ties over to Brian. He put the bag over Brian's head and taped it around his neck. Over the duct tape, he tied Brian's ankles to the chair with the plastic ties, to make it that much more difficult for the fucker, and did the same with Brian's hands. He patted Brian's pockets and found cigarettes, a lighter, and another joint. He pocketed all of them. He stood, smoked the joint and watched the plastic bag go in and out as Brian breathed. When it slowed to every five seconds, Eddie tore a hole in the bag where Brian's nose was and kicked the chair over. He threw the duct tape across the room and stumbled out of the shed and into the twilight.

CHAPTER FORTY-EIGHT

Jack knew it was a risky play. The price? His brother's life. But he wanted to get Chris Ryan dead to rights. He needed to catch him red-handed. So, he waited.

And doubted.

Chris played the part of grieving relative with the perfect mix of gravitas and grief. He held up Mary Doyle as she walked down the aisle of First Methodist Church, drugged up to her eyelids with Valium. Amy's mother followed, the children on her arms, and Joe Doyle walked behind them all, rigid, staring straight ahead with an expression of fury Jack suspected was more due to the DEA agents combing over his businesses than for the death of his family or his daughter being in custody for the murders.

Jack stood at the back of the sanctuary and surveyed the room. He knew a quarter of the congregation by name, and half by sight. Ellie, sitting near the rear, caught his eye. She raised her eyebrows and gave him the once over. The uniform. He shrugged. She smiled slightly, dipped her head in prayer, and pushed her hair behind her ear. Jack hid his smile out of respect for the dead.

Ellie liked the uniform.

Kelly sat with her son, Seth, on the other side of the room, staring purposely ahead. Jack wondered vaguely why Kelly wasn't sitting with Ellie when he saw Ethan sitting next to Olivia, Troy, and Susan Grant. Susan turned around in the pew, searching for Brian no doubt. She saw Jack and turned back around quickly. The fact Brian wasn't here, and Susan didn't know where he was, gave Jack hope his twin was still alive.

The interminable service finally ended, and Jack snuck out the back before the family filed out, followed by the congregants. There would be no graveside service since Matt and Amy had made it clear they wanted to be cremated and their ashes sprinkled on Kyle Field at A&M. Jack shook his head. Aggies.

He got in his car and drove off, not wanting to get sidetracked by the newspaper editor or gossipy citizens who wanted to know why Michelle wasn't there. Was it true she'd been arrested for murder? He waved as he drove past Lincoln Bishop, parked on a side street in his personal car. Five law enforcement officers were on Chris Ryan—Jack and Bishop, a sheriff's deputy, Tom Hunter in an unmarked Suburban, and Miner Jesson, whose job it was to stay close to the Doyles and to alert the others when Chris Ryan left the reception at Joe Doyle's house.

"He's settled in," Miner said through the radio twenty minutes later. "He doesn't look like he'll be leaving for a while."

"Bishop, where are you?"

"Parked outside the house."

"Eastman?"

"Drinking coffee at the Chevron."

"Hunter?"

"Doyle Industries."

"I have to stop at my house. Tell me as soon as he leaves."

"Roger."

A minute later, Jack pulled into his driveway, killed the engine, and got out of the car. He hoped Ethan was at the reception. He didn't want to do this with him in the house, but he would if he had to.

Jack walked through the house and up the stairs. Julie lay on the bed, typing on her phone and grinning. When she saw Jack, the grin fell from her face. "What are you wearing?"

Jack looked down, forgetting for a moment about the uniform. He didn't bother answering and held out the divorce papers.

She looked from the papers and back to Jack. "No."

"Yes."

"I'll take Ethan."

"He won't go."

"I'll tell him how you cheated on me."

"He knows who cheated on whom. You shouldn't have left your phone last year. All of those messages and texts from your boyfriends? I've made copies of them all to present as evidence if you contest the divorce."

"My father will hire the best lawyer money can buy . . ."

"Julie, for once in your life, take the easy out. Divorce me. Find some rich man who won't care what you do in your free time as long as you're there to look good on his arm and let him fuck you when he wants. It's the life you've always wanted to lead. Your mother's life, right?"

She rose and walked to Jack. "Do you think I'm going to let you take my son away and start a new little family with your pregnant girlfriend? Yeah, I figured it out. With a little help from Kelly. What will Ethan think when he finds out?"

"I already know."

Ethan stood in the doorway, staring at them. "I guess I should be happy you both want me around."

"Of course I do, sweetie," Julie said. She moved forward, arms outstretched.

Ethan moved away from her and into the room to stand by Jack. "Don't touch me," he said.

"Ethan?"

"I wouldn't go live with you if you were the last person on earth. If a judge rules I have to, I'll run away. I'll do a better job than you did, though. I won't be found."

"Ethan, why are you acting like this?" Julie said.

"I heard you."

"Heard me?"

"And Uncle Eddie the other morning. The walls are paper thin, Mom, and my room is right next door. Jesus. It's like you wanted to be caught."

Jack's stomach twisted. He put his arm around Ethan's shoulder and was relieved when he didn't flinch away. Jack held out the divorce papers again. "The terms are good. Better than you deserve. Have a lawyer look them over then have him call my lawyer."

Jack's radio crackled and Miner's voice came across. Jack turned it down before Julie and Ethan could hear it. "I have to go."

"Of course you do," Julie said. Jack walked past her. "You haven't even tried since I got back." Jack stopped in the doorway and turned. Julie's chin was lifted in triumph, at her ability to reel him back in. Every time.

"Ethan, I'll be home late."

"Sure, Dad. No problem."

Jack turned to Julie. "You need to be gone when I get home."

"You would leave your fourteen-year-old son home, alone?"

"The difference between him and you, Mom, is I know he's coming back." Ethan walked out the door, and Jack followed.

CHAPTER FORTY-NINE

The groundskeeper's shed sat two hundred yards off the twelfth green and thirteenth tee, on a gravel access road that led to the highway. A line of fir trees mostly camouflaged it from the golfers, a pathetic attempt to fool everyone into thinking the greens and fairways were maintained by mystical fairies instead of an army of illegals.

The officers tasked with raiding the shed were dropped off at the end of the gravel road and ran, with only the moon to guide them, to the woods bordering the golf course. Not wanting to alert anyone who might arrive at the shed from the back, the cop cars and emergency vehicles drove on and waited at a nearby farm.

Jack and Tom Hunter found Lincoln Bishop crouched at the tree line. "Is he in there?" Jack said.

"Someone's tied to a chair, a plastic bag over his face."

"He's alone?"

Bishop nodded. "The chair's been knocked over. I didn't see any blood, but I couldn't tell if he was alive."

Jack's gut twisted. He activated his radio and said, voice low, "Eastman, where's Ryan?"

"Still in the clubhouse. Wait. Here he comes. He's getting in a golf cart. Coming your way."

A voice came over the radio. "A car is turning down the drive."

"Get the plate number."

"Roger."

"Eastman," Jack said. "Is Grant's truck in the parking lot?"

After a brief pause, "Yes, sir."

"Where's Grant?" Jack said to Bishop and Hunter.

"No one has come or gone since I've been here," Bishop said.

Jack keyed his radio again. "Eastman, stay there and keep an eye on Grant's truck. If he shows up, arrest him."

"Yes, sir."

A black Chrysler 500 with blacked-out windows rolled up to the groundskeeper shed and stopped at the same time Chris Ryan arrived in his golf cart. Three men got out of the car. Two looked around the darkened landscape, the other walked up to Chris Ryan and shook his hand.

Jack keyed his radio. "Time for the cavalry."

"Pretty sure that's Miguel Pedroza," Hunter whispered.

"Eddie's made some high-level enemies," Jack said.

"You have no idea."

One man stood by the car, the other accompanied Ryan and Pedroza to the shed. Using the shadow of the woods as cover, the three cops ran in a crouch around the perimeter until the building was between them and the guard.

Jack took out his gun and ran across the small open area and flattened himself against the wall. He motioned for Bishop and Hunter to follow.

"This isn't McBride!" Pedroza's thickly accented voice easily carried through the metal wall.

Jack took a deep breath, ran around the corner, and stopped at the edge of the doorway. He peeked around and was immediately spotted by the inside guard. Jack raised his gun, pivoted into the doorway, and put three bullets in the man's chest before he was able to draw his gun. Bishop ran past the doorway to the edge of the building and waited for the outside guard.

Chris Ryan and Pedroza turned. Pedroza's hand went into his coat.

"Don't move," Hunter yelled.

Jack heard a sickening crunch and then a thud as Bishop took care of the second guard. Hunter stood to Jack's left, gun trained on Pedroza. "Pull your hand out nice and easy, Pedroza. Hands on your head. You, too, Ryan. On your knees."

"All clear," Bishop yelled.

The crunch of tires on gravel announced the arrival of the cavalry.

Jack holstered his gun, went to Pedroza, and removed his gun from his body holster. He handed it to Hunter and cuffed Chris Ryan with a black plastic tie. Hunter shoved the gun in the waist of his pants and cuffed Pedroza. Jack walked to the man on the floor.

Brian Grant lay on the floor, mouth taped, a plastic bag partially torn from his head. His bruised cheeks and blood-coated mouth couldn't disguise his expression of fear and regret. Jack lifted Brian and his chair upright, pushed the bag completely from his face, and ripped the duct tape from his mouth. "Where's Eddie?"

"I don't know. I was out cold when he left."

"He's alive?"

"He was last I saw."

A swarm of police flooded the shed, guns raised.

"Put your guns away, boys," Hunter said. He lifted Pedroza to his feet. "I've waited a long time to get my hands on you," he said.

"No hablo ingles."

"Uh-huh."

Hunter handed Miguel Pedroza off to one of his agents and turned his attention to Ryan, whose smug expression hadn't changed.

"Is Eddie hurt?" Jack asked Brian.

Brian nodded.

"Bleeding?"

"Doubt it. Chris worked him over some. He was saving him for the Pedrozas."

Jack bent over to get on Brian's level. "What were you thinking, Brian?" he said, voice low.

Brian worked his jaw. Tears rimmed his red eyes. "My family needed the money."

"And now you're going to jail."

Jack stood and walked up to Chris, who knelt on the concrete. A couple of sheriff's deputies started unbinding Brian from the chair.

"You've killed four people and kidnapped a federal agent, and for what?"

Chris stared straight ahead. "I don't know what you're talking about."

Jack inhaled and counted to ten, hoping the urge to pummel this bastard would pass. Bishop eased next to Jack and, somehow, his six-foot-five presence calmed him. "Take him to county," he ordered Bishop. He nodded and lifted Chris Ryan to his feet.

"I played against you, you know," Chris said to Bishop.

"Did you?" Bishop grabbed his elbow and propelled him along.

"Baylor guard, '88 to '90. I was on the sideline when you blew your knee. Nasty injury."

"And here I am, taking you to jail."

"Funny how life works."

"Hilarious."

Miner entered the shed as Bishop left.

"Listen up!" Jack yelled. "Grab some flashlights. We're searching the surrounding area for Eddie. Miner, you're in charge."

He nodded in acknowledgment and started drawling orders to the other men. Jack turned to Brian who rubbed his wrists before the sheriff's deputy cuffed him again. Jack pulled his iPhone from his pocket, opened the voice app, and hit record.

"Brian Grant, you're under arrest for kidnapping Sean Edward McBride Junior." Jack pulled a card from his shirt pocket and read Brian his Miranda rights in front of the deputy then ordered him to go join the search. Jack sat Brian back into the chair, pulled a stool up in front of him, and sat. He tucked the card back into his pocket and buttoned it. "Do you understand these rights as I've read them to you?"

"Yes."

"I'm recording this interrogation. The resulting audio may be used in your prosecution or defense. Do you understand?"

"Yes."

"Do you want a lawyer, or will you willingly answer my questions?"

"If I do, will it keep me out of jail?"

"Since Eddie's a federal agent, the final decision is up to the Feds, but your cooperation will go a long way and, if you don't lie to me, I'll do everything I can to help you."

"Even though it was Eddie?"

"I'm not doing it for you. I'm doing it for Susan and the kids."

Brian's shoulders slumped. He bowed his head.

A paramedic came into the shed to look Brian over. "Want me to wait?" he asked Jack.

"Give me five minutes."

"I'll be at the rig," the paramedic said.

"Your brother, Kyle Grant, stated he called you on Tuesday, November 6. What did he say?"

"He told me Eddie was a DEA agent and for me to tell Chris Ryan."

"Not Michelle Ryan."

"No. Chris. I told Kyle I worked for Michelle."

"Since when?" Jack said.

"Monday. She offered me a job."

"To make up for losing Matt's contract?"

"To keep me quiet about what I heard at the truck yard after the bonfire."

"What did you hear?"

"Michelle threaten Matt."

Jack filed the confirmation of Fred's story away. "So, you told Kyle you worked for Michelle. What did he say?"

"That her days were numbered and that Chris would take care of me."

"What did you do?"

"Went to Chris."

"Did you talk to Michelle at all?"

"No."

"Did you call Chris? Go see him?"

"I called, told him Kyle had a message. He told me to come out to the club. I came out and demanded he tell me what was going on before I gave him the message."

"What did he tell you?"

"He told me Michelle was about to be arrested for murdering Matt and Amy, and she killed the men in the Old-Armed Soldier's House."

"Chris told you yesterday that Michelle was going to be arrested?"

"Yes."

Jack tried not to let his elation show. His theory that Chris had planted the gun in Michelle's dresser was looking more and more likely. "Go on," he said.

"Chris said Michelle was going to go away for a long time and he was going to take over. He offered to bring me in, but I had to show my loyalty by helping him take care of Eddie."

"You agreed."

"Yeah. I went to DI last night and waited for Eddie to get back. I talked to him, distracted him, while Chris snuck up behind him and knocked him out. We brought him out here, and Chris beat him up, then left me to guard him."

"How did he get free?"

Brian looked away, ashamed and angry. "He taunted me into it. Stupid thing to do."

Jack stood. "All right. On your feet."

Brian rose. "Is it enough? Will you help me?" Jack grabbed his arm and propelled him out of the shed. He passed him off to the paramedic at the ambulance when Deputy Eastman ran up, out of breath. "They found him."

"Where?"

"Curled up in a ball and shivering at the bottom of the sand trap on the thirteenth green."

"How is he?"

Eastman shook his head. "High as a kite and beat to hell."

CHAPTER FIFTY

Jack's hand trembled from too much caffeine, sloshing the scalding coffee onto his hand and the floor. "Shit." He turned around, searching for a trash can, and saw Ellie standing in the door of Stillwater Medical Center's family waiting room. His burned hand lost its importance. "Hey."

She walked toward him, eyes on the coffee in his hand. "You okay?"

Jack switched the Styrofoam cup to his dry hand and flicked the coffee onto the ground. "Yeah."

Ellie picked up a thin paper napkin from the table, grasped his hand gently, and dabbed it dry. She noted his shaking coffee cup and glanced up at him in amusement. "Overdosed on coffee?"

Jack smiled for what seemed like the first time in weeks. "Yeah."

Ellie tossed the napkin in the trash, took the coffee from Jack, and sniffed it. "Seriously?" She threw it in the trash.

"The Book Bank's closed."

"I should have thought to bring some." She crossed her arms over her chest. "How's Eddie?"

"Collapsed lung, broken left orbital bone. Five broken ribs. Sprained ankle from falling in the sand trap, we think."

"And Brian?"

"A couple of black eyes, courtesy of Eddie. Chastised. Saying whatever we want to hear in hopes to get out of this mess."

"Will it work?"

Jack shrugged. "I honestly don't know. Have you talked to Susan?"

"Not yet. Is Brian going to jail?"

"Probably."

Ellie sighed and glanced out the window. "Poor Susan."

"Brian cooperated. I told him I'd do whatever I could to help."

Ellie smiled up at him. "Thank you."

They held each other's gaze for a long moment. There was so much to say and never the right time to say it. "Are you busy tonight?" Jack said.

"Work."

"Can you make time to talk? Maybe meet out at your lake house?"

"Jack, I'm not going to sneak around behind your wife's back."

"We won't be. I gave her the divorce papers last night."

Ellie straightened. "You did? But it's only November."

"I'm tired of waiting. And, with you being pregnant . . ."

"I don't want you to do it because of that!"

"I'm not. What's the difference between now and six weeks from now?"

"The holidays. Ethan."

"What's worse, Ethan seeing two people in a miserable relationship or two people who love each other? Frankly, I'd rather model the latter for him. With you."

Ellie closed her eyes rubbed her temple. "This might be the worst scandal of my life, and that's saying something."

"What's the scandal?"

She dropped her hand and looked up at him again. "Everyone thinks I've been dating Eddie for the last six weeks. Now, I'm switching to his brother? And I'm pregnant?"

"So, we tell the truth. We started seeing each other right after I arrived and stopped when my wife got back. With all this other shit going on, people won't care in the least about our personal life."

"Don't count on it."

"What are you saying? Don't you think we're worth it?"

Her expression softened. "Of course we are."

Jack grinned. "So, tonight after work?"

"Tonight after work." Ellie reached out and touched his uniform shirt. "What brought this on?"

Jack looked down. "I figured it was an easy thing to do to appease my critics."

"Smart move."

"Do you like it?"

"I don't *hate* it. But, I like the suit better."

"God, me too. I feel like one of the Village People."

Ellie laughed and dropped her head on Jack's chest. He pulled her forward and gently wrapped his arms around her. She did the same.

"You're all bulky. Have you been working out?"

"It's the Kevlar."

A familiar voice interrupted them. "Don't you two look cozy."

Julie stood in the waiting room door. Ellie stepped away, but Jack put his arm around her waist and pulled her to his side. "Julie."

"I knew it." She sniffed. "You aren't even his type."

"Apparently I am."

"You'll bore him in a month. I'm bored looking at you two."

"Give it a rest, Julie."

"Do you even know which brother is the father of your bastard?"

Jack tried to move forward, but Ellie held him back. "Don't. She's trying to bait you." Instead, Ellie stepped forward and stopped in front of Julie. "I want to thank you."

"Thank me?"

"If you hadn't been such a narcissistic bitch and left Jack and Ethan, Jack would have never ended up in Stillwater, and we would have never fell in love."

"In love? He sure didn't act like he was in love with you when he was fucking me."

"Funny, that's exactly what Eddie said about you."

Julie laughed, but had an appreciative expression on her face. "Remember what I told you yesterday morning. Don't say I didn't warn you."

"Warn you about what?" Jack said.

"Regression to the mean, darling." She looked the two of them up and down, "I give it two years, tops."

"Okay," Jack said, stepping forward, "that's enough. Ellie." He put his arm around her and kissed her on the cheek. "I love you. I'll call you later." He grasped Julie's arm. "You, come with me."

Jack propelled Julie down the hall. "I cannot believe you are leaving me *for her*?"

Jack found an empty hospital room and ushered Julie inside. "You left me, remember?" Jack sighed. "Did you come here to check on Eddie?"

She crossed her arms. "Yes. How is he?"

"He's got a long road to recovery."

"Where is he going to do that? Here?"

"I haven't thought that far. I'm sure when Mom gets here . . ."

"Your mother's coming?"

Jack looked at his watch. "She should be here in the next hour or so."

"Is she staying with us?"

"She's staying with me. You need to be gone by the time I get home."

"I'm not leaving."

"You can go to our house in Emerson if you need a place to stay. I left some furniture for this eventuality."

"Eventuality?"

Jack stepped forward. "I decided to divorce you the moment I saw you at that hotel with your little photographer friend. I've got pages and pages of documentation about how we tried to get in touch with you, and you never responded. I have every voice mail and text each of your boyfriends left last year. I have a dated picture of you with Ansel Adams. And I have the audio of you telling Eddie two days ago you wanted to continue to fuck him behind my back. If you even think of contesting this divorce, I'll trot every scrap of it out and plaster it all over the news."

"Ethan would never forgive you."

"You forget, Julie. I'm the one who stayed. It carries more weight than you think." Jack walked to the door. "You need to be gone. Today. Or I take the gloves off."

CHAPTER FIFTY-ONE

Eddie opened his eyes and tried to figure out where he was.

"Well, Sleeping Beauty awakes."

He turned his head and saw a policeman who looked remarkably like himself sitting in a chair next to his bed. Eddie squinted and licked his dry lips. "Barney Fife called. He wants his uniform back."

Jack grinned. "Fuck you."

Eddie lifted his arm, which weighed a hundred pounds. "Get me some water, will you?"

Jack stood and offered Eddie the bendy straw protruding from a sturdy plastic cup with STILLWATER MEDICAL CENTER emblazoned on it. The cool water flooded his mouth and slipped down his throat. He couldn't remember anything ever tasting or feeling so good. "Thanks," he said. "So, I'm in the hospital. Give it to me."

"Collapsed lung. Broken left orbital bone, fractured skull, five broken ribs. Two black eyes."

"Damn."

"And a sprained ankle. You fell into a sand trap."

"Nice."

"What do you remember?"

Eddie closed his eyes. "Brian at the truck yard. Chris with a set of brass knuckles." He smiled. "Putting that bastard Brian in a chokehold."

"No details?"

Eddie opened his eyes. Yeah, he remembered the details. In a halting voice, he told Jack how Chris confessed to killing Matt and Amy and setting Michelle up for it with each blow, saving the revelation of his prime motivation till the last one. How Chris grabbed Eddie's hair and pulled his head back and said, "I knew she was fucking you and didn't care. Until you fucked her in the woods at the bonfire. There's only so much a husband can stand, you know?"

Eddie said, "I asked him why not kill Michelle and he said, 'Too quick. Too easy. I wanted to make her a spectacle in her hometown, just as she's made me one.'"

Eddie closed his eyes and turned his head away. His eyes stung from the oncoming tears. Of all the things he'd done in his career, he could say with confidence he hadn't killed anyone, or been the cause of anyone's death, who didn't in some way deserve it. Until Matt and Amy Doyle. Fucking Michelle hadn't been necessary to the job, but Eddie'd never been one to turn down pussy when it was offered. It was one of the perks of being untethered emotionally. He would have to learn to live with the guilt his selfish actions created.

The door to the hospital room opened and a nurse walked in. "Well, look who's awake."

"Nurse Lowe," Jack said.

"Chief. You McBride boys are going to keep this hospital afloat," she said. She looked down at Eddie and shook her head. "Your poor mother." She reached for the blood pressure cuff and started her routine.

"Speaking of Mother," Jack said, "she'll be here in the morning."

"You didn't."

"I did."

"Nurse Lowe, could you double my pain meds? I'm going to need to be as loopy as possible to deal with my mother."

Nurse Lowe kept at her tasks, unimpressed with the request.

"I hope you don't mind, I told her your secret."

"Which one?"

"The heroic one."

Eddie's head throbbed when he nodded. "And?"

"She was crying too hard to say much."

Jack went to the other side of the bed and held Eddie's hand. "I'll let you get some rest."

"Did you ever talk to Ellie?"

Jack glanced at Nurse Lowe, whose face was so blank as she inserted a needle into Eddie's port she could only be mentally recording everything they said. "Yes. We've worked everything out. I gave Julie the papers last night. She should be gone today. Thanks for the audio file, by the way."

"Sorry I had to do it."

"I'm glad it's over."

"Does Ethan know?"

"Yeah."

"Shit." Eddie closed his eyes and started to float.

"Don't worry about it right now. Rest. It'll work out. I promise."

There was pressure on Eddie's hand. A feather caressed his forehead and a soft voice said, "I love you, brother."

Eddie smiled and groaned his reply before falling into a deep, painless sleep.

CHAPTER FIFTY-TWO

"You know what the problem with modern-day criminals is, Ann?"

"No, Jack, what's the problem with modern-day criminals?"

"James Bond."

Jack and Ann Newberry sat across the interrogation table from Chris Ryan, who stared vacantly at a point above their shoulders. He clasped his handcuffed hands lightly before him and smiled to himself.

"Oh, Daniel Craig," Ann said. Jack glanced at her and saw her blush.

"I'm a Sean Connery guy myself."

"No surprise there."

"But the problem is those Bond villains. They always think they're smarter than they really are. And they talk too much."

Ann nodded. "They always have to tell Bond how brilliant they are and how completely they've bested him."

"When they should just put a bullet in Bond's head."

"Because he always wins."

"He always wins."

Chris smirked and stayed silent.

"Of course," Ann said, "Cops are as bad. They list every single thing they have on the criminal and then, voila, the criminal breaks down and confesses."

"Courtroom confessions are my favorite."

"Damn *Law & Order*," Ann said.

"It never happens like that in real life," Jack said.

"Our lives would be easier if it did."

"Yes, it would."

"So, Chris, we're here to give you some good news, some bad news, and to give you a choice. You ready?" Ann said.

Chris looked between the two officers with amusement, but didn't speak.

"I'll take his silence as a yes," Jack said.

"Start with the bad news. Always better to get it over with, like ripping off a Band-Aid."

"You've killed four people, Chris. Four counts of first-degree murder. That's four life sentences, if you're lucky. More like Texas will try to execute you four times."

"You can't prove I killed Matt and Amy."

"He speaks," Ann said.

"We have a piece of evidence you don't know about that will convince the DA to take it to the grand jury."

Chris looked interested for the first time.

Ann leaned over to Jack and stage-whispered, "This is where the police always tell them the evidence."

"Mistake number one."

Ann nodded in agreement.

"We have other bits of evidence which, alone, don't amount to much, but taken together will surely be enough to indict you," Ann said.

"We could indict a ham sandwich with our evidence."

"We could."

Chris lifted the cuffed hands and inspected his fingernails with a bored expression. "What's the good news?"

"Oh," Jack said. "I'm not finished with the bad news. You kidnapped and assaulted a federal agent. One of the best undercover agents the DEA has. That's forty years, easy."

"No way the Feds go easy on him," Ann said.

"No way."

"He looks sad, Jack. Give him the good news."

"Let me guess," Chris said. "If I cooperate, you'll see what you can do with the DA and the Feds."

"He watches TV," Jack said.

"Yep."

"That is one thing they get right, though," Jack said. "So, that's the good news. You cooperate, tell us everything, the DA won't seek the death penalty. Pigeon's already agreed to it. You remain silent, it'll be death row."

"You're assuming I'll lose."

Jack grinned. "I'm confident you'll lose."

Chris shook his head. "You have no actual evidence I did anything. I'll wait for my lawyer."

"You sure?" Ann asked.

"Last chance," Jack replied. "The offer walks out the door with us."

"I'm sure."

Jack shrugged and stood with Ann. They walked out the door and into the hallway. A sheriff's deputy went inside the room to guard Ryan as DA Pigeon walked out of the viewing room. Andrea Armstrong sauntered toward them, a shiny new briefcase clutched in her hand. "Hello, Chief McBride. I'm seeing you everywhere I go."

"Ms. Armstrong."

"Andrea, please. I've been retained by Chris Ryan. Looks like we're going to be seeing a lot of each other over the next few months." The lawyer looked to Ann and Pigeon with raised eyebrows.

"Sheriff Ann Newberry, District Attorney Oliver Pigeon, Andrea Armstrong. Newly minted lawyer. You just passed the bar, right?"

Andrea's confidence wavered a fraction at being so transparent.

"Don't be alarmed," Ann said, "he's trying to make you think he's a mentalist. We looked you up."

"Know your enemy and all," Jack said.

"I'm alarmed you think I'm your enemy," she said. "Not a good way to start a professional relationship."

"He didn't mean that," Pigeon interjected.

"It's a conflict of interest for you to defend Kyle Grant and Chris Ryan," Jack said.

"Why?"

"Grant's testifying against Ryan."

She furrowed her brows. "No, the agreement was Mr. Grant testifies against Michelle Doyle Ryan. Not Christopher Ryan. There is no conflict of interest. What is my client being charged with?" She directed the question to Pigeon.

Pigeon hesitated before answering. "Kidnapping a federal officer, assault of a federal officer."

"You don't seem too confident, District Attorney Pigeon."

Pigeon grinned. "I think I'm going to like you."

Andrea smiled. "I'm sure I don't need to tell you, don't talk to my client without me present. Nice to meet you, Sheriff, Mr. Pigeon. Chief." She pointed at the door. "In here?"

"Yes," Ann said.

Andrea Armstrong entered the room. The deputy who'd been guarding Chris skirted around the other three and went into the break room.

Pigeon said, "Just like they said."

"What?"

"I called a friend of mine, professor out at Tech law school. She's top of her class and completely ruthless. Overconfidence is her weakness."

"No kidding," Ann said.

Pigeon waved thoughts of Andrea Armstrong away. "Good call, not mentioning Eddie's testimony about Chris's confession."

"I felt sure he'd realize his mistake with our Bond villain speil," Ann said.

"They're never as smart as they think," Jack said.

"Besides Eddie's statement, all we have putting Chris at the Doyle murder scene is Matt's voice mail to Eric Sterry."

"And any trace evidence they find can easily be explained away by family gatherings," Jack said.

"What can we charge him with?" Ann asked.

"Feds will charge him with kidnapping and assault. Search the club, see if you can find any evidence of his book. We can charge him with gambling. Let's see if we can't turn Kyle Grant, or come up with some physical evidence before we charge Chris with murder."

"And Michelle?" Jack said.

Pigeon sighed. "Drop the murder charges and amend it to intent to distribute and bribing a police officer. With the amount of drugs we found at her business, and her confession about bribing Jesson, we can charge her with two felonies," Pigeon said and walked away.

Jack sighed. "I've had six murders in eight weeks on the job and still no arrests." He rubbed his face. "Jesus Christ."

"We have Matt's call to Chris and Eddie's statement in our back pocket. We put enough pressure on Kyle Grant, he'll turn on Chris to save himself. I know you want arrests now, but you know building a solid case takes time." Ann put a hand on his shoulder. "You aren't going to get fired tomorrow."

"If Joe Doyle has anything to say about it, I will."

"Rumor is Doyle's being pressured to resign his city council seat. Might be a first, resigning a seat you haven't taken yet." Ann slapped Jack on the shoulder. "Between that and your fetching uniform, I think your job is safe for a little while longer."

Jack chuckled and shook his head. "I don't know that my job is ever going to be safe."

"Come on. We've got to break the news to Michelle that not only has her dad betrayed her, but her husband has, too."

CHAPTER FIFTY-THREE

"I don't believe it," Michelle's brow furrowed, as though trying to connect the version of her husband Jack presented to the man she'd been married to for years.

"Because you don't think he's capable of murder or you don't think he'd betray you?" Ann said.

Michelle considered for a moment. "He *liked* Matt and Amy."

"Apparently, he hated you more."

"He told you that?" Bob Underwood asked.

"No. He's not talking. But Brian Grant, Kyle Grant, and Eddie are. The Feds have made a number of arrests at Houston Heavy Equipment. Your operation is crumbling, Michelle," Jack said.

"Go ahead and gloat, McBride. If Doyle Industries goes out of business, you'll have put one hundred Stillwater residents out of a job."

"*You'll* have put them out of a job."

"You think they're smart enough to understand the difference? They'll see you, an outsider, coming in and going after a business and family who's done much more good than harm."

"Debatable."

"You don't get it. These people are willing to look the other way, to forgive a shitload of stuff from us they'd never forgive from others because we're one of them. We employ people. We support the community. The other stuff? Never touches 95 percent of them. They can look the other way and take our charity with a clear conscience. They did it with Buck Pollard for years. He knew who to fuck over and who to coddle. He was a master at it. You? You're like a bull in a china shop. By the time you're done do-gooding the town to death, Stillwater'll be like fucking Detroit."

"Thanks for the civics lesson," Jack said.

"Are you amending the charges against Michelle?" Bob asked.

"It seems Kyle Grant is sticking to his story that you pulled the trigger on Vazquez and Morales," Jack said.

"We've checked Michelle's calendar for October thirty-first and November first. Halloween night, she was working the Meals Ministry booth at First Methodist's fall festival. There are at least two hundred people who can account for her presence until 10 p.m. She arrived at work at 7 a.m., as usual, and had conference calls and meetings all day."

"We know she likes to do business late at night," Jack said.

"If you'll remember," Bob said, "there was a thunderstorm that night. Jordan, Michelle's daughter, is terrified of storms. She slept with Michelle that night." Bob looked a little smug.

Michelle's right eyebrow and corner of her mouth raised in sync, as if lifted by a puppet string. "I can tell you where Chris was at the time of both murders, if you're interested."

"What?" Jack and Bob said at the same time.

"You heard me."

"Just a minute." Bob leaned over, and the lawyer and client had a brief, whispered conversation. Bob's expression lightened, and he smiled. "Well, this changes things."

"We don't know the evidence, yet," Jack said.

"Drop the bribery charges, and you will."

"Not the murder charges?" Ann asked.

Bob laughed. "Even if those would stick, which they won't, you'll drop them soon enough with this evidence. You need to call Oliver," he said.

Jack and Ann exchanged a look, and in silent agreement Ann stood and left the room.

"Now we wait," Bob said cheerfully.

Jack studied Michelle, who looked extremely smug. "Thinking of ruining my career?" Jack said.

"Among other things."

"If you didn't murder these people, I don't want you to go to jail, but rest assured, Michelle, you will be going to jail for distribution, at the least. The Feds are keeping me in the loop and it doesn't look good."

"We'll see."

"You can mitigate the fallout. Tell us about your operation. Testify against your father."

Michelle laughed.

"Haven't you wondered where your father is?"

Michelle pursed her lips and tried not to look interested.

"He hasn't asked about you once." Jack turned to Bob. "Has he called you, Bob?"

"Mary called," Bob said as much to Michelle as Jack. "She's taking care of your children."

"Have you forgotten your father gave us your motive to kill Matt?" Jack said.

Michelle sniffed. "I've known my dad is a ruthless motherfucker my entire life. Where do you think I learned it from?"

"Apparently you didn't learn his self-interest, because your 'loyalty,'" Jack put air quotes around the word, "to your father will land you in prison for a long time."

Ann returned. "Plead guilty to bribing a public official, and the DA will recommend probation. No jail time."

"And the murder charges?" Bob asked.

"I suppose that depends on how good the evidence is," Ann said.

Bob nodded to Michelle, who had her arms crossed over her chest. "You want me to plead guilty to a felony? I don't think so."

Jack stood. "Then take your chance with a trial. Ann still knows some of the guards up in Gainesville. Maybe she'll put in a good word for you."

He and Ann started to leave.

"Wait." Michelle sighed. "There's a GPS tracker on Chris's car."

"Why?" Jack said.

"Because I'm a control freak."

"Does he know?"

She paused, looked a little panicky, but covered it quickly. "Maybe."

"We'll check into it," Ann said.

"Better hope he didn't destroy it."

Michelle laughed. "He's not that smart."

"He was smart enough to frame you for four murders," Jack said.

"Fuck you, McBride."

"You've fucked my brother. That's as close as you'll get."

"Jack," Bob said sternly.

"Stand up, Michelle," Jack said. "You're under arrest."

"What?" she shouted. "I just gave you Chris on a silver platter."

Bob stood and his chair fell back onto the floor in his rush. "What's going on, Jack?"

"You're under arrest for conspiracy to commit murder," Jack said.

"Against whom?" Michelle was incredulous.

"Fred Muldoon. You forgot about old Fred, didn't you? Eddie delivered him to the DEA along with Kyle. Fred's been using your truck yard as a place to flop for no telling how long. He knows a lot, and he's singing, too."

"An eighty-year-old drunk doesn't scare me," she said, but her expression betrayed her surprise and unease.

Jack leaned on the table and got in Michelle's face. "Three witnesses have you dead to rights on this, Michelle: Fred, a federal agent, and Kyle Grant. It's a first-degree felony with a possible ninety-nine-year sentence. Add that to the case the Feds are building against you and your father? Well, your grandchildren can visit you in prison."

Michelle crossed her arms over her chest and met Jack's gaze. "I'm not turning on my father."

"Give me Buck Pollard."

Michelle's eyes widened, and in the almost imperceptible flicker of relief, of triumph, Jack knew he had her.

"He's alive, isn't he?" Jack said.

"Can you give us a minute?" Bob said.

Jack and Ann left the room. "Goddamn, Jack. I hate to admit this, but with everything going on I've almost completely forgotten about that old fucker."

"Which one? Fred or Buck?"

"Both of them."

"I wish I could forget about Pollard." Jack stared at the interview room door. "Why is she so loyal to her father?" he mused.

"Same reason you've stood by Eddie all these years."

Jack shook his head. "If Eddie lied to get me arrested for murder, I guarantee you I'd turn on him in a second."

Jack pulled his phone out and dialed Tom Hunter.

"What do you want to bet DI has GPS trackers on all of its vehicles?" He left a voice mail for Hunter, telling him the new information.

"Think Michelle will take the bait?" asked Ann.

"She might not today, but she will. All the Doyles' assets are frozen. We get bail set high enough, she won't be able to make it. Every day she sits in jail and her father doesn't retract his statement or come to visit her gets me one day closer to nailing Buck Pollard."

CHAPTER FIFTY-FOUR

Ellie collapsed in her office chair, leaned her head back, and closed her eyes. Christ, what a day. What a week.

It was another record sales day for the Book Bank, and it wasn't even five o'clock. Word came down about noon, where from no one could say—Joe Doyle was denying any knowledge of the drug operation Michelle had been running through DI for years. He was appalled it had happened under his nose and was cooperating fully with the authorities. Customers flooded the Book Bank within thirty minutes, cementing its reputation for the place to be for information. Ellie wasn't sure she wanted her passion project to be known as the local gossip mill, but she couldn't deny her sales projections had been shattered.

Ellie's customers were pretty evenly split on those who believed Joe and those who thought it was bullshit. Ellie liked to think the bullshit faction had voted for her, but her 30 percent showing at the polls belied that theory. She didn't need to hear everyone rehash what was known, suspected, or theorized about the goings-on at Doyle Industries. She knew Joe Doyle'd been behind the Yourke County drug trade for years—hell, everyone knew it, but no one wanted to admit it—and she wasn't surprised in the least he was throwing his own daughter under the bus.

Joe Doyle and Big Jake Yourke were cut from the same bastard cloth. One thing did surprise her: she felt sorry for Michelle Doyle. The only person Michelle had left on her side was her mother, Mary, and even Ellie wasn't sure Mary would stand by Michelle. Ellie doubted Mary Doyle knew how to think for herself and she knew Mary would do and say whatever Joe told her.

Ellie allowed a small flame of triumph to burn deep within her being, a flame she would never share with anyone. Not Kelly (not that Kelly was speaking to her) or Jack or Susan. To everyone in Stillwater, she would be classy, would take the high road when it came to Michelle's downfall and talk of innocent until proven guilty, letting the system take its course, believe none of what you hear and half of what you see. But Ellie believed Michelle got what she deserved, finally. Karma was a bitch, and you can't do the things Michelle'd done for thirty years without those chickens finally coming home to roost.

Privately, she hoped Michelle went to jail until she was old and haggard and was turned into some big, ugly butch lesbian's wife.

But Ellie would never say it or admit it. Even to Jack.

A knock on the door jolted her from her uncharitable thoughts. Ethan McBride lifted his hand in an awkward wave and said, "Hey."

Ellie sat up. "Hey."

"Dad told me to meet him here?"

"Right. We were going to, um, get a bite to eat I think. Are you hungry?"

"Yeah. I'm always hungry," Ethan's face reddened and he looked away.

"Your dad texted and said he'd been held up."

"Okay. I'll wait out here." Ethan turned to go.

"Wait." Ellie stood, desperate to make a connection with this young man who, if things went the way she hoped, would play a big part in her life. "We can go grab something, you and me. I can take you. If you want. It's fried chicken night at Mabel's. Have you had Mabel's fried chicken?"

"No."

"It might be the best fried chicken I've ever tasted."

Ethan shrugged so half-heartedly, Ellie knew the last thing he wanted to do was be seen with her eating fried chicken. Alone. With Jack? Maybe.

"If you don't like fried chicken, Mabel's has good fried fish. Or we could get Dairy Queen. Whichever."

"I'm good."

"Why don't I go to Mabel's and get two meals to go? Three. We'll save one for your dad. We can eat them upstairs in my apartment." As soon as she said it, Ellie thought it sounded weird, as if she was trying to lure an unsuspecting teenager to her lair and take advantage of him. God. Would people think that? No. Yes. Maybe. "Or we can eat it down here, in the store. I'll see if Paige wants one. We may be busy all night with everything going on."

"Do you always talk this much and this fast?"

"No. I'm nervous. I want you to like me but I'm afraid you hate me." She stopped. Way to lay it out there, Elliot.

Ethan read the sign on the inside of the safe door with instructions on what to do if you were locked in. He pointed to it and turned to her. "Seriously? There's no way out?"

"There wasn't when this was a bank, but I had them remove the lock so you can't get trapped. There's a little window to open for oxygen."

Ethan stood on his tiptoes and opened the window. "Cool." He opened and closed it a few times and said, "Troy and Olivia like you a lot."

Ellie smiled. "Glad to hear it."

"They act like you're a saint."

"I'm far from a saint." Ethan stopped messing with the little window, but kept his back to her. Ellie took a deep breath and dove in. "Ethan, I love your dad very much."

"How is that even possible? Y'all barely know each other. Unless y'all've really been sneaking around for the last six weeks."

"We haven't. I swear to God. When your mother came back, we stopped seeing each other."

"You both keep saying it, but I don't know if I believe it."

"Why not?"

Ethan fidgeted and looked away. "I can't imagine staying away from Olivia for six weeks."

Ellie smiled and wondered if Susan knew, or even suspected. Or cared, considering everything.

"It was as awful as you imagine it would be." Ellie wanted to reach out and touch him but knew better. "I know this is going to be weird for a while. All I ask is you give me a chance, okay?"

The silence stretched uncomfortably between them. Ellie hadn't felt this nervous around a teenage boy since senior prom. Finally, Ethan said, "Fried chicken sounds good."

Ellie exhaled and smiled. "You won't regret it."

"I hope not."

They smiled at each other, shyly, and looked away.

"Did I hear someone say fried chicken?"

It took a moment for Ellie to associate the cop who stood in the office door with Jack McBride. Apparently Ethan had the same problem because he burst out laughing. "Dad, you look *so* weird."

"Says the kid who's worn the same hoodie every day for a week."

"It's been two weeks, and I like this hoodie."

"I seem to remember you started wearing it around your birthday," Jack said. "Someone special give it to you?"

Ellie was afraid Ethan's face was going to catch fire it turned so red so quickly. Behind Ethan, she shook her head in warning to Jack. He nodded and said, too brightly not to sound forced. "So, everything good?"

Ellie waited for Ethan to respond. "So far so good."

Ellie felt a smile spread across her face. It wasn't much, but it was something. Then Jack had to go and push the envelope.

"Where's your mother?"

"Gone when I got home from school."

"Should I ask?"

"She didn't leave a note." Ethan raised his finger. "But she took her phone, so she's making progress. How's Uncle Eddie?"

"Dreading the arrival of Lieutenant Governor Grandma."

Ethan groaned. "Join the club. Are y'all ready? I'm starving."

"Yeah, go on up front. We're right behind you."

Ethan rolled his eyes and walked off. "Gross."

Jack and Ellie raised their eyebrows at each other. Ellie shrugged.

"So."

"So."

"We're pregnant," Jack said.

"We're pregnant." Ellie looked away and fiddled with the corner of a stack of papers on her desk.

Jack stepped forward. He stilled her hand with his and said in a low voice, "You don't seem happy about it." He put his finger under her chin and lifted her head to meet his gaze. "Are you not happy about it?"

"Of course I am. It's just . . ." She leaned her head back and searched the ceiling for what to say. Tears welled in her eyes and her throat thickened. She closed her eyes and dropped her head. "I'm forty-two years old, Jack. I'll be sixty when it—he—she—graduates from high school."

"So will I."

"What if something's wrong with it? I've been drinking, more than I should. Plus, being over thirty-five, the chances of the baby having some sort of condition increases by—" Jack placed his fingers over her mouth but Ellie kept talking. "I don't know how much, but a lot. Jane wants me to run for mayor. Apparently she thinks I'm supposed to save the town. Save it from *what* is what I want to know. And, there's rumors Doyle's going to resign as city councilman even before he takes office, which will mean they'll appoint me. And I think Jane is dying, and she said once, in an offhand comment, but Jane never makes offhand comments, that she's leaving the bank to me. I mean, come on!"

Jack laughed. "Ellie, stop." He put his hands on her hips and pulled her toward him. He brushed the tears from her cheeks and pushed her hair behind one ear. "I don't care about any of that other stuff. The town and Jane Maxwell can go to hell. All I care about is you, Ethan, and the little baby inside there." He placed his hand over her stomach. "I'm not going to tell you everything will be okay. It might not. But worrying